The Cave of Bones, an .... site, has stood
silent for centuries. Now, the white men have come to disturb it,
to dig for artifacts for their universities and museums. But the
Native Americans are not so easily pushed aside. They fight
against the dig: in court, in the newspapers, in the halls of government.

Some, more militant, more in touch with the old ways, carry the
fight to the shadowed forests, to the sacred ground itself. And
one of these, who sees himself as a medicine man, calls on the
Ancient Ones for help.

From the flames of the fire over which he chants, he receives an
answer . . .

And the killing begins.

PRAISE FOR ROBERT C. WILSON AND
HIS PREVIOUS THRILLERS . . .

"Intense horror, compellingly told."

—*The Washington Post*

"Fascinating . . . a gripping, terrifying tale."

—Frank De Felitta, author of *Audrey Rose*

"Flat-out terrific . . . but don't read it alone at night!"

—*Detroit Free Press*

"High powered and very suspenseful . . . exceptionally well
written."

—*Publishers Weekly*

Novels by Robert C. Wilson

CROOKED TREE
ICEFIRE
SECOND FIRE

SECOND FIRE

ROBERT C. WILSON

JOVE BOOKS, NEW YORK

SECOND FIRE

A Jove Book / published by arrangement with
Crooked Tree Industries, Inc.

PRINTING HISTORY
Jove edition / March 1993

ISBN: 0-515-11070-1

Jove Books are published by The Berkley Publishing Group,
200 Madison Avenue, New York, New York 10016.
The name "JOVE" and the "J" logo
are trademarks belonging to Jove Publications, Inc.

PRINTED IN THE UNITED STATES OF AMERICA

10 9 8 7 6 5 4 3 2 1

For

Michelle, Paul and Marie

SECOND FIRE

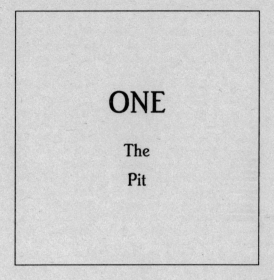

ONE

The
Pit

Chapter 1

IT USED TO be the killing was hard and the rest was easy. Now, the killing was easy. And the rest was a chore.

Especially when he had to seek refuge in the forest. Especially when he was being pursued.

His was a primal life. At its most basic, it was kill, or die. That's the way he looked at it anyway. That's the way he had to look at it. He held nothing against his victims. Indeed, he held nothing but respect for them. He was merely acting out the primeval directive scripted for all beings of his kind. Why don't *they* understand that? Why don't they leave him alone?

From his hiding place under the canopy of three-lobed ferns, Buck Billings watched as the lawmen came closer, as their lights began to sweep across his position. He looked toward the light, toward the shadows put in motion by the light. They were long and sinuous, blackened twins of dangling branches, dark projections of viney tendrils. They were the shadows of fern stalks and dead limbs and narrow-trunked saplings. With the erratic motion of the light, the shadows moved across the forest floor, turning it into a nest of vipers, a living mass of serpents that crawled on and near and over the figure lying prone under the ferns.

With each new angle of the light, with each shift of the shadows, it was as though the snakes were more real. It was as though they were twining around him, taking him for one of their own. He closed his eyes and buried his head into the ground, shielding himself from the light, from the shadows, from the images conjured from the shadows.

Though his eyes were closed, the images did not dissolve. They pursued him into the darkness, and from there, there was no more retreat. He wanted to scream, to get up and run, to escape. The impulse was nearly overpowering, but somewhere within the rhythm of this high-tempoed urge beat his last remnant of rationality. And it was this meager touchstone to reason that kept him where he was, that prevented him from betraying his position, that held him back from charging toward the road. That slowly brought him back to his senses.

When he looked up again it was dark. Buck climbed to his feet, hoisted the carcass to his shoulder, gripped his rifle in his left hand and headed deeper into the woods. He didn't stop until he reached his sanctuary. Until he reached the pit.

It was a steep decline with broken chunks of rock littering pathway meanders caused by rainwater. Buck zigzagged down the slope, following the meanders, until he reached the floor of the pit.

He unloaded the carcass, and using his belt, tied two limbs together. Then he hoisted it as high over his head as he could reach and hooked the belt over a broken nub on a branch. His kill safe from ground scavengers, he started to collect firewood.

There was no longer any pretense of the internal fire that was an adjunct to his tension. He was cold, and sweat-dampened clothes clung in chill swaths to his skin. The act of gathering wood, of breaking twigs, of positioning all of it on top of dried leaf litter, was enough activity to keep him from shivering. But even as he struck the match, the chill was already beginning to sink deep inside.

The leaves flared hot and fast, and in less than a minute had burned down to ash filaments held together by their network of veins. The kindling had been ignited, and a blue flame hugged tight to the gnarled twigs like velvet gloves over arthritic fingers. He went down to one knee and leaned close to stoke the tiny flames with his breath. As he began to blow, the wood glowed red, the flames rising higher. He shifted, tilting his head, bending closer.

The fire danced and moved, responding to the fuel of oxygen, sucking it in, using it as nourishment, coming more fully to life. As he looked directly into the fire, the flames seemed to cease their sway and instead bend closer, toward him.

He started to blow lightly again. There was a snap and a quick hissing sound. An air pocket in the wood was suddenly breached and a tiny jet of fire shot out. Toward him. Toward his eye.

There was a fizzing, crinkling sound, the sound of hair singeing. He jerked his face away, but the flame had been so bright, so close, he was momentarily blinded. He pulled back, sitting up. He felt his eye, and his lashes disintegrated into dust at the touch.

The bright image imprinted on his retina faded, and he looked again at the fire. There was another crack, another tiny air jet, as the fire grew. He smiled, allowing himself a private laugh. Of all the black thoughts he had harbored that evening, the last thing he'd imagined was being blinded stoking a fire. He laughed again, this time out loud.

The fire was taking hold well now, the kindling burning steadily, the bigger logs ignited, the flames curving up and around them from below. He leaned closer again, letting the heat work its effect on him. As his face, then his chest, began to warm, the damp cloth clinging to his back seemed to grow chiller by comparison.

He stood up and began to unbutton his shirt. As he did, looking down, he couldn't help but noticed that the flames were concentrated on his side of the fire pit. They rose higher as he did, and it was almost as if he were attracting them, as if he were the source of a secret draft the fire actively sought.

It was too hot, and he had to circle to the other side. He slipped out of his shirt and draped it open, holding it close to the flames. As he stood there, the fire began to change. It began to creep along the old wood, moving across the pile, migrating toward the other side. More than merely adjusting to the source, the tips of the flames seemed to be changing the slant of their reach. They seemed to be curving in the opposite direction. Toward the secret draft. Toward him.

He watched the fire closely as it moved toward him, as it sent out flickering fingers in his direction, as if beseeching him, as if reaching for him, as if seeking him out.

He stepped back and swung his shirt over his shoulders, slipping it on. He circled round to the other side and again sat down. As he did, he couldn't take his eyes off the fire—the weaving, flickering flames, the flashes of yellow, the glow of the coals, the graying of surface ash as it curled outward from the face of the wood, revealing new fire, new life beneath it.

New life. Born from the old. Taking its first breath as the outer layer takes its last. There was no mercy in the flames, no value placed on life. It was kill and survive. Existence at its most primitive. Like his own.

He clenched his eyes shut, not from the fire but from the glare of his own thoughts. They were crazy, the things that were jumping into his mind. Irrational. And yet he couldn't shake the images that continued to alight in his mind with the clarity of full vision.

He opened his eyes. The fire was changing again. Moving again. Migrating across the top. Coming back toward him.

He licked his lips, already beginning to crack from the heat. He tried to bring moisture to his mouth, to force a swallow, but all he could manage was a gummy phlegm. It did little to soothe his throat, which was dry and raspy. And hot. His throat seemed to have been touched by the fire. It seemed to be giving in to the flames.

His chest rose and fell with a deep breath. He wanted the burning to cease, but the cold air only served to make it worse. It made it burn more. He grabbed his throat and began to massage it, all the while keeping his eyes locked on the flames.

They were swaying, flicking, jumping into the air as if the fire sensed its effect on him. As if reacting to its creeping influence. As if coming alive with its own heated tempo of excitement. Alive with its own designs. Alive with tension. Alive!

He shook his head. He arched his neck. He stretched his shoulders back. Anything to shake the sensation, to chase the thoughts, to maintain his grasp of reason.

No matter the diversion, the thoughts would not die. He could not rid himself of the notion that the fire had control over its movements, that it was guiding its own actions, that it was acting on its own secret agenda. As he stared at the fire, at the dance of the sharp-lobed flames, he watched closely the movement, the gradations of color, the patterns of light and dark as they played across the stack of logs. As he stared, it suddenly began to seem plausible. After all, in a sense it *was* alive. It consumed, it grew, it gave off energy. It reacted to its environment. What more was there to life? What else was required to be deemed a living organism? What more—

There was a sharp crackle, and a tiny knot of flame erupted out of the pit and landed on his hand. He slapped at it, crying out in surprise. There was a sharp, stinging pain, from a burning sliver of wood.

He shook his hand, then brushed at it with his fingers. The splinter dropped away. The tiny flame died. Bringing his palm to his mouth, he sucked the burn, and as he did, he looked toward the fire. It was flicking rapidly back and forth, curling upward faster than before.

Slowly, his hand dropped away from his mouth. Pointed arches of flame pulled the fire higher, then snapped off and floated untindered for a flash of a second before dying out. As the tips of the flames snapped, as dark patches appeared in the bank of yellow and red, the abstractions of light and dark began to lose their disconnected pattern. They began to come together in a cohesive design.

A deep, trembling rush of breath escaped from his chest. He hugged his arms tight to his stomach, hunching forward. It didn't seem possible. It *wasn't* possible. And yet it was happening, in the fire, right before his eyes.

Suddenly his mouth dropped open. The air froze in his lungs. The flames had parted, drawing upward, revealing black holes, spaced evenly apart. But just that fast, they were gone.

As the fleeting image replayed itself in his mind, he looked for it again in the fire. With the suggestion planted, it was as though every flicker, every flash from light to dark, showed traces of what he had seen. Were the images the same as the snakes on the floor of the forest? Were the shapes in the fire the same as when he had lain under the ferns and lights flashed over his position, giving life to the shadows?

It was crazy. *He* was crazy. Others said he was. They'd said it for years. Had they been right all along? Despite the surface heat of the fire, a chill rippled across his skin. Falling more under the spell of the flames, he started to shake his head in a spasm of denial. He knew he was in control of his sanity. If he weren't, how could he be rational enough to pose the question? Or was this how it began? Would the illusions grow stronger? Would the hallucinations become real? Would the fire for him really come alive?

Trying to break the spell, he looked away, his eyes catching on his kill. The flickering of reflected light seemed to give it movement. It seemed to bring expression back to eyes already dead. He had to look way again, turning his face skyward. Above him, the draft of the fire was fluttering the leaves, causing them to twist and bob and turn. Leafy undersides reflected new variations of light and dark, and on this overhead canvas new shapes could be imagined in the shadows and nervous movement of the tree.

Quickly, he looked down, before the new patterns could work their effect. The fire before him was raging, shooting tongues of flame too fast for him to imagine detail. Too fast for him to notice the change. The change in the pit, near the base of the coals.

The fire had left its enclosure and was snaking across the ground, forging a path through the forest debris. It spread neither to the right nor to the left, but maintained its narrow channel, as if drawn forward by an unseen hand, as if acting out some purposeful plan of action.

As his focus shifted, as the column of fire inched forward, he sensed the change before he saw it. After all, his sight was an untrustworthy ally. He saw snakes in the shadows, shapes in the flames. But this time, the illusion was real. The fire was moving. It was coming toward him.

He rolled to his knees and without thinking brushed at the dirt with his bare hand. As he did, the fire leapt at him, scorching the cuff of his sleeve. Covering his wrist protectively, he sprang to his feet. The fire was only momentarily deterred. It continued, circling the divot he had caused. He stepped forward, kicking at the fire, scattering it again. Then turning his foot sideways, he began sweeping it frantically into the dirt, scraping the fiery column back toward the pit.

Beads of sweat appeared on his forehead. The internal fire of the chase earlier that night was reignited. The fear of that pursuit came rushing back. He kicked faster, harder, sending up a cloud of dust, causing a pall to settle over the flames. The dust shaded once-distinct lines, making the stark purity of the yellow bursts of light seem somehow tainted and dirty and unclean. Caught in the draft, the brown particles of earth billowed along the edges of the flames, outlining them with ugly shadow.

A sharp report suddenly crackled in his ears, like the sound of a small-caliber rifle.

My God!

His first thought was that he had been shot. He had taken a bullet to the chest. He grabbed at the wound, looking down, ripping his shirt open.

A black circle discolored his chest. To his touch it was hot, and inside it burned. He looked closer, using the light of the fire to see. There was no penetration of his skin. No entry hole of a bullet. No blood. Instead, where he was struck, his skin was charred.

In the manner of horror's slow comprehension, his eyes lifted toward the fire. As they did, there was another crack and another fiery projectile spit out of the flames, striking him in the shoulder. Staggered by the impact, he grabbed his shoulder, trying to smother the pain and the searing heat.

Barely able to maintain his balance, frozen by shock, by fear, his gaze was locked in place on the flickering bands of light. As he stared, the patterns began to come together again. The dark holes, the matching shadows among the flames, slowly took shape. And below them, another parting of the flames. They yielded grudgingly, drawing out in distinct lines, narrowing further as the space opened wider, until the lines were mere strings of fire, until they parted completely, in the middle, leaving sharp pointed spikes of light.

The fire flared suddenly higher, and a lobe of flame broke off, shooting toward him, hitting his arm below the shoulder, wrapping around his biceps. He screamed from the pain, from the unrelenting heat as it seared into his flesh. But more than from the burning, he screamed because of something else he felt. A tug. A slight pressure on his arm, as if the disconnected lobe of fire were trying to pull him forward.

He grabbed at the thing on his arm as if it were something corporeal he could remove. But fire is as substantial as a wisp of steam, and nothing he could do had an effect. And yet the flame died.

His chest heaved, the air rushing through his mouth, the sound of panic taking control. He stumbled back a step, then two. He turned and without looking tried to break away, but crashed square into the carcass dangling from the branch.

He staggered back as it began to swing on its tether, the body spinning, as if engaged in a mocking, whirling, celebratory dance. Its face passed before his own, its eyes seeking his. It was as though it were trying to communicate, as if trying to deliver a message of welcome. A message from the dead to one who soon would be.

A wavering, high-pitched cry vibrated from his throat. He lurched to the side and began to stagger into the dark, toward the woods. Before he had managed three steps, there was a violent burst of flames and his shadow was suddenly outlined in stark relief in front of him. And then he felt it. A narrow, burning band of pressure across his stomach.

He leaned forward, striving to pull away, but the grip was strong. Then with one powerful tug he was spun in place, completely around, and suddenly he was face-to-face with the excited bands of yellow and red, staring straight into the fire.

The fire! It was energy in its most primal state, an uncontrolled expulsion of heat and color and noise. It lashed upward with spikes of flame in an unsteady display that flickered and fluttered and flitted back and forth with the randomness of frantic motion. The quickly changing pattern of bright colors and deep shadow, the nervous, flicking quality of its aurora, disturbed the air, creating its own waves of energy, of tension, of trembling movement, and all of these things entered the man, infecting him with their intensity, transmitting their message of panic through every neuron, mixing with the blood in his veins and making it pump faster, harder, hotter.

He could barely breathe. He was losing all muscular control. The most dominant sound was quickly becoming the pounding at his temples. But through it all, instinct survived, and he found himself turning, striding, lunging away from the fire.

Though it seemed as if he had been running forever, in reality he had managed only a few steps when it happened. The explosion. It was another projectile from the fire, stronger, more powerful than before. The impact struck hardest square in the middle of his back, and he crashed forward, plunging face-first into the dirt.

Fighting to regain his wind, he forced himself to his hands and knees. He raised his eyes. There was no time to waste. He couldn't have the luxury of waiting for his breath to return to normal. He had to get away. Into the woods. Away from the fire.

He reached awkwardly forward with one hand, then dragged a knee after it. Again, struggling forward, crawling, scrambling, anything to propel himself from the pit.

A whispery, hissing sound cut the air. The sound of a whip lashing out. And then it struck him. Diagonally across his back, curling over his shoulder, around his neck. It burned like acid, it gripped with the hold of a thousand teeth, each barbed extremity digging into his flesh.

He screamed, but the hold only strengthened. It started to pull him back. He fought it, his fingers digging into the soil, gouging at the earth, seeking their own hold.

The pressure suddenly increased, he was yanked over on his side, and again he was face-to-face with the fire, a shimmering curtain that seemed to be gathering more definition from the shadows, more depth from the curves of the flames. But it was a gathering clarity he could not see. He could no longer focus clearly. He couldn't think clearly. It was as if the fire were gathering body and strength from the bits of life it took from him.

His solitary awareness was becoming the pain, his agony. The frustration. There was nothing he could do, no way to fight. He was powerless to resist.

His only outlet was through his voice. His only protest became his screams.

His voice shrieked from deep in his throat out into the protected hollow where he had set camp, into the mantle of trees, to the lip of rocky heights above him, and from there into the lifeless night of the forest. Every ounce of reserve he possessed, every bit of energy that still pumped through his body, became focused in his lungs, in his throat, in the raw expulsion of his unintelligible cries of terror.

Though his sight had become again an untrustworthy ally, he was aware of the movement, of the shadows, of the fleeting shape he had imagined earlier, which now seemed to be holding its pattern.

He shut his eyes tight, but despite the voluntary surrender of vision, the brightness continued to grow. The image continued to come closer. The illusion of fire come to life became even more real, confined within the parameters of his mind.

Like the snakes. Like the initial suggestions of form he had read into the fire. This was just one more deception. One more self-induced fantasy. One more step downward into insanity.

Had the descent become complete? Had his reason been irretrievably lost? Was there a point where the insane accepted their world of dream and illusion, ending the torment, existing in peace with false suggestion and half-drawn reality? Or were the insane doomed to live as part of the delusion, smears of oil on a blank canvas ready to be stroked by some unseen artist into whatever demented landscape his tortured psyche envisioned?

How did the insane distinguish reality from hallucination? How did they ultimately survive in either world? How did they know, when for them both worlds no longer existed?

How did it end for the insane?

How did it end?

Chapter 2

"THEY EXIST. THE same as they always have, since my people first set foot on this land."

The attorney standing before the witness turned and strolled across the courtroom, letting the witness's words resonate for as long as he could in the judge's mind. His back to the bench, he glanced at the two men seated behind his table, revealing the patient stalker's confident grin of triumph at hand. He stopped at the jury box and rested his hands on the rail, leaning forward, staring at the empty chairs. Slowly, he turned. "They are . . . alive?"

Jean Shawshequay's expression did not change. She kept her eyes on the attorney as a cornered badger would keep its eyes on the wolf, knowing the hole it was backed into was its own. She didn't fear him. She didn't fear the process. Indeed, she welcomed it. "Yes," she said. "They are alive."

Attorney John Meachum started to walk toward her. "You are an expert in native beliefs, are you not?"

"I have a degree in Anthropology. And presently I am editorial director for Native American publications at the University of Oklahoma. Any legal characterization of me as an expert is up to the judge."

At the table opposite the one where Meachum's two clients sat, counsel for the petitioner Larry Wolf could not repress a smile. His witness was born to testify.

"Be that as it may," Meachum continued, "your attorney has offered you as an expert witness."

She looked at her attorney, then back at Meachum as if such a self-evident fact needed no confirmation. But she answered anyway. "He has."

"And the reason you came all the way from Oklahoma to northern Michigan was to testify as an expert."

"I came to help in the effort to protect against the desecration of ancestral burial grounds."

"By testifying as an expert."

"If you insist on characterizing me as an expert, I'll cede to your opinion."

Meachum's eyes narrowed almost imperceptibly as he evaluated his opponent. "Thank you," he drawled, without a trace of any real gratitude, "for your kind offer to yield to my opinion. But it is *your* opinion that concerns us. Your expert opinion. And so there can be no misunderstanding, I ask you, is it your *expert* opinion," he said, pronouncing the word *expert* in a manner that suggested it was a synonym for quack, "that these spirits, these supernatural beings, are in fact, alive?"

"Yes. That is my opinion."

"And a university sponsored archaeological expedition should be prevented because it offends these spirits?"

Larry Wolf exploded to his feet. "Your Honor. If counsel wishes to belittle this woman's religious beliefs, I suppose there's nothing I can do to prevent that. But the issue here is the desecration of a possible Ojibwa burial site. Not the underlying validity of her religion."

"Mr. Wolf has offered this individual as an expert," Meachum said. "In other words, she's here to offer her scientific opinion as to why this court should issue an injunction to stop a perfectly legitimate scientific expedition. As such, the basis of her scientific opinion is something this court must evaluate."

"The basis of her religious beliefs is beyond the purview of this or any other court."

"Not when it is offered as justification—"

"Gentlemen," Judge Hayes interjected loudly, raising both palms toward the attorneys. "I fully understand the issue and what is or is not probative of it. Since this is not a trial, and since I assure you when the time comes, I will present on the record clearly and unequivocally the reasons for how I rule on the preliminary injunction regarding excavation at the Cave of Bones, I suggest you both cut each other some slack." The judge leaned back slowly in his chair. "Now, if you don't mind, I'd like to ask a few questions of my own."

The attorneys eyed each other like two boxers forced to their corners.

"Ms. Shawshequay," Judge Hayes continued, turning toward the witness box. "You say these ancient spirits, of your ancestors, and indeed, of the animals, are alive. Could you explain more fully what you mean?"

Jean Shawshequay had the unhurried delivery of a person content to let things unfold at their own pace. Perhaps that was due in part to where she was raised, but more than that, it was due to the simple fact of her confidence. Confidence that she was right, the other side was wrong, and that in civil discourse such absolutes can never be confused.

She showed none of the outward traits of a crusader. Rather, she looked like a business executive. She wore a dark green suit with a check hard to see from a distance, a white blouse open at the collar, and a malachite necklace. Her hair was swept to both sides from a part on the left and tied in back with a scarf so that it hung in a straight black column well below her neck.

Cocking her head just slightly so she could look toward the judge, she responded. "The spiritual beings that populate the natural world of the Native American are alive in the same sense that ordinary bread and wine at a Catholic Mass become the body and blood of the Son of God."

"A court must afford supernatural beings legal respect because they are part of someone's religious beliefs?"

"True religious belief is given life by the act of believing. Whether certain tenets of faith are demonstrably provable or not, faith transforms the believers, and it is they which we in science, and the law, must respect, if not the beliefs themselves."

Judge Hayes rocked back slowly. "So you are suggesting that if a group of people believe something strongly enough, to the point it qualifies as a religion, then courts should treat their beliefs as the truth?"

"The Constitution protects their right to hold certain religious beliefs as true. To allow acts which are a desecration of those beliefs would be inconsistent with the protections prescribed by the Constitution."

"So this is a freedom of religion issue?" the judge asked.

"In part."

"Oh, for crying out loud," one of the men at Meachum's table exclaimed in disgust.

"Mr. Heath," Meachum cautioned quietly. "Please."

"You're going to let that go unchallenged?"

"Nothing will go unchallenged."

"If Mr. Heath has something to say," the judge said, "I have no objection to letting him speak his mind."

With client and judge of the same mind, there wasn't anything Meachum could do but yield.

Curtis Heath stood behind the table, buttoning his suit jacket, gray with just the trace of a herringbone pattern. Bald on top, with a neatly trimmed tuft of hair around the sides and back, Heath was a man in his early fifties who had the soft appearance of someone who spends most of his time in an office.

It hadn't always been that way for him. He had built his reputation in the field and because of that reputation had been tapped to run the Great Lakes Natural History Museum in Detroit, and its renowned collection of Native American woodland artifacts.

Heath looked from the woman on the stand to the black-robed figure behind the bench. "Your Honor," he began, "the witness would like it to become a freedom of religion issue, but if it is a matter of freedom of religion, I'd like to ask, whose religion?" He paused to let his question hang in the air for a few moments; then he continued, offering his own view of things. "She and her side have no more right to claim a religious interest in this site than I do. It is an abandoned and forgotten location on the edge of a sinkhole overgrown by trees, and to suggest it is a sacred place held in great reverence by these people now is not only patently absurd, it is a thinly disguised grab for power or some supposed financial control over what could be an important archaeological discovery."

"Because my people didn't build pyramids or carve gaudy monuments to mark the last resting place of their ancestors doesn't mean we revere our dead any less. All we seek is to allow their spirits to rest in peace."

"These aren't even your people," Heath said, exasperated. "From all indications, this is a prehistoric site, from before the time tribes of the Algonquin stock inhabited this area."

"If by prehistoric you mean pre-white, then any lack of clarity over lineage is a fault of yours, not ours. You seem to think that there's a line that divides time, with no connection between before and after. But there is a connection. We are the sons and daughters of those that came before on this land the same as you and others like you are the sons and daughters of those who lived in England or France or Italy. We don't have family Bibles inscribed with generations of names, but there is a kinship that extends back over the years. It is a kinship which we honor and hold sacred, and which places certain duties upon us. Foremost among them is the duty to protect the bones of the Ancient Ones from desecration."

As she spoke, the man still seated at Heath's table watched her carefully. He was drawn to the dignified bearing of her composure, to the exquisite control she exhibited over even the most minute of moves. Her back was as straight as the flagpole next to her, her face as hard as chiseled granite, and if black could ever be the color of fire, her eyes were twin discs at the heart of an inferno. She didn't blink, her head barely moved, and even the power of her speech disguised a quietly stated passion. But Fielding could see the passion; he could feel it; he could sense it in her every turn of phrase. It was more than a single person's conviction. It was as if she were the fountainhead for the past convictions of a people whose voices had been stolen from them.

As he listened, Christopher Fielding felt as though he were immersed in the flow of her words, cascading onto his shoulders, tempting him to enter the current. The pull of her voice wasn't something he was inclined to resist.

"Miss Shawshequay," Meachum said forcefully, cutting off his client. "You are Potawatomi, are you not?"

"Yes. I am."

"Though you speak very eloquently about kinship and responsibility, surely you don't mean to suggest that the Potawatomi too have a stake in this matter."

"Mr. Meachum," she said evenly, the toneless quality of her voice carrying more anger than if she had shouted at the top of her lungs. "The Potawatomi are the Keepers-of-the-Fire, the sacred fire that was never to die. Along with the Ojibwa and the Ottawa, we were known collectively as the Three Fires. We were a confederation of sorts, of peoples related by language and traditions. Most of the Potawatomi were resettled in the west on arid land as different to the land they were accustomed to as the Sahara would be to you. Some may have been moved by force, others because there was no reasonable choice. As for my own ancestors, they were resettled in Kansas during the last century. But hear me clearly, Mr. Meachum. Though you may move the ground under my feet, and tear the children from my grandmother's bosom, there is nothing that you can do or say that will come between me and the dead of this land."

Fielding felt his blood rise as he listened to her. Internally, he felt the same sense of outrage she radiated. It was a strange sensation, for in effect he was enraged at his own complicity in the affair. It was he, after all, who led the archaeological expedition to the site. It was he, Christopher Fielding, who had drilled the cores and uncovered the crucial evidence that verified the importance of the find. And it was he, Associate Professor of Archaeology at the University of Michigan, who had convinced the museum to underwrite the initial phase of excavation.

"Miss Shawshequay. We are not the enemy. Judge Hayes," Meachum said, turning toward the bench. "We are as concerned about native rights as anyone. More than most, for that matter. Our collection of Great Lakes Indian artifacts is one of the most complete anywhere. The scholarship the museum has sponsored in partnership with university scholars has enriched the national understanding of native cultures. All we seek is to continue the good work that we have accomplished."

Larry Wolf countered, "What you seek is a continuation of your paternalistic hold over the lives, the effects, and the afterlife of a living culture which to you is little more than an interesting field of study, fit for nothing more than a source for curiosities to stock the glass shelves of your museum."

"That's a slanderous outrage," Heath cried, leaning forward, bracing himself against the table. "And what I find an even bigger outrage is that radical elements like you would deny to others of your race the chance to rediscover their lost culture."

"If you think I'm a radical, then you have no idea of the depth of opposition to you out there."

"What's that supposed to mean?"

"It means that my client Miriam Goodmedicine as president of the Ojibwa Association has tried to be reasonable about this from the very beginning. She has rejected what some of the more radical voices in the community have advocated. All she seeks is the basic right of being able to speak for her dead ancestors."

"What you really want is for us to turn our backs on antiquity because of some fanciful notion that people dead for centuries will somehow take offense at having their bleached bones pulled from a forgotten hole in the ground."

The crack of the gavel was like the sound of a rifle shot in the cavernous room. Heath jerked to attention; Wolf spun toward the bench. Judge Hayes eyed both men in turn, twisting the head of the gavel in his palm as if hoping for the pretext to hurl it at the first person who broke the peace.

It was all so unnecessary, Fielding thought. He had never imagined what had begun as an exciting discovery could devolve into this. But he should have seen it coming, he realized, when Curtis Heath had insisted on coming north for the hearing. He had battled with him over everything from plans of excavation to Heath's insistence on joint authorship of his papers. He should have known that in a situation that demanded sensitivity and compromise, Heath was preordained to incite conflict.

Fielding rested his forehead on his fingertips, his elbow planted on the table. He felt ashamed and frustrated and angry all at the same time. But what could be done about it now?

When he looked up, he saw that Jean Shawshequay was staring at him, her black fire trained directly on his eyes alone. And then she looked toward Heath, her expression unchanging. To her, they were one and the same.

"Ms. Shawshequay," the judge said. "What do you believe happens if the bones of your ancestors are disturbed?"

"It is believed that the afterworld is very much like the world in which we live, with the same environment, the same kinds of challenges. Though the spirits of our ancestors are of the afterworld, they are linked to where they came from. If their remains are dishonored, the violation will affect them in the next life, making it more difficult to meet the challenges they face, preventing them from reaching their final peace. Some even say that the spirits can never truly be at rest until their bones have been left long enough so as to be reduced to dust. Only then is the link to this world severed."

Fielding released a wavering breath. There was no reason for the dispute. There was every reason to be working on the same side. It just didn't make sense. To be adversaries. To be in conflict. To be arguing over a matter that was so patently of mutual interest. But they were arguing. They were in conflict. They had become adversaries.

As his frustrations mounted, the attorneys continued to talk.

"Every venue that has considered the issue," Larry Wolf said to the court, "has come down on the side of the Indian. The Smithsonian Institution has formulated a new policy to repatriate the remains of all identifiable specimens. Stanford University has recently agreed to return the bones of over five hundred Indians for reinterment. The Senate Select Committee on Indian

Affairs has said that museums should inventory their Native American artifacts and seek out Indian groups that have an interest in them. The trend is clear and unequivocal. Where a dispute arises over Native American remains, it is up to the descendants of those people to decide how that dispute should be resolved."

"With all due respect to those fine institutions you mentioned," Meachum began, and as he countered with his legal argument, his words seemed to fade from Fielding's hearing. The man's voice was lost to the clamor of his own inner voice.

Fielding shifted nervously in his chair. He leaned forward, his forearms pressed against the edge of the table. They were all so intent on their own narrow views. But they were all missing the point. Worse, they were fabricating controversy out of consensus. It just wasn't right.

Fielding closed his eyes, as if trying to shut out the affair. He threw himself back, his face lifted toward the ceiling. A helpless, frustrated sensation began to take root within him. It grew of its own accord, giving off its own heat. All he could think of was the lost opportunity. The endless words. The look of black fire. He felt hot, and sick. And angry. And finally, he could be still no longer.

Fielding slammed both palms on the table in front of him and jumped to his feet. "Stop!"

The room came to a sudden and forced stillness. Fielding looked from the judge to the attorney representing his institution, to the witness on the stand. In each was his or her own individual mix of anger or irritation or dislike. But Fielding was blind to all that now. He was blind to the black fire the same as he was blind to the glare of his benefactor.

"What has happened to us?" he cried out, venting his frustration now like uncapped steam. "Why have we become adversaries over this? Why do we insist on perceiving only the worst in each of us?" Looking to Wolf, he said, "I have no desire to desecrate ancient graves." Then turning to the witness, he continued, "I don't wish to hinder your people's quest for a current identity. And I don't think you wish to turn your back on legitimate historical inquiry which can only aid in defining that identity. What this is all about," he said, throwing his arms up, indicating the court itself, its proceedings, "is distrust and misunderstanding. Don't you all see that? Don't you share my frustration?"

"We *are* frustrated," Larry Wolf said. "The problem is—"

The gavel cracked again crisply. "Counsel. I don't think Mr. Fielding was finished." The judge sensed a building accommodation, and he didn't want anything to derail the momentum.

"We are frustrated, Mr. Wolf," Fielding continued, "because we all know, at its core, all of what we are doing here today is a waste of time. Worse than that. It's absolutely senseless. It's senseless because we are arguing over graves that we don't even know to exist. It may be called the Cave of Bones, but it's no cave, and I think we're all agreed the origin of the name has nothing to do with human bones.

"All we know for certain based on the test cores is that on the lip of that sinkhole in the middle of the woods some centuries ago some unnamed people lived. That's all. There is absolutely no indication that this is an ancient grave site. In fact, there is every indication that it is not. The evidence suggests that this site was strictly one of habitation."

"Where people lived, people died," said Jean Shawshequay. "And where they died, they were buried."

"But not under the floors of their homes. If there are burial sites within a hundred yards of the village, for all practical purposes they could be on the moon. The time and effort to excavate a mere ten-foot square precludes even the remotest chance of expanding so far afield that we would accidentally uncover a grave."

"Just because no actual grave site has been uncovered," she said, "that does not mean we don't have the right to prevent the possibility of desecration before it occurs."

"She's right, isn't she, Mr. Fielding?" the judge said. "The existence of a constitutional right implies the power to prospectively protect that right, does it not? To wait until a right has been violated before redress is offered is to, in this case, deny the right itself."

"My point is there is no possibility that what she speaks of will happen. And to issue an injunction on an unfounded fear is to unfairly close our minds to the advancement of knowledge."

"Are you suggesting that the Ojibwa Association rely on your assurances alone that no grave site will be disturbed?" the judge asked.

"I'm suggesting that we work together on this. It's a relatively simply matter. Join me at the dig. I welcome your participation, at whatever level you choose. If all you care to do is observe, to keep an eye on me, that's fine too."

Fielding paused, letting the suggestion hang. Whether what he had said was being accepted or not, there was a definite shift in the atmosphere. Most noticeably with Curtis Heath. The man's jaw was clenched like a vise.

"I'm not a grave robber," Fielding continued. "I'm a scientist. I'm interested in uncovering evidence of past civilization and then reading the record. If we work together on this, we not only will broaden our general knowledge, we can ensure that there will be no violation of anyone's religious beliefs."

Larry Wolf began to move slowly to the center of the court, drawing the focus of attention to himself, while at the same time giving himself a few moments to think. Standing near the bench, he turned toward Fielding. "We appreciate your sentiments, Mr. Fielding, and your candor in identifying the problem that concerns us as nothing more than robbing graves. But what you've said brings us to an issue we haven't yet discussed. The matter of artifacts and quite simply—assuming there is an excavation—who should take an ownership interest in them."

Attorney Meachum responded quickly, speaking before Fielding could open his mouth. "Surely you don't mean to suggest that as a legal principle there is anyone alive today who can assert ownership over mere objects of daily life that have been abandoned and buried for centuries?"

"What may be *mere objects* of daily life to you may well have a sacred function to us."

"The broken shards of a cooking pot? Flakes of stone chipped off an arrowhead?"

"Objects that contribute to the cultural identity of a people whose culture has been practically obliterated, by all moral rights *must* belong to the descendants of those people."

Meachum's chin rose a fraction as he considered his adversary. "Is this some new law out of the legislature I haven't heard about?" he asked, the derision thick in his tone. "Or is it something that has been passed down to you directly from some higher source?"

"Gentlemen," Judge Hayes said. "And ladies. Before we go too far afield, I think it might be useful to evaluate more fully Mr. Fielding's suggestion. Perhaps if a framework for understanding can be worked out, maybe the rest of it will fall into line."

"Your Honor," Meachum said. "I fail to see how Mr. Fielding's extemporaneous remarks would form the basis for a framework for understanding, given Mr. Wolf's rather peculiar grasp of the law."

"I'm sorry to hear you are afflicted with such a case of blindness. For your sake, I hope the condition is temporary." The judge stood behind the bench. "Let's give ourselves ten minutes to catch our wind. Then we'll gather in my chambers, where I think an informal assessment of where we stand will be more fruitful."

And where he can twist arms toward a compromise, the two attorneys realized.

The gavel sounded and the judge was off the bench.

"Hey, Fielding."

The archaeologist was too caught in the grip of his own thoughts to hear the court officer. He kept walking.

"Hey, Fielding. Wait."

This time he noticed. He turned to the man in uniform, a deputy sheriff. "Yeah?"

"When you're done in here, the sheriff wants a word with you. If you don't mind."

"Something about the case?"

"No. He just wants to ask you a few questions about some things happening out in the woods. You're out there every day, aren't you?"

"Just about."

"Good. His office is just down the hall. If that's okay?"

"Sure," Fielding agreed. "I'd be glad to." Some things happening in the woods?

"Chris!" It was Heath, waiting for him.

Christopher Fielding's sport coat was an all-purpose jacket. He wore it hiking in the woods as readily as in a court of law. At the moment, it was doubling as his formal attire. Underneath he wore a light blue canvas shirt with wrinkles that would resist any iron, if he had chosen to iron it. His tie was thin and yellow with two vertical blue lines that ran down along the left edge.

The contrast between him and Curtis Heath was as complete in every other regard. Where Heath was soft, Fielding was conditioned by the outdoors. It was where he received his energy, whether at work or on his own time, which more frequently than not overlapped.

Mustached, with hair naturally waved so that it found its own order, Fielding was a man moved by the pursuit of new discoveries, whether a recognizable form taking fuller shape out of encased dirt with each swish of a brush, or the undetected approach to a beaver floating gnawed branches to its lodge. He was energized by the world of ideas, and whatever innate aggression he possessed was directed not at personal accomplishment, but rather toward the vigorous defense of his beliefs. He had the singular capacity to see the same attributes in other people, and it was to them he was attracted, even if those beliefs were diametrically opposed to his.

Curtis Heath may have been like him when he was younger. But if he had been, something had happened that changed him.

Seeking a few minutes of seclusion, Meachum had directed his two clients into the witness waiting room. As soon as the door clicked shut, Heath turned on Fielding. "What in the hell is wrong with you?"

Despite past confrontations, Fielding was still thrown off guard. The museum director was coming on even stronger than he usually did.

"What right do you have," Heath continued, "to compromise the museum's position without consulting us?"

"We were going backwards in there," Fielding said. "What we have to do is build bridges, not set down the gauntlet."

"Some conflicts are unavoidable. And you don't make things better by giving in to the other side."

"There is no other side. This isn't an athletic event. It's the search for knowledge, and understanding. And if we stop insisting on being their adversaries for just a minute and reach out to them, they'll understand. And they'll want to join us."

"Are you crazy? Give them standing to interfere, and the first chicken bone you uncover, they'll bring everything to a screeching halt."

"The way positions have hardened in there, things have already come to a halt. We'll be in court three years before the first shovel of dirt is tossed on the sieve."

"That won't happen," Meachum said. "What they say may sound good, but they don't have a legal leg to stand on."

"Forget about the legalities," Fielding said, pressing his point. "Don't you think they have a right to protect the sanctity of their ancestors' final resting places?" Turning toward Heath, he continued, "Don't you think we as archaeologists owe them that?"

"As archaeologists, we owe it to the museum not to bend under pressure and superstitious hokum. We owe it to the museum to return to it something for its investment. You heard Wolf in there. Give in to one demand and there'll be another. You concede on the bones and he's after the artifacts. You give him a position to observe the excavation, and he'll want to control it."

"Who cares who controls it?" Fielding exclaimed.

"I care," Heath blurted, stabbing himself in the chest with the fingertips of one hand tented tightly together. "And don't give me that sanctimonious crap about truth and the pure pursuit of knowledge. You might like to think you stand apart from all the dirty business of fund-raising and kissing ass, but no matter how morally convenient that all is for you, without me and the institution I represent, *you* don't have a leg to stand on."

Three quick raps struck the outer door. "The judge is ready for you now," the court officer called.

Heath turned to his attorney. "So what the hell are we going to do in there?"

Meachum pressed his lips tightly together and shook his head once. "I'm afraid Judge Hayes loves Fielding's idea. Our only hope is that the other side dislikes it more than we do."

At a glance, it was apparent to Fielding that Meachum's hope had been realized. Larry Wolf, Jean Shawshequay, and Miriam Goodmedicine were already seated when they entered, and it was on Fielding that the attorney and the two women focused their gaze. Wolf eyed him warily, and in Shawshequay the black fire smoldered, while Miriam Goodmedicine, at fifty years old or so, with short hair waved by a permanent, seemed the least threatening and least threatened. She looked like a kindly grade-school teacher—which is exactly what she was—and her reason for focusing on the archaeologist was curiosity.

Miriam was seated on a sofa, Jean near her in a lightly padded chair, and standing next to her with his hands on the back of a matching chair as if it were a lectern was attorney Wolf. As soon as the others greeted the judge and sat down, Wolf began. "Let me just say that we appreciate Mr. Fielding's sentiments, and though his suggestion on its surface may seem to have some merit, I'm afraid at this point there is no way the Ojibwa Association can agree to be party to his project. No matter how benign his suggestion may sound, without clearly stated rights and lines of authority, the situation would be unworkable."

"And why is that?" asked the judge.

"I would envisage a situation that when disagreements arose, we could be forced to run to the court on a daily basis, exhausting the finances and perhaps even the will of the Association."

"Oh, I don't envisage that," Hayes observed, rocking back in his chair behind the desk. "Do you, Mr. Fielding?"

"If you please, Your Honor," Meachum interrupted. "Mr. Fielding is a scientist, as he said, and an idealist. I'm not confident he can appreciate the technical nature of the problems that may arise."

Judge Hayes still had on his robe, but it was now unzipped down the center. Folding his hands across his middle, he said to Fielding, "Is that true? You simply don't understand the nature of the problem?"

"No, sir, that's not true," Fielding said. "I've directed a number of excavations, both here in Michigan and in other Great Lakes states, working with Native Americans as my students and alongside them as my colleagues, and there have never been any problems that were not resolved. As for the artifacts themselves," he added, nodding toward Larry Wolf, "I'm interested in scholarship and learning, not in acquiring a treasure trove of objects."

"Would you let them know your plans in advance?" Judge Hayes asked, leaning forward.

"Yes."

"Would you let them take part in the planning?"

Fielding nodded. "I'd welcome their suggestions."

"You'd talk over every procedure, in advance?"

"Whatever they wanted."

"They'd have open access to the site?" Hayes continued to press. "They'd be able to watch everything that goes on?"

"We could work side by side, if they'd like."

The judge's expression softened. His eyebrows lifted, and slowly he eased back again in his chair, looking at the other parties in turn. Heath's face was white as bleached limestone. Shawshequay's eyes were darting nervously, angrily, between the judge and her attorney.

Hayes said, "It seems a reasonable grant of permission."

"Permission can be withdrawn," Jean Shawshequay said, a harsh edge to her voice. In the courtroom, on the witness stand, she hadn't let her anger show so openly. Perhaps that was because it was easier to maintain composure in the face of an unbending foe. After all, it wasn't so easy to marshal righteous passion in the face of moderation. And that's what made her so mad now. Fielding was beating her with reasonableness.

"What she means, Judge," Wolf said, "is that permission implies authority, and if there should be any authority over that site, it should rest with the Indian. Then if permission is to be withdrawn, it will be the Indian who withdraws it."

"I'm not so sure it matters all that much who's in charge from that standpoint," the judge replied. "What makes sense to me is that the person running the show knows what he's doing, and it's fairly obvious to me that not only is Mr. Fielding the one who knows this site best, he at least," the judge emphasized, pointedly excluding Heath from his observation, "strikes me as eminently reasonable."

Swiveling his chair so it faced Miriam Goodmedicine, Hayes addressed her directly, bypassing her attorney and the expert witness. "The question is, Miriam, who would the Association have to adequately represent itself at the site of the excavation?"

"I haven't heard any acceptance of that man's proposal," Jean Shawshequay said, edging forward in her chair. "In principle or in any other regard. So with all due respect, discussing a possible representative is a waste of time."

"Hypothetically then," Hayes said, still eyeing the president of the Ojibwa Association. "Can you think of someone who could represent your interests?"

Ignoring her only increased Jean's agitation. She said, "I believe we are entitled to a ruling on the injunction."

"Miriam, humor me." Hayes cocked his eyes, silently repeating the question.

Goodmedicine rested a hand on Jean's knee, stopping her before she could interrupt again. "I'm not sure I can answer that, George," she said, thinking. "For starters, it would have to be someone with the background to understand what was being done."

"You'd need a lot more than that," Jean said.

Goodmedicine nodded. "We'd need someone experienced in

archaeology, with a working knowledge of techniques and procedures."

"Someone who could understand what they were told," Jean said, her eyes locking distrustfully on Fielding. "And who could determine if they were being deliberately misled."

"We'd need someone who understood the culture and the old ways, and what was important to us."

"Someone who believed strongly in the cause and who could be trusted."

"We would need someone who was not afraid of standing up to the powerful interests against us."

"Someone who was aware of the issues, and of past patterns of sacrilege," Jean said, turning her gaze on Heath.

"We would need," Miriam concluded, "someone like Jean Shawshequay."

"Someone who could recognize—" The Potawatomi anthropologist from Oklahoma stopped in mid-sentence. The black fire in her eyes was extinguished with the efficacy of water on coals. She looked toward Miriam. "What?"

"You have the background. You have the knowledge to observe and interpret and understand."

"Yes. But surely . . ." she said, her speech trailing off, her head beginning to shake back and forth in a tight spasm.

"There are others? Not me. And not anyone else that I can think of. Not like you."

"But I can't do this."

"Why?"

"I just can't. I've got a job. I've got a full list to worry about. I haven't even finished editing everything for the fall."

"You spoke well of kinship before. And duties. Foremost among them, protecting the Ancient Ones from desecration. Is what you have to do in Oklahoma more important than that?"

Jean's breath came erratically, and she found she was looking toward the judge for help. He would understand. But in his face she saw the same look as in Miriam's.

"They are alive," Miriam continued. "If you do not protect them, who will?"

"It won't be that long," Fielding said, and at the sound of his voice the black fire was back. He continued, "And if you want, you can bring your work to the site. We have a tent."

It was all his fault. He had originated the problem. He had offered the solution. "It's out of the question," she spat out angrily, her voice poisoned by the venom she held for the archaeologist.

The harsh finality of her proclamation silenced the room. Hayes rocked back slowly, studying her as if making secret judgments. When he spoke, his calmness was a counterpoint to her anger. "I can't order you," he said, his eyes locked on hers, his silent evaluation continuing. "But I can deny the injunction."

For a second her eyes flared wide in defiance, but just as fast, reality set in. She glared at the judge, then Fielding, then all of them in the chambers. She was livid, but in the end, she was left with no real choice.

"You will have unrestricted access to the site," the judge said in summary. "If any bones are uncovered, the excavation at that location will cease immediately. All artifacts are to be under Mr. Fielding's control for at least a reasonable period of study. After that, if both sides can't work out an agreeable arrangement, the matter will be brought before me. Neither the museum nor the university is to sell or destroy anything without the express authorization of the court. Does that about cover it all?"

The attorneys nodded.

"Then let's go in and put it on the record."

The session didn't end soon enough for Jean Shawshequay. She bolted from the court and was down the steps in front before Fielding came through the door.

"Wait!" he called, but she didn't stop. She didn't turn. She didn't acknowledge him in any way. "Jean!"

Fielding ran down the county-building steps after her. Striding quickly, he had closed to within a half dozen paces when she spun around. He stopped in his tracks, and for a few seconds they eyed each other across a silent gulf. Fielding forced a swallow, then said, "I'm sorry this is going to cause you so much trouble."

"You could care less," she said. "It's your work that's important, and to hell with everybody else."

"I didn't plan for all this to happen."

"You didn't do anything to stop it."

Fielding took a deep breath, turning away from her for a moment, looking down the street, up at the trees. He was struggling for a way to get past her anger. "Listen," he said at last, "being enemies isn't going to help anything. What's important is what

happens between us from this point on. We'll be working together, and whatever I can do to make things easier, I'll try to
do. If you let me."

Shawshequay eyed him with stony contempt.

Fielding nodded in the direction of his truck. "I'm going out
there in a little while. Perhaps you'd like to go with me. To see
the site."

She raised a finger and leveled it like the barrel of a gun at his
chest. "We'll stop you. One way or another, we will stop you."

The weapon that was her hand slowly came back down to her
side. When she turned and started walking away, Fielding
didn't pursue her. He could only stand and stare, her threat
eclipsing all other thoughts that tried to take shape in his mind.

"Fielding!" The voice came from the courthouse steps.

It took a second to strike home, and when it did, he turned.

It was the court officer, the deputy sheriff. He called, "The
sheriff?"

The sheriff, he thought. He wanted to talk to him. Fielding
nodded, then walked back toward the county building.

In a town like Watersdrop, there weren't many manhunts. In
fact, last night's was the first one Sheriff Dick Halstead had ever
taken part in. It was unusual, but it was a special case.

"I understand you're out there every day," Halstead said to
Fielding. "Sometimes late?"

"Yeah, that's right."

"Have you noticed anything out of the ordinary lately?"

"Like what?"

"Like a truck parked in the middle of the woods. Anybody
acting strange. A guy doing his best to stay clear of you."

"No."

"Ever hear any gunfire?"

"Gunfire? Why? What's this about?" The Indians, Fielding
was thinking.

Halstead was tired, and he looked it. He motioned to a well-
worn wooden chair and Fielding sat down. Settling himself, one
haunch on the edge of his desk, the sheriff told Fielding about
last night's vigil, the interdepartmental effort, how close he
thought they had actually come. "The only way we didn't have
covered was straight back into the woods," he concluded. "Toward the sinkhole."

Fielding thought for a moment, then shrugged. "Sorry. I haven't noticed anything unusual at all out there."

"You ever talk to any of the people who live out that way?"

"I didn't know anyone lived out there."

"Oh, there's a few. Not necessarily on the road to the sinkhole, but out there in the woods. Mostly your standard recluse, get-away-from-society type. I thought you might have bumped into some of them."

"No. I never have."

"Have you heard of somebody called Buck?"

"No."

"His real name is Henry Billings."

Fielding shook his head, then asked, "He one of the recluses?"

"Yeah. He's got a little shack of a cabin out there. Always was a real strange character."

"Is he the one you were looking for?"

Halstead raised his eyebrows, hesitating. "I think he might be. But the brown shirts . . . they don't seem to care much for my hunches." Halstead suddenly cleared his throat, glancing at Fielding as if he might have said too much. "So, uh, no gunshots?"

"I don't think so."

Halstead showed his impatience. "You mean you wouldn't recognize them if you heard them?"

"I mean I don't remember hearing any. Then again, I didn't have any reason to remember."

Halstead breathed heavily, then slid his leg off the desk, coming to his feet. "Well, if you do hear anything, let me know right away. Okay?"

Fielding agreed, then walked with Halstead to the door.

"He's a crazy son of a bitch," the sheriff said. "So if I was you, I'd be careful."

By the time Fielding had reached his truck, he was no longer thinking about the sheriff's warning. He was thinking about Jean Shawshequay. He was thinking about her threat.

Chapter 3

THE JEEP COMANCHE rolled slowly over the familiar path, rocking from side to side, dipping one tire at a time into depressions that in the typical summer, if they weren't filled with rainwater, at least showed the muddy residue of it. Now, they were bone dry.

Dust hung like a dirty mist in the wake of the vehicle. The trees were a buffer to whatever breeze there was, and under their canopy it seemed still and quiet. And tame.

Christopher Fielding couldn't afford even one wasted afternoon. Working by himself, there was a lot to do. Despite what Heath had said, Fielding was not unaware of the dirty business of seeking backing. He just did it on a different level.

Archaeological sites vied for limited dollars, and Fielding had used his early examination of the site to secure the museum's investment. Their funding had made possible a limited excavation, which he in turn hoped would be grounds for a government grant that would allow the excavation to begin in earnest next summer, with a full crew of student interns.

As the truck took a sandy rise, Fielding stepped harder on the accelerator. At the top, the road curved left, and as he guided the vehicle loosely through the turn, he glanced out the side window.

It was the high point on the trek into the site, and a rocky outcropping provided the only vista of the sinkhole from a distance. The Jeep had already slid past it and back behind the trees when Fielding hit the brakes. Something wasn't right. He glanced over his shoulder, but the truck was being overtaken by the drift of the dust.

He shifted into reverse and shot back to the opening. Grabbing his binoculars, he climbed outside and stepped through thick tufts of grass to a boulder that broke through the soil. Looking out over the sweep of the forest, he could see the circular mark of the sinkhole, set in the continuous, rolling carpet of tree crowns like the imprint of an elephant's foot in wet grass. He had just enough altitude to see the depression, but not enough to look down into the pit itself. But that wasn't what had caught his attention anyway. It was what was in the air, trapped in the arboreal bowl, hovering in long bluish streaks like the smoggy residue of cigars in an unventilated room.

Fielding sensed a nervous uptick to the pace of his heart. A fire? He jerked the binoculars to his eyes and worked the focus back and forth. But even in focus, a cloud at best was just a blur.

He lowered the binoculars, trusting his own vision to bring distinction to the scene. Was it simply a layer of dust? But kicked up by what? There was no wind, at least not enough to penetrate the canopy.

Fielding stalked along the crest of the rise, trying to get a different perspective. And for a second it seemed to work. The afternoon sun backlit the forest, and the haze suddenly seemed just a function of the glare. His heart quickened again, this time from relief. It had been an illusion. He had imagined the smoke, anticipated the worst. The suggestion of problems had already been planted by all that had happened in court, and for Fielding, the expectation of trouble was just waiting for the slightest reason to emerge.

Despite the explanations cycling rapidly through his mind, Fielding's anxiety did not lessen. Through it all, he realized that the smoke was indeed real. It was trapped in the hollow of the sinkhole. There had been a fire at the site of the dig.

"Damn it!"

Fielding spun in place and dashed back to the Jeep. He fired the ignition, dropped the stick into first, and the truck lurched back onto the trail.

There was movement amid the stillness. Clandestine, furtive, but nonetheless discernible amid the branches and the ferns. It was a mark of restlessness perhaps more than anything, restlessness brought on by waiting.

At least that's how the movement would be perceived, in human terms. But those that caused the movement bore only a superficial resemblance to things human, and if they truly were as they appeared, could beings of such otherworldly design be thought to exhibit the thoroughly human trait of impatience?

The plants and animals had changed since the retreat of the last ice sheet, but the land itself had changed very little. It had been shared by a succession of life forms, some still surviving in their own particular niches.

Man had come twelve thousand years ago, at first living at the edge of retreating glaciers, then prospering and suffering with the changing climate, with the changing times. Some people immigrated into the area, then emigrated out a few generations later. Some people came and were moved out by others; some came and died, leaving no heirs.

The people who had shared this land over the millennia might not have all been directly related by blood, but they shared certain things that linked them to one another more significantly than the strict criteria of the geneticist's code. From the people who brought down sixteen-thousand-pound beasts with nothing more than chipped bits of stone, to those who first witnessed the strangely clad visitors from a new world, they were linked by their philosophy of nature.

It was a philosophy that nurtured religions with a pantheon of gods and demons that could rival the most imaginative mythic creations of the Greek or Roman worlds. In these woods where successions of native peoples hunted and camped, worked and slept, the spirits of their invention survived. They survived in the stealth of a fox, in the spring greening of the leaves, the majesty of the black bear, in the whisper of the wind. The spirits survived in the claps of a summer storm, in the grace of an eagle.

And they survived in the beings that moved restlessly in the brush and trees that enveloped the dirt-track road. Representatives of the Ancient Ones, they had witnessed enough sacrilege. Now it was time to stop the desecrator. It was for him they waited.

Fielding had one hand on the wheel, leaving the other free for the stick. He worked it hard, downshifting in the turns, then stretching it out at every opportunity.

It was a tight course the road laid, not meant for speed. It was one of the old lumber trails that ribboned the north country, kept from being completely overgrown by the occasional traffic drawn to the geological curiosity of the sinkhole.

After a storm a year ago, a hiker, who was one of the curious, noticed a small round stone with a concave pit on one side lying at the bottom of a newly cut drainage ravine. It was just a piece of granite, but it was so perfectly formed, the visitor knew it had to be man-made. He brought it to the University of Michigan Department of Archaeology, and Associate Professor Christopher Fielding confirmed at a glance that first impression. And Fielding realized there was much more to the story.

The worked piece of granite was a grinding bowl used for pulverizing nuts and grains into flour. Indians of the area were quick to make use of European trade goods, and the fact this was a stone implement told him it was probably pre-contact, or at least Early Historic. The similarities to other pieces already identified made him feel it was more likely Late Woodland, a period not as well documented as both earlier and later eras. Most significant to Fielding, that first day he saw the granite bowl, was that the artifact would have been used in a sedentary process of food preparation. That meant it was probably close to a habitation site. In other words, the true importance of the find was not so much the tool itself, but the fact that it could well mark a much larger discovery.

Fielding came and drilled exploratory cores, turning up charcoal in spots, bits of pottery in others. Strong evidence of a habitation site. Evidence that he used to secure Heath's sponsorship for his solitary excavation.

Since he had begun the surveying and plotting, no one but him had been out there. Until now.

The native peoples believed not in the transcendence of man over animals, but in the equality of living things. Each species had the same claim to the land, and each had its own spirits to protect it. Sometimes the traits of man were ascribed to the spirits of animals, and the traits of the beasts, to man's. And sometimes, the spirits seemed a mix of the two.

In the woods, along the wheel-rutted trail, creatures of mixed design continued their vigil. They were at once grotesque and fantastic, inexplicable and yet undeniably real.

Individually and collectively, they displayed a mélange of features. Flesh and hide, fur and feathers were matched with beak and claw, talon and fang in an order that made sense only in the mythic inventions of the peoples who had shared this land.

The creatures appeared wild and ferocious, qualities not diminished by the hot fluids that pumped through their systems. Yet they were far from beasts of wanton violence. They knew precisely what had to be done. Layered firmly beneath their otherworldly rage was cold, humanlike reason.

Archaeology was a science of mysteries. It was a science of discarding surface truths in favor of buried complexity. It lent to its practitioners a different perspective on the world. By its nature, it made them see mystery where others were unable to see the contrivance.

For Christopher Fielding, the mysteries extended beyond the source of the haze in the sinkhole. The trees that flashed by the side windows seemed a solid curtain, blocking his vision to what lay beyond. The very road was no longer the familiar path into the site. The forest itself had become his adversary, working against his progress. Soft dirt tugged at the wheels, countless trunks of oaks and pines posed danger at every bend. Even the woody stems of bracken fern down the median scratched at the undercarriage of the Jeep, brittle claws of the forest itself trying to get a hold.

As these and other common things began to change, as the initial rush of anger ebbed lower, he began to consider the situation more thoroughly. What could the fire have destroyed? The tent. Survey stakes, cord, the dumping platform. Perhaps the screen frames. But nothing that couldn't be replaced. Unlike the stratified evidence locked in the ground itself.

And yet if they had wanted to stop his activity, would they have stopped at destroying mere tools? Or would they have scrambled the careful stratigraphy of the excavation so thoroughly as to destroy its scientific value?

He decided the fire might only be an adjunct to their strategy. If they truly wanted to stop his work, they would have taken pick and ax to the ground itself. Jean Shawshequay would have known that the site would be worthless if it could not be dated stratigraphically.

A mix of anger and anxiety began to rise again within him. As he continued working the clutch and the wheel, it never occurred to him that the best way to stop his work was to stop him.

Glassy eyes stared without blinking through the cover of vegetation. The shuffling, restless movement had ceased, as if all of the beings were controlled by a single switch.

The sudden stillness had gripped them all, and paradoxically, it was now the trees and the bushes that seemed restless. With a flutter of leaves, a rippling of fronds, it seemed a nervousness had come to the forest. It was as if—as the native peoples who had shared this land would have believed—the flora had their own spirits, and now they too were coming alive, joining the representatives of the fauna, anticipating the arrival of the desecrator.

The beings of mixed design became still because they could hear it. They could hear the distant clamor, the discordant sounds so alien to the ancient forest. Even the quiet was desecrated by the intruder.

As the noise came to them alternately lower then higher, so did the passions within them cycle in recurring waves. It was as though an offshore storm, seen in the distance for so long, were finally hitting the beach. The waves were coming harder, faster. The wind was increasing. Each new trough was deeper; each new crest, higher.

The creatures sensed the rising tide. They sensed the impending violence. They sensed that the full impact of the storm would soon strike.

It was a land of mystery. And of tension. And at this moment, fighting the constraints of the dirt trail, Fielding was increasingly subject to the effects of both.

Danger had not even been a consideration when he began his charge to the site. All he could think of was the possible senseless destruction of so rare an opportunity to glimpse a past world. It hadn't occurred to him that the starters of the fire might still be there, that caught in their crime, they might be forced to commit another.

As that thought began to slide into his consciousness, his grip on the wheel seemed to grow slippery. He hunched forward, stiffening his back, then almost immediately he shifted again, bracing himself back against the seat. He swallowed, then exhaled a wavering breath, conflicting reactions seeking the same end, an expulsion of the fear that he knew threatened to take control.

Fielding knew they might well still be there. In a practiced denial of involuntary fears, he told himself he hoped they were. He wanted to confront them.

The face that rose slowly above the brush displayed the stoicism of the Ancient Ones who had called this land their own. It betrayed no emotion. It seemed to lack any hint of expression. Its cheeks and forehead were covered in short brown hair that resembled the hide of a white-tailed deer. But that's where the resemblance ended. The face was flatter, the chin more elongated, and where the eyes should have been were placed instead black pits.

Though the face concealed its inner passions well, it was a visage that nonetheless portrayed a depth of conviction that could not be shaken no matter the strength of the forces it opposed. It was as though the creature had faced worse challenges, as though it had already made the ultimate sacrifice. Its dried skin and faded hair made it appear a creature once dead come back to life, returned to this world for this one important purpose, returned to this world to stop the desecration.

Despite their seeming connection to the otherworld, their strategy was firmly rooted in this one. To stop the desecrator, they must first stop the vehicle. And for that purpose, the plans had been well laid.

The Jeep Comanche's suspension was tough enough to absorb the worst of the jolts, but a wheeled vehicle had not been designed that could smooth the ruts and surface roots of the old lumber trail. From the asphalt highway into the sinkhole was three and a half, maybe four, miles. Usually it was a drive of fifteen to twenty minutes. At his current rate of progress, Fielding was going to cut that in half.

Just ahead was a sharp bend. Fielding recognized the spot, and he geared downward. As the woods began to close in, the vehicle slowed.

The eyeless deer that wasn't a deer jerked its head toward the flash of reflected light. Then through the trees came a flash of color. It was a shiny, metallic black, flickering with the patterns of the forest.

All the creatures perceived the approach of the vehicle. And they all reacted as if controlled by a single entity, holding their position, maintaining their camouflage. There was nothing to be done until the desecrator was separated from the metallic beast.

It wasn't supposed to happen this way. Field archaeology was a discipline of tedium: digging with trowels, breaking clumps of dirt to sand-sized particles, piecing together shards of earth-colored ware. The only violence was what might echo across the years. The mortality archaeologists faced was in the examination of bones lifted from centuries-old graves.

There shouldn't have been any dispute about the value of Fielding's work. Knowledge, though an end itself, also brought new understanding. And understanding instilled self-pride as it encouraged respect from others.

It was all so senseless. The only controversy in archaeology should come from conflicting analyses of ambiguous clues, not from the process of discovery itself.

Falling victim to the frustrations, feeling the heat of fading opportunity flare across his skin, Fielding slowed to a near crawl. He pulled hard on the wheel as he made the turn.

At the first sight of the nose of the vehicle, a hooting call pierced the air. It was suggestive of a great horned owl, and yet also strangely human.

The living creatures of myth reacted to the cue. A heightened tension was telegraphed from one to the next. Whatever manner of internal organs that powered them began to beat faster, harder. They sought a common rhythm, a joint exercise of will. The collective power generated seemed to coalesce above them, swirling together into one, coordinated assault. Even the leaves sensed the change. They fluttered as if reacting to the effect of rising heat.

The metal beast was almost there. It was almost time to act.

Coming round the tight curve, at first Fielding didn't see it. He was intent on the road directly in front of him. His attention was on—it had to be on—the pitted, rutted, rocky trail. He had to be ready to react, to brake, to steer, to shift. It was that way on every trip out to the site. Only this time it was worse. He was pushing himself, the vehicle, as far as he could. And he was handicapped by his thoughts. By the frustrations. His misgivings. His impatience. His fears.

He didn't notice the change because of all the things competing for his attention. The woods was the woods. It was always the same. Why would he expect anything different? But it was different. It had changed. The trees had changed.

It was as he started to accelerate, as he geared upward to second that he saw it. Directly ahead. In the road.

Fielding hit the brakes, and the front end of the Jeep dove toward the ground. The truck skidded forward, the tires gripping ineffectually at the loose soil. His hands tightened on the wheel. His wrists stiffened as he pushed backward, as if that act would have some effect on the motion of his vehicle.

The bumper hit the fallen tree and following the curve of the log, rode upward. Instinctively, Fielding dropped the stick into reverse and popped the clutch. The rear wheels dug into the dirt; the front two spun against the bark of the tree.

Dust kicked up by the skid, by the reverse thrust of the wheels, enveloped the truck. Fielding stepped harder on the pedal. The engine revved higher; then suddenly the bumper tore loose, the front end dropped down, and the Jeep jerked backward.

Fielding quickly took his foot off the gas, stomping hard on the brake. The truck ground noisily to a halt.

The representatives of the Ancient Ones watched the settling cloud. From the trees, from beneath the ground cover, they maintained their unspoken discipline. They were ready to act—they wanted to act—but it was not quite time. The dust had to settle. The desecrator had to make his move. He had to act as they anticipated he would act.

Despite the dust, the creature nearest the black metallic beast did not even blink. Its control was that of a raccoon concealing itself from a pack of hounds. Indeed, it resembled that midnight forager of the forest, the ancient cousin of the black bear, the masked animal with paws more nimble than a human's hand. It resembled a raccoon, but its size made the comparison falter.

It was as large as nearly a dozen of them, and indeed, it appeared as though the skins of numerous raccoons had been melded into one, as if this single creature were the repository of multiple souls. Scattered across its assembled frame were its individual heads, each with its eyes fixed on the road, each with needlelike fangs bared in a silent snarl.

The multiple creatures that it represented, the spirits they all represented, were as alive at this moment as they ever had been. They were alive and anxious and waiting for the desecrator to leave his protected enclosure.

Fielding sat behind the wheel, staring directly into the dirty cloud. As the dust settled, he sighed deeply, trying to settle the unwanted rush of adrenaline through his system.

He had been driving too fast, he told himself, not paying attention. It wasn't a maintained highway. There was bound to be deadfall on occasion blocking the trail. He couldn't let the evidence of a fire at the site make him careless.

An act of nature was the logical explanation, he thought, but the coincidence of timing was too pronounced for Fielding to dismiss. Was blocking the road part of the effort to stop the dig?

He reached for the latch and opened the door. Despite the sobering realization of a moment before that he had allowed himself to lapse into carelessness, it did not occur to him that he was exercising incaution still.

The desecrator was out of the vehicle.

The creatures that appeared not quite human, not quite animal, sensed the challenge to their self-control become greater. Inside, each battled a dual imperative: an almost feral drive to attack, and at the same time an equally strong directive that told them not to move.

A hulk in the shape of a black bear fairly shook under the strain of the competing demands. The beast it represented was not used to tempering its behavior, and filled as it was now with the ageless fury of the desecrated past, it could not for long hold itself back.

The bear, the deer, the owl, the spirit of the raccoon were animals not only of altered appearance, but also of altered natures. No longer operating under the natural instinct to survive, they were motivated strictly by revenge.

Fielding stopped when he came in front of his car. The tree lay perpendicular to the road. The work of a storm was his first thought. But as he started walking toward it, he realized there hadn't been a storm last night. There hadn't been a storm in weeks.

Where the bumper had run up the trunk, the bark was gouged deeply. Even from several paces away he could see the glistening, fresh wood. He followed the tree with his eyes back into the woods. Toward where the stump should be.

Fielding stopped dead in his tracks. The dirt road was the interloper here, yielding to the overall primacy of the woods. Trees grew right to the edge and the undergrowth was thick. Despite the cover, he could see it. The stump. It had been cut cleanly.

The first rush of blood to his face was a result of anger. Fielding thought of all the work he had done, all the work that remained to be done. His eyes flashed through the vegetation back to the road. To the tree blocking the road. He had a winch on the front of the Jeep. Could he pull it free?

As he studied the tree trunk, as he glanced back at his Jeep, the surge of anger ebbed. The exercise of reasoning through the problem forced him to be calmer. And with the calmness came the ability to notice the little things. The brush of twigs against one another. The gentle rustling of the leaves.

He listened closer, his eyes scanning the canopy, and as the idle of his truck receded into the background, he began to hear the sounds of the woods. As with everything in nature, on its surface there was no apparent order. But as Fielding listened, the minute sounds seemed to fall into a kind of pattern. As if there were order to each shift of a branch, to each brush of a leaf. As if in this land of mystery something lay concealed just beneath the surface of the vegetation. Something that was beginning to come to life.

Carefully, the creature that was part bear, part something else, pulled aside the long-stemmed grass. The desecrator was there, moving in the manner of such beings, each bit of motion a clumsy attempt at duplicating the stealth of the animals of the forest.

The representative of the bear ached in its reserve. Still subject to competing directives, it strained under the command to wait for the common call. But claws that for too long had not touched blood, teeth that for too long had not tasted flesh, could not resist its own private call forever.

Its jaw frozen in a muted growl, the black-furred creature designed not according to the dictates of the natural world, began to ease forward.

Fielding's tongue lapped at moisture collecting on his lip. There *was* order to the apparent chaos. He could sense it. He could hear it. He could see it.

Amid the patches of light and dark, lost against the lines and curves of the forest, new shapes began to emerge. At least Fielding imagined he saw them emerging.

His eyes darted from a bushlike clump of scrub oak to the low-slung frond of a white pine to the even canopy of the three-lobed ferns. He saw contour in the shadows, things of corporeal substance taking shape from the trees and brush.

They were moving. The vegetation was moving. Catching the wind.

He could hear the leaves rustling. But it was more than that. More than branches gently rubbing against each other. There was a loud cracking sound, a heavy thrashing of brush, of leaves, of brittle twigs snapping all at once.

Fielding spun in place. Back toward the car, beyond the car, he could see the movement, the sudden plunge toward the earth.

A birch tree was falling. Its crown snagged on another, causing it to spin off to one side. As the branches twisted, as the network of leaves meshed with others, the birch tore off one limb after another, and together all the debris crashed toward the ground cover, toward the forest floor. Toward the road!

To the creatures of mixed design, the fury of sound unleashed by the tree was a match for the forces active within each of them. More than that, it was the common call, the signal that the dual imperatives could now merge, the guarantee that the desecrator could not escape.

The tree hit the ground, came up a few inches, then settled back into the imprint it had made. Twenty feet behind the Jeep, it lay directly across the road.

The archaeologist was slow to react. He stood there as though paralyzed, trying to comprehend, listening to the echo of the leaves thrashing against one another as the tree hit the ground. But the forest produced no echo. What he heard was something new, the sound of ferns being pushed aside, the brush being flattened, the branches above him creaking and moving.

Though the paralysis lasted only a few seconds, given how fast things were happening, the moments of indecision seemed an eternity. It all changed for him when he at last saw the movement, in the brush, just off the side of the road. It changed when he saw the flash of black fur.

The creature whose upper jaw was that of a bear and whose lower jaw was somehow human, whose breast wore the plumage of the bald eagle, scrambled on all fours up the short rise to the narrow dirt clearing. It grunted audibly with the exertion, with the release of its passion. Directly ahead, the desecrator stood immobile.

Fielding moved instinctively toward the far side of the road. His eyes were locked on the fur, pushing its way through the brush. Though recognition was almost immediate, he refused to accept what he saw. His mind resonated with the thought, This can't be happening.

And yet it was. As the creature began to emerge from cover, he could see the eyes, the muzzle, the bared fangs of the carnivore.

He looked toward his truck, but the bear was between him and it. He started to turn slowly, careful to make no sudden movements. Bears don't attack people, he thought. At least not around here.

Though Fielding had snapped out of the initial shock, he had yet to make the logical connections—between the felled trees and the bear. And if there was a connection, the black-furred beast must be something more than a bear. Instead of evaluating things, he was simply reacting to the latest stimuli, thinking how to get away, where to run.

He turned, but it was as if he hadn't turned at all. There was another creature, another bear coming out of the woods. And next to it . . . "My God!"

Fielding spun back around, toward the first of the bears. It had elevated itself to its hind legs and was raising its claws to the sky. As it did, as Fielding saw the true nature of the creature that straddled the lines of different species, it began to howl in a voice as otherworldly as its appearance.

The sound itself froze Fielding to the spot. It was a churning, rasping, shrieking cry that seemed to be powered by some unspeakable torment. And rage. It rose above them all, collected in the branches, then came crashing down in an audible assault that by itself seemed enough to subdue its prey.

But Fielding was no ordinary prey. He was one of the few modern men who could recognize and understand who these creatures were. Or rather, who they represented.

"Listen to me," Fielding shouted, but as he did, the bear that was not quite a bear shrieked louder. It stepped closer.

"You don't know what you're doing," Fielding cried out, trying to overcome the volume of the approaching beast.

The desecrator's voice only served to heighten the bear-thing's fury. It shook its head violently from side to side, as if trying to escape the sound, as if the words themselves were things of substance driven with the force of rusty spikes into its ears.

Deep within its lungs the bear called forth even higher expressions of its anger, its pain, its outrage over the violations. Its voice—like its appearance—was a mix of varied creatures. It was the sound of a bear, yet within the gravelly cadence of its growls was the hint of language, a dead, forgotten language.

Fielding found himself trying to answer, but he could barely hear his own voice. It was being drowned out, by the bear, by the beings that approached from behind him, from both sides.

He turned in one direction, then pivoted again, his eyes darting from the hooked-beak visage of an owl to the strange, flat expanse of an undefined creature with facial hair that resembled a deer, a white-tailed deer with black pits for eyes. Next to them was a multiheaded raccoon the size of a man, with teeth like miniature daggers, and beyond that a brown-furred beast with snake scales coiled around its neck. And there were others, approaching from every angle, and each of them adding its own brand of incoherent raving to the growing babble.

At the center of this mix of cries and growls and screeches, this cacophony of sounds from the spirit world, the archaeologist gave up any effort at communication. It was senseless to try. It was senseless in every regard.

There wasn't any hope of reasoning with them. They were little more than wild beasts, touched by some manner of insanity. And yet they weren't insane. They were acting according to some well-defined purpose. And in that purpose he could sense the anger.

For the first time, the archaeologist felt afraid. He realized that the creatures meant to do him harm. They meant to kill him.

What he felt in the center of his chest suddenly flared outward in every direction, spreading into his limbs, rippling over the surface of his skin, threatening to take control of his thoughts. It was a hot and febrile flow that at once seemed debilitating and energizing. Though every one of his muscles seemed suddenly limber, he felt little control over them. He was moving as if by instinct, without any conscious design of what he should do, controlled simply by a single determinant: to get away.

Fielding lunged forward, toward the bear-spirit representative, catching it by surprise, knocking it off balance, spinning past. But with the move his element of surprise was spent, and they all surged forward.

Fielding felt a heavy paw at his shoulder, then the claws raking across his back. He staggered to the side but kept moving forward. Toward the truck.

The verbal rage reached a new crescendo, and as it did, the archaeologist felt new assaults coming from both sides. He twisted to evade the holds, and though he felt he was succeeding, suddenly he was plummeting toward the ground. It was a dizzying, uncontrolled moment, until his chest banged into the dirt. His legs had been pulled from under him.

Fielding forced himself to his knees and, grabbing at spiny tufts of bracken fern, pulled himself forward. As he did, they were touching, stroking, clawing at him from every angle. All the while, the growls and grunts of animals gone berserk rained down upon him. Still, he was moving forward. Getting closer to the Jeep. Just a little farther.

A black shape collapsed beside him. Out of the corner of his eye he could see the muzzle of the bear. He could see the yellowed canines exposed in its jaw. And then he could feel them, at his neck, pressing into his skin.

"No!" he screamed, but his voice was now as incoherent and meaningless as them all. It only added to the din, to the atmosphere of terror.

The bear was forced to drop back as Fielding scrambled along the side of the truck. The passenger side. He dropped to his belly and rolled underneath. The engine was rumbling like the sleeping voice of one of his attackers, and the smell of fumes was strong, but neither detracted from his plan of escape. With the eighteen-inch clearance of the Jeep, he could roll shoulder to back to shoulder to stomach, and he did, clear to the other side. He shot to his feet and yanked the door open, flinging himself inside.

But the creatures were just as fast. A flash of feathers rolled or flew across the hood, and before Fielding could get the door closed, it was reaching in, grasping his arm, threatening to pull him outside.

With his right hand he dropped the gear shift into reverse, then worked the pedals hard. The Jeep bolted backward, and as it did, Fielding was almost yanked outside. But instead the feathered creature lost its grip. It crashed to the ground. And then the Jeep plowed into the birch.

First it hit the branches, snagging for an instant, and with no hand on the wheel, the truck veered off line. Off balance, Fielding fought against the forces that sought to fling him to the ground. His foot braced hard against the floor, against the accelerator. The Jeep bounded back. The rear wheels hit the trunk of the tree and the tail end was knocked upward. Fielding was thrust upward too, cracking his head against the frame of the door.

The sound of bone against metal carried a sickening crunch, and for an instant everything went black. More gray than black, a kind of cloud, a swirling mass of dense air that conspired to steal his breath. Fielding moaned, reaching out blindly for something to grab hold of—the dash, the stick, the wheel.

His foot slipped off the accelerator, and the Jeep jerked once and stalled. The cloud spun faster, but Fielding had a grip on the wheel. He clenched it tightly, trying to steady himself, trying to leap free of the dense air that was sucking him in deeper.

He had to open his eyes, to see. But they were already open. He was staring straight through the windshield. His vision started to clear, but what he saw only brought confusion. He had the sensation of floating, and he saw leaves. He was in the trees. How could that be?

He grabbed the sides of his head and squeezed. His skull felt as if it were going to burst. He felt sick and pained and disoriented all at the same moment. And then he saw the face. Coming through the trees. The visage of a raptor frozen in its last, lethal plunge from out of the sky. Coming through the branches, onto the hood of the truck, it was this face, this creature of otherworldly invention that paradoxically inched him back toward reality.

Fielding turned the key, pulling the door closed at the same time. He started back again, but the Jeep was now straddling the trunk of the birch, the rear end over it, the front wheels still blocked. It wasn't moving! "Jesus," he implored. "Move!"

He glanced back toward the front. The creature was at the windshield, clawing at the glass with its talons, talons that had the hefty force of considerable weight behind them. It was trying to break through. And behind it, to the sides, the branches were moving. The others were coming.

Fielding turned his head quickly to the rear, and as he did, the pain from the point of impact sank like an iron wedge deep into his skull. The cloud intensified its circular motion. It flashed darker, then lighter. Almost without conscious control, Fielding's foot was slowly pressing harder on the gas, trying to give the wheels an opportunity to seek their own traction.

Each of the wheels gripped at dirt or tree or leafy debris. The left rear was digging a hole; the opposite tire in front was gouging into the slick bark of the birch. But through it all, the truck was rising. "Come on!" Fielding shouted, throwing his back against the seat.

Over the sound of the engine, the spinning of the tires, he could still hear the shouts, the cries, the animal grunts of his tormentors. And he could hear and feel them striking the car, in the front, along the sides, and now, on the roof.

The car jerked up six inches in one move, but then branches snagged on its undercarriage. Fielding stomped hard on the accelerator, the engine whined shrilly, and then in a cracking, snapping tumult the Jeep shot free, rocketing backward.

There was a heavy thump as the body on top fell to the hood, then rolled off to the ground. The same force knocked Fielding forward, his chest thrust up against the wheel. The car careened wildly, seeking its own course. Without guidance, it veered off the narrow trail and bounded into the woods, flattening brush, snapping low branches, splintering saplings.

The Jeep plummeted deep into the cover before Fielding could stop it. As it lurched to a halt, he slumped forward, gasping for breath. The cloud had never lifted, and now as he hunched forward, fighting the pain, the nausea, it seemed to spin even faster, threatening to pull him into the vortex.

Keeping his eyes open, fixed dead ahead, he inhaled greedily. Before him was a clear swath cut through the ferns. As he looked, the swath became like a tunnel, darkness closing in on all sides. He was losing it. He had to keep going.

Fielding threw the stick into first, and the Comanche roared powerfully as it started back toward the road. It took the bumps and fallen humps of·mossy deadfall easily. Fielding suffered a light-headed thrill. He was going to make it. He was going to get out of there.

The trees slid by to the side. The downed brush fluttered passively at the undercarriage. It was going well. He increased his speed. His hands gripped tighter on the wheel.

Suddenly, there was a heavy bang at the lower front. The

truck shuddered. He had gone over a stump. The sound of the underbrush began to crack noisily, no longer yielding as it did. He swallowed, leaning forward. The tunnel had vanished. He had strayed off the course.

A flicker of panic flitted across his mind. He swung his head to the right. As he did, he caught new movement. Vertical shapes. Were they still coming? Or was it the trees, in motion because of his own movement?

Fielding looked forward, licking his lips. The last thing he should do, he realized, was increase his speed. But that's what he did. He had to get out of there. He had to find the trail.

The Jeep was deflected by a tree; another forced him to change course. He didn't even see the small trunk of a sapling until he knocked it down in front of him.

Where was the road? The swirling mass of congested air billowed suddenly fuller, heavier. It seemed as though it were gathering substance, becoming an obstacle to the truck no different from the branches that tugged at its forward progress, the ferns that slapped at the doors.

Fielding breathed harder, deeper. Rather than bringing greater clarity, each new breath seemed to power the force of the cyclone. He was a scientist, for God's sake. Didn't they understand? He wasn't an enemy. His work would only help to keep them alive, to increase common awareness of them. Why did they object? It wasn't fair!

Fielding felt suddenly weightless, as if the cloud had finally succeeded. It had snatched him into its pull, lifted him bodily off the ground, sucked him into its vortex. And then the truck crashed back to the surface. It hit the ground hard, falling into the depression of the road.

It was the ruts that brought the wheels into line with the trail, not Fielding, but he quickly recognized where he was. He shifted, picking up speed. He acted on instinct, following the ribbon of light above him as much as the road itself. Leaves and grass and barren branches starved from lack of sun flashed by his side window. It was all a blur. Like the cloud. Like the thoughts that tumbled crazily in his head.

He drove hard, or at least it seemed he was pushing it as much as he had coming in. Each turn began to seem the same, each rough bump sent the same waves of pain through his head. Around each bend he began to expect the highway. But it wasn't there. He was being teased. He sensed the motion, but how could he be moving when he never sensed progress? Were the things around him just conveying the illusion of motion? As he looked at the trees, they indeed seemed an illusion. The trunks seemed to waver like columns of heat in the desert.

He eased back on the accelerator. It was all going too fast. He was out of control. The truck slowed even more.

He had driven one mile. Maybe two. Three? He had no idea. He had no idea when he would meet the paved highway.

The Jeep passed the high point where he had first noticed the trace of smoke at the sinkhole. But that event, at this moment, was not even a memory. He just had to keep going. Keep driving. But it was hard. He felt sick. His vision was fogged. He had not had a single moment to try to recover from the blow to the head. He needed to stop, to let the pain subside, to let his faculties regain control.

The truck glided on the mere crawl of momentum. Without making a conscious decision, Fielding had taken his foot off the accelerator. The truck drifted, until finally it stopped.

He leaned his head forward, resting it on his hands, which still gripped the wheel. But that was no relief. He sat back, and as he did, he started to feel hot. Feverish. He needed air. The dense cloud was back, spinning around him.

He flung the door open and staggered outside. Almost immediately, he began to cough, to retch for oxygen. The plume of dust kicked up by his passage had enveloped the truck, and Fielding was caught within it, within the swirling mass that had bedeviled him since his head struck the inside frame of the door. At last, it had become something real, a mass of substance that clogged blank air with particulate matter that sought to choke off all life caught within it.

Fielding collapsed to his knees. He closed his eyes to escape the cloud, but the swirling motion only got worse. He forced his eyes open again, and through the cloud he saw shapes beginning to emerge.

The shapes were actually nothing more than trees, coming back into view as the dust settled. But to Fielding they were surreal images that had their own vitality. As they had back there. Deep in the woods. The images were like things he had encountered on his drive to the dig. They were like the . . . The what?

Suddenly, the mix of animal parts seemed to become even more jumbled in his memory. The more he tried to reconstruct the creatures in his mind, the more they seemed just part of his sickness, his dizziness, the delusions that continued spinning in his mind. Was that all it was? A dream?

He had had an accident. Of that he was sure. He had hit his head.

"No!" he cried. It *had* happened. What he saw was real. What happened was real.

Yet how could it be? How could what he remembered have really happened?

How could the bear that was a bird that was a man be real? How could the other creatures he remembered be real?

How could any of them be real?

How could it be real?

Chapter 4

His name was Blackbear. Makwamacatawa.

He didn't have a surname, or rather he no longer had one. In the open-time, the years before the white man, his people had not used first names. Most had adjusted since then, adopting the new ways, as had Blackbear's parents. But he had changed all that.

In the open-time, names were not a family legacy, but were earned during life. They were descriptive of a person's character, or given to him or her because of a powerful incident that happened to the person, whether that incident was real or came in a dream. Which is how Blackbear had acquired his name. It had come in a dream, four years ago, when he was twenty-one years old. Before then, he had been known as Joseph DuBois.

The passage for him back to the spirit of the open-time had begun years earlier, though at the time he hadn't known he was beginning a journey. At the time, he had only felt humiliation.

DuBois was his mother's name, and he knew that she was Chippewa, or at least mostly Chippewa. His father he didn't know. He could have been Chippewa, or Miami, or Sauk, or like himself, a mix of tribes, or possibly even a mix of the races.

He and his mother lived in Wyandotte, just downriver from la cité de détroit, the city of the straits, the connection point between Lake Erie and the St. Lawrence River, and Lake Huron and the Upper Great Lakes. It was a strategic position for the Wyandotte Indians, whose village remained intact there until 1818, but it was even more strategic for the Europeans, for whom conquest and retrenchment of territory were so much more important.

A basement or a foundation could not be built in the DuBois neighborhood without uncovering relics of the past, and most of these ended up in the Wyandotte Indian Museum. For the local school kids, the museum was a primary destination for field trips. It was at the museum, on a field trip, that his journey had begun.

He was at an age when kids first begin to notice differences among themselves. As usual with kids, the one who was different was the last to know the difference has been noticed.

There was a skeleton on display, in a glass case at the museum. It had been dug up from a grave near the site of the museum itself. It was the main attraction for the kids—far more interesting than stone tools or arrowheads or tattered bits of deer hide decorated with quills.

As they crowded around, one of the kids said, "Hey, Joey. Is this your grandfather?" They all laughed, and the laughter fed more taunts. It *was* his grandfather, they said, in a glass case, hanging up for everybody to see. Things got worse on the way back to school, when the bus passed a cemetery. It was a cemetery with gravestones and impressive wrought-iron fences and monuments, and with graves dating back to the eighteenth century, from the time when the Indian in the glass case had lived. "That's where the white people are put," the kids said. "But don't worry. They'll save you a place in the museum."

The taunts hurt terribly, that day of the field trip. But as he grew older, the memory of them hurt even more. Not because of the unfairness of what the kids had said. But because he came to realize that they may well have been right.

Wyandotte was a name that encompassed the four Huron Indian tribes, and for the Hurons who had settled on the straits between the lakes, it was the name they preferred to use for themselves. Joseph DuBois's mother held nothing but disrespect for the Wyandotte, so when he was young, he felt confident that he had no Wyandotte blood in his veins. Later, it occurred to him that maybe he was half-Wyandotte, and that was the reason for his mother's contempt for that tribe. The nature of his bloodline didn't matter, though, until years later, after he had already decided to drop out of college.

He was at the university for two years, and at first he did well. But the isolation he felt—as on the day of the field trip, but ever so much more subtle—sped him on his journey back to the open-time. He came to resent the alien culture that treated his own with such contempt, but more than that, he resented having to try to assimilate himself into that culture.

In the end, he rebelled against the notion of making it in the white world. And that's when his bloodline became important.

A one-hundred-and-twenty-five-year-old treaty that had been
honored only by the red man had given rise to a lawsuit. It was
settled in the seventies, and one provision of the settlement provided for the grant of ten-acre parcels of land in the Upper Peninsula to descendants of the Chippewa, or as many preferred to
be identified, Ojibwa. The question became, Who were the descendants? Only those who were 100 percent Chippewa? At
least half? Or was as little as a single drop of Chippewa blood
enough to allow participation in the treaty settlement?

The Ojibwa Association decided that a one-quarter bloodline
was a fair resolution. Though Joe DuBois couldn't say for certain what his exact lineage was, he could prove that he was at
least one-quarter Chippewa on his mother's side alone.

The land that was the focus of the settlement was in the Upper Peninsula, in the ancestral territory of the Chippewa/
Ojibwa. Joe came north and claimed his ten acres, building a
log cabin near the shore of Lake Superior, near the town of
Watersdrop.

Many of the old Indian names survived, spelled phonetically
in English, or in translation. Joseph Dubois chose to use both.
He didn't want to dishonor the spiritual nature of his acquired
name by using it in white society, so in it he was called
Blackbear. At other times, the translation would be an insult to
the spirits, and so he was called Makwamacatawa.

He had become Makwamacatawa as the result of a vision that
came to him in the sweatlodge. His vision quest had come late
in life, but for him, life as an Ojibwa only began when he came
north.

In his dream, brought on by the heat, by the fasting, he was
visited by the spirit of the black bear. It told him to be strong, for
his people. To lead them. To guide them back to the open-time.
To do what was necessary to protect and preserve the heritage
his people shared.

It was appropriate to his brothers that he was visited by the
black bear, that he was to be called Makwamacatawa, because
the black bear was the strongest, most vital creature in the world
of their ancestors. And Joseph DuBois had a voice and presence
that matched the power of the black bear.

The younger Ojibwa were drawn to him, and for those who
had never had the chance to go to college, his presence among
them was proof that rather than feeling deprived, they should
feel proud in not being forced into the white man's world. They

admired him for what he had given up, and for the life he had chosen to lead.

They followed him. They listened to him. And when he spoke of the desecration that was to come, they felt some of the same outrage Makwamacatawa had held close to his heart since the day of the field trip when he saw the skeleton of one of his grandfathers in the glass case in the museum.

In the realm of the black bear, Chris Fielding was on his knees, leaning back on his haunches. The dust had settled, and the woods had become again the woods. The trees were steady, and the only movement was the gentle sway of greenery. Most significant of all, the internal vortex had given up its hold, and what had clouded his mind and threatened to eclipse his reason had disintegrated. His head still hurt from the blow, but at least the visions of otherworldly creatures had forfeited their haunting.

He felt his neck where the teeth of the bear that was a bird that was a man had pressed into his flesh. There was no wound. His back felt wet, and Fielding reached his hand under his shirt where the claws of an unnamed beast had raked across him. It was sweat, not blood.

Had they been real?

It was the same question that had reverberated in his mind a few minutes before as he fought to bring himself back under control. But this time, the question was more analytical.

He looked at the car and saw the dents; then he stood up quickly. As soon as he got to his feet, the dizziness came back in a rush. He had moved too fast. He clenched his eyes tightly shut and grabbed his forehead with one hand, stabilizing himself against the truck with the other.

Slowly, equilibrium returned and the sudden pounding that had erupted in his head scaled back to a dull throb. He opened his eyes.

Across the length of the hood were two sets of vertical scratches, running from the windshield to the grill. Caused by the branches when the truck had plunged into the woods?

Fielding edged around the side of the Jeep to the front. He visually traced the scratches down and over the front of the hood, and in the grill, snagged in a chrome square, was a long, dark shape.

Retrieving it with his forefinger and thumb, he held it close to his eyes, inspecting it carefully. As he did, the sweat on his back went cold. It was a black feather. The feather of a bald eagle.

The creature with the head of an eagle but with the limbs of a land animal pushed its way through the leaves that blocked the road. It showed no signs of injury from the slide off the metallic beast, almost as if the hot rush of timeless anger had cloaked it with the invincibility of the ages.

Next to it, behind it, came the rest of the beings of mixed design. They had pursued the intruder for a short distance, until it had come out of the woods and found its way back to the trail. And then they had retreated, at their own pace, with no more sense of urgency, regrouping in the space between the felled trees where they had staged their ambush.

They were no longer restless; in each the tempest of rage had been stilled, replaced by a feeling almost as powerful. It was the sense of accomplishment. Of victory. Of atonement for past wrongs.

They had succeeded. The desecrator had been driven off.

Still holding the feather, Fielding looked back down the dirt-track road. It had all happened so suddenly, so unexpectedly, that it was natural to be confused. Adding to that confusion was the dizzy state of mind induced by the crack to the head, a swirling, nearly unconscious state more akin to dreaming than wakefulness. Because of that, and because of the nature of the beings he had seen, it was understandable that he questioned whether what he thought had happened had really occurred.

But standing there at this moment, free of any lingering instability of thought, he saw again the various creatures as he had first seen the bear after it rose to its hind legs. And with the cold certainty of lucid thought, he knew that they were alive.

The creatures that seemed lifted from mythology did in fact exist. And he felt certain he knew who had sent them.

Makwamacatawa slipped his fingers out of the cloth ringlets sewn into the underside of the bear's paw. He unhitched the chest strap that secured the hide to his body, then very carefully he eased the head of the black bear off his own.

Near him, the young Ojibwa men who looked to him for leadership began to emerge from under their own cloaks of spiritual disguise.

A flat mask fashioned of deer hide and perforated with deep-sunken eye holes was removed, revealing the core human nature of that creature of mixed design. Another human took shape from under a drape of raccoon pelts that had been sewn together, complete with individual heads and fangs bared in silent snarls.

The traits of men predominated again, all around. Tanned hides and fur and feathers plucked from bird flesh long ago gave way to manufactured clothing and shapes of recognizable form. The representatives of the Ancient Ones had fulfilled their duty. Now they were relinquishing their brief grip on immortality.

Makwamacatawa carefully laid the black bear hide on the ground. He circled it, stretching it out flat, adjusting the claws that for too long had not touched blood, positioning the bared teeth that for too long had not tasted flesh, making sure his cousin the black bear was comfortable in its state of repose.

Kneeling in front of its head, Makwamacatawa deposited a small cone of tobacco on the ground. He lit it, fanned it with his hands, and then, as the smoke began to rise, curling upward in solid wisps of visible air, he bent low and blew gently across the burning tobacco, sending drafts of the particulate haze into the face of the bear.

The smoke wafted between the teeth frozen forever in a muted growl; some entered the flaring nostrils of the black bear, and the rest dispersed into and through the thick fur.

Makwamacatawa leaned back. "Oh great makwa," he whispered, "accept our gift and our prayers in gratitude for the life of your representative who gives us life. Who gives us the means to honor you. Who helps us protect the Ancient Ones.

"Accept our gift," he repeated, bending low, blowing more smoke into the creature's face. As he did, as he continued with his prayer, his own image was reflected in the glassy eyes of the bear, and the bear accepted his offering silently, expressing neither approval nor dissatisfaction.

The sacred cloaks fashioned of animal hides were all folded and ready to be carried back to the vehicles.

Makwamacatawa was fulfilled. The Ancient Ones would have been proud.

Pausing to let the satisfaction spread, he surveyed the array of nature that surrounded him: the delicate fronds of the ferns, the long needles of a pine, the acrobatics of a chickadee, and directly overhead, splayed limbs like leaded lines patterned throughout a mantle of glass stained various shades of green. It was a scene little different from what his grandfathers would have observed in the open-time.

"Blackbear," a voice said to him, and Makwamacatawa lowered his gaze. "Do you think he will return?"

Blackbear looked in the direction the Jeep Comanche had retreated. "At least he knows the nature of the opposition has changed," he said. "He knows that not all the fight will be on the white man's terms."

Chapter 5

MIRIAM GOODMEDICINE'S HOME rested in a stand of red pines in what had used to be the outskirts of Watersdrop but now was well in from the farthest spread of roadside businesses and scattered homesteads carved out of the woods. It was the only part of town where the roads weren't paved, and because of the drought, a perpetual layer of dust clung to the walls, the trees, and even took a bit of the color off the flowers. The neighborhood was called informally Ojibwa Village, not because it was any sort of legal entity, but because the pattern of settlement years ago had resulted in the Indian homes being bunched together.

Miriam lived in a high-peaked, wood-frame bungalow whose roof and walls were splotched in places with spots of pine needles and dirt stuck in sap. It was a constant battle keeping the paint clean, but Miriam never considered cutting the trees.

The house was a small place that once had been filled with voices but now was quiet more often than not. Her husband had died in his prime, her three daughters were all away, two married and living downstate and one in veterinary school, and the only child still at home was her eighteen-year-old son Raymond. He had made a room for himself in the basement, and usually Miriam knew he was home only by hearing the shuffle of his steps below her. Most times, he entered and left through the fruit-cellar door that came up directly into the sideyard.

The quiet was one reason Miriam insisted the expert witness from Oklahoma stay with her during the hearing. But now that Jean Shawshequay's visit would be longer, Miriam could take little extra comfort in the continuing company. She knew how Jean felt about staying, but as leader of the Ojibwa Association, there were many things Miriam would rather not do that she did. The gulf between the reality and the hope of her people's economic position meant that some things just had to be done.

Carrying the stack of neatly folded clothes two of the ladies had brought over, Miriam began ascending the stairs.

Jean had heard the women arrive, but chose not to come down to greet them. She was angriest with Fielding because it was all his fault. But she couldn't help but feel betrayed by Miriam. She had come all this way to help, and for that was manipulated into giving more than she could afford.

At the knock, Jean waited several seconds before saying, "Come in." Then, as the door opened and shut, she stayed hunched over her notes at the desk, finishing her list of what she would need from her office.

Miriam stood patiently near the entrance of the three-bed attic-dormer. It was the girls' room. She waited until her guest looked up from her work. "You probably didn't pack the right kind of clothes for the woods," she said, "so a few of the neighbors collected some things you may need."

"That was thoughtful," Jean said evenly.

Miriam placed the jeans, sweatshirt, and shirts on a dresser. "You're so skinny you can probably fit into my girls' things. There in the closet."

Jean managed a strained smile. "Thank you."

"There are boots there too, and here," she said, pulling out a drawer, "are thick socks. Underwear. Whatever you'll need. Just put your laundry by the door and I'll make sure it's done."

"I can do my own laundry. Really, you're doing too much."

"No, it's not too much," she said.

Jean put down her pen and got up from her chair, moving toward Miriam. "Don't worry about me. I can take care of myself. I do appreciate the clothes, though. These wouldn't be much good," she said, indicating her green suit, "at the dig site."

Miriam flashed a half grin, then looked past Jean, toward a far bureau. There was something else on her mind.

"What is it?" Jean asked.

Miriam took a deep breath, then walked toward the bureau, toward the array of pictures on top of it. She selected one of the frames and handed it to her guest.

"Your husband?"

"Yes," Miriam said. "He died twelve years ago come September. Of liver disease."

Jean looked up, still holding the frame in her hands.

"He was a good man. The problem was, he never thought that he was. He always felt he should be doing more for his family. He tried, but I think he felt there was something about his race that meant no matter what he did, he could never compete with the white man. You have to understand, people of his generation—of my generation—didn't grow up learning about the good things in their heritage. They grew up instead learning firsthand why they were at a disadvantage. You know what I mean. I'm sure it's the same, with some people where you come from."

Jean nodded.

"I don't know if it is entirely fair to say," Miriam continued, stepping toward the window, looking out at the red pines, "but I've often wondered, if Wes hadn't been trapped in that . . . that malaise, if there had been some deeper meaning in his life, if as a child he had been raised with pride in his heritage . . ." She turned away from the window, looking back at Jean. "If someone back then had fought to protect our beliefs, I wonder if Wes would still be alive today."

And if there is no one to fight now, will the children suffer the same fate? Though the point went unstated, Jean understood the reason for the story.

Miriam reached into her pocket and pulled out a small animal carving. "Your name translates as mink, but I suppose you know that."

"Yes, though my brother always used to say that, for me, Shawshequay really meant weasel."

"Wes carved this. He said he couldn't afford a real mink. So he made me one." She held it out to Jean. "I think it's appropriate you have it now."

The body of the mink was only about two inches long, its tail adding another inch. The detail was so fine Jean could see the rich texture of its fur and, between the creature's slightly parted lips, the trace of teeth so tiny they must have been carved with the aid of a magnifying glass.

"The girls loved his animals," Miriam said, gesturing toward a wooden menagerie on a shelf.

"I think it's beautiful," Jean said, clutching the mink.

Miriam looked away, her lips quivering. Then she walked to the door, where she paused, saying, "I think young Ray has inherited his father's talent." She turned and left Jean to herself.

The birchwood mink had never been painted, but nonetheless the normally light wood had acquired a dark patina from handling. As she studied it, Jean wondered how many times in the last twelve years Miriam had held this tiny piece of wood close to her heart.

Before Miriam had come upstairs, Jean had been dreading her call to Oklahoma. What was she going to tell her director? She had decided to take a few extra weeks and join an archaeological dig? "And oh, by the way, you can send me my manuscripts up here. If I get time, I'll finish the editing."

She wasn't supposed to be part of a story. She was supposed to be a reviewer, an appraiser, a witness to other people's stories. It had always seemed to be that way, even though at the beginning that had not been her intent.

Sitting there in her attic room, looking at the tiny mink on her stack of notes, she thought of her plans and goals not that many years ago. When she was a student, she had wanted to be a field archaeologist. If she were honest with herself, she'd admit she had wanted to do the things that Fielding now did. Except that she would have brought an Indian perspective to the search for her people's roots. More importantly, she would have brought the proper sensitivity to a profession that too often disregarded the sanctity of the ancient lives it was unearthing.

As she thought about those days, as she considered how she was going to handle her job, outside on the street a vehicle slid to a halt on the hard-packed dirt, sending up a cloud of dust. The door slammed, but as someone used to the city, Jean didn't notice it.

Had she really had opportunities to pursue her plans? Jean wondered. Or was it that she had succumbed to the easier path? She had wanted to be at the heart of the Indian revival. Instead, she read about other people who were.

There was a loud banging on the door out front, and she jumped, startled.

Jean had not been able to make out what was said when the two women were over, but after Miriam opened the door this time, she could hear the voice clearly.

"I thought we had a deal," she heard the archaeologist say. "Where is she?"

"There *is* a deal," Miriam said. Jean got up and started down the narrow staircase that led directly to the front door. "What are you talking about?" she heard Miriam continue. Fielding didn't answer. He had heard Jean on the steps. When she entered the living room, he was facing her. He was dirty and sweaty, but the biggest change from before was the look in his eyes.

Fielding spoke as she was still absorbing what she saw. "If you thought that was going to stop me, you were wrong."

"If *what* was going to stop you?" Jean asked.

Fielding leaned back, appraising her contemptuously. "I thought you were a person of conviction. But now you try to hide it?"

"Hide what? I don't know what you're talking about."

"You said you were going to find a way to stop me. Well, I'm sorry to tell you, you missed your chance. The only way they could have stopped me was to have killed me out there."

Jean stared at him, astonished. "What the hell are you talking about?"

Fielding didn't respond right away. Instead, he watched her, not because he believed she wasn't an accomplice in the assault, but because he was impressed with the sincerity of her performance. "You know what I'm talking about," he said. "You know exactly what I'm talking about."

"Well, I don't," Miriam said. "What's going on?"

Fielding inhaled deeply through his nostrils, as if seeking air to cool his inner fire. His eyes still locked on Jean, he said simply, "She set me up. She told her friends I was coming, and they were there, waiting for me."

"At the site of the dig?" Miriam asked.

Turning toward her, Fielding began to explain. "Short of it a ways. Out in the woods. I came around a bend and the road was blocked by a tree. When I got out, they came at me from every direction. Men draped with animal skins and masks."

"I don't believe you," Jean said.

Ignoring the interruption, he continued. "Totemic cloaks. Funerary masks. It was like a museum display come to life. At first I tried to talk to them, but they were the ones who had a message to deliver. In their own fashion."

Miriam exhaled a wavering breath as she listened. Turning away, walking toward the front window, she asked, "Did they say anything to you?"

"Their only speech was the language of the spirits. Animal sounds. Maybe some Ojibwa phrases. It was hard to tell with all that was going on. I couldn't even hear my own voice."

"Did they hurt you?"

"No. I hurt myself, getting away."

"Listen, Mr. Fielding," Jean said. "It's true I don't like what you're doing here, or more to the point, how you and Curtis Heath have gone about it. And in anger, I may have said some things I shouldn't have. But let me make this clear: I had nothing to do with whatever happened to you."

"You're real clever, Miss Shawshequay. And so were your friends out in the woods. The costumes, the ambush, the scare tactics. But in your cleverness, you fail to see what's really important. You don't understand the value of what I'm doing, not for me personally, but for your own people. You think you've got all the answers, that you're the expert, that no one who is not an Indian can be trusted. But you're wrong, and if you're not going to help with the solution," Fielding looked toward the Ojibwa Association president, "maybe someone else should be chosen to observe the excavation."

"They couldn't have been her friends," Miriam said. "She hasn't been here long enough."

"But there's a kinship," Fielding said, stepping closer to Jean, parroting her testimony. "She holds it sacred and it places certain duties upon her. For like-minded people, it's stronger than any other kind of tie."

"You think you're so clever," Jean said. "That you've got everything figured out. But what it really indicates is that you don't understand us at all. If you think that native peoples are so single-minded they'd jump to the bidding of someone they don't even know, then to me that's proof you're not the great white friend you want us to believe you are."

"Tell your friends to be careful. I'm going to the sheriff now, to report the assault, the damage to my truck. The interference with a court order. Tell them if they try anything more, they'll end up in jail."

It was no use trying to deny everything again, and at this point, Jean Shawshequay didn't care what he believed.

After he left, Miriam turned away from the window. "You're going to have to go after him."

"What?"

"To the sheriff. Fielding was hot and wouldn't listen. But the sheriff will listen."

"Do you think it's true what happened to him?"

Miriam didn't answer her directly. Instead, she said, "If it is, it's important—for the sake of the court and our agreement—that the Association is not part of what may have happened out in the woods."

"Who could have done it?"

Miriam sighed, then walked to a straight-backed chair and sat down. "Not all of the Ojibwa back the Association. Some say we are too conservative in our approach to issues. They think we should be more strident in our demands. That the sins against us are so great that we can never be part of this society. They may well be right, I don't know. But if they are, I am not the one to lead them."

Jean watched her, and suddenly Miriam seemed an old woman. It didn't seem fair. There should be some rest for a person like her, who had fought so long and so hard and so nobly.

She walked to the foot of the steps. "I'll change," she said to Miriam. "Then I'll go see the sheriff."

Miriam stayed in her chair until Jean had left. As the front door closed, her gaze shifted from the exit to the closet next to it. She remained where she was for a few more seconds, as if resisting what she had to do. But as on so many other occasions, Miriam Goodmedicine found the energy and the will to do what she must.

On the floor of the closet was a cedar chest. Miriam slid it out far enough so she could open the lid. Inside were neatly folded traditional clothes, a buckskin dress decorated with beads, a breastplate of silver and agate, a ceremonial pipe, several birch-bark boxes decorated with quills, a beaver-skin pouch.

After carefully shifting through the contents of the chest, Miriam sat back on her ankles. What she was looking for was gone. The elongated deerskin mask had been removed from the chest.

When Fielding first asked to see the sheriff, Halstead assumed it had something to do with last night's manhunt. When it became apparent it did not, Halstead couldn't disguise his disappointment. As he listened to Fielding's story unfold, he settled back on the top of his desk, his hands braced on the edge, his fingers tapping impatiently.

He was tired. He had been chasing around in the woods too much lately. He was getting ready to go home early for a change, and now this. At worst, it sounded like kids playing a prank on the outsider. If it had really happened at all.

"Let me ask you a question about these half men, half animals," the sheriff said when Fielding was finished. "Did you see them before or after you hit your head?"

Deputy Sheriff Jerry Cole snickered from his place behind Fielding, near the glass door of the office.

"Okay, have your big laugh," Fielding said. "But it did happen, just as I've said. And they weren't trying to be funny. And yes, I hit my head as I was trying to get away. Just before I drove into the woods."

"Oh. So you *drove* into the woods."

"After they ambushed me, after I hit my head, as I was trying to get away."

Halstead heaved a deep breath, then folded his arms across his chest. "Okay, Fielding. Let's just look at it from a different angle. Here's a guy from the university, his head's all filled up with Indian myths and legends, he has a taxing morning, he's tired, he goes out to the woods and gets into an accident. He's dizzy—you said you were dizzy, didn't you?"

"Yes. After I cracked my skull on the doorframe."

"Okay. So you're dizzy, you're off the road in the trees, and you start imagining things. Now, does that strike you as the least bit possible?"

"No."

"Come on, you're a scientist. Be objective."

Fielding came to his feet. "Sheriff. Maybe you should take a look at my truck."

Halstead started to get the uncomfortable feeling that for the second night in a row, he was going to be tromping around in the woods. But he was not ready to concede. "Okay," he said. "We'll have a look."

The truck was dented and scratched all right, and the fiberglass cap over the back bed was cracked on top. As Halstead and Deputy Sheriff Coles ambled slowly around the vehicle, Jean Shawshequay got out of her car and came toward the men. Fielding only glanced in her direction, irritated. He didn't want to be distracted.

After Halstead and his deputy had completed their circum-ambulation, the sheriff said to Fielding, "I don't suppose you can tell me which of those bumps came from you driving into the woods, and which came from the animal-men?"

"What difference does that make?"

"Well, if this is your proof that what you say happened really happened, I'd say we'd have a tough time proving it in court, with the tale you've got to tell."

Fielding reached in through an open window and retrieved the eagle feather. "I picked this out of my grill, after one of them slipped off my hood."

Halstead took the feather from him. "You know, killing a bald eagle is a federal offense."

Fielding couldn't believe what was happening. In disgust, he turned his back to the sheriff, resting an elbow on the cab of his truck.

Tapping the feather between his fingers, Halstead looked over at Shawshequay. "You know anything about this?"

"No," she said. "Except that I believe him. I believe that it happened."

Fielding jerked his head in her direction.

Halstead grimaced; then, massaging his eyes with one hand, he turned and took a few steps away from them. "Say it's true," he said, turning back. "What do you want me to do? Go out and arrest somebody for assault? Malicious destruction of property?"

"I don't care about that," Fielding said, animated again. "I told you, there was a fire out there. There's a tent at the site. Equipment. Survey posts. That site is an important and irreplaceable archaeological discovery, and needs to be protected. At the least, I want you to come out there with me to see if they're still there, to check what damage they've done."

"I suppose you want to go now."

Fielding glanced at his watch. "It's not quite five o'clock. We've got plenty of daylight."

"It would make sense," Jean said. "The fire, I mean. If they were trying to adhere to the old ways, they may well have kindled a sacred fire, allowing its smoke to carry their prayers up to the soul villages."

Halstead was resigned. "How many of these bear-men did you say there were?"

"Two. But there were others, wearing different cloaks. Seven, eight. Nine, ten. I'm not sure."

"Okay, Jerry. You're driving out there too. I think the two of us can handle ten ghosts. Don't you?"

"Sure, Sheriff."

Besides, Halstead thought, if anybody had to stay out there, it was not going to be him.

As the lawmen went for their cars, Fielding climbed into the Jeep. Jean walked around to the passenger side and opened the door.

"What are you doing?" Fielding said.

Jean climbed in and slammed the door. "I'm supposed to be the observer here. Well, I'm ready to go out for a look."

Fielding eyed her silently, and for a second, he saw her as he had in the courtroom: as a woman of confidence and conviction; as a woman passionate about her beliefs and even more passionate about defending them. He saw her again in that same light, as a woman with eyes of black fire, a woman of strength and determination. And beauty.

Without saying a word, Fielding fired the ignition and began easing away from the curb.

The Chippewa Lodge was the old Watersdrop Gun Club, a cinder-block building with a fan-shaped spread of woods behind it cut for a skeet range. When the club folded, the Ojibwa Association had purchased the building and grounds with federal grant money, to use as a headquarters for community events and programs—day care, health, alcohol and marital counseling, social affairs—and sometimes an informal gathering place.

When Miriam Goodmedicine pulled into the sand and gravel lot, there were four other vehicles already there. Before she reached the front door, she could hear the voices, the laughter. But all that stopped as soon as she stepped inside.

Miriam stood just inside the door, quickly scanning the group of ten or eleven young men. Her son, Ray, was seated at a folding table, his back to the door, and was one of the last to turn around. He had a can of beer halfway to his lips when he saw her.

There was nothing she could say to him now that she hadn't said before, about drinking, about his father. But that didn't mean she didn't suffer seeing him sitting there, eighteen years old, poised with a can of beer in his hand.

One of the men emerged from the group. "Mrs. Goodmedicine," Blackbear said. "Welcome."

"Celebrating something?"

"You could say that."

Indicating her son with a quick jerk of her head, Miriam said, "Since when does the Lodge allow minors to be served alcohol?"

Blackbear turned slowly, then cast a gaze at Johnny Penay. As soon as Miriam saw Penay, her eyes flared. Like Blackbear, Penay had come from downstate. But unlike Blackbear, who had come in search of something, the suspicion was Penay had come to escape. Without a word being uttered, Penay walked over to Ray, took the beer out of his hand, and went back to his place.

To Miriam, Blackbear continued, "I apologize. It won't happen again. Is that why you came?"

Miriam didn't answer him right away. Instead she stepped past him and made her way into the middle of the room, taking her time to catch the eyes of each of the young men, most of whom had at one time or another studied in her classroom.

She turned to face Blackbear. "I understand you stopped the archaeologist's car on the way to the Cave of Bones. And then you attacked him."

Blackbear's eyes narrowed as he studied her. "Did he say it was me?"

"I know who it was. Cloaked in your robes, and your masks," she said, glancing toward her son.

"Maybe it was the Ancient Ones who attacked him. After all, they are alive. Some even say that when provoked, their wrath turns hot. And then it has the power to scorch those who disturb them. Was he burned?"

"You don't know what you're talking about."

"It's happened before, over the years. I've heard."

"What you've heard you don't understand. And what isn't understood has a danger all its own."

"Since when is knowledge of the old ways dangerous?"

"Misinterpretation of old stories is not knowledge. And passing them off as the truth harms all of us. There are enough false impressions of the Indian as a savage without adding fuel—"

"—To the fire?" Blackbear completed for her, and then he began to laugh. His confidence strong, with nothing to hide, he added, "Your Mr. Fielding wasn't harmed, physically. We just wanted him to know the Ancient Ones disapprove of what he is doing."

"And you are the keeper of the Ancient Ones?"

"Someone has to be."

Miriam Goodmedicine, president of the Ojibwa Association, felt the blood pulse to her face. "What do you know of the Ancient Ones?" she said. "What do you really know about the old ways?"

"I might not know all I should about the old ways. I don't know how any of us could, given their systematic destruction. But at least I know that the color of my blood is the color of my skin."

As fast as the blood had come to her face a moment before, it now drained away. But Miriam's battle was not so much for Blackbear's mind as it was for the others in the room. As it was for her son's. "You are a proud man, Makwamacatawa. And that is good. There is much that a man of your conviction and intelligence can accomplish for our people. But one thing that you will never be able to accomplish is to take us back to the way it was before the Europeans."

"We can do whatever we choose to do, if we do it together. If we unite and follow a single path."

"You mean if everyone else unites behind *you*. Follows *your* path."

"It is not my path. It is a path based on harmony and the natural balances. It is a path based on respect for those who have gone before us."

"In the open-time, there was harmony and balance. And respect. But there was also hardship, and there was change. Change that is irreversible. To try to go back is to follow a path that will ultimately be a dead end. A spiritual life and a respect for the old ways is an important part of our existence. But it is only one aspect of living. Just as important is survival in the world in which we now live, and respect for those who will come after us is just as important as respect for the dead.

"To turn our back on this society is not as easy as changing your name. It is our society too, and to exclude ourselves voluntarily from it is to relinquish our fair share of what it has to offer."

"What has the white man's world given to us?" Blackbear said. Then, turning to the others, he added, "Whatever it is, I want no more."

"To say we want nothing from society is another way of saying we have contributed nothing. Which is false. We have contributed. We have contributed with our blood and our labor and our land. And by all that is just, we must share in its bounty. As full, participating citizens."

"And as a full, participating citizen, have you stopped the desecration?"

"While you were planning your act of terror, in court we were negotiating protections that will accomplish the things you thought you were going to achieve."

"In court," he said disdainfully. "When will you ever learn? It's been the white man's courts and the white man's words that have been used against us for all this time."

"That's not the way it is anymore. That's not the way it will be at the Cave of Bones."

"Why? What have you . . . negotiated?"

"We will have an observer at the excavation, one who is trained in archaeology and who will have complete access to everything that is done."

"Who?"

"The witness who came in from Oklahoma. Jean Shawshequay."

"She's working with Christopher Fielding?" he said in surprise.

"Yes," Miriam answered.

Blackbear stiffened as he considered this information. The Ancient Ones would have their own means, he felt certain. He just did not know yet what they would be. He did not know yet how he could serve them.

Blackbear turned, making eye contact with Johnny Penay, and Penay got up and took the floor. "If it is your decision to work with the desecrators," Penay said, "then be advised: We will be there as well. To observe."

As Miriam stared deeply into his eyes, she saw the blank look, a dead look, and she felt chilled. It was as if the warning were directed as much at her as at Fielding, as if he would be there to watch the Association as much as the archaeologist.

In even the most unruly child, deep down there was always a look that explained the behavior. But in Penay's eyes there appeared no emotion of any kind. And that was why she was chilled. He looked like a man who would stop at nothing, if the stakes were high enough.

Chapter 6

TRAVELING SLOWLY OVER the bumps and jolts of the dirt road to the dig, Jean Shawshequay tendered her first remarks about the archaeological site. In what seemed like a tentative forward foray out of the trenches, she began by asking generally about the location itself. By her questions, Fielding could tell she was interested in more than simply the exact spot of the excavation. Would any grave site, no matter how removed, disqualify this site in her eyes from being excavated?

"Why exactly is the sinkhole called the Cave of Bones?" she asked. "If it's not a cave. And if there's no bones." Fielding looked over at her, not sure if she was serious or not. "It seemed to be common knowledge in court that the name at least had nothing to do with human burial."

"You really don't know?" Fielding asked.

"I'm not from around here, you know."

Fielding glanced in his mirror. The two sheriff's cars were still there but had spaced themselves well back to avoid the trail of dust. "Because of the fossils," he said simply.

"The fossils?"

"It's all limestone, formed by the deposition of primeval marine creatures. You can't break open a rock without finding some kind of fossil. Crustaceans, fish, brachiopods, corals. Some forms must have been recognizable to the early Ojibwa; others, long extinct, would not have been."

"As a place of death for so many creatures," Jean observed, "it must have been a very powerful location."

Fielding looked over at her, trying to read her train of thought. But staring straight through the windshield, her profile showed a blank page. "Yes. I suppose it was," he said, looking back to the road.

They passed the rocky outcropping where Fielding had first noticed the smoke. He slowed for a look, but the haze had lifted. The camp fire had been out now for sixteen hours.

• • •

The bottom of the pit, as the local woodsmen called the sink-hole, was a world unto itself. Shut off by its circular ramparts, it was a quiet place. A fitting place to die.

Close to the light gray ash pile of the camp fire, the carcass was still strung from the branch. Nearby rested the man who had brought it to this place, the man who had spent so many nights killing.

The pit was a fitting place for both of them.

"I said, are we close?"

"Sorry," Fielding said. "I must have been thinking about something else." He had been. He had been thinking about his last frantic drive over this same road. Coming out of the woods, crashing into the twin ruts, the branches and trees and vegetation all flashing by in a blur, as all the while he fought to maintain his consciousness, fought the effects of the cloud, the centripetal force that increased its hold with each revolution, the pain that throbbed in his head.

It had begun to hurt again, as he thought of it. The pressure wasn't as intense, but it was still there, where his skull had cracked against the rim of the door.

Intermixed with memories of the escape, he saw the frozen snarl of the raccoon, the black fur emerging from the brush, the raptor clawing at the front windshield—bits and pieces of the entire incident thrashed together in a fashion not constrained by reality. Everything blended together to re-create the tension he had felt then, and it was the tension—not the memories—that was affecting him now.

"Well? Are we?" Jean prompted again.

Fielding glanced at her quickly. He was hot again. Sweaty. His breath was coming harder. He realized by her look that it showed, and he turned away, back toward the road. "Yes," he managed to say. "We're close." Fielding looked at the trees, trying to recognize points of familiarity. Downshifting, he said, "Right around this bend."

At least he thought the ambush had taken place right around the bend. For some reason, everything appeared so different.

As Fielding took the turn, he didn't even look in the mirror. He was supposed to stop and wait for the two sheriff's cars to catch up. But the thought didn't even cross his mind. He was too anxious to see what was around the bend, to prove to the others that the assailants had really been there. To prove it to himself.

There shouldn't have been any doubt, but everything seemed so peaceful again. Peaceful, except within the confines of his own thoughts.

The road straightened and Fielding looked ahead. His eyes traced the dual tracks as they followed an unbroken course, weaving slightly around a large white pine, dipping with the contour of the woods, finally disappearing around another bend.

As he looked at the road, as his truck glided slower, Fielding sensed a rush of heat come to his face, along his sides, down the center of his back. Where were they? Where were the trees that had blocked the road?

The sequence of events seemed suddenly less clear. It was as if the cloud had come swirling back, blurring the entire incident. Had it all been an illusion? Could the half men, half animals have appeared after the accident?

He had been convinced that they were real. Yet he had been convinced that the creatures had pursued him, taking shape in the swirl of dust after he had stopped the truck and fallen to his knees outside, gasping for air. But they hadn't been real then. The images had been simply trunks of trees, wavering in his vision due to the dizzy near-incapacity from the blow to his head.

"This is it?" Jean said.

Was it? Fielding was uncertain. As it had a few hours before, the doubt suddenly seemed to have more credibility behind it than what he thought had happened. It remained that way, until he saw it. Until he saw the silvery underside of a fallen birch off in the woods.

The Jeep chugged and he hit the clutch. "Yeah," Fielding said. "This is where they were."

By the time the sheriff and Deputy Cole pulled up behind the truck, Fielding and Jean were already outside. Halstead was skeptical until Fielding showed him the trees and the fresh stumps. A short distance up the road, past the next bend, they found a place where several vehicles had flattened the brush.

"Okay, Fielding," Halstead said. "Someone was here. Let's go to the sinkhole. See what they did."

At first glance, it appeared as though nothing had been touched.

The Cave of Bones was another half mile past the point of the ambush, and when Fielding saw the untrammeled tent line through the trees, he began to feel a nervous relief. They parked and approached cautiously.

The site of the ancient settlement was a partial clearing, roughly semicircular in shape. It was in the lee of a bald knoll, only slightly higher in elevation, yet enough to form a windbreak from the northerlies. The clearing was cut by a shallow drainage ravine, which led to the edge of the sinkhole.

It was a typical, unordered patch of rocky north woods, except for the grid. Superimposed over the grass and dirt and scrub bushes, like an architect's overlay, were Fielding's carefully surveyed markers.

Stakes, connected with white twine that was leveled to take the contour out of the ground, were placed at precisely measured points. At selected spots scattered throughout, narrow holes punctured the earth, where Fielding had drilled his core samples.

Near the start of the ravine, a peaked tarp, held aloft with poles at the corners, covered the beginnings of an excavation.

"You've begun," Jean said it like an accusation.

"Yes," Fielding said, stepping down into the flattened dirt surface. "Good strata were already visible here," he pointed, indicating the side-cut, "and down here," gesturing farther along the ravine, "was where the hiker found the first artifact."

She nodded, tight-lipped, then turned and followed the drainage ravine toward the sinkhole.

Fielding watched her for a moment, then climbed back up to the surface.

"No sign of fire," Sheriff Halstead said. "Everything else look okay?"

"So far." Fielding eyed the large green tent at the edge of the clearing. Extending outward from its entrance was a porch area sided with mosquito netting. "Let me check over there."

As the men were moving in the opposite direction, Jean Shawshequay reached the lip of the sinkhole. If someone had come up to it from the woods unawares, it would have appeared to be another clearing. Until the surprise at the edge.

It was a strange site, as if the forest floor had suddenly dropped out from underfoot. Standing at the brink, Jean was looking out over the rolling humps of tree crowns, level with the surface. It was a leafy green carpet, and for a few seconds, it had the same effect on her as looking down on clouds from an airplane. It seemed so solid and permanent, as if a person could walk straight across to the other side.

The other side was about 250 feet across, and by eye the sink-hole appeared a perfect circle. It was an anomaly of geologic science, one that struck modern man as curious, and one that, she thought, must have struck ancient man as something more than a mere curiosity. How would their mythology explain such a feature? Would it be a sacred place? An evil place? Whatever they thought, she felt certain, they could not have been neutral.

Peering straight down, she noted that the trees effectively blocked the surface of the sinkhole from easy observation, concealing whatever secrets the Cave of Bones held. Jean wondered what was down there. She wondered what ancient man would have found at the bottom of the pit.

Turning in the direction of the tent, she shouted, "Sheriff, I'm going down."

Halstead was just outside the mosquito netting, watching Fielding check his gear. He turned. "What was that?"

"I'm climbing down into the sinkhole. I want to see what's down there."

"Why don't you hold on a second? It can be a tricky climb."

Jean glanced down the slope. It didn't look so difficult. "I can handle it," she said, then leaned down to get ahold of a rock edge. Reaching one leg backward, she felt solid support, then eased herself down.

Halstead watched for a second, then as she dropped from view, he looked at Deputy Cole and nodded in her direction.

The deputy took one last drag on a cigarette, then flung it to the ground. Crushing it underfoot, he said, "Let me just toss my hat in the car."

The descent was steep and arduous, but it was not a climb calling for any degree of technical skill. Jean alternately followed rain gulleys or angled sideways over exposed cornices of rock, sometimes balancing herself with a hand, but more often than not able to take the descent upright.

The deeper she descended, the quieter it became. If the woods near dusk were peaceful, the pit was serenity itself. There was no sound, no movement of any kind. If indeed there was a parallel world the dead migrated to, it could be imagined that this was the kind of place they would be sent. As in fact many had been, as evidenced by the remains of creatures millions of years past their time, and the body that still hung from a limb near the center of the circle.

Below the upper story of leaves, the odor was stronger. Once she identified it, she realized she had been smelling it all along. It just hadn't been distinct enough to notice.

Jean stopped and did a quick scan. She didn't see any smoke. But the smell of charred wood told her this was the source of Fielding's fire. She glanced back up the incline, but no one was there. Turning back, she shouted, "Hey! Is anybody down here?" She waited, then cried out again, cupping her hands around her mouth.

For a moment the peace of the pit was disturbed by her voice, but then just as fast, the quiet returned, smothering her calls without an echo. If any heard, none responded.

Jean resumed the descent, and at the bottom, seventy-five feet below the surrounding forest floor, she stopped again. It was a lost world she had entered, cut off from the normal development and depradations of the surface by the rock walls that surrounded this spot of land. Everything seemed larger down there, from the ferns to the trees, and over all was a kind of musty smell, an earthy aroma of thick black dirt that had somehow maintained its pungency even in drought.

The ground itself was uneven, the result of chunks of rock debris—some pieces small, some as large as an automobile— that littered the surface of the sinkhole. Most of the hard edges had been reclaimed by the buildup of vegetation, but in places, the stone lay exposed.

There was a mix of tree species, as at the surface, but dominant overall were the oaks. Not the scraggly versions that sprouted like weeds throughout the cutover timberlands above, stunted because they grew too close together, but massive oaks, untouched by the lumberman's ax, that spired straight up in a vain attempt to tower over the horizontal world that began seventy-five feet above their roots.

Roots spread wide rather than deep, because of the rock, and shielded from the wind, the only trunks to fall were those whose centuries-old grasp on life had expired. Where the viney stems of ground cover and the tendrils of tree roots spread across crevices between rocks, they acted like a net, over time catching leaves and twigs and all manner of forest debris, until they became matted webs of spongy soil capable of nurturing life by themselves.

Feeling the ground begin to sink under her feet at the first of these soil mats, Jean pulled back quickly. She went around, placing her feet carefully on thick roots near the base of an oak, hugging the bark as she moved. But soon she realized that the matted webs were everywhere, and to make any progress at all, she had to test them. As she did, as she reached a tentative foot forward, the dirt began to give, sinking under her weight. There was an eerie creak like the sound of rope netting being stretched taut, but as with any net of thin strands, the sum resilience of its overlapping pattern was strong. The matted floor held.

She continued forward, moving from solid ground to soil hollow under her feet. Inside, she began to sense a lively rise to the tempo of her heart. This is how it had been. The place was unchanged. It had been the same for centuries. What she saw was what had greeted her ancestors: the same trees, the enormous ferns, the same earthy aroma. And if they had camped down here, the same odor of burnt wood would have lingered under the leaves, trapped by the stone walls, just as the smell of smoke lingered now.

At the surface, Jean had roamed off from Fielding to get an overall picture of the archaeological site, looking for evidence of human activity and, in particular, for hidden signs of ancient burials. On her descent, discovering the source of Fielding's fire had become a second reason for her survey. But now, walking in the steps of her ancestors, captured within the draw of history, sensing the same awe the Ancient Ones must have felt, she began to forget the other reasons why she was there. She began to forget the dangers.

The rifle was propped only inches from his hands. It remained on safety, but the chamber was fully loaded. His kill hung nearby, protected from scavengers. Protected from whoever threatened to take it—and the way he chose to live his life—away from him.

Jerry Cole steadied himself after jumping down to a rock. "Whoa," he said to himself, breathing deeply.

Could it have been high school the last time he had been down here? Drinking beers and shooting holes in the cans with his .22?

However long it had been, though the pit had not changed, he had. He wasn't quite as agile as he had been. Or perhaps he was just more mindful of the dangers. Whatever the reason, he knew he would have to be more careful continuing the descent.

It wasn't the same for Jean Shawshequay. No matter how much she wanted it to be, it was not. It was not the same, because she was different. She was not of that time. She never had been; nor could she ever recapture how they must have thought, what their reactions truly must have been.

Around her, she saw nothing more than quiet, dead woods. She hadn't been born out here. She didn't depend on its bounty for survival. She lacked the perception of the Ancient Ones, who could notice the little things. Who could hear the subtle noises, distinguishing the sounds of life from the natural sounds of swaying branches and leaves. She was at a disadvantage, lacking their perception. For no matter how serene the woods appeared, there were always dangers. And they were dangers she could not recognize.

Deputy Cole frowned, staring into the dense matting of trees and brush. For those at the surface the sun had not yet set, but for those at the bottom of the sinkhole, it had set hours ago. And now, as the sun neared its final horizon, it was getting dark in the Cave of Bones. Cole didn't see her.

"Hey!" he shouted. "Where are you?"

She heard him, but something told her to remain quiet. There was a clearing, she could tell, just ahead. And the smell of the fire was strong.

Carefully, silently, she continued forward, as if she had indeed inherited an instinct for stealth. Why it was necessary, she wasn't sure. Maybe it was because of the stillness, the earth that absorbed all sound, the deathly quiet that hung in the air. For whatever reason, she tried to cover her approach.

There was a shape there, in the clearing. It was upright and appeared to be holding its position. Why it maintained silence she could not guess.

The killer lay prone on the ground, absolutely still. They had said he was crazy. They had hunted him in the night. And only now did he risk discovery. Not by the law, but by an academic turned editor from Norman, Oklahoma.

He risked discovery, but looking at where he lay, it was not immediately apparent that a human form was even there.

"Damn it." Cole's foot had slipped between two roots and partially broken through the matted soil. He tugged once, twice, until it was freed. Speaking to himself, he said, "I'm going to break my fucking neck looking for you?" Then he shouted, "Hey! Talk to me. Where the hell you go?"

Jean flinched. Be quiet, she wanted to shout. Someone was there. Some*thing* was there. She was sure of it.

Her first impulse was to call out to the figure who was taking shape with each bit of her progress closer. But she chose to remain silent. And as the reasons for maintaining her secret approach cycled through her mind, she began to sense fear. It was a prickling, vibrant feeling that fanned upward along her spine to the base of her neck, spreading its electricity up and over her scalp. Whoever it was chose to remain silent as well.

She eased herself closer. Somehow, it wasn't quite right. The shape was moving slightly, she could see now. It was moving too easily, as if moved by a breeze she couldn't even feel, as if it wasn't supporting its own weight. As if . . .

The air at her lips whistled between her teeth. It was a short, quick gasp of breath, involuntarily inhaled. And it remained in her lungs, frozen by her surprise, by the sudden flare of electricity that sparked throughout her nerves.

Only when she stepped fully into the clearing, letting the branch she parted snap back behind her, did she exhale. From the carcass her eyes darted around the open area. There was a fire pit, a few scattered logs, but nothing else. She did not notice the hunter, lying within easy range of her.

Approaching closer, her full attention was on the deer. She noted how its front legs were tied with a belt, and how the belt was looped over the stub of a branch. Along its underside ran a vertical cut, where it had been gutted.

She walked up to the carcass and grabbed a lower leg, bending it, testing the flexibility. Then she turned it so the stomach cut faced her. She parted the incision and leaned close, taking a deep whiff. Then she reached inside to feel the chest cavity. It was sticky, but still moist. A day old, no more.

As she turned from the deer, as new questions began to come rapidly to her mind, she came abruptly to a halt. Someone was there, in the woods. Approaching.

She looked quickly around. At first the footsteps seemed to be coming from the same direction as her own path of approach. But the brush of footsteps through old leaves was a directionless sound. She pivoted, seeking a potential avenue of escape. But escape into the brush seemed more dangerous than where she was.

Backing away from the hanging carcass, Jean's eyes caught on some movement. Back in the trees. Coming closer. It was at that moment, when the figure was pushing its way into the clearing, that she first noticed the gun.

"Hey!" Deputy Cole called, pushing through the leaves. "Where the hell you been?"

Jean's chest sunk. "Jesus. You scared me."

"Sorry, but—"

"Why didn't you say something?" she said quickly, cutting him off.

"I did. I was yelling my head off. Why didn't you answer?" Cole stopped dead in his tracks. "Holy shit!"

Jean turned and glanced at the deer, then gestured toward the dead camp fire. "I'd guess we've found Fielding's fire."

Cole looked at the fire, then around the clearing. "What's that?"

Jean looked where he was staring. "The hunter's gun, no doubt."

"No. I mean that."

Her eyes narrowed. Near the gun were some of what she'd thought were logs, blackened and charred.

Cole stepped toward the burnt heap. With each step, he grew more tentative. Jean watched him, then the logs. What was it?

"Oh, Christ," Cole exclaimed. He spun away, his eyes tightly shut. He bent over at the waist, one hand braced against a knee, the other at his forehead. He tried to swallow, to keep down what was rising from his gut.

Jean's eyes gaped wide, staring at the deputy, then looking toward the logs. She couldn't yet see what he had, but she could certainly sense his dread. She took one step closer, then another. They were logs, weren't they? Two branches splayed from a larger trunk. And the other end?

Another two steps and Jean froze. At last, visual confirmation caught up with what she had already suspected in her mind. At the deputy's first reaction, she had thought immediately what it might be. But perception and acceptance of what is perceived do not always run apace.

Things that are too horrifying to comprehend have a way of carrying their own denial. For Jean Shawshequay, the state of denial had ended.

Chapter 7

"WELL," SHERIFF HALSTEAD drawled, standing over the charred corpse, "at least the DNR will be happy."

Fielding shot him a look.

"Hey, that's how the brown-shirts are," Halstead said defensively. "Personally, I didn't think it was that big a deal. A guy up here, lives by himself in the woods, taking deer for his own use. But jeez, it drove them crazy. You know what I think really did it?" Halstead said, turning toward Fielding. "The time he took down a buck with a radio collar." The sheriff broke into a big laugh, before adding, "Four months of study, then poof."

Fielding moved away from Halstead, walking around the other side of the corpse. Studying the remains intently, he asked, "How could this have happened?"

"He got too close to the fire. Maybe he fell asleep."

"But would he be burned so . . . thoroughly? I mean, look at him. He looks like a charred piece of coal."

"I don't know, Fielding. I do know fire burns until there's nothing more to burn." Staring at the corpse, he snorted, "Maybe his blood was half alcohol."

Fielding ignored him, continuing to study the body. The dead man was laid out in a line radiating away from the camp fire, with his legs closest to it. His body was partially curled inward, about halfway between flat on his stomach and on his right side. His elbows were bent, but both hands extended beyond his head.

The sun had set, but the sky straight up was still bright enough for them to see. There were no shadows, however, and because of that, surface features lacked definition.

Fielding crouched near the body's outstretched hands. He had almost missed it altogether. "You got a flashlight, Sheriff?"

"Jerry?"

The deputy pulled out a penlight that had been clipped into

his shirt pocket. Edging forward, he reached it toward Fielding, never once looking directly at the charred remains.

Fielding clicked the light on and shined the narrow beam at the dirt just beyond the reach of the cinders that once had been fingers. There were marks there, gouges in the soil. Fielding held the flashlight level with the ground, shining it across the marks so shadows highlighted the pattern. "What do you make of this?"

Both the sheriff and Jean stepped closer to look, Halstead going down to one knee. There were two sets of vertical gouges, four in each set. Both sets were about four or five feet long, beginning at the fingers and stretching in a straight line away from the fire pit. "He did that?" the sheriff said.

"Looks like it."

Halstead was puzzled. He looked at the gouges, the position of the corpse, and the camp fire. He was strained to offer an explanation. "He must have caught on fire," he said, still eyeing the pit, then shifting his gaze to the finger grooves in the dirt, "and he was trying to pull himself away from the flames that had ignited him."

"But, Sheriff," Fielding began, "if he was trying to crawl away, his trail would lead in the other direction. His marks would be under him."

The sheriff continued to study the problem. He knew what it really looked like, but that wouldn't make any sense. "So what does it look like to you?"

Fielding peered down again at the narrow grooves, the twin sets of shadowed marks extending outward from the corpse. He knew what it looked like as well, but for someone trained in the sciences, to state observations that suggested an illogical cause was not an easy thing to do. He stared intently at the marks as if fighting to grasp an explanation.

Before he could answer, Jean Shawshequay spoke for all of them. "It looks like he was moving toward the fire. Like he was being dragged toward the fire."

Halstead rose slowly to his feet. "Maybe we'd better leave him where he is. Call in the State Police evidence boys. See what they make of it."

Fielding shined the beam into the corpse's face. The man had been left with empty pits for eyes, a bump that suggested a nose, overall more skull than head. Continuing downward, the light passed over a blackened ridge at the neck—a thick collar, probably, a jacket or a wool shirt. As the beam crossed the chest, there was a glint of light. A reflection. Fielding looked up. Halstead had seen it too. "May I?" Fielding asked.

Halstead gave him a nod. "Go ahead."

Fielding opened his pocket knife and with its narrow blade scraped at the crusted ash, revealing a small metal object. Fielding extracted it with the same care he reserved for unearthing centuries-old artifacts. He stood and held out the metal object between his forefinger and thumb. It was roughly oval in shape, a cap with a nozzle in the center. All that remained of a disposable butane lighter.

"Well," Halstead said, "that explains how the fire flashed so hot so fast."

"Think so?" Fielding said, not convinced.

"Maybe there was some other kind of fuel," Jean said. "He was using it on the fire and it flared up in his face."

Fielding eyed her silently, thinking. Handing the lighter to the sheriff, he walked toward the camp fire. Blackened logs rested in a bed of gray ash. There was no smoke, no sign of the fire in the remains from last night.

Fire is an entity of dual natures. It is a ravager, flaring fast and hot, that destroys wantonly. It is also an unhurried killer, deliberate in its pace of destruction. By its first nature, it dies as fast as it consumes. In its second, covered with ash to limit its breath and with the right kind of hardwood fuel, it can last for days. Entire forests have died because of its second nature.

Fielding began to sift through the ash with the blade of his knife. He couldn't help but notice that the logs were little different in appearance from the limbs of the corpse. As he rolled one of the chunks of wood over, a tiny patch of red came to life.

Fielding didn't notice it because as soon as it was exposed to air, it flared and died. Its first nature. The ember still lived, underneath, but it was sheathed with a thin flake of black carbon.

Scraping through the ash in patterned strokes, he searched for scraps of metal, a weapon, a fuel container, anything that might give a clue as to what happened. As on an excavation into forgotten till, he didn't know what exactly he was looking for. Whatever he turned up would tell him its own significance, even if there was nothing there at all.

● ● ●

The carbon layer was as thin as an orchid's membrane, and just as fragile. The heat below it gradually caused it to curl, until finally it cracked. Exposed again, the ember came to life, this time erupting with a tiny jet of flame. It shot upward an inch, no more, seeking oxygen, desperate for survival. It wavered, one direction then another; then, as quick as a switch being turned, it was snuffed out.

Even as it died, it had grown, increasing the area in which the ember smoldered, boring into new wood, insuring that it was only a matter of time before its second nature yielded again to its first.

Fielding wedged his knife under an ash-buried object, pried it loose, and rolled it to the edge of the pit.

Jean Shawshequay was standing over him, watching. "Anything?"

"Yes," he said, and she bent closer. "Looks like a Paleolithic gas can."

It was a rock, she could see now, and for the first time, a semblance of warmth passed between them. It was only a smile, his to hers, and hers in return, but compared to their interaction so far, it could have been an embrace. It seemed so incongruous, making a joke under these circumstances at this time, but Jean couldn't help but be touched by the humor. She stared into his face, at his easy grin, for a moment at least forgetting what had happened. But as their eyes connected, something began to change. It began to change within him. As she watched, there was the briefest of flickers in his eyes, as if his pupils widened then narrowed, all in a split second. At first she thought he was mocking her. But then she saw the surprise. The shock. The pain.

Fielding started to fall backward. His right hand was moving to his left wrist. His eyes were shutting tight, the skin crinkling in fleshy folds below them and to the sides.

Jean could observe every detail of his face. It was all happening fast, but to her, it appeared to be happening in slow motion. She saw him fall. She saw him roll to his back. She saw him pull his left hand close in to his chest. And she saw his mouth turn round in a scream.

It was the noise, the sound of Fielding's unintelligible cry of pain, that shook her out of the suffocating pall that smothered any reaction. She started toward him.

Fielding continued to wheel away from the pit, rolling to his side. "Aah!" he shouted in a continuous, wavering syllable powered not by any source of rational thought, but springing forth from the raw, physical nature of the stimulus.

"What is it?" Jean cried frantically. She had collapsed to her knees next to him.

Jerry Cole instinctively went for the gun at his waist, but it was not there. It was on the floor of his car. Halstead stormed toward the fire pit, kicking at the log.

Fielding was bringing his knees up to his waist. His right hand was still at his left, but instead of holding it protectively, he was yanking at it as if trying to pull something free.

Jean grabbed his shoulder and tried to roll him to his back, toward her. But he fought her. He was fighting everything. "Chris! Stop it! Let me see."

"Let go!" he cried.

"I'm trying to help." Fielding's muscles were so tensed, she had little effect on him. It was as if he didn't even notice her efforts. She leaned back, not sure what to do.

Fielding's jaw was clenched tight, but his voice was a mix of power and pain too strong to be held in. "Damn you. Let go!"

Jean rocked back in horror. Not from his curse, but because she was no longer trying to roll him over. She had already let go. "Chris! What's wrong?"

Fielding moaned and dropped over to his back, this time on his own. But his right hand was still at his left.

Jean grabbed him again and tried to pull it free. "Sheriff. Help me!" she shouted.

Halstead was already coming to Fielding and now dropped down next to him. He grabbed Fielding's other arm and together with the anthropologist pulled his hands apart.

Fielding grimaced, letting out a guttural expletive. But no longer was he out of control. He lay there, panting, trying to hold each breath in as long as he could. But the effort was too much to ask, and his breathing devolved into a rapid series of exhales.

Jean raised Fielding's left hand. There was a trickle of blood from it, or rather, the dark, crispy residue of blood already dried. And there was the pungent aroma of charred flesh.

"Jesus. I thought the fire was out," Deputy Cole said.

The heel of Fielding's palm was burned and raw, but the

sharp impact of the pain had lifted. His breathing steadied as he brought himself under control.

As he tried to rise, Jean held him back. "Just hold on."

"I'm okay," Fielding said. "Let me see."

"It was my fault, Chris," she said. "I'm sorry. I distracted you."

Fielding forced himself up to a sitting posture. "What the hell was it?"

"You really okay?" Halstead asked.

"Yeah." Fielding twisted his hand carefully, then began to brush away the gray ash that had stuck to his skin. He grimaced, then blew on his hand to clear most of the ash away. He was burned, but it was not a surface thing. It was more like a puncture. On the inside of the heel of his palm were two marks, about an inch apart. Slowly, Fielding rotated his hand to examine the other side. There were two more burn marks, about an inch and a half apart.

"Christ. You must have stuck yourself good on something," Halstead said.

Fielding didn't say a thing. He studied his hand, the wounds, then looked at the fire pit.

"Jerry," Halstead said, "is there any wire or something in there?"

Cole swallowed, then approached the fire pit cautiously. He toed a log over, then, without bending down, scuffed the side of his shoe across the ash. "Doesn't look like it, Sheriff."

"There's nothing in there," Fielding said.

"It must have been a splinter of wood," Jean said.

Fielding looked at her, holding a thoughtful expression for a few beats. Then he nodded. "Yeah. Must have been."

Halstead exhaled heavily, looking up toward surface level, then at the sky. "You can make it out of here, can't you?" he said to Fielding.

"There's nothing wrong with my feet."

Halstead smiled, then said to his deputy, "Come on. Let's bury these coals."

At the surface, Halstead told Jerry Cole to stay at the site. "I'm sure the forensics boys won't come until tomorrow. But I'll send Kinsey out at midnight. Your shift lasts until then, doesn't it?"

Actually, it was over at ten. But Cole didn't mind. There were worse ways to get a couple hours of overtime than sitting out in the woods at night.

Standing next to his patrol car, watching the Jeep truck and the sheriff's car disappear through the trees, Cole reached into his shirt pocket and pulled out a pack of cigarettes. He flipped his wrist, then pulled one out with his lips. Sliding the pack back into his pocket, he fingered a book of matches.

Snapping open the cover, Cole's eyes caught on the print inside. "Be an Entrepreneur," it read. "Run Your Own Business!" My own business, he thought, smirking. He remembered telling Julie all his big plans, at this very site. Between sips of beer and awkward attempts to slide his arm around her back. What had he been then? Nineteen? Twenty? Well, there was still time.

Cole broke off a match; then before striking it, he pulled the cigarette out of his mouth and tried to clear his throat. He had a thick, raspy feeling in the back of his mouth, and his throat was still raw with the taste of bile. The climb and the heavy breathing hadn't helped.

Cole slipped the cigarette back into the pack and cleared his throat again, trying to bring some moisture to his mouth. It was hot and raw, as if it were on fire.

Fielding's hand was wrapped in a bandanna, and he had it raised above his head, his elbow balanced on the back of his seat. Jean was driving.

She took her eyes off the dirt road for a moment, glancing over at him. "At least you'll have a good anecdote, when you present your findings."

"I don't think telling the Society that I stuck my hand into hot coals will do much for my field reputation."

Jean laughed. A few moments passed as she steered around a rutted depression, the branches of a jack pine scratching alongside the truck. Pulling squarely into the trail again, shifting into second, she said, "You going to be able to dig?"

"I don't know," Fielding said. "Maybe you'll have to do the heavy work."

"Ah. Now I understand."

"What's that?"

"Why you were so anxious to have an observer. All you really wanted was free labor."

Fielding smiled, looking out his side window. He did not disagree.

Jean downshifted, then eased her foot onto the brake to nego-
tiate the round top of a boulder protruding through the dirt.
Coming back to speed, she eyed him again. He seemed quiet,
content, not the least in any pain from the burn. "You know, I
didn't set you up."

Fielding turned toward her, the easy contentment suddenly
gone.

Glancing at the road, then looking back at him, she added, "I
had nothing to do with the people who jumped you."

The crease that had appeared between Fielding's eyebrows
evened out. He studied her impartially for a time, watching as
she divided her attention between him and the road. He watched
as her expression began to change, from patience to concern.
Finally, she said, "You don't believe me?"

Fielding looked away, gazing out through the windshield. "I
was never your enemy. I'm not out to steal your heritage."

Jean settled back in her seat. "I know," she said.

Fielding didn't understand. "What do you mean, you know?"

Jean licked her lips and swallowed before answering. "Do
you know Professor Oaten? Adam Oaten?"

"Yes, of course. As a matter of fact, I once delivered a lecture
for him. Four, five years—" He stopped in mid-sentence, turning to look at her.

She smiled, reading his thoughts. "Yes. I was there."

Fielding stared at her, his lips parted in surprise. "You were
there," he repeated, as a statement of fact.

"I was there."

Fielding exhaled a quick gust of air through his nose, then
turned away, shaking his head. "You were what? A grad student?"

"Yes."

"Do you remember what I talked about?"

"Oh yes," she said. "And I was impressed."

Fielding waited for her to continue, but when she did not, he
said in frustration, "With what? My good looks?"

Jean laughed out loud. "No. Or not only."

"Come on, you know what I'm asking."

"I was impressed with your sensitivity," she said. "I had
never heard anyone talk about the respect archaeologists owed
to the remains of those they studied."

Fielding brought his left hand down to his lap. "Then why,"
he said evenly, "did you come on like you did in court?"

"I 'came on' the way I did because of some of the things you said that day in Oklahoma. And then I came on hard because of your boss."

"He's not my boss."

"You were with him. On the same side. I just assumed . . ." She trailed off, not finishing her sentence.

It seemed an admission that she had been wrong. At least that's how Fielding took it. He settled back, and as he thought about her, and Curtis Heath, and the courtroom, he began to laugh.

"What's so funny?"

"Prehistoric equals pre-white. I thought I'd heard that before."

Jean began to laugh too. "I said you were impressive."

"No. You were," Fielding said. "In court. You were beautiful." He meant how she had acted then, the passion with which she spoke. But as his last word lingered in his mind, as he stared into the eyes of black fire that now showed heat of a different kind, he couldn't help but let his description take on a fuller meaning. *She* was beautiful, he thought.

The reception on the radio was so weak, the song was more Jerry Cole than Diana Ross. But he needed her voice to follow the lyrics, so when she faded out even more, he joined Mary and Flo instead. His melody was even worse than the scratchy sound coming out of the speakers, but he didn't mind—there was no one to hear. The only thing that would stop him would be the end of the song. Even then, he carried on for a few bars because he didn't realize it was over.

Motown static he could take, but not the static of a commercial. He leaned forward and clicked the radio off. His throat was still dry, and for that he blamed Sheriff Halstead. If he had known he was going to have to stay out there, he would have come prepared.

As he sat there, he started to imagine being stranded, partly to amuse himself, but also because that's how he felt. They could simply forget about him. Then his car wouldn't start. Maybe a war would break out. Any number of emergencies and he'd be stuck out there in the middle of nowhere.

Of course. An emergency. "Jesus. Am I a dope?" He slapped his forehead with the fingers of one hand, then got out of the car. At the back, he opened the trunk.

It was rapidly getting dark, and the trunk light wasn't bright enough for him. He used the flash. At one side, braced in the fender near a box of emergency flares, were four twelve-ounce bottles of water.

Cole released one from its plastic yoke, then cracked the seal. He smelled it first, then sampled the liquid. No telling how long it had been in there. It was warm and tasteless, which for him was okay. Better than warm and bacteria-filled.

He drained the plastic bottle, then screwed the cap back on and dropped it in the trunk. The second bottle of water he drank more leisurely. Sitting back on the open lip of the trunk, Cole pulled out his pack of smokes and drew a cigarette from it with his lips. He struck a match; then after touching the flame to the end of his cigarette, he shook the match out and flicked it to the ground.

He took a long drag on the tobacco, then followed that with a drink of water. Just like the old days, he thought. After dark at the pit. Drinking beer and shooting the cans with his .22.

As the memories played themselves out in his mind, Jerry Cole stood up and looked back in the trunk. He fished out the empty, then walked around to the driver's door. Reaching inside the window, he pulled out the headlight switch, and the woods in front of the car were suddenly cast in equal parts glare and dark shadow.

As artificial lights drowned out the natural darkness, back near the trunk, on the ground, there was the flicker of a different kind of light. Amid last year's leaves, a red glow was climbing up a brown strand of grass. At its base was the match. Its extinguished heat was too low to keep the cardboard burning, but the dry tinder of the forest wasn't quite as reluctant a combustible.

Natural fire comes to life in stages, with threshold events having to happen in sequence. Usually, a casually tossed match, even if lit, is not enough to ignite a fire. To survive and grow, it has to find a ready host to accept its heat before it dies, and then the new carrier of the heat has to nurture it, allow it to spread, and transfer it to new fuel, where the process is repeated on a slightly larger scale. At any stage, the sequence can be halted. The fire can die.

For the small red glow near the right rear fender of Jerry Cole's car, it was all happening in the right sequence. It was almost as if it were happening by direction.

• • •

Light through the plastic bottle had a greenish, almost turquoise hue. Amid the shades of emerald and jade in the forest, it was a false color. Like the glare of the automobile headlights themselves, it was an intrusion, and intrusions have the quality of changing the character of the location they intrude. For this patch of woods near the edge of the sinkhole, the effect was to make it suddenly an unnatural place.

Both bottles were on a log about two feet apart. Deputy Cole stood with his rump against the grill, dead set between the headlights. He leveled his revolver straight out, bracing his right wrist with his left hand. Slowly, he squeezed the trigger.

The red glow in the forest debris had spread. It had touched the lobe of an oak leaf, then radiated inward from that point. As the red line advanced throughout the leaf, filaments of veins remained, keeping the structure of the leaf intact.

Below it and to either side, new fuel was ignited, and the spreading glow began to build on itself. Red turned to yellow as the first flame jumped to life, but just as sudden as its birth was its death. Though the rise of its first nature had been premature, the second nature of the fire was keeping it alive.

"Damn!"

Cole adjusted his stance, then took careful aim again. As he squeezed the trigger a second time, the controlled explosion of the cartridge cracked through the night air. The sound was a dramatic rent of this quiet realm, but to Cole, because of the lingering impact on his ears from the first report, the second gunshot didn't seem as loud.

The barrel flash was the opposite. "Jesus!" Cole shut his eyes tight and shook his head. When he opened them again, the brightness was still there, imprinted on his retina.

At the moment of discharge, the flash of fire erupting out of the barrel had seemed twice as big as usual. Only gradually did the glare recede, returning Cole's eyesight to normal.

Was it just the night or what? Cole checked his weapon, then extracted the unspent rounds. They appeared to be all right. So one by one, he reloaded the cartridges. It was only then that he noticed he had struck his target. It wasn't much of an accomplishment, but a gun and an accurate eye give a man a sense of invulnerability.

Near where the first bottle had been, the second one still stood.

The second nature had yielded to the first.

The fire was expanding in a circle, growing outward at the same time that it pulled heat into its center. Small flames flickered and jumped in a nervous, jittering display of tension or impatience. Or excitement.

The flames seemed anxious to spend their energy. They seemed anxious to seek out more fuel.

The gun fired a third time. "Aah!" the deputy cried. The discharge was even brighter. He felt it on his hands. It backfired through the cylinder into his face.

Cole collapsed to his knees. He dropped his gun and grabbed his eyes. They stung from the flash, and he squeezed his hand tightly over them, trying to stop the burn. Gradually, the pressure seemed to work, until he relaxed his grip and opened his eyes. Wherever he looked, dots and flashes moved with his sight. It wasn't just one flare, but the imprint of many, as if he had fired not once, but a hundred times.

Cole spit in his hands and rubbed them over his closed lids. Another test glance, and the images of multiple discharges had dimmed. The deputy breathed easier, then, with exaggerated effort, pushed himself to his feet. Damn cheap ammo, he thought.

He breathed heavily again, then started around the front fender. He needed to rinse his face with water. As he came along the side of the car, as he passed out of the forward cone of the headlights, the glare was suddenly back. Near the tail end.

What the hell?

It took a moment for him to realize that the glare wasn't a continuation of the retinal imprint from the faulty discharge. That it was something else entirely. A fire!

"God damn!" he shouted aloud; then in the next instant he charged toward the fire.

His first thought was to stamp it out. He didn't think of the flares in the trunk. He never even considered jumping behind the wheel first and moving the car to safety. What did occur to him was that the fire wasn't large, but it could spread rapidly in this dryness. He had to act fast.

• • •

From a distance, the headlights were a meager crescent set against the dark, parting the black curtain like an ivory blade passing through tar. The moving brightness lasted for a few seconds, then it surrendered to the forces of night as the vehicle passed on. Within a matter of minutes, this battle between light and dark wouldn't matter anymore, because the Jeep Comanche would be in town.

"Chris?"

"Yeah?"

Jean Shawshequay kept her eyes on the highway straight ahead. She tried to make her voice sound natural and uncontrived, but that's not at all how she felt inside. "There was something else . . ." she said, and trailed off, as if she had felt that, once unleashed, the words would flow on their own. But nothing was going to come easily.

"What is it?" Fielding prompted.

Jean licked her lips, then plowed onward. "When you burned your hand, you said something. After you fell back. Do you remember?"

Fielding leaned back, as if willfully seeking the shadows of the cab. He did remember, but instead he asked her. "What did I say?"

"You said, 'Let go.' And then again, 'Damn you, let go.' " She paused, waiting for Fielding to offer his explanation, but when he did not, she turned her head toward him. "What did you mean by that? You wanted *what* to let go?"

The dash lights reflected off Jean's face, giving it a reddish tint, but Fielding's visage in the passenger seat was cast more in blackness than in light. He held on to the silence as he held on to the shadow, but he knew that neither offered permanent sanctuary. "I didn't know at first I stuck it in the coals," he said. "It didn't feel like that anyway. It felt more like . . ." He paused, searching for the right word or perhaps, more accurately, searching his memory to decide if the word fit how it actually had been. "It felt more like a bite," he continued at last, looking over at her. "I thought something had bitten me."

The glow like firelight from the dash played off Jean's skin, and the dark cavities that shadows brought to Fielding's face seemed to deepen. A moment passed, maybe two, and then he added, "That's what I thought at least, before I realized it was only the fire. And I just wanted whatever it was to let go."

• • •

Deputy Sheriff Jerry Cole stomped on the fire. Though he crushed a portion of it under his foot, the motion of his leg only seemed to fan the remainder. The flames near him leapt higher. Faster. They seemed to fling themselves toward him. Toward his leg.

"Christ!" he exclaimed, jumping back. The fire was already too large to stomp out. The ground was too dry. It was spreading too fast.

Cole stood there for a second, on the verge of panic. He could visualize it roaring out of control. Flashing through the entire forest. And all because of him. It took only an instant for the horror of that scene to spark throughout his system. Every nerve came alive, signaling its own demands, reacting individually to the threat, creating a state of agitation that prevented the reasoned flow of logical thought.

Cole began acting before he realized what he was doing. With the vision of a forest-wide inferno lingering in his mind, he began kicking at the fire, sweeping his foot sideways, trying to shuffle it back in on itself.

It was a mistake. He only helped to spread the fire, kicking burning bits of leaf and twig farther from the circle, igniting new tinder in an instant.

The fire grew. Lobes of flame snapped and broke off in its greedy reach for greater height. Individual shoots wavered and flashed and twitched in an excited dance of light and sound. It was dance without choreography, a free-form exhibition of writhing, twisting figures, an orgy of tortured bodies, the performance of a gifted repertory company depicting damned souls reaching out in agony at final judgment.

Cole stumbled backward until he hit the car. His chest heaved, his mouth was as dry as the fuel at the core of the fire. He licked his lips, and his eyes began to dart randomly from the fire to the woods to the car. The car!

His eyes flared wide. He had to move the car! Cole pushed off from the rear fender, and as he did, there was a sharp crack, like the explosion of a sap-laden tree, and Cole felt a sudden stinging at his side. He looked down. My God! He was burning. A slash of fire had slapped across his bicep and along his side. It stung like a whip, a whip laced with acid that continued to burn.

Cole began to spin in place as he slapped at his arm, then his side. The brief flare of flame was extinguished, and Cole stumbled sideways, all the while keeping his eyes fixed on the fire.

It was now as high as the rear of the car, and it was coming together in the center. The individual flames were seeking one another, their heat drawing them higher, pulling more combustibles from the forest floor.

Cole grabbed the side of his face in shock, in horror, in panicked indecision. He couldn't believe what he was seeing. Was it like the after-flash from the discharge of the gun? An imprint that wasn't really there, but that had burned an image into his eyes, into his optic nerve, into receptor cells in his brain that controlled his vision? Was his fear painting scenes on a canvas that provided its own inspiration?

The fire flared with a sudden roar, and a bolt of flame flashed against his chest. Cole screamed as he looked down. His shirt was afire. He brushed frantically at his front, but his fingers suffered the heat even worse. He clenched his fists and scraped it away with his forearms. As he did, he was jostling up and down, stumbling haphazardly, twisting, spinning, knocking his knees against each other, kicking his ankles with his feet.

Cole fell heavily, directly on one knee, then over to his side, catching himself with an outstretched hand before he went all the way down. He yelled from the pain, from the impact. But he didn't stop moving. Clawing, clutching, pushing at the dirt, he forced himself upright, to both knees.

He remained there for a moment, trying to catch his breath, his chest expanding and contracting with the force of an internal gale. As he hovered on the brink of reality, his body already having given way to the raptures of the insane, he stared at the fire. At once transfixed and horrified, he tried to give meaning to what he saw. To what was happening.

The fire had a shapeless quality, an ever-changing mix of distinct lines and blurs of light. But within the disorder, within the shadows and curves, there seemed an overall design, or rather, there seemed an emerging pattern. He thought he had seen it a few moments before. He thought he saw it now. Parts of it only, but within the flickering nature of the flames, there was a strobelike consistency to the whole. And within his mind, the bright flashes remained alive as after-images for a few seconds, and it was in that fashion that the overall image seemed to come together.

Cole leaned back, his eyes opening wider involuntarily, reacting in opposition to what would have been the natural reflex in the face of such glare. A tremulous, razored breath escaped from the back of his throat. Within him was an abject forfeiture of will and reason and all manner of muscular control. He saw it. It was moving.

"No!" he screamed, and as the sound erupted from the deepest part of his mouth, as the single syllable of terror and pleading and denial burst out of his chest, he began to move. Energized by some untapped reserve to survive, by a voice that seemed barely his own, Cole found himself rising to his feet, backing away, about to turn.

A ripping sound of fire preceded a sudden flare of light. Twin spikes of flaming heat rocketed out of the column of fire, the shifting curtain of yellow and red and black that was now taller than a man.

Cole's head snapped back as if it had been hit with high-caliber projectiles. "Aah!" he screamed, and immediately he was back on the ground, clutching at his face. The twin missiles had struck him directly in the eyes.

A rolling, continuous cry of agony and terror blared out of the man on his knees in front of the fire. He appeared a supplicating idolator before a pagan's sacramental element, but within him was neither devotion nor a willingness to die. Within him instead was a tortured blend of mental and physical torment.

His fingers gouged at his eyes as if in an attempt to extract the pain, the burning feel of the flame that seemed to penetrate still, delving deeper through soft tissue, sinking steadily farther, igniting new charges in the center of his skull. But despite the torture, he suffered a fear strong enough to eclipse the sensation of pain. It was only going to get worse, he knew. He had to get away.

Cole tore his hands from his face and opened his eyes, but what he saw was no different from what he'd seen with them closed. It was all bright, absolute glare, as if he now resided in the center of the fire, as if the fire had entered him directly, as if he had become part of the fire.

He moaned another inarticulate cry, then let himself fall forward, catching himself with his hands. He started to scramble away, and even on all fours he seemed to stumble. Blind, he didn't know what was in front of him. All he knew was the direction of the fire. He could feel the heat.

As he gouged at loose debris, as his shins scraped on sharp

projections, as his toes dug into the soil, there was a sound like a rush of wind, like combustible heat being blown across a prairie. And then he felt it, at his waist, lashing across the fleshy part of his thigh. It was the fire, and it burned, but more than that, it was sharp and penetrating and it seemed to slice into him.

Cole screamed as he was stopped momentarily. But then the pressure lifted and he lunged forward. Another blow of fire caught him, and Cole collapsed to the ground. His face pressing against dead leaves and the trails of insects, he could only groan as the burning intensified.

Steeling himself for another lunge, another desperate break to escape, Cole listened to the throaty rush of hot air. It was the sound of heat forced through a flue, except that it was not constant. It came in spurts, in spasms of advance and retreat. It was a rumbling, gravelly sound, like dry rock being churned at the bottom of a tube, its muted rumble turning over and over until its echo escaped the enclosure. It was almost a guttural sound. It was almost the warning growl of a predator.

"Nooo!" Cole screamed. Galvanized by his terror, he started to rise up. But at the moment he moved, he felt the fire upon him. It stabbed and burned and tore all at the same time. He tried to resist, but the force against him was too strong. He managed to hover above the dirt for a few seconds, his arms trembling under his own weight, but then the crooks of his elbows cracked and he crashed to the ground.

No longer able to move, no longer even trying, he was as though paralyzed by the scorching blaze that seared his flesh. His eyes were open or closed, it didn't matter, because all he could see was the yellow-white glare of the fire. It was an incendiary blur that came not from actual sight, but from an optic impression it had gouged in his brain.

As he lay there, as each nerve suffered the incalculable pain of being burned alive, the brightness at last began to die. The fire was going out. But before it did, before the blinding flash in his brain died, one last image forced itself into the glare. It was the image of the charred corpse at the bottom of the pit. The image that upon first sight had made him ill. But as this visual memory entered his mind, it was not sickness that he felt. Only relief.

The white light turned to black.

• • •

When the explosion came, the drama had already ended. The flares ignited first, then the gasoline. The rear of the car lifted off the ground, then settled. It was all over in a few seconds. Except for the sound. The sound that no one heard.

Chapter 8

FIELDING'S ROOM WAS actually a cabin, one in a series set back in the woods that the proprietor called a motel. With the windows open, at night, there was the constant sound like wind through a canyon. It came from the rapid rush of the Burning Creek stream as it cascaded over a dolomite ridge on its last leg toward Lake Superior. It was one of four streams that converged in the area, dropping over the same ridge, giving the town of Watersdrop its name.

Because he was drifting on the wind that was the distant cascade, when the knock came, Fielding didn't know if he was awake or dreaming. It wasn't until he heard the news from the sheriff on the phone in the motel office that he came fully alert. As soon as the sheriff broke the connection, Fielding dialed Jean Shawshequay.

The sky was beginning to brighten when they got to the archaeological site. It was about the same degree of brightness as when they had left the dig the night before.

As the Jeep Comanche rolled in amid the police vehicles, Sheriff Halstead made his way toward the driver's door. Fielding climbed out slowly, keeping his eyes on the sheriff as he approached. He looked weary.

"I guess you were lucky," the sheriff said.

Fielding didn't catch on immediately to what he meant. "Lucky?"

"They got Jerry. They could have gotten you."

Fielding glanced across the hood at Jean. He had been told on the phone about the fire that took the deputy. But not that anyone else had caused it. Fielding shut the door firmly, then looked back at Halstead. "Was what happened to Jerry like what happened to Billings?"

The sheriff nodded in the direction of the fire-blackened patrol car. Portable klieg lights fully extended on aluminum tripods illuminated the area to the rear and right side of the car.

They were wired to a gasoline generator. Even from a distance, Fielding could see that centered in the lights were the charred remains of the deputy. "You say somebody did this to him?"

"And to Buck. I think that's obvious now."

"Who?"

The answer to Halstead was also obvious, as it should be to Fielding. The sheriff regarded the archaeologist narrowly, as if evaluating whether he was going to be an ally or not. He said evenly, almost as a test to see if he would disagree, "The same ones who went after you."

Fielding took a deep breath and began to pace in a circle. When his back was to the sheriff, his eyes latched on Jean's. She felt as he did. The sheriff was wrong. Fielding turned back toward him. "I'm sorry, Sheriff. I don't see the connection between men in ceremonial garb and these burnings."

"A simple killing wouldn't be good enough for their . . . spirits. They needed to do it with some kind of hocus-pocus. Like they did to scare you."

"What they did to Chris may have been wrong," Jean said angrily, "but the basis of their beliefs is not hocus-pocus."

Halstead looked at her with raised eyebrows, then shifted his gaze toward Fielding. *They* sure had become allies mighty fast. And here they were together, after the early morning call.

As certain conclusions were settling in the sheriff's mind, Fielding added, "To think those men would resort to murder simply because Jerry and the poacher happened to be in the area of the sinkhole doesn't make sense. If they were willing to kill to stop the excavation, they would have killed me."

"I suppose that would have been more fitting," the sheriff said, and beneath the weariness Fielding could see the anger. "But then again," Halstead continued, "if they had taken you out, there'd have been another one like you. Next week, maybe. Or maybe not until next year. But sooner or later, another archaeologist would have come. This way, they deliver a message, and you walk away voluntarily, putting an end to it yourself."

Fielding could see it wasn't an argument he was going to win. Yet what did happen to Deputy Sheriff Jerry Cole? And Henry Billings? And what had happened to him when he leaned over Billings's fire?

Fielding had turned away from the sheriff and was looking toward the burned-out car. The kleig lights shut off. The body of

Jerry Cole had been zipped into a black plastic bag and lifted into the back of a truck.

"I want you to tell me more about the men who jumped you," Halstead said.

The archaeologist turned slowly, reluctantly. "I told you about them."

"I want to hear it again. In detail this time."

Fielding nodded toward the evidence techs, the state police officers milling about the scene. "What do they say happened?"

A look of distaste passed across the sheriff's face. "They think he ignited emergency flares in the trunk with a cigarette or something, and blew himself up."

"Could it have happened that way?" Fielding asked.

"Yeah. But if it did, why did Jerry fire his gun three times?"

Fielding turned all the way back around.

Halstead pointed toward the car. "We found his gun on the ground in front of the car, apparently where he dropped it. He managed to get off three rounds before they got to him. Now, if it was an accident, who do you suppose he was shooting at?"

Fielding had no idea. "What did they say about Billings?"

"The lieutenant said it was a crazy thing, two accidental burnings a night apart. But not so crazy it wasn't possible." Halstead made a clicking sound, a sign of disgust. "I guess where they come from, this kind of thing happens all the time."

Fielding turned toward the state police crew. They seemed to be wrapping things up, collapsing the lights, getting ready to leave.

"He was nice about it though," Halstead continued. "Offered to give us one of his body bags so we could haul up the remains."

"I don't see how anything I have to tell you about the guys who jumped me is going to help you figure out what happened to Jerry."

"That depends on how much you can tell me, doesn't it?"

"Even if I gave you a photograph, you'd still need evidence. Something concrete to tie those men into what happened here."

"Oh, we'll find something," Halstead said. "I can guarantee you that. We'll find what we need."

By the time Fielding finished describing in detail the ceremonial garb on the men who attacked him, the state police were gone. The sheriff and his men left a short time later, leaving Jerry's car for a flat bed wrecker they said was coming.

Fielding used a stick to raise the trunk of the charred car, and right away he noticed the odor of gasoline. As he stepped closer, he could see the deep black flash marks of the flares.

It looked like it could have happened as the state police said. Who was he to say differently? What was he looking for that would tell him differently?

Jean called back from the driver's side window, "The lights were on."

It took a second for Fielding to shift gears. Lights? "The headlights?"

"Take a look."

Fielding leaned in through the window. The headlight knob was pulled out. He tried to push it in, but it was frozen in place.

Pulling back out of the car, he looked into the woods, in the direction the lights would have been shining.

"What do you think he was looking at?" Jean said.

What did he see? Fielding wondered.

Except for the crunch of footsteps, the woods were quiet. What little dew there had been was already gone, so dry it was.

Sheriff Halstead and his men were spaced more or less evenly apart as they traversed the area, searching. They looked under ferns, behind trees; they swept aside vegetation with their feet, all the while looking for something out of place. Something left inadvertently. A dropped pocketknife, a scrap of cloth snagged on a twig, or perhaps a footprint cut into the moss.

They had driven back to the area where Fielding's attackers had parked their vehicles, and where very possibly they had changed into their totemic cloaks. It was here Halstead hoped to find his evidence.

Low to the ground as the sheriff walked past, a face well camouflaged against the dried grass and moss watched him in silence. It was a face that lacked human definition, but then again, it could hardly have been described as a common animal of the forest. Lying there against the base of a tree, it gave no hint of its presence. It did not move. Its eyes didn't even blink. It was as if an intelligence behind those eyes knew the purpose of the search. As if it were gifted with preternatural insight, because of whom it represented.

● ● ●

"Look at this," Fielding said, pointing at the ground. It was a perfect cup of rotten bark, freshly exposed. The dead log had been picked up and pivoted eighteen inches, making it perpendicular to the direction of the headlights.

Fielding crouched down to inspect the log. It had been leveled at one end by a smaller chunk of wood. He looked up at Jean. She deduced what he did, and together they walked past the log, deeper into the woods.

Jean found the first of the plastic water bottles, ensnared in some brush. Fielding found the other, at the bottom of a shallow depression. The labels were old, but they had not been exposed to even a single night's rain. Staring back toward the car, Fielding could almost visualize Cole standing there. "Two hits and a miss," he said.

"If all he was doing was target practice," Jean said, "why do you suppose he just dropped his gun in the dirt?"

Fielding shrugged. "Maybe it wouldn't have been effective," he said, "against whatever he saw."

"Hey, Kinsey," Halstead shouted. "Nothing?"

"No, Sheriff. Sorry."

Halstead took a deep breath as he evaluated the situation. Maybe he'd find something at the site of the ambush itself, where they had cut the trees down.

As he started walking back to the dirt trail, his mind was already jumping ahead: to the next site, to the step after that if the search still proved fruitless. And that's when he saw it.

Sometimes it happened that way during an investigation. Stop looking, and vision is clearest.

At first he saw the deep black eyeholes, and that startled him. He actually jumped back a step. Then he caught his breath and came forward. Near the base of a tree, where it must have been left behind because of the rush, was a mask. An elongated totemic mask fashioned of deer hide.

Chapter 9

LINDSEY VERHOVEN CAREFULLY snugged the silver nib into place, then held the rod up and sighted along the handle to the tip. She approved, then continuing her inspection, she lowered the rod, checking where the bamboo was planted into the cork handle. That's when she stopped, looking up at her dad in surprise. Her name was drawn in black underneath the lacquer.

Lindsey wasn't given to wild expressions of excitement, but John Verhoven could see the delight in her eyes. The rod wasn't just another one of her dad's, but her very own. And a good one. Made by Uncle Bob from his carefully hoarded Chinese bamboo.

Her professionalism quickly returned, and like a true fisherman, Lindsey tested the flex by flicking her wrist. She was tall for twelve years old, but still coordinated, with good hand and arm control. She was an athlete, a fine basketball player.

"Dad," she said, the happiness finally bubbling through, "this is perfect."

Everyone else was surprised that she had taken to fly fishing. But very early she had shown an interest in nature: bugs and snakes, flowers and trees. She was a quiet girl; her mother said she was shy, but that wasn't quite true. She just wasn't moved to demand attention the way most kids did. Usually she was content to listen, letting the others talk.

From those standpoints, it was not all that surprising to John that she was interested in fly fishing. There was no more perfect outdoorsman's sport for combining the primal drive of capturing game with the gentle appreciation of wilderness. The fly fisherman's skill required stealth and solitude and a close recognition of the subtleties of nature. All of which came naturally to Lindsey.

The back door opened. "Oh for heaven's sake, John. What are you two doing out here? We were supposed to leave at nine. It's already nine-thirty."

"Okay, Mags. We'll be right there." He was looking at Lindsey when he said it, and she giggled. The conspiracy of the river.

"If we're not to Watersdrop before dark," Maggie continued, "we're staying in a motel. We're not driving into those woods when we can't see a thing."

"We'll make it, Mom," Lindsey said, pulling the rod sections apart. From inside the house, Jimmy cried, "Mom! Sharon hit me!"

Maggie's chest sank. "This is vacation?"

John walked over to her and clasped her by the shoulders, then leaned forward and pecked her on the cheek. "By tonight, everything will be like it usually is, up there. No sounds of traffic, the stars not blocked by city lights, and after the kids are in bed—"

"We'll have a fire."

"We'll curl up on the floor in front of a crackling fire."

Word spread fast throughout town. And so did the rumors. Officially, Deputy Cole's death was an accident, but the only people who really believed that wore blue uniforms and were headquartered out of Lansing. Everyone else felt the Indians were behind what had happened. The non-Ojibwa suspected it, and the Ojibwa feared it.

In the Warbler's Nest, Blackbear and Johnny Penay hunched over coffee at a small, round table, their backs to the room. They were speaking quietly but forcefully to each other, Penay in particular expressing strong opinions.

So absorbed were they in their conversation that they didn't see Sheriff Halstead enter the restaurant and head in their direction. They didn't notice him until he laid the deer-hide mask on the table between them. Slowly, both men looked up.

The sheriff watched them for a moment, trying to gauge their reactions. But both men concealed their thoughts well. He said, "Was it some kind of ritual slaying?"

Their expressions did not change.

"A cult thing?" Halstead said. "That's what you are, aren't you? A cult. The Three Fires. I know about that." The men remained impassive, and Halstead continued. "You can't just kill somebody; you must do it in a certain way. Feed him to the eternal fire. Is that what you do? Sacrifice your victims?"

Finally, Blackbear spoke. "You don't know the first thing

about us. About our way of life. About our beliefs. If you did, you wouldn't speak with such ignorance."

"Come on, Blackbear, Or Mukwa-whatayacallit. I grew up around here. I know these Indians better than you. And they've always been reasonable, regular folk. Before you got here."

"They've been docile," Penay said.

The sheriff's eyes lit up. "And so now you're changing that. You're out to restore their old ways. The aggression they needed back then to survive. Their . . . savagery."

Penay thrust back the chair and started to shoot to his feet. As he did, Blackbear grabbed his forearm, practically pinning it to the table. "He's doing it deliberately, Johnny. To provoke us. Don't you see?"

The sheriff managed a secret grin. That's exactly what he was trying. Hoping for a mistake.

"He doesn't have shit so he's fishing for a reason to place us under arrest. Get us where he thinks he can exert pressure and get us to break."

Penay hung in his half stance, the tendons in his neck like guy wires under canvas. He wasn't ready to give up on his urge, yet he was listening to Blackbear.

"He thinks he can get us to turn on each other," Blackbear added.

"You got a reason to fear each other?" Halstead asked quickly.

"You watch too much bad TV, policeman."

"Don't we all, Blackbear." He shifted, standing straight. "Where else do you think I should get my inspiration?"

"Pray. To your God. If you have one."

"To keep your Indian spirits from doing this again?"

This time it was Blackbear who almost swung at the sheriff. But he held back.

Halstead smirked. He had hoped to get lucky. But on the other hand, pressure needs time to build. And it would continue to build, as long as he pushed the right buttons. As long as he found the weakest point.

The sheriff looked toward Penay. "Just where did you come from, Johnny? Back home, were you this much of an . . . activist?"

Penay only blinked, maintaining the fire in his glare. But Blackbear could feel the change in his muscles. It was almost as if he flinched.

"I wonder if someone's looking for you back there," Halstead continued. "I wonder if your name's in the LIEN? Or do you have a new name too?" He paused, maintaining eye contact for several beats. Then he picked up the deer-hide mask and turned toward the door.

Blackbear did not understand the things that had happened. He never sought rational explanations when it came to the spirit world, but somehow he expected some manner of logic to its actions. Why had the Ancient Ones destroyed the poacher and the deputy and not the desecrator himself? Were they blindly lashing out at anyone near? He didn't think they were like that. They were beings of justice, to be sure, but benevolent justice.

The door to the restaurant closed and Penay leaned close. "It was the kid's mask."

"I know."

"What are we going to do?"

"About Ray Goodmedicine? Nothing."

"No," Penay said. "About the sheriff. And the archaeologist."

Blackbear looked at Penay, his eyes shifting nervously. He didn't know.

"You expect the desecrations to stop?" Penay was speaking in a forced whisper, his face mere inches from Blackbear's. When Blackbear didn't respond immediately, he continued. "I told you we would have to be ready to follow through, wherever it leads."

Blackbear leaned away. "We don't know where it leads. We have to wait until things become clear."

"Until the Ancient Ones speak?" Penay said with sarcasm.

"Until they let us know what is happening. And show us how we can help them."

"You don't need them to tell you what to do. You've got your own power. Use it!"

"I have no power," Blackbear said. "What are you talking about?"

"You have power over the men you lead. They'll listen to you. They'll do what you tell them. They'll carry out whatever you tell them is the will of the Ancient Ones."

Blackbear eyed him silently.

"We have an opportunity," Penay whispered. "The deaths of the hunter and the deputy show us the way. If it were to happen again, those responsible for the first burnings would get the blame. And despite what the sheriff may think, you know there's nothing that ties us to them."

Is that what it came down to? Blackbear thought. Murder? With the posing of the question, he felt his strength return. He wasn't sure what to do. But he was sure of what shouldn't be done. "It is not for us to kill," he said. "It is for us to serve the Ancient Ones. And to wait for them to instruct us."

"They have instructed us. By the means with which they destroyed the others. That is not a sign?"

"It may be a sign, but I'm not sure what it means for us."

Penay leaned back. "Then maybe you should go talk to your spirits directly." He slowly slid back his chair and rose to his feet, his eyes never leaving Blackbear's. "After you do, you come get me." Penay turned and walked out.

Penay did not believe. Blackbear knew that. The old beliefs for him were merely a unifying focus. But perhaps there was some truth in his ridicule. Perhaps he should talk to the Ancient Ones.

"Johnny Penay is dangerous," Miriam said to her son. "He's not a man we can trust with the welfare of our people."

"At least he's a man who speaks directly," Ray said. "Who is honest with those who listen to him."

The way he said it made Miriam turn rigid. "Speak directly yourself if you have something to say to me."

Ray had long hair parted in the middle, which more often than not hung in black spears across the sides of his face. Raising his chin, he shook his head slightly, brushing his hair behind his ears. "What did Blackbear mean when he said it had happened before?"

Miriam was caught off guard. Her lips parted but no sound came out.

"About people being burned by the Ancient Ones?"

"That's not true," she said weakly, turning so he couldn't see her face.

Ray waited in silence for a few moments, then strode to the basement door. "You expect me to trust you," he said bitterly. "And yet you refuse to trust me with the truth."

Miriam was shaken by her son's words, but the longer she sat alone after Ray had gone down to the basement, the more convinced she became that the conscious decision her generation had made to tear up certain pages of their history had been correct. She knew that no matter how it came out, it would be misinterpreted, and old stereotypes would be resurrected.

As she listened to the angry movement of her son in the basement, she felt little comfort in the correctness of her decision. Instead she felt consumed by the worries. When the knock came at the front door, at first she didn't notice. But then the rap came louder.

Her first thought when she opened the door and saw Sheriff Halstead was that she had been too late with her warning to Ray.

On the coffee table he unwrapped the newspaper, revealing the deer-hide mask. Perhaps it was because she was already emotionally spent, or maybe because she had such good control, but for whatever reason, she showed little reaction to seeing her husband Wes's ceremonial mask. He had been a member of the deer clan, and one day he had hoped Ray would wear the mask, if that was what the dreams decreed for him. But Wes died before Ray came of age, and Ray never had his vision quest. Though he had finally donned the mask, Wes would have been disappointed by the manner in which Ray had assumed it. But for Wes there had been many disappointments.

All of these things were flashing through Miriam's mind as the sheriff asked her a question. "Miriam?" he had to say again, breaking her fixation on the mask. "I said, do you recognize it?"

Though she could conceal emotion, it was more difficult for her to manufacture false expression. She stammered as she shook her head, saying, "N-no."

"Then do you think you can help me find out whose this is?" Halstead said.

Miriam looked at him, her eyes wide, trying to think. "I-I could try. I'm not sure if it would do any good, though."

Halstead studied her reaction, then took a deep breath before going on. "I understand it might put you in a sensitive position. And I wouldn't be asking you if it wasn't important. I think you know how I feel about you folks. But the men I'm looking for are killers, and until I catch them, they're not going to do any of us any good."

Killers? "I heard that the deaths were accidental," Miriam said quickly.

"That's not how I'm treating it," the sheriff said. "And I think whoever wore this had a hand in the killings."

Miriam was practically breathless as she gave a series of one-word assurances that she would try to help. She was afraid her air would not sustain her through an entire sentence.

The sheriff wrapped up his evidence, and as he began to leave, he said, "I intend to do whatever it takes to find him. And I appreciate anything you can do."

She was unable this time to even mouth a word of assurance, and so she nodded. It wasn't until she shut the door behind him that she became aware of a hollow thumping in her chest. It was all she could hear, so deathly still had the house become.

She knew Ray would have been able to hear everything that had been said. And as she stood bracing her back against the door, listening to the tumult of her heart, she could tell it was even quieter in the basement.

Chapter 10

CURTIS HEATH DRUMMED his fingers nervously next to the phone on the desktop. His attorney, Meachum, had just told him that the two burning deaths could have no impact on the agreement approved by the court. But he wasn't so sure there wouldn't be other, even more detrimental repercussions.

Timing was at the crucial stage. Heath knew only too well how the federal grant procedure worked: how far in advance decisions were made, who he was competing against. Any more delays could cripple his effort to put together a convincing application for funding for next summer.

He was already handicapped by the weather in the upper Great Lakes, at best providing only five to six months when work could be done. And his competitors for the research money had the additional advantage that the governing board was dominated by Western Indian interests. That's where the glamour sites were: cliff dwellings that would last as long as the mountains, a dry climate that would preserve bones and artifacts forever.

The destructive nature of the Great Lakes climate was all the more reason archaeological sites there should take priority, Heath had often argued. There were fewer of them, and they couldn't be set aside for future archaeologists, as some sites out west were. He had made all these arguments before, and though they were always received with sympathy, they rarely worked by themselves. Results were what counted. Demonstrable discoveries. Artifacts.

Heath's frustrations were turning to anger. At the process itself for being unfair. At the sheriff for not accepting the obvious. At Christopher Fielding for staying in a backwoods cabin without even a god damn phone!

Heath grabbed his jacket and stalked out of the room. He hadn't even seen the site yet. And it was time he did.

• • •

"The sheriff has his own agenda," Fielding had said to Jean after coming out of the woods with the bottles Cole had used for target practice. "I'm not sure this will convince him his theory is incorrect."

"But we have to tell him," Jean said.

"We will, but . . ." But there was no rush. They were out there, at the site. And though he didn't say it, to Fielding it seemed time would better be spent seeking explanations right there, rather than trying to extinguish blind leads. Though he had no rational basis for thinking that, at the same time he couldn't stop thinking about the burn that had felt like a bite.

The thought made him uncomfortable, and he felt foolish for dwelling on it. He felt foolish for considering even halfway seriously the crazy ideas that kept arising in his head. But emotions are not governed by reason, and it was his emotion—his fear?—that kept bringing him back to the sensations of the jaw locked around the fleshy part of his hand as he leaned over the fire pit, next to the incinerated corpse of Buck Billings.

And so they stayed for a while after finding the bottles, and Fielding went back to the excavation he had begun at the head of the water-cut drainage ravine. It seemed the thing to do. Besides, he was on a tight schedule and had already lost too much time.

They lasted past lunchtime, working side by side in the dirt, but since they had come out so early, without a chance to make provisions for eating, they were tired and hungry. They drove back into town and dropped the plastic water bottles off at the sheriff's department. Halstead wasn't there, but they left word of their findings. Then they got something to eat and went to Fielding's cabin to rest.

Jean fell asleep on the couch, but Fielding couldn't sleep. He was standing on the porch when Curtis Heath arrived. Fielding met him halfway to the car.

"The State Police say it's all an accident," Heath said, "but the local guy's in a lather. He thinks it's murder, for Christ's sake, and that makes him a bigger threat than the Indians."

"In what way?" Fielding asked.

"For all we know he's out there right now, roping off the area as a crime scene."

"He's not doing that."

"Not yet," Heath said. "Because he hasn't thought of it. But he might, or Lord forbid, if some other crazy thing happens, he'll have us out of business. He already blames us for stirring things up around here."

That was true, Fielding acknowledged to himself. "So what do you want to do?"

"I want to go out there. See for myself what's going on, where we're at. I've got to start making calls when I get back, and I want to have something to report."

Archaeological excavation was a slow process, but necessarily so. It wasn't something that should be rushed. Fielding had a sense of what Heath would want to do, but on the other hand, he couldn't keep him away. Besides, they had planned on going back there today anyway.

Fielding told him they'd take just a few minutes to get ready. He had to wake up Jean.

"She's in there?" Heath said, surprised.

"Yes," Fielding said. "She's resting. The sheriff had us up early."

Heath didn't say anything as Fielding disappeared inside, but his mind worked feverishly. Jean Shawshequay was the enemy, and Fielding at best was marginally trustworthy. Fielding no doubt figured she was there to help him. Heath's concern was that the situation in reality was the other way around.

The field of desecration was the appropriate place. It was like an open wound that continued to bleed. It was here that the voices would be strongest. But to hear them, the listener had to be strong.

As with his journey back to the open-time that had begun with the field trip to the museum, Makwamacatawa knew that another journey without signposts lay before him. At present his head was filled with the interference of events and moods and personalities, but he knew that that would pass, as long as he could focus the power of his mind. As long as he could sink into an altered consciousness, a state of being more akin to the ephemeral nature of the Ancient Ones than to all that passed for normal existence. To attain that state, to be deemed receptive to the communications from those who had walked before him, he had to purge his body of impurities. He had to become a pure vessel, sustained only by the cleansing solution of water drawn from a free-running stream.

Like the vision quest when he dreamed of the black bear and acquired its name for his own, it would not be easy. There would be pain, but physical pain he could endure. If there was anything he feared, it was the mental agony, the doubts, the uncertainties he knew he would be forced to overcome before he could learn about the fires. Before he could learn what they meant.

As they sat three abreast in Fielding's truck on the drive out to the site, Heath belittled the sheriff's theory that protestors of the excavation were responsible, but the more he talked, the more apparent it became that he was concerned. After all, they were on their way out there, where it had happened. What if it hadn't been an accident? What if the protestors were back? What if . . . ?

The questions were never posed, but instead went unstated just beneath Curtis Heath's nervous chatter.

"What keeps coming back to me," Jean said, "is not who or what caused it, but how the fire could have done what it did. When I walked up, I thought he was a pile of logs. I mean, he was burned so . . . so thoroughly."

"Have you ever seen a person burned to death before?" Heath asked.

"No, but I know what fire does. Especially with something as thick as a human body. It burns from the outside in. This, it seemed almost as if . . ." She broke off as if stymied by the illogic of what she had been about to say.

"As if what?"

"As if the fire penetrated him, and burned from the inside out."

As if the fire penetrated him, Fielding repeated silently.

As the truck rocked over the trail road, as the plume of dust behind them billowed into the narrow cut between the trees, Fielding's mind began to wander, back to his studies of the old beliefs, their logical extension. "Are either of you aware," he said after several quiet moments had slipped by, "of any sort of Ojibwa fire being? Some kind of spirit that arguably could have done something like this?"

Both Heath and Shawshequay looked at him oddly.

Fielding glanced over, then managed a weak smile. "I mean, is it possible according to Algonquin mythology? Are there any beliefs that taken literally might explain what has happened?"

"You mean someone could be duplicating the myth?" Heath said. "I hope that's what you mean."

"Fire was a sacred element," Jean said. "As it was in most aboriginal societies. It's both a destroyer and provider. It purifies the old and decayed, and gives life through its heat and light."

"I know," Fielding said. "But is there anything else, specifically, that relates to fire as a spiritual entity, an avenging angel so to speak?"

"It's used in ceremonial functions, of course. Its smoke carries prayers up to the heavens. It's a symbol of the links between the Algonquin peoples. It's something brought to earth by the Thunderbirds. There's the festival of the new fire, not too different from the pagan rites in northern Europe." Jean was simply running down a list of every connection to fire she could think of. Fielding knew of these things, and nothing seemed to fit what was happening now. She concluded, "But there's nothing like what you describe. That I'm aware of anyway."

Heath said, "A local aberration, perhaps?"

Perhaps, Fielding thought. And perhaps Miriam Goodmedicine would know if there was one. What it would mean, Fielding wasn't sure. Just as he wasn't sure about so many things that had happened. Just as he wasn't sure why he was looking to the supernatural to explain the burning deaths.

When they reached the site, something was different.

"What the hell's that?" Heath said.

Fielding looked toward the flatbed trailer. "It's here to pick up the deputy's car," Fielding said. "The sheriff told us it was coming."

"Not that. Up there."

Fielding stopped the Jeep and looked where Heath pointed. At the top of the knoll squatted a figure cowled with the head and pelt of a black bear. For a second, Fielding was touched with the same vibrant state of anxiety he had felt when he first saw that bear figure, rising out of the brush in ambush. Then as he climbed out of the truck, as he stared up at the cowled figure, he was touched with curiosity. Why did he do it? What were his beliefs? And who was he?

Fielding started to walk toward the knoll, but Jean stopped him, grabbing his forearm. "Don't," she said.

He looked at her and hesitated, debating what to do. Then Deputy Kinsey reached them. "I already called in about that guy up there," Kinsey said. "It's a good thing you're here. You can identify him to the sheriff."

Halstead arrived just a few minutes later, and this time there was nothing Jean could do to stop them from ascending the knoll. Makwamacatawa didn't budge as they approached. He was sitting on the ground with his legs folded, the bear's head fixed over his own and the skin draped over his shoulders down his back and spread out on the ground. His hands wore the front paws, and the bear's claws rested on his knees. When the sheriff greeted him, he did not respond. It was as though, garbed in the representation of a makwa manitou, Blackbear were denying his humanity. He was denying any possible link of communication. But just under the upper jaw of the bear, which extended over his forehead, within the daggered shadows caused by the teeth, Fielding could see the man's eyes. They were locked on his own.

Fielding thought of the black fur ascending out of the brush; he thought of the animal he had imagined it to be before Makwamacatawa rose to his feet, revealing himself; and he pictured that animal as it had been in life. The fur would have been blacker, shiny almost, the eyes penetrating and intelligent, the muzzle sheathing incisors glistening with moisture, and overall, the animal would have possessed a languid almost lazy movement that at the crack of a twig could be tensed into a muscular display of agility and grace.

"Well?" Halstead prompted impatiently. He was waiting for Fielding to identify the man under the cloak. He'd arrest Blackbear on the assault, and sooner or later, he was convinced, he'd have him for murder.

The animal that it had once been no longer existed. But within the strange melding of man and beast, there remained a bit of its former wildness, a suggestion of its once unchallenged dominion over this land.

Blackbear hadn't killed anybody. He hadn't leapt out of Billings's fire pit and bitten Fielding's hand. Why the latter was proof of the former, Fielding would have been hard-pressed to explain. He would have been hard-pressed to admit even to himself that there was a connection. "No, Sheriff," Fielding said. "This isn't one of the men who attacked me. I don't recognize him at all."

Halstead stiffened. He turned slowly toward Makwamacatawa as if to deliver a silent message. Perhaps because of the heat under the heavy cowl, a single bead of sweat started near Blackbear's temple and meandered across his cheek. Halstead didn't look back to Fielding until the drop of moisture stopped at the curve of Blackbear's jaw.

Every concern he had had about Fielding had been proven right, in an instant. He was on their side. She had turned him. He was the enemy. "You may think you can deal with them, Fielding. But I guarantee you'll be disappointed. And when they turn on you again, I hope it's not too late. For the rest of us."

As Halstead turned and began to walk away, Fielding glanced at Makwamacatawa. In the shadows the eyes were set straight, the expression unchanging, as if he were neither witness to nor stakeholder in what had just transpired. Fielding followed Halstead back down the rocky knoll.

Jean Shawshequay had stayed below, near the vehicles, and though she had been out of earshot, she could read what had happened. She could read it in Halstead's stump-legged retreat, and when he got close enough, she could read it in Chris's face.

The sheriff halted abruptly when he reached her. He gave her a long look, then turned on Fielding. "No matter what you do, you're not of their kind. You're an outsider. You'll never be accepted by them." Another glance at Jean, then back at Fielding. "By any of them."

As Fielding watched Halstead climb into his car, he couldn't help but glance toward Jean. She returned his look, and when their eyes caught briefly, they immediately looked away, as if embarrassed by what the sheriff had said, embarrassed that they might have been thinking what he'd implied.

Whether the discomfort forced her away, or she was drawn by the lure of ancient whispers, after the sheriff's car pulled out, Jean wandered off by herself toward the lip of the sinkhole. That's what seemed to draw her interest at this site anyway, the living legacy of a past world where her people had once walked, not dead mementoes that might or might not have lain buried here.

"Are you crazy?" Heath said to Fielding when they were alone.

"Having him in jail wouldn't do us any good."

"It would keep him out of our hair."

Fielding looked up toward Makwamacatawa atop the knoll. "He's not going to bother us."

"Yeah? Look what the Mohawks did in Quebec. Look what they may have done here, to that deputy and the old bum."

Fielding didn't respond. It wasn't an argument he cared to continue. For him, the matter was settled. "You want to look around here or what?"

Heath spit into the dirt. "Yeah. I want to look around here. Where's the mag?"

The magnetometer. Fielding flinched. "What do you want that for?"

"I can see your markers. I want to see what's below them."

"You read my notes, didn't you? I sent you copies."

"Yeah. Strange, no apparent copper signatures. Here, of all places."

Here was in the range of a copper-producing culture that dated back five thousand years. Where twentieth-century mines had been sunk a mile deep, native copper the size of boulders had once protruded through the surface, making it possible for aboriginal peoples to cross into the age of metal centuries before other civilizations made the jump. Not only were copper tools like awls and gouges, spear points and adzes, as well as decorative breastplates and beads, common in Great Lakes archaeological sites, but due to the extensive trade well established thousands of years before European contact, Lake Superior copper could be found as far south as the Gulf of Mexico, and as far west as the Rocky Mountains. So for no copper artifacts to be here, of all places, would be highly unexpected.

Either Fielding had missed the indications, or he was holding something back. Heath hadn't cared earlier if Fielding chose to play it close to the vest to avoid a leak about the possibility and location of valuable artifacts. That was how Heath would have handled things, if he had been in Fielding's position. But the time for masking findings was past. Events dictated otherwise.

By the time the electrodes were set in the ground, Kinsey, the flatbed trailer, and the burnt hulk of Deputy Cole's car were gone. Heath set the mag near where Fielding had begun digging, and when the needle jumped, he was not surprised. "You chose here because of the drainage cut," he said in a factual tone of voice. "It was the 'natural' place to begin."

Fielding edged over to the machine's display. It confirmed what he had earlier established: the presence of metallic objects, and a profile putting them about a meter deep. "There was a reason for not putting that in writing."

"Maybe. But not for not telling me."

"I had to make a decision about what was best for the project, in the long run. If word got out, from whatever source, someone would've been here in the middle of the night with a backhoe."

Heath inhaled deeply through his nostrils as he looked at the mag results. He didn't much care about Fielding's explanations. He already had him pegged as untrustworthy. The problem was how to deal with him now. He slowly rose to his feet and looked the archaeologist in the eye. "We're going to have to take it out."

Fielding broke into a humorless grin. "You wonder why I didn't tell you?"

"I don't care what you decided not to tell me because it didn't matter. But now it does."

"Nothing's changed, as far as I can see."

"You know damn well things have changed. The delays have put us back as far as setting up next year. And just because we won in court doesn't mean the people in Washington won't be sensitive to the local Indian opposition, if we give them enough time to build up a head of steam."

"We've got an agreement with them."

"How about that guy up there," Heath said, indicating the knoll. "Do you have an agreement with him? And what happens when Washington starts hearing about the deaths associated with this site?"

Fielding tried to be conciliatory. "I recognize the importance of getting to the copper artifacts. That's one of the reasons I began here. And soon enough, I'll get to them."

"We don't have the time to do this by the book. If we don't move on it now, the money you hope will finance a full expedition next summer will be paying some cultural anthropologist in New Mexico studying petrified shit."

"Better to lose the financing for a year than hack up the site."

"Hack up the site? Who do you think I am? Indiana Jones? What I'm talking about is a limited, careful dig, not much larger in scope than your core samples. You know it's possible."

He was right, Fielding thought. It was possible. Given the profile from the magnetometer, they pretty much knew exactly where to go and how deep.

"You've been in this long enough to know compromises have to be made. Remember the bank that was going in along the Tittabawassee in Saginaw? They gave us thirty days, and look what we accomplished."

He was right again. Frequently, compromises had to be

made. Matter of fact, more often than not, archaeological digs were an exercise in negotiation and compromise. Over time. Technique. Goals. The world did not stand still for the saviors of time to carefully brush away past histories.

"Nothing is ideal," Heath urged. "We just have to do the best under the circumstances."

So they began to dig, carefully setting aside each layer of dirt in separate boxes for later sifting.

Outside of the scorched earth where Cole had died, there was no reminder of the fires. Fielding's hand no longer was bothering him, and with his attention on the buried copper artifacts, the search for understanding what had happened here was the furthest thing from his mind.

As Jean walked away from the area of Fielding's grid, the voices of the men soon faded, until she could no longer hear them at all. She was following the perimeter of the Cave of Bones, stepping over rocky protrusions, brushing low-hanging vegetation from in front of her face. She had never completed her survey of the entire location, and that's what she told herself she was doing now. Mapping the geography in her mind. Evaluating how the physical features would have related to the habitation site. Looking for other evidence of early man's residence and use of this land. But the farther she walked into the woods, the less technical her survey became.

This wasn't like any other site. There were things happening here that told her that. They were not the kinds of things she as a woman of science and scholarship could easily express, but within the confines of her mind, such barriers were easier to breach, especially as she stepped deeper into a primeval world where science was a distant echo, and scholarship a foreign concept.

She and others of her discipline lived much closer to the world of superstition than most. So wasn't it perfectly understandable, she asked herself, for persons like her to consider the supernatural in searching for explanations to unexplained events? Beyond that, was there something internal that drew her to such a field? Like the psychiatrist on the edge of sanity whose interest is generated by a desire to understand himself, were anthropologists subconsciously looking to assign credibility to the pre-science world, where spirits had taken an active role in daily life?

Moving steadily, Jean came to a notch in the ground that deepened and spread wider until it reached the brink of the sink-hole. It was similar to the water-cut drainage ravine where Fielding had begun to dig, except that it was overgrown. If she had been thinking like an archaeologist, she would have noticed the similarities. But she was not thinking that way. She was caught within the spell of ancient magic.

Ancient mud yielded to the gentle probing of the trowel. The first artifact uncovered was a rolled copper bead, tarnished by the soil but nonetheless readily identifiable. It wasn't what had caused the mag needle to jump earlier, but it hinted at what might lie below it.

Before extracting it from the dirt, Fielding took his measurements and photos, then labeled it and slipped it into a plastic bag. Heath continued working, slowly scraping at the soil, carefully breaking up clumps cemented by moisture or pressure, adding the loose till to the boxes set aside for later examination.

What under Fielding's normal progress might have taken days, they accomplished in forty-five minutes. They reached the source of the anomaly in the magnetic field that had registered on the magnetometer. At first they thought the metal object was a rock because it was rounded and larger than they would have expected. But as the trowel edged to the side of it, as the dirt was brushed clear, the distinction between metal and stone became apparent.

The object was very dark, much more so than the rolled copper bead, and it had a formless, shapeless quality. It seemed to have folds, or rolls, to it, like a mass of wax that had hardened as it overflowed from a vessel.

Words spoken between the two men were scarce, because each was perplexed. And so they worked in concert and almost in silence, troweling away the dirt, brushing the newly exposed surface clean.

With each stroke, with each bit of the object to come to light, the men became more subject to a simmering tension, an intensity of nerves, of mental activity. It wasn't what they had expected. They weren't quite sure yet what it was. Only what it wasn't.

The people who had lived in the area over the last few millennia had used copper because it existed in its native form at the surface. The bridge from the technology of extracting and shaping an existing malleable metal, to the techniques necessary for mining and smelting ore, was a span that in most civilizations lasted centuries. If indeed that gap was ever bridged. Yet here was evidence that the link had been forged.

A series of mysteries silently expressed both enlivened and numbed each of the men. As the object was lifted from the dirt, the first of the mysteries was resolved. The rounded, once molten object was iron.

It wasn't dark yet, but shadows had begun to meld together, bringing a dimness to the woods. Objects lost their sharp distinction, softening at the edges, hinting at the mysteries night brings. Ferns were the fabric of the forest, and in the failing light they became like old lace, obscuring the ground. Leafless twigs became all but invisible.

As Jean reached her foot carefully over a log, there was the sudden feel of a pointed object stabbing her cheek. She snapped her head back and tried to twist away, but it seemed to follow her, scratching along her face. Then it was in her hair.

She hadn't seen anything. Yet the thought instantly came to her mind that neither had Fielding when he pawed through the dead camp fire. She stumbled backward, slapping at the thing in her hair. All she could think of was getting rid of it. Getting it off her. Any other danger was eclipsed by the sudden flash of fear, by the memory of Fielding rolling away from the dead fire, gripping his hand. She wasn't thinking about the sinkhole. But it was that precipice she neared. Twisting again, she half stepped, half fell closer to the edge.

"Damn it," she cried. Then, reaching her hand into her hair, she combed forcefully through it. There was a snap and she could feel the sharp object. It broke in pieces as she yanked parts of it free.

As she held the pieces in front of her face, the breath steadied in her lungs. Pieces of wood. A stick. A gnarled twig. That's all.

She dropped the pieces of broken twig and felt her cheek. There was no blood. The skin was not broken. As she stood there feeling her face, her thoughts returned to what had sprung into her head a moment ago at the feel of the sharp but invisible object. She was too jumpy. Too ready to accept the irrational. She had let herself fall prey to ancient whispers.

Angry at herself, thinking about Fielding rolling away from the camp fire, she was slow to recognize where she was standing. There was nothing to see but open space, and so it took a few moments for her to realize that she was on the brink of the rock drop-off.

"Jesus," she gasped on a blow of air. A moment of vertigo dizzied her, and she staggered back. And for a few seconds she was struck with a renewed sense of panic as she realized that the real danger had not been illusory.

Jean reached behind herself for support, found a tree trunk, then let herself slide to the ground. She settled on a log, and though the dizziness and panic dissipated quickly, she was left with a vibrating nervousness.

It might have been just a leafless twig in the dark, but was there some equally rational explanation for what had happened to Fielding? There had to be, she told herself. There usually was for such things. Spirits don't exist. Creatures invisible to the eye do not take substance from the air and come alive in the ashes of a dead fire. Yet human bodies are not spontaneously combustible. They are not penetrated and then consumed whole by fire. There are no longer any unknown properties of fire. It consumes fuel, grows stronger, then dies. There are no secrets about it. At least in the present day.

Jean thought of the countless prayers that had been said over fire, the sacrifice of tobacco, the words canted into the smoke, taking substance from the rising cloud, ascending to the soul villages where their message was heard. She thought of the ancients stripping flesh from the dead with great respect and love, then burning it, sending the remains skyward so the departed could begin their spiritual life.

She thought of these things, how fire was perceived as an element of magic and mystery, and as she sat quietly, she began to hear the sound of wind. Or what she thought was wind. Slowly at first, then building to a torrent of air. She eased forward, leery of the edge, parting a branch with her hand.

A black cloud was rising above the canopy. At first sight it struck her as the mark of another fire; another death, another incinerated corpse. But there was no odor of smoke, no sign of any flames. And the cloud itself . . . it did not behave like rising smoke. It was not a column of darkness that reacted to currents of air, spreading over the tops of the trees, but rather a solid band of black that seemed composed of individual parts that moved collectively. It seemed to have life of its own, and as the impression settled, Jean edged closer to the brink of the sinkhole. It was as if her thoughts had given life to this stygian pillar, as if indeed it were a column of souls rising into the sky, as if the ancients were playing out their spiritual trek before her very eyes.

The dark column was the source of the wind, a kind of frantic, leathery sound, the hurried, rushing echo of something beginning to happen. It carried the cadence of motion, the element of speed. The sound of flight.

Jean let the branch slip from her fingers, then slowly, carefully, rose to her feet. The column was not the rising cloud of another immolation; nor was it the frenzied flight of departed souls to heaven. She knew exactly what it was, and as this reality hardened, more importantly she knew what it meant about this place called the Cave of Bones.

Iron. At a supposed Late Woodland site, prior to the coming of the Europeans.

After the surprise came disappointment.

"These grounds are filled with iron ore," Fielding said. "Do you think it's possible . . ." He trailed off, realizing the folly of what he was suggesting.

"That aboriginal peoples leapt into the iron age overnight, and nobody knew about it?"

No, it wasn't possible, Fielding realized. And with the realization, the disappointment deepened. After all, the hoped-for value of this excavation was a pre-contact site. Every indication had been that it was, until now.

But on the other hand, concluding that the iron was the result of one of the early European incursions did not seem to offer a ready explanation either. The iron was no mere artifact, a manufactured relic from an early explorer. It was evidence of iron-ore smelting itself, at this very site. There were no known European settlements here, and would Jesuit missionaries or itinerant fur trappers have had the need or the ability to set up a smelting operation?

As the digging continued, as more of the iron fragments were uncovered, the initial flush of excitement was regenerated. Fielding looked over at Heath. "Who the hell could have done this?"

Heath continued to study a large piece of the metal, taking his time before he answered. "I think the key to that is, when was it done?"

Fielding let the implications settle. "You saying it could pre-date the explorers?"

"There's nothing in our historical records about it. And all your nondiagnostic tests indicate the age of this settlement is early sixteenth century, at the latest."

"But the indigenous people couldn't be responsible for this. We already settled that."

Heath nodded, then looked up slowly from the globular iron piece in his hands. "Maybe someone was here before we thought."

Fielding rose to his feet and turned away from Heath, slowly, thoughtfully, drawing his hand down his cheek. Contact prior to Cartier, Champlain, Marquette? And not a mere passing exposure, but an actual settlement. It would be a discovery with nearly as shattering an impact as revealing that the Ojibwas had entered the iron age on their own. Just the kind of discovery, Fielding realized, Heath would do anything to engineer.

Is that what was happening already? Was Heath lining things up to lead to a conclusion he hoped to reach, rather than letting the facts determine the path? They had already accelerated the process of excavation past what Fielding would have preferred. Had they made a mistake? Could they have merely stumbled into a garbage dump sunk into the earlier stratigraphy?

"Are you familiar with the bog-iron method of smelting?" Heath asked.

"I'm aware of it, but that's about all."

"Fairly primitive, before blast furnaces were used to fire the ore. The heat was provided by peat, which was not the best source, and so consequently was not too efficient. You'd end up with lots of low-grade waste that looked exactly like this."

Fielding picked up a flattened sliver of the metal, smooth on top and showing the mark of soil granules underneath, where it apparently had cooled on the earth. "Primitive, but simple. Perhaps that explains why someone on the frontier would use it."

Heath shook his head. "It's more than primitive, technology-wise. It's practically medieval." Heath set the iron hunk back onto the ground. "Let's assume a metalsmith was here, say in the 1600s. He'd be familiar with the forging methods of his day, not some historical methods out of a different time, fit for a different place."

"But if he didn't have what he needed, he'd use a simpler method."

"Possibly," Heath said. "But it'd be like expecting a good car mechanic to be an expert on the care of horses. It doesn't always follow that a tradesman knows all the historical antecedents to his craft."

"So you're saying because this iron looks like it was made by a medieval technique, that means that Europeans were here before the historical record?"

"What I'm saying is, it's reasonable to assume that whoever smelted iron here using the bog-iron technique had not been exposed to later advances."

Fielding considered that, turning the flat piece of iron over in his hand, studying it from every angle. "You've seen this kind of material before?"

Heath nodded. "It was common eight hundred years ago and before. All over northern Europe. The Norse. The Celts. The Gauls. They were all related, you know, more or less. We don't think of them as a single civilization, because there was no unifying political force. Like the Roman Empire. But it was a single culture. Unified by their ideas of independence. Material culture. And religion."

Fielding sensed a growing discomfort. The discussion was outpacing the facts. An early Norse settlement? They were in Newfoundland around the year 1000. And for nearly a century people have been claiming that the Kensington Stone proved they were in Minnesota in 1363. Was this what Heath was suggesting?

Fielding scraped his thumbnail along the surface of the iron, shaving off a fire-blackened residue. He placed the sliver of metal in one of the boxes, then turned toward Curtis Heath. "So what is it you think this all represents?"

For just a second there was the flash of something undefined in Heath's face. It was a wild look, a brief glimpse into his private thoughts, and it was that one, unguarded moment that most heightened Fielding's feeling of caution.

But Heath recovered fast. "We're scientists," he said, grinning humorlessly. "Fortunately we don't have to guess at such things. We can carbon date the charcoal residue."

The way it should be done, Fielding thought. But he couldn't rid himself of the thought that Heath was already formulating the results. And what he would do with them.

From the area of the sinkhole, there was the sound of movement through the woods. Jean Shawshequay emerged.

"If this is not an Indian site," Heath said, making an effort to keep his voice between him and Fielding, "you know what that means."

Fielding only looked over at him, waiting for Heath to continue.

"It renders any agreement with them inapplicable."

The headlights jerked with the spastic motion of a swordsman flailing in the dark. As the car dipped and rolled, the light jabbed and feinted with the trees and brush of the forest.

Maggie Verhoven bent her head down so she could look toward the sky, as if that were her last hold on things familiar. She hadn't really meant her threat earlier about staying in a motel if they didn't get to Watersdrop before dark. She wasn't afraid of the woods. She just didn't like the . . . lack of order.

The front end of the car suddenly dipped lower as her husband hit the brakes. Maggie was thrust against the harness, then fell back. "John!" she cried out, more in surprise than reproach.

An uprooted jack pine lay across the dirt-trail road, its roots having raised a black pod of the matted forest floor. "It's just a blow-down, Mags," he said. "No problem."

Maggie took a deep breath, controlling her rising fear, seeking to stave off her anger.

"It's okay, Mom," Lindsey said. "We're almost there."

"Oh, great," Jimmy said. "Almost to nowhere." For him, a week in the woods meant a week without skateboards, without Nintendo, without soccer in the field behind the house. His sister Sharon, at ten one year older than him and two younger than Lindsey, was asleep in the middle. But she would have appreciated his sarcasm.

With the door open and his feet outside on the ground, John turned and looked into the backseat. He knew it wasn't worth losing his patience now, but ten hours in the car had lowered his threshold for guff. "You're right, in a way, Jim. This is nowhere. If you define wilderness by a lack of civilization, then we are almost there. But don't for a minute make the mistake of thinking that being in the wilderness limits the things that you can do with yourself."

Jimmy sighed, turning away from his father. He's heard this kind of stuff before.

John slowly pushed himself outside, rising to his feet. He moved the pine from the road, then looked in the backseat again before getting behind the wheel. "Tomorrow things will start to happen. There's the river, hiking in the woods—"

"They only get two channels on the TV up here," Jimmy said, lashing out, "and they don't even work good."

John paused a few seconds, letting his son's tantrum subside, before saying, "Well, you won't have to worry about that this year. I didn't bring the TV."

Jimmy's entire face swelled. "What?"

"Didn't I tell you?" He glanced at his oldest daughter, and she grinned back. "Lindsey and I decided."

Sharon had come awake. "What are we going to do all week?"

"We can go fossil hunting. At the sinkhole. You like that." He turned toward his wife. Her jaw was set like a vise, her eyes searing into his. He said, "You're always saying to turn that thing off. We figured we had your vote."

"Let's go," she said evenly, carefully gauging the tone of her voice.

As John shifted into gear, Jimmy threw his head back against the seat. It was going to be the worst trip ever.

The cabin was musty, but it cleared out fast with the windows open. After the car was unloaded, it didn't take any convincing to get Jimmy to go to his room. He was more interested in sulking than anything else. Sharon was asleep first, but Lindsey could barely draw herself away from the riverbank. She only went to bed when her father insisted.

With Maggie still putting things away in the kitchen, John started on the fire: a few crumpled newspaper pages, some kindling, a couple of logs from the stack out back. Long-stemmed matches were stored in a cardboard tube by the hearth, and John selected one of them. But as family tradition dictated, he was waiting for Maggie before he lit the fire.

The cabin was cedar logs with the kitchen, eating area, living room and fireplace all open to one another. The ceiling vaulted two stories, and a staircase and open balcony at the back led to three bedrooms. When Maggie noticed John by the fireplace, waiting for her, she paused, looking at the things in the kitchen that remained to be done. She was tempted to forget it all till the morning.

"Ready?" John said.

She took a deep sigh, then shook her head. It was too late.

She was too tired. They'd have all week. "I think I'm just going to go to bed, John. I'm beat. And you should be too."

He nodded, but didn't get up from the stone ledge of the hearth. He sat there, tapping the wooden match between his fingers.

Maggie came over to him and hugged his head to her stomach briefly, then looked down. "You coming with me?"

"Yeah. In a bit."

"We'll have a big fire. Tomorrow."

He nodded again, and she left him for the bedroom. As she prepared for bed, John remained seated on the stone ledge, fingering the match, staring at the pile of kindling as if the fire were alive and the flames were curling up and around the pieces of wood. It was almost as if he could see the yellow and red, as if he could hear the cracking sounds of the tinder being consumed. Almost as if he could feel the heat.

The fire came alive in his face. The flames seemed to roll with the curve of his cheeks, dipping into the cavities of his ocular sockets, turning his jet-black eyes to red. The fur reacted to the fire in its own way, seemingly shifting position with each upward flicker, its filaments of shadow dancing with the light. And the scimitars of ivory once again seemed alive, the flames making them appear glistening with internal moisture.

Neither the man nor the beast showed any changes as the fire played out its dance of death in front of them. The movement was reflected in the sweat of his face, and squatting close to the small fire, Makwamacatawa could feel the heat on his skin. His back was exposed only to the night, but the cowl of the black bear kept him warm.

He was hungry, and he knew that the pain would get worse before it would go away. But go away it would, and then his biggest enemy would be fatigue. For if he succumbed to its gentle urges, he could not dream the living dream scripted for his benefit alone. He would not see what he was meant to see. He would not hear the Ancient Ones.

As he sat by the small fire of kindling and forest debris, atop the knoll overlooking the place of desecration, on the first leg of his vision quest, Makwamacatawa suddenly came alert. His eyes seemed to grow redder as the whites expanded, accepting more of the reflected light of the fire. His chin lifted so he could better see under the jaw of the bear, and slowly, he leaned closer.

It had been a gradual thing, the coming together of the edges of the flames, the shadows created by the gaps, and at first he hadn't noticed anything different. He had been sitting there so long, staring at the fire so intently, that he had been blind to the subtle changes. He had been blind to the coming together of shape and shadow. It had taken a while, almost as if it were a struggle to call forth its own distinction, as if the act of bringing itself to life was an exercise as tortured as the flames themselves, as if with each flickering attempt at defining itself it required more fuel, stealing the life of its tinder, metamorphosing that life into its own.

Though he was tired and hungry, Makwamacatawa had felt very much in possession of his physical nature. He hadn't expected anything like this so fast. Were the spirits here so strong? Or was his mind too eager?

Makwamacatawa eyed the flames with a keen sense of expectation, and uncertainty. He saw the subtle changes, the flits and flickers, the advances and retreats. And yet he also saw the fire for what it was, an abstract design in constant motion showing infinite variations, each variation—given a receptive imagination—a recognizable shape.

Makwamacatawa's shoulders slumped forward as he leaned even closer, as he watched and studied. As he began to pray. He began to pray because he knew what he saw was no random shuffle of the flames. It was a repeated pattern, a very deliberate attempt at organizing the flames and shadows into a cohesive design.

Makwamacatawa shivered. Something was trying to take shape in front of him. He sat stock-still, waiting for the thing of the fire to come alive.

Chapter 11

THE WORDS WERE spoken in a rush, almost as soon as Heath had gotten out of the truck. Fielding knew something was coming. He had seen it in her eyes when she came toward them from the woods. He had sensed it in her lack of interest in the evidence of iron-making they had discovered.

When she finally felt free to speak, the words came in a sibilant torrent not unlike the leathery rush of wind she had heard while standing by herself on the brink of the sinkhole. "There's a cave!"

Fielding pushed himself back in his seat, his arms straight out against the steering wheel. He looked over at her. A cave? "Did you go inside?"

"No, not inside," Jean said. "I just saw it."

"Where?"

"It's at the bottom of the sinkhole."

Fielding was even more surprised than before. "You climbed down there tonight?"

"No, but I walked all around the perimeter of the sinkhole, and that's when I saw the cave."

"From the surface?" Fielding couldn't hide his disbelief. "How could you see a cave from up there?"

Jean had already made the obvious connections in her own mind, and on the ride back to town had even gone beyond that to speculation. She was excited, but she had to pull herself back and start from the beginning. From when she had let herself slide to the ground after a touch of vertigo, as she realized she was staring straight down the drop-off.

"How did that happen?" Fielding interrupted her.

She had been stabbed in the cheek by a twig, and for just a second she had thought it was like what had happened to him at Billings's camp fire. She thought . . . "Jesus, what difference does it make why I was sitting there? I was, okay? And if I wasn't, sitting there quietly I mean, I might not have noticed it."

"The cave?"

"No, the wind." She told him about the wind, building like a gathering storm, then the rising black column, which she thought was smoke. Another immolation. But it wasn't smoke. And it wasn't the wind. What she had heard was the leathery brush of wings. The sound of flight. "Bats! Thousands of them. Tens of thousands, probably. All rising at dusk from a cave at the bottom of the sinkhole."

Fielding shifted behind the wheel. He had been down there, pacing off every square inch of the sinkhole and had not noticed a cave entrance. Wouldn't he have seen it? Wouldn't someone know about it?

"You listening to me?" Jean said, exasperated. "I saw the bats, rising from a cave."

She had nearly fallen over the edge. She panicked. Was she even sure of what she saw?

"You realize what a cave down there might mean?"

"You saw bats," Fielding said. "Not a cave."

"Where the hell you think they were coming from?"

"The sinkhole itself would be good shelter. Dark. Protected. They could perch in the trees. Under rock ledges. Maybe some under the mats of earth. Who knows?"

"It was a single column," she said, an angry rasp to her voice. "So thick I thought it was smoke. It was no scattering of bats taking flight at their leisure. They were all aroused at the same time, the commotion building on itself. And that indicates a colony. And the only place that could shelter a colony like that is a cave."

Fielding wasn't ready to accept her explanation, perhaps not even what she said she'd seen. He glanced over at her for a second, then back through the windshield, keeping his eyes on the road. "If it is a cave, what do you propose to do?"

She expelled a gust of air. "Do? We go down there. That's what we do."

He had just uncovered evidence of a significant archaeological find, and now he was to leave it to search for a cave at the bottom of a pit? Heath was taking the iron for carbon dating at the lab, but there was so much more to do on-site. They had ripped through the earth to uncover the metal as revealed by the magneto, and now he had to carefully reconstruct the stratigraphy they had penetrated: examine the dirt, the artifacts, set the complete stage.

"Christ, Fielding, what's wrong with you? They would have known about the cave. The people who lived there. And you know they would have used it. For shelter. For storage. For religious events. Who knows what we could find in there?"

"If it exists at all. If we can find it. If we can get inside."

"And it's my job to find out," Jean said. "You had something to do with that, remember?"

The Jeep turned onto the dirt road into Ojibwa Village. Fielding took a deep breath. He was tired. He needed time to think. To rest. He pulled to a halt in front of Miriam Goodmedicine's house. "There's a lot that has to be done. At the site, and yes, in the pit, if there's a cave. But we have to come up with a plan. We've got to list the priorities. Maybe we can sleep on it, and talk about it all in the morning."

Jean climbed silently out of the truck and walked around the front, coming up to the driver's side window. "You're afraid of what I'll find down there. Afraid it'll stop you. If it does, then so be it. All I've got to say is, I'm going to find that cave tomorrow. And I'm going in."

Fielding only acknowledged her intentions, said good night, and drove off. Watching the red taillights retreat, she was angry. But in a way, she was also sorry. She had expected something more from him. Excitement. Encouragement. A desire to investigate.

She had assumed, on the drive back into town, that they'd be up late, talking, making plans. Getting ready for something exciting to happen. But instead, she was standing by herself on the curb.

Jean turned and went inside.

She had discovered something, off in the woods by herself. Curtis Heath was sure of it. It was all she could do to keep it inside.

After they dropped him at his hotel, he had taken the bog-iron globules—carefully packed in sand and wrapped in plastic—into his room. He had told Fielding he was going to head downstate in the morning, but even as he said it, he wasn't so sure. And as he sat at the desk in his room thinking about Jean Shawshequay, he was even less certain he should leave without finding out what she had found.

Fielding had sensed what he had, but had done nothing to get it out of her. It was as if an unspoken conspiracy had been forged. He had kept the mag results from Heath. He'd keep what she told him secret too. And what was it? Another habitation site? An artifact? Something that bore on the discovery of iron?

Whatever it was, the stakes were too high to trust everything to Fielding. The stakes were simply too high not to be there himself.

Ray Goodmedicine drove his mother's '77 Toyota station wagon over the ruts of the road. The suspension was bad enough when it was new; now, it was brutal. All he could do was drive slower. He should drive slower, anyway, as dark as it was. As close as the trees came to the trail.

Though he grew slightly more confident of his feel for the road, the nervousness did not subside. It didn't subside because of Blackbear. What he was doing out there. What Ray might see.

Ray remembered his father describing the vision quest. He remembered how he described the fever that wasn't a fever, the hunger that wasn't hunger. And he remembered the descriptions of the dreams that weren't dreams. They were personal visits from the dead, from the spirits of the natural world, and they were as real as he was at that moment sitting there telling him all this.

His father told him this as if it would be a great moment in his life, but at five or six—whatever he was—it only scared him. And for a reason he could not explain, that's how he felt now, driving out to where Makwamacatawa was on his vision quest. Were the spirits real, as his father said, as Blackbear said they would be? He never did have his own vision quest when he should have. He never tested his beliefs. He never gauged his reaction to his fears. And at this moment, as much as anything else, he was afraid of how he would react to his fears.

The woods suddenly opened up and he saw the twine and the stakes. He was there. Ray glided to a halt then cut the engine and got out.

It wasn't hard to see where Makwamacatawa was, because of the fire. He was at the top of a small rise overlooking the excavation site. Ray stood there silently for a moment, not knowing if he should call out, hoping Blackbear would call to him. But the man was silent. If indeed it was a man, Ray suddenly thought, and as he did a chill rippled across his skin with the feel of winter ice.

Ray shook his head, as if to shake the thoughts clear. Child's fears, he told himself. That's all they were. Child's fears.

He went to the back of the wagon and lifted the tail gate, then pulled out the two five-gallon plastic jugs of water. He didn't know how much he was to bring, so he brought both jugs, filled at the Burning Creek stream, as he was told.

He eased the tailgate shut, then with a jug in each hand, he started up the knoll. He had the feeling he was intruding, that he shouldn't be there at all. Maybe he should just leave the water and get out of there. Blackbear would find it. He would know he had come.

It was a tempting thought, but was this how he faced his fears? Ray felt drawn up the slope, slowly, step by step. Drawn by his promise to Blackbear. The words of his father. The fears of a child. All of these things took hold, propelling him into the ascent, drawing him up the hill, toward Makwamacatawa. Toward the fire.

For a small camp fire the flames seemed large. They seemed to move and flicker as if stoked by an unfelt breeze, as if sucking more energy from the wood than the wood had to give. The flames curled and snapped and leapt into the black with a kind of excited urgency, a jittering, quaking display of Ray's own tension, come to life before him.

Increasingly, Goodmedicine was drawn to the fire. To the motion of the fire, to fast-paced flickers that seemed a counterpoint to the stillness all around. He felt the sweat beginning to form across the nape of his neck, down his sides, in the narrow of his back. Was it from the exertion, moving up the hill, carrying the plastic jugs? Or was it his fears?

Ray paused to rest, setting down the jugs. As he did, his eyes didn't leave the fire. Its glare seemed to black out everything else, and focusing as he did on the bright flashes of yellow, he was aware that something about the fire was different. It wasn't simply that the flames seemed to be rising higher, that the frantic motion seemed to be gaining momentum. It was the shape of the flames, the rapid coming together then parting of the individual tongues. It was as if the same thing was happening over and over, as if the fire was being controlled not by the whims of nature, but by another force. A force that called the flames together, that was seeking to tame them, that was bringing some manner of order to the shimmering curtain. An order that included something recognizable. A head? A face?

Ray felt himself fall back a step, almost involuntarily. His hand came up across his mouth, gripping his cheeks, squeezing hard, as if to stifle a scream. Was this what he had heard about? Was this what his father spoke of twelve years ago? Were these the creatures of past lives come to visit the living?

Ray Goodmedicine could only stand and stare at the yellow and red furor, at the black holes that seemed to suggest a visage sculpted by the sharp lines of fire. And then he heard it. A moan, a deep-throated sound that became a voice. A voice not of the fire, but of the bear, of the man cowled under the bear. He was chanting, praying, trying to communicate with the thing of the flames.

Ray turned and started down the hill. Powered by his fears, pulled by gravity, he moved fast, lunging, stumbling, barreling forward in the dark. His left foot came down on loose stones, and he fell, coming down hard. He rolled to the side, gasping for breath, the impact practically knocking the air from his lungs.

As he lay there he looked back up the slope at the fire, at the representation of bestial form that was seeking to control the fire. If this vision was Blackbear's personal quest, then how was it he could also see? How could he dream the same dream?

Ray let himself roll with the slope, coming to his feet again in one deft move. A few more steps he was on the level, then at the car. He fired the ignition, then popped the clutch into reverse. The car shied, then conked out. The parking brake! He grabbed the black lever between the seats and dropped it down.

In a moment he was moving, backward, then the headlights were slicing wildly to the side as the car spun around. He had shifted again, pulled powerfully on the wheel, both acts as though involuntary movements.

He drove the old station wagon hard, working the brake and the clutch and the stick almost nonstop, slowing only when he had to, stomping on the accelerator every time a narrow passage opened up straight before him. The sight of the fire was still very much in his mind. It was as if he could see the flames still, coming together, pulling apart, gyrating, flickering, flashing, all the while struggling to maintain the same design, a consistent shape, a recognizable form. As he replayed the images, as he delved deeper into what he had witnessed, he kept coming back to the same question: Were these the spirits of the Ancient

Ones? Delivering the message that Blackbear sought? Playing out the ancestral heritage his father described?

Each time he posed the question, on the drive back to the asphalt highway, on the way back into town, as he lay in his bed in the basement, he kept coming back to the same answer. Somehow, it didn't seem right. No matter how scared he had been as a kid when he listened to his father talk about the vision quest, these were not the spirits he described. What he saw—if indeed he saw anything more than a coward's illusion—was not a being about to impose wisdom or guidance. It was a being of non-benevolent design, a creature of carnage, a visage of horror. It was the face of evil.

Lying there in bed, staring at the naked rafters of the basement ceiling, he wondered about the connections between the people who had died, and the thing in the fire. He began to worry about Blackbear, and as he did, he felt the heat of the timid come to the surface of his skin. It was shame he felt, and whether it was the shame. or the questions that refused to quit their haunting, he could not sleep. He could not sleep until the morning sun began to light up motes of dust that hung in the space near the narrow windows at ground line. Only then did his eyes close. Only then was he able to risk entering the world of dreams.

Sheriff Dick Halstead showed the deer-hide mask to every Indian he had had any personal contact with in the past. Not one admitted even to seeing the mask before, much less knowing to whom it belonged. In a way, he should have expected that kind of reaction, but it still made him angry. Surely the Ojibwa community as a whole was not involved in some arcane conspiracy of fire worship or some such nonsense. So why would they protect a killer?

He felt certain that somebody must know. In fact, he felt it probable that they all knew. At the powwows and other functions they conducted, masks like this one would be brought out every time. The sheriff never attended the ceremonies himself, though outsiders were welcome, but he remembered the pictures in the Watersdrop Newsfall. Every time, the Indians made the front page. And that's what gave him the idea.

Halstead went to the newspaper office, a two-story wood-frame building on Main Street that had been the publishing home of the Newsfall for some ninety odd years. An index?

Helmi Tuisko only laughed. So the sheriff began flipping through the pages, issue by issue, looking for pictures of Indian celebrations, festivals, whatever.

The paper was only a weekly, and it averaged twelve pages. So that speeded his search. And after a while, he came to know the yearly schedule of events. The July powwow. The November 1 Feast for the Departed, the Ceremony of New Fire, and then some of the more restrictive pan-tribal clan gatherings.

He came across numerous pictures of the local Ojibwa in various ceremonies, wearing various traditional garb. But he did not see the deer-hide mask. Until he had gone back fifteen years. It was a crowd shot, with a number of figures sitting in a circle watching a dance. One of the people in the dance was wearing the mask. Halstead looked closely. It was the same one, he was sure of it. But the picture's caption revealed no identification; nor did the story accompanying the photo link any names with what had been worn.

Halstead continued, and his thoroughness was rewarded by a few more photos where the mask could be identified. But as with the first photo, the individual behind the mask was not. The sheriff tried to maintain the same thoroughness, but after he had been there almost all day, his attention to detail, as well as his optimism, slipped. The pattern was clear. Where a masked Ojibwa was caught by the lens, he was not identified. Even if he found a dozen more photos, could he expect that pattern to change?

He started flipping faster through the pages, skipping whole issues after a glance at the front page. He started concentrating almost exclusively on the dates of the major festivals. It was because of that that he almost missed it.

The issue was twenty-eight years old, the first of September, and Halstead had already flipped the paper over when a photo caught his eye. It was on the back page, where the obituaries usually were, and what caused him to take a second look was that the photo was not the standard head-and-shoulders shot of a deceased. It was a picture of several men, apparently at a funeral ceremony, and one of them was holding in his hand the deer-hide mask with the deep eye sockets and elongated chin. The man looked so much like his son that he didn't need any identification. But he checked the caption anyway. Below the photograph, the holder of the deer-hide mask was identified as Wes Goodmedicine.

Chapter 12

THE BATS WOULD rise at dusk.

That's what she told Fielding. That's what they were waiting for. But the closer it came to the right time, the more nervous she became. Despite her certainty about what she had seen, the doubts still leaked into her mind. Below the canopy, they'd have to be close to see them.

But they were close, she figured. When they arrived, they had parked near the storm cut, barely noticing that Makwama-catawa was not at the top of the knoll. She had led Fielding to the same spot on the rim where she had seen them the night before. They took their bearings, then descended into the pit, moving into the quadrant where the bats had risen.

The mosquitos made everything worse. The only saving thought was that they would soon be bat food. Jean smiled at herself, and for the first time the progression of anxiety was broken. But the tension returned almost instantly.

It was the noise that did it, like last night it was the sound of wind. At first a slight blow, then quickly, a gathering rush. It was the leathery sound of frantic motion, the sound of flight. It was the sound of the bats.

"This way," Fielding said, and they headed over the hump of an uprooted stump. He was already disappearing into the brush when Jean came down the other side. Her foot slipped, and she had to catch herself with a hand to the slope of the hump. Short hemlock needles stabbed the heel of her palm, but she didn't slow down. Moving into the brush after Fielding, she swiped her hand across the thigh of her jeans.

He was up there, another ten feet, standing still, looking around himself intently, listening to the wind. When she reached him, he said, "Can you tell?"

The noise seemed to be coming from behind them, in front of them, all around. She wheeled first one direction, then the other, staring up into the trees, searching for movement of the leaves, a branch, the trail of smoke. But there was nothing. "You start to circle that way," she said, gesturing. "I'll try this way."

They split up, trying to walk soundlessly over the spongy humus soil, succeeding except for the wheeze of matted roots stretched taut, the occasional snap of a twig. There was a strong, earthy smell of dirt eternally moist, and yet at the same time there was the smell of dry leaves, of a forest in the middle of a drought.

Jean moved carefully, forced to watch her footing as much as scan the overhead canopy. Jagged rocks smothered by moss and black soil provided for uneven footing, and webs of roots concealed hidden cavities between the rocks. Crossing the gaps, she'd test the soil like a mountain climber testing a snow bridge. Then, tentatively, she would cross.

The bats were rising in a tight column until they passed through a hole in the canopy cleared by countless passages. As a waterfall can seem an unmoving feature, the rising colony seemed a solid mass that held its position. Their dark coloration made them harder to pick out against the background, but for all the illusion and camouflage, they were not invisible.

"Chris!"

From a distance away, Fielding wheeled around.

"They're here!" Jean glanced over her shoulder for Fielding, then decided not to wait. She started to inch forward, slipping between the trees, until she came to the point at which the bats were being disgorged from the ground. She eased herself down to one knee and watched as the black column spewed upward.

The exit hole was in a cleft of boulders, mostly covered by a rooted mat. The opening itself was semicircular, about three feet across, and, if it weren't for the bats, probably would have been closed off long ago by the creep of the roots.

When Fielding reached Jean's position, he came down beside her, touching her lightly on the shoulder to let her know he was there. The dusk exodus gradually lessened, until the flow stopped.

Jean looked over at Fielding, excited, expectant. "Let's go."

She moved between the boulders and went down to both knees at the hole, flicking on a flashlight. Sandy soil granules, stuck to dangling tendrils of capillary roots, glinted in the beam. Parting them like a curtain, she peered beyond the threshold. "It looks like it drops away pretty fast. But I can't really tell."

Fielding slipped his small day pack off his shoulders, then

came down next to her and flicked on his own light. At first it looked like a shallow hole that angled in no more than five feet. "Let me get a better look," he said, easing forward. Going down onto his elbows, he pushed his head through the opening, then inched through the uneven curtain of capillary roots. It was a black hole he was sinking into, one that seemed to absorb the meager beam of his light. Overhead, sharp-edged stones were stuck in the thick web of dirt and roots, and wherever he looked was the evidence of spiders.

The sweep of his arm halted. His light had caught the glint of tiny eyes, a few feet from his face. It was a bat, dangling from a woody stem, and as Fielding reached closer with the barrel of the light, the bat fluttered its wings and bared its teeth. He nudged it, and the bat loosened its grip and dropped free. Fielding ducked as it flew past his head toward the exit.

"Ooh!" he heard Jean say from behind him.

"Sorry."

"At least you could have warned me."

"There'll probably be more, I imagine."

Jean hunched her shoulders, then drew her hair back tightly behind her head, tucking it under the collar of her jacket. Then she zipped her jacket up to her neck.

There was a cool, dank feel to the air rising into Fielding's face. It wasn't a draft, more like a stationary zone that he crossed, a line of climate between the atmosphere induced by the weather above, and the subterranean conditions, which varied little. Within the dankness was the hint of an acrid odor that he could feel in the back of his throat.

"What can you see?" Jean said.

"It drops away all right, but I can't quite look down. Hand me the shovel, will you?"

She pulled a small, folded shovel—an army-surplus entrenching tool—from Fielding's pack and locked the blade open. "Is it big enough for us to get through?" she said, passing the shovel forward.

"As far as I can see, yes." Fielding swung the shovel to sweep away cobwebs, then used the side of it to hack away some of the roots. As he did, he was showered with particles of sand and clumps of dirt. Crawling forward, he came to where the hole fell away. Shining his light down, he could see more rock than dirt. But to get there he had to widen the narrow tunnel. He jabbed the shovel at the edges, dislodging soil and stones, then chopped at more of the feelers from the trees above. Taking another look down, he could see that the descent was clear, at least to a floor maybe eight feet down.

Fielding backed away from the edge, then managed to turn around so he could go down feet-first. "It'll be easier if you enter this way," he said to Jean. "And bring the pack."

Fielding started over, reaching his foot blindly below him until it felt an edge, then lowering his weight. Before the next step he felt with his hand for a grip. Where his natural reach extended, he felt a nub of stone. He paused as he let himself sense the texture of the stone, as he considered what it meant. Unlike the jagged edges of the crumbled limestone, it was smooth and rounded.

He eased himself down until he came to the flat section, then called for the pack. Jean passed it down, then followed him into the hole. They were in a narrow chasm, seemingly formed more by the random pattern of large chunks of rock than dissolved out of solid stone. There were narrow crevices in every direction, a network of passages, and the acrid odor was strong and biting, stinging the eyes and the throat.

"Ammonia," Jean said.

Fielding flashed his light along the jagged walls and on the floor. It was marred by the accumulation of bat guano. In the crevices and along the ceiling there was still a scattering of bats that had yet to take flight, but with the light and the disturbance, several flapped their wings in annoyance, and a few of those dropped free and flew by the intruders.

Fielding led as they worked their way into the network of crevices, until they came to another drop. Unlike the first descent, it wasn't a hole they could climb into, but rather a wall they had to descend.

At the bottom, Fielding flashed his beam throughout the chamber. They were in a long passage, rounded and relatively smooth, unlike the passages above. Obviously, it had been created by the seepage of water over the years, part of the overall process that had ultimately undermined the surface level.

Fielding trained his light the length of the tunnel. If it was a remnant of the drainage system, where would the water have leaked into? The passage descended gradually until it seemed to stop at the far end. "Let's go down there," he said.

As they walked, he kept his light focused at the end wall, at what appeared to be a fracture, or slippage, along a fault line.

Behind him, Jean was flashing her light throughout the tunnel. Along the ceiling, proto-stalactites cast mini-shadows over the greenish surface. It was because of the shadows that she first looked past the dark lines above her. But there was something about the contrast between them and the shadows and the folds of stone that made her stop. She shined her light straight above her head. There was a pattern. "Chris! Look."

Fielding wheeled around, first toward her, then up at the ceiling where her beam shone. There was a figure there, on the ceiling. He stepped closer.

It was a pictograph of a man, reddish from the ocher paint. The figure was about twenty inches tall, and at its feet were a series of long, rectangular paired lines, radiating from a central point.

"A sweatlodge?" Jean asked.

"It resembles Spider Cave, yes," Fielding said. "But not quite the same."

"Not a complete representation maybe, but the arrangement of radial logs at his feet for a fire to heat the messenger stone, the ritualistic figure . . . it's too close not to depict the same thing."

Fielding directed his light in wider arcs around and above the figure. Finally, he said, "There's no lodge."

Jean's gaze narrowed. "What do you mean?"

"At Spider Cave, and other pictographic representations of the sweatlodge, the figure is enclosed by a double line, indicating the sweatlodge. Here, there's nothing."

"Look there," Jean said, her beam spotlighting the ceiling to the right of the figure. "Can you see it?"

"Yes," Fielding said. He could see it. Under a glistening coat of lime, there were more pictographs, or a continuation of this one. The next one seemed a geometric shape, a triangle perhaps, but because of the encrusted lime, it was impossible to be sure. And beyond the triangle, there were more, or so it seemed. The ceiling slanted downward as the tunnel did, and the lime crust grew thicker. "Lineally arranged, they tell a story."

"Beginning with the preparation of the sweatlodge, with the fire in front of the man."

"Is it?" Fielding said, going back to the only clear pictograph. "In front of him, I mean."

"The fire? It's placed below him. With no spatial perspective to their painting, that's how they would indicate that it is in front of him."

"But what if the artist wanted to depict them on the same plane?" Fielding said. "How would he do it differently?"

Jean focused on the area between the man's feet and the radial-legged representation of a fire. There was no space there. His legs seemed to grow out of the fire, not much different in appearance from the logs themselves. "It's as if he's . . . in the fire," she said at last.

Fielding didn't respond. He had already come to that same interpretation.

A figure of a man standing in a fire. Was he coming out of the fire? Was he being burned? Or was he resisting the flames? Was it a god? A man? Or something else?

The questions turned over slowly in Fielding's mind, and he began to try to envision the artist, brushing the natural pigments on the stone arcade with a sponge of moss. Was it religious fervor that moved him? The historian's duty to record? Or was it a warning?

"Do you think . . ." Jean began to ask, then trailed off, not sure how to phrase the question.

Do you think what? Fielding echoed in his mind. That some Ojibwa belief is at the root of the burning deaths that have occurred? As posed within the privacy of his own thoughts, the question did not strike him as the least bit absurd. And perhaps it was that realization more than anything that caused an electric tingle to rise up the back of his neck.

He turned toward the far end of the tunnel. "Let's go on."

The fault lines of the dolomite layers slanted at an oblique angle toward Lake Superior. The downward tilt was caused by the great weight of ancient glaciers that had settled in the earth's crust like a biscuit in the hardening skim of a plate of gravy. Between the layers fissures had formed, and some of these were later filled with magma from below. The tunnel appeared to end at one of these granite dikes, but it was obvious the underground river had to have gone somewhere.

Near the floor, at the border of granite and limestone, was a pile of stone rubble rising up about three feet against the wall. It was too symmetrical, too localized, to be a natural formation. The exit hole for the tunnel had been deliberately blocked.

They started pulling the rocks away one by one, but progress was slow. So Fielding took the shovel and began scraping them away with the side of the blade. Within a few minutes the outline of a passage appeared. It was circular and smooth, descending in circumference the deeper it went. A natural funnel.

Sliding on his belly into the narrow aperture, Fielding jabbed the shovel in front of him. The last rocks of the blockage fell away, rebounding down a stone face he couldn't yet see. "It opens up again up here," he said, trying to restrain his excitement. And he *was* excited. From the deep, echoing refrain of the dislodged rocks he could tell the next chamber was larger than what they had been through. What had the barricade been designed to keep inside?

He asked for his flashlight and Jean slipped it forward. Ahead of him, the funnel narrowed to no more than twelve inches. Swallowing hard, he eased himself forward, until he could feel the stone pressing against his chest and his shoulders. Whether from the struggle, or the feeling of being closed in, he began to feel warm. The vision of being trapped flashed through his mind, and the heat flared hotter. He rested his chin for a moment, then tried to inch backward. He couldn't move. He forced his forearms against the stone, but it just seemed to make things worse.

"What's wrong?" Jean said.

Her voice seemed strangely muffled, as if he were already closed off. As if he were already buried.

"Chris. What's wrong?"

Nothing's wrong, he said silently. He was fine. He just had to maintain control. Not panic. He felt himself taking a few deep breaths. He had come this far. He could get out. It was simple physics. If he maintained his composure.

Jean had him by the calves. "Can you hear me?" She tugged.

"Wait. Yes, I can hear. I have to back out." His voice even to his own ears was disjointed, and scared. It must have sounded that way to Jean too, because she fell silent, waiting.

Fielding closed his eyes and began to review his entry into the hole. Mentally reversing each movement, he could visualize backing out. He took another breath, exhaling deeply as if to compress his chest even more, then began to move.

He wasn't stuck, really. It was more a function of his shoulders being constricted, of the difficulty of pushing himself backward versus pulling himself through. But slowly, in measured increments, Fielding backed out. He slipped his legs out of the funnel, then turned and rested on its edge. He was soaked with sweat, and with the hot fears draining away, he felt chilled.

Jean edged past him for a look into the opening. She pulled back. "I can fit through that. Let me try."

Fielding looked at her, then back into the opening. "I'm going to see if I can hack it away a bit. I should be able to reach the shovel into where it narrows."

He started to move, but Jean stopped him with a hand on his shoulder. "I'll clear it away, from the other side." She paused, then added quickly before he could disagree, "It'll be easier, standing up. I'll have much better leverage."

She was right, of course. And what possible difference would it make if she was through first?

"There's nothing in there that can hurt me," she said, almost as if reading his thoughts.

Indeed, what danger was there? Beyond the normal hazards of being in a cave, that is. Still, it was with a trace of reluctance that Fielding pushed himself to his feet, clearing the way for Jean. He was reluctant not for any specific reason, but because of a sense of quiet dread. It was a feeling for which he could give no rational explanation, but could any of the events of recent days be explained in rational terms? How could a poacher and a cop be seared to a crisp in an almost identical fashion? How could they be reduced to mere charred representations of the human form, as if the fire had entered them and consumed them whole? How could a man of science imagine the bite of an invisible creature?

Fielding suddenly looked at his left hand. The marks were still there. *Punctures.* Two on the top side and a matching pair underneath. Like fangs.

Fielding closed his eyes almost in disgust. What was making him think these things? In an attempt to bring himself back to reality, he bent down to watch Jean. She was on her belly, up to the narrow gap where he had turned back. She was grunting with effort, but nonetheless moving steadily. Inch by inch she slid forward, her toes lifting and scraping in minute fractions. And then she stopped.

"You okay?" he called.

"Yeah," she said, panting. "Just resting. I can feel the edge, though." Her voice seemed distant, as if muffled by more than her own body. It was as if her words were being stolen away from her, cast into the next chamber only to be quickly smothered by the dark, absorbed by the space. "I can't see much, but there's an opening. That's for sure."

An opening, Fielding considered. The dread of indeterminate origin returned. It was the feeling of a child staring at a closed closet door. The feeling that comes in the night woods. Investigating creaks in the basement with a kitchen knife in hand.

Jean's feet dropped from view as she entered the chamber. A moment later her face appeared at the far end of the aperture. "You brought the lantern?"

"Yes."

"Can you pass it through?"

"What's it like?"

"Hard to say. Except it's big."

Fielding checked the gas lantern in his pack. Protected by a wire cage, the glass shade was uncracked. Inside, the mantle was still intact. The propane canister was snug.

Pushing the pack with the shovel and lantern into the funnel, Fielding sensed a flicker of private embarrassment. Why was he suffering these fears? He should be excited instead. He was on the verge of discovering valuable archaeological information. What they'd discovered so far was already valuable. And perhaps the sealed chamber held the key to what it all meant.

Maybe that's all it was, he thought. Excitement. Anticipation. Nervous energy. He was simply anxious to get in there himself. Anxious for the answers.

Fielding could hear the heavy metal of the shovel blade being placed on the ground. Then the clank of aluminum and glass. "Where are the matches?" Jean asked.

"You don't need any to start it. It's got an auto light. Place it on something flat and turn the knob to the right. It'll ignite."

There was the sound of stones skittering across the rock surface as she brushed a ledge clear.

"It might flash a bit when the escaping gas catches," he added. "Don't let it startle you. It'll flare down quickly; then adjust the gas so the mantle's an even white."

"Okay." A moment passed. "To the right?"

"Yes. You might have to force it."

Fielding heard the click of the auto switch and a hiss of gas, then saw a flash of light. His eyes squinted involuntarily, it was so bright. Was it the contrast? With the lightning speed of terror's shock, his mind was instantly electrified. It was more than a flash. It was an eruption. A bursting of incandescent material. An explosion without sound.

The observations came with the rapidity of electric impulses through prime conductors. In the next moment came the beginning of a scream. It was all happening so fast, but the paradoxical effect of his suddenly heightened awareness made everything—sights, sounds, reactions—come in slow motion. It was her voice—Jean Shawshequay's—and it wasn't. Somehow, it was strangely altered. It started low, guttural. An expulsion of her own shock. Then fear. It was an unintelligible gasp of surprise, heightened in fractions of a second to a shriek. A scream of agony. She was on fire!

He couldn't see her, but he could see the blaze of light. He could hear her tortured cries. "Jean!" he shrieked, diving head-first into the funnel.

She didn't answer. She couldn't answer, her voice captured by the twin demons of panic and pain.

Fielding scrambled forward into the narrowing split of stone. His head ducked lower as the ceiling rushed down to him. Stretching one elbow out front, he pulled himself deeper with his forearm, then alternated with the other. Each new reach became more cramped. His progress slowed.

Jean's scream took on a whirling tone, a rise and fall in cadence as if she were falling away, reeling away, from the entrance aperture. And then, for the first time, a recognizable syllable: "No!"

"I'm coming," Fielding tried to shout, but his chest was already constricted and he couldn't give his cry much power. The rock was at his back, jabbing into his shoulders. He could barely move.

"Help!" It was a whimper more than a cry.

Fielding stretched his hands forward, searching for a grip, a hold, a corner of stone. Anything to give himself leverage. Anything to grasp and use to pull himself through.

Ahead, the light seemed to have acquired a bluish glow. Less intense than before, it seemed the color of the sky. The sky as viewed through desert heat. Trembling, vibrating, flickering.

He was in deeper than he had been on his first attempt to pass through the opening. And the sensation of being trapped rushed in on him with an even greater strength. The image of Jean burned to a cinder took hold in his mind, but the fear he felt was not for her. It was for himself. He would be stranded, pinched for all eternity in the stone jaws of the funnel. At least her death would be fast. His pain would be as intense, but gradual, lasting days. Weeks.

Fielding blurted out a syllable of defiance, an inarticulate expulsion of sound shouted between teeth clenched against the horror he envisioned, against the strain of his muscles, against the mere thought he would not succeed. Exhaling heavily, his chest sunk, and for just an instant the pressure of stone subsided. He slinked forward another fraction. And then he froze, iced not by his own terror, but by Jean's voice.

Like an echo across time, she cried, "Let go!" And Fielding was suddenly thrust back to the camp fire. It seemed an age ago, but the sensations were suddenly back. He could feel it all over again. The pressure, the jaws. "Get away!" he heard her cry out, and with the energy of that past event, with the power of his fears, he pulled himself mightily forward. The pressure left his shoulders. He moved faster. It was at his buttocks. He twisted, pulled, scrambled, and he was past the obstruction. He was at the edge, and a dozen feet, two dozen feet—in the eerie void it was hard to tell—she was facedown, bathed in light. Blue flame of a propane fire. And yet it wasn't fire. More like a glow, a cobalt aura that hovered around her body, that projected the impression that she was floating, a smudge of noon sky against the midnight black.

"Ooh!" she moaned and struggled at the same time to push herself up.

"I'm here," Fielding shouted. "I'm coming."

She rose on her elbows a half foot, then collapsed again, moaning.

Fielding came down head-first out of the opening, catching himself with his arms. He swung his legs under him, rolling over and rising to his feet in a series of motions that flowed together into one swift move. He came down the rock incline toward her, stumbling over the uneven features, fighting the awkward twist of his ankles.

Nearly to her, he tripped and came down hard on his hands, his wrists bending painfully with the force. She moaned again, and her head seemed to rise and fall like the head of a cloth doll. The bluish haze that hugged tightly to her was fading. It was as if she were fading with it. He reached forward, plunging his hands into the blue fire. But there was no heat. It was a cold fire, and at his touch it flickered and died completely. Somewhere behind them her flashlight lay on the ground, shining aimlessly into space, casting only the dimmest of reflected glows over them. He had her from behind, his hands at her sides, but she was just a shadow. He rolled her over, and she grunted.

"You're okay now," he said. "It's over. The fire is gone."

She only moaned in reply. If conscious at all, she was only hanging on by a tether. Her body was like deadweight. He got her to her side, then adjusted her legs and pulled her lower arm from under her so she could lie flat. His hands came up behind her back, trying to gently ease her down. Her head suddenly lolled back and her mouth drooped open. And the light was back.

From black to glare so fast, Fielding flinched, at first only because of the sudden light. But it was more than a mere light. It was in her, in her mouth. It was the fire!

Her mouth was parted in a silent scream, and within it stretched narrow spikes of fire. But it wasn't fire. It couldn't be. The lighted spikes were possessed of a distinct shape and design. And they were expanding, narrowing in the center like gummy phlegm stretched taut within a carnivore's jaw. A carnivore's jaw! The fangs of a killer. The spikes opened in the center, breaking apart, becoming pointed daggers of light.

Her head suddenly lunged forward, toward Fielding. The fangs slashed at his neck. Fielding shouted out his horror, letting her fall from his grasp, reeling backward. She fell flat back on the stone, collapsing heavily. He rolled to his side, coming flush in to a boulder. He pushed flat against it, sliding upward to his feet, all the while looking back in horror at the thing on the ground, at the fangs of fire, at the—

There was no longer any blaze of oral flames. The only light came from the flashlight, on the ground. It was Jean Shawshequay before him, bathed in shadow, moaning almost inaudibly, thrashing in slow motion from side to side.

Fielding stared down at her, transfixed by the image of a scant few seconds before. But that image did not fit with what he saw now. There was no fire. No daggers of flaming teeth. Nothing but a woman on the verge of unconsciousness.

What was happening? his mind screamed.

He tried to think, but there was no order to his mind. He saw again the fangs of fire, but this time they were rising from Billings's pile of dead ash. He felt the closed, constricted panic of being trapped in the neck of the aperture and flashed back to his vision of slow starvation. Trapped because Jean was dead, burned like the others. The flash of the lantern had preceded it all, had set in motion a series of conclusions, each building on the last, nurtured by his imagination, powered by his fear.

Was that all it was? Fielding thought. Bits and pieces of what had happened suddenly merged into seeming coherence because of his fear? As a dream assembles disparate thoughts into a whole?

Fielding found that he was shivering, quaking against the rock. He felt as if he were losing his mind. He must be, if he had imagined all that he had seen. Then he thought of the blue fire. Had that been imagined?

Quickly he found the propane lantern on the ground. The glass shade was broken, the mantel turned to dust, and the canister of gas pulled free. He shook the canister. Empty. He looked over toward Jean. The gas jetted out, then flared so fast it didn't ignite her clothes. Could it have happened that way? He took two steps and knelt at her side. Her shirt was damp, like his own.

She reacted to his touch. "Chris?" Her voice was weak, trembling.

Fielding hovered over her, observing, the breath practically stilled in his chest.

"Chris!" This time it was said more forcefully. A touch of fright.

He wanted to grab her, to hold her tight, to tell her everything was all right. But for whatever reason, he felt he could not move. He felt he could not speak.

She opened her eyes, staring at him, questioning.

When he finally did recover the ability to speak, his voice trembled like hers. He reached out tentatively, touching her shoulder. At his touch she rose quickly from the waist, rising up to him, throwing her arms around his back. Fielding tried to push her away. But her motion was too swift. Her grip too strong. Her own fear too great. Her arms latched around him, hugging him tight.

Burying her face into his chest, she began to sob. Quietly at first, then growing more uncontrolled. And as her heaves worsened, her grip tightened around his back.

Fielding suffered a sense of shame. For resisting her needs. For being frightened by his . . . dream? Already, what had hap-

pened had become little more than a dreamscape, a collection of
facts and fictions blended into a confusing whole.

He felt her loosen her grip. A function of fatigue, to be sure,
but also a sign her panic was lessening. Over time—Several
seconds, a few minutes? Time itself seemed to be as elastic as
the new reality—she relaxed her grip completely, letting herself
back down to the ground. She began to massage her left temple
with her hand.

"You think you're going to be all right?"

She took a moment to answer. "I feel so . . . dizzy, I guess.
And my stomach, it's—" She suddenly spun away from Fielding, hunching over. She convulsed in the middle and vomited.

Fielding knelt down quickly, placing his hand across her
forehead. She moaned, her body shuddered, and then the sickness returned in another violent episode.

Another few minutes passed, all the while Fielding trying to
soothe her, until she was at rest again. She looked up, fixing him
with her eyes, composing herself, waiting for the strength to
speak. "What happened?" she said simply.

"We'll talk about it later," he said. "You rest while I try to
widen the opening."

She nodded, and Fielding took the shovel to the horizontal
split in the rock. The limestone chipped and broke easily, and
soon he had made the gap fractionally higher. It would still be a
tight squeeze, but not as it had been before. When he came back
to Jean, she was sitting up against a boulder. "Ready?" he said.

She didn't look at him. Nor did she speak. She only nodded
to Fielding's right. Toward a crevice in the floor. Fielding
looked. An object, several inches across, was caught in the
crevice. Rounded, it had the appearance of a stone that had
rolled into the gap. But it wasn't a stone. He went down to one
knee, training Jean's light directly on it. He reached down,
gently prying it loose and picking it up. The light penetrated
through holes in the front, illuminating the object's hollow interior.

He looked over at Jean, then very carefully laid the object on
the ground so that it was upright, balanced along its relatively
flat lower edge. Sitting back on his haunches, he stared silently
at it, thinking. He was eye to eye with a human skull.

There was more than one skull. The cave was strewn with
bones. Human skeletons. Dozens of them. Some complete as

they lay, others disarticulated, as if having separated and fallen apart.

It was a huge chamber, compared to the outer passages. It had a high vaulted ceiling that seemed broken and uneven, and the beam was unable to penetrate the craggy black holes that pitted the roof. The floor was in some respects a reverse image of the ceiling, partly because of the rocks that had fallen from above. There were cracks and fault lines, veined throughout the cavern, some of the fissures traveling up and into the walls.

The bones were in flat areas, atop boulders, and slipped into the cracks. And they were of all sizes, from children to adults. But the most striking feature about them was that they were all charred. They had died together, at one time, in a massive inferno that had blackened the walls of the cave.

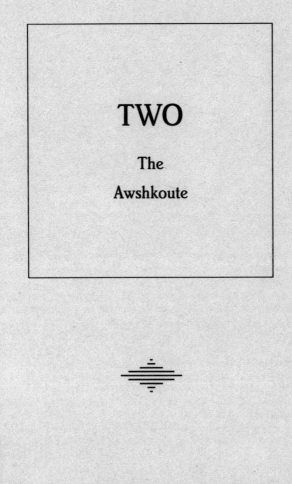

TWO

The
Awshkoute

Chapter 13

TIME HAD LOST its meaning for him. Which was appropriate, because it was a timeless world into which he sought admission. A world not divided into lifetimes, but a world marked by a continuation that stretched back as long as his people had walked this land. He was one with the past as they were creatures of the present, parts of the same whole, dependent as much on each other as the brain is dependent upon the heart.

As merely a single moment on the continuum, a day didn't matter. Or two. At least that's the conclusion he had arrived at, over the course of the day. It hadn't been that way, however, when he first awakened, lying on his side next to the small heap of dead ash atop the knoll overlooking the site of desecration.

Makwamacatawa had been disappointed in himself when he awoke. He had been on the verge of communicating with the Ancient Ones, and he had failed. He had fallen asleep without receiving their wisdom. Or was he already asleep when he saw them trying to take shape in the fire?

In the light of day he wasn't sure if they had appeared in his dreams or had actually begun to draw shape from the flames. But that distinction mattered little, Makwamacatawa decided, because the object for a man on a vision quest was to erase the line between reality and dreams. And if beings not of the natural world—entities from a different point on the continuum—chose to make contact by drifting into his dreams, it was no different than if they took substance from the elements of this world and appeared physically before him. It was up to the Ancient Ones to decide.

And it was up to him to be receptive. To free himself from the constraints of this world. To tear down the barriers between the two. To cleanse his body and soul so he was as pure a being as the spirits beyond his point on the continuum.

He would build a sweatlodge, he had decided shortly after he awoke. A solitary hut of meditation where the heat would purify his body, and steam rising from the messenger stones would carry his petitions to the Ancient Ones.

Removing the cowl of the black bear, he had begun his work, collecting what he would need from the forest. That's where he had been when the man and the woman arrived in the Jeep truck. He saw them through the trees, but it was a mark of his success at retreating from the natural world that he took little note of their presence. It was the same way when the third individual appeared. Makwamacatawa barely noticed him at all, particularly because he entered the place of desecration on foot. If he had come in a vehicle, it was parked well out of sight. To Makwamacatawa, his behavior was of no consequence. Nor did he pause to reflect upon his apparent stealth as he followed the path of the first two down into the Cave of Bones.

Jean Shawshequay was firm. "The bones stay." She was supposed to be the observer at the archaeological site, the court-sanctioned representative of the Ojibwa people, there to ensure that no ancient graves were disturbed. So despite the dizziness and the fatigue that still gripped her, on the matter of removing the remains from the cave she remained strong.

"It's important that we take a sample for fuller analysis. You know it is."

"Not every blank footnote in history has to be filled in. Some things are more important."

Fielding was frustrated. He looked down at the row of nine skulls they had gathered. Some had been complete where they laid; with others he had to search around for the lower jaw. When he found the matching mandible, he fitted it to the maxilla as if piecing together a puzzle. Each of the nine skulls connected in the same manner. Fielding knew Jean knew what that meant. And that's why he was frustrated. She just refused to accept the obvious.

Fielding took a deep breath and pushed himself to his feet. He'd try a different tack. "This isn't a consecrated place. It isn't a carefully laid-out grave where these people were sent on their journeys with the respect and preparation they would have wanted. It isn't a burial site at all," he said, raising his voice. "This was a massacre."

"We don't know what it was."

"Which is why we can't turn our backs on it now. We have to find out. There's too much at stake not to."

"You mean like your academic credentials?"

The words were spoken with a biting edge, and for a second Fielding saw in her eyes the same look she had harbored for him the first day he saw her, in the courtroom, when she was on the witness stand. He had to turn away. "No. Not my credentials. It's important for the sake of the archaeological record."

"Is that all?"

Fielding turned slowly back toward her. "It might help explain . . . what has been happening."

"Professor Fielding. You mean to suggest that these massacred people are somehow seeking their revenge?"

"No," Fielding said quickly. He didn't know what he meant.

"Well, that's what the public would say. Some kind of Indian voodoo is responsible. And we've had enough of that over the years."

Though her words were forceful, her voice was not. To Fielding the fatigue was evident. He should have taken her out of there right after the lantern flared. It was only because of his— What? Academic interest?—that he had stayed on at risk to her health. The bones weren't going anywhere. He could come back. The important thing was getting Jean out of the cave. "You're right. We have had enough of that." He bent down to help her to her feet. "Let's get out of here."

He picked up the pack, and together they walked to the entrance hole in the wall. Jean was ready to crawl in, when she backed off and looked at him, as if embarrassed to admit she was afraid. "You go first."

He agreed, and as he was about to slip the pack in ahead of himself, she took it from him. "I'll bring it out," she said. "You have enough trouble fitting through."

Fielding went in head-first. Having heightened the ceiling of the tunnel with the shovel, he was able to get through easier, but it was still a matter of inching forward bit by bit. At the other side he picked up his flashlight and shined it back, calling for Jean. She didn't respond.

"Jean?" Fielding listened intently. He could hear something, some manner of movement. And there was the glow of her light, somewhere away from the hole. "Jean!" A few moments later she appeared at the other end. "Anything wrong?"

"No."

"You okay?"

"Yes, I think—" She trailed off, not sure what she thought.

"Just the dizziness, I guess." And the next thing she knew, she felt Chris's hands at her shoulders, slipping under her arms, helping her out of the narrow entrance. It was as if she had jumped forward in time, skipping the intervening moments. Or was it that there was a gap in her memory? She was watching him climb into the hole, then he was helping her, then she was out. Like someone watching clips of a film spliced together with intervening frames removed, she was not witness to the full scene.

Jean gripped her forehead and let herself sway back against the rock wall.

"What's wrong?"

She began to shake her head, "I, I don't—" She threw her head back and took a few breaths, seeking to recover from the dizziness, the emptiness, the sensation of floating. The feeling of burning up inside.

"You've got a fever," Fielding said, feeling her forehead. "Come on. Let's go." He tried to take the pack from her shoulder, but she snapped it back with a strength that surprised him.

He let her keep it. There was no reason not to, he told himself. The main thing was to get out. But as they walked through the narrow passage under the pictographs, then scaled the wall to the next, smaller chamber, he realized there was something more behind his concession to her than the need to get out of the dampness.

For just a second, as she regained control of the pack, as she locked her eyes on his, he had been afraid. It was as if he expected to see again the illusion. As if he expected her mouth to bare white-hot daggers of fire.

The fire in the Verhoven cabin hearth crackled like crumbling snack-food packages.

"That was some firewood you had delivered last spring," Maggie said. "Already cured, you said."

John held his cards down and scowled at the fire. "He said it was."

"Oak, too, he said." Maggie smiled across her hand at her partner, young Jimmy. He grinned. "It sounds more like pine, if you ask me."

John laid his cards flat on the table and went to the fire, putting the screen across the opening. How was he to know if it was oak or pine? He could tell the grain of finished lumber, but how the hell could he tell the difference between cut logs with their bark?

"Face it, Dad," Jimmy said. "You got took."

John looked over at his family. They all seemed to take such amusement in this. "So I'm not a woodsman," he said loudly, throwing up his hands. "I've got more important things to work at. Right, Lindsey?"

Lindsey was his partner in the canasta game. "Right, Dad," she agreed.

"You don't mean fishing," Sharon said. She looked over her magazine from her place on the couch.

"That's exactly what I mean. It's an endeavor of consummate skill," he said, flipping an imaginary rod, "a one-on-one contest, man against nature, a sport that requires patience, and most of all, intelligence."

"Must be some darn smart fish out there," Maggie said. "They out-thought you all day."

"They didn't out-think me," he said, taking his seat again at the card table. "That was our plan. Wasn't it, Lindsey?"

She showed a moment of surprise, then tried to cover it, not sure what he was getting at.

"We were just tempting them today," he continued. "Letting them get used to us. Letting them get nice and relaxed. Setting them up for tomorrow morning. Nice and early, that's when they'll strike."

"Oh, jeez," Jimmy said as his father drew a card from the pile and laid it down. "Another red three."

"It's all in the wrist," John said, discarding as if he were casting a line. "You just be ready by mid-morning for the best pan-fried trout breakfast you ever had."

"Ugh," Sharon said. "Don't make me puke."

"Maybe you'd like to join us," he said to his younger daughter.

"Oh, no," Maggie answered for her. "She's going grocery shopping with me in the morning. Just in case you decide you haven't done enough . . . tempting."

Even Lindsey laughed at that, and so it went, until the game was done and the cards put away. The kids went to bed, and John and Maggie were about to follow, when Jimmy appeared at the bottom of the steps, sleepy-eyed and in his pajamas. "Daddy?"

"Yes?"

"Can I go?"

"Go where, Masterblaster?"

"With you and Lindsey. Fishing."

John raised his eyebrows, and he looked over at Maggie. Then back at his son. "You know, we'll be getting up early."

"I know."

"It'll still be dark outside. We have to be in the river before sunrise."

"That's okay. Can I come?"

Another glance at Maggie and she shrugged. "Sure, Jimmy. I'll come get you in the morning."

"Okay."

"Now get some sleep. You'll need it."

As he climbed back up the steps, Maggie looped her arms around John from the side. "I've lost another one to the river."

John smiled. "Pretty soon you might have to join us."

She shook her head. "No. I'll just have to learn to take you when I have the chance." She started to tug him toward the bedroom.

John didn't resist at first, but then he thought there was something he had to do. He pried her arms off of him.

"Not anything to do with your fish, is it?"

"No," he said. "The fire. I'll be right in."

She kissed him, lingering close, then left him to the fire.

For some reason he approached it cautiously, as if coming up to an animal in the woods. He pulled the screen back. It had burned down quite a bit and he hadn't added any more logs, but still there were remnants of flames, dancing in tiny shoots across the charred surface of the wood.

He watched it for a while, and though he couldn't quite explain it, something just didn't seem right. There was a nervous, flickering quality to the flames. It didn't seem to be a dying fire, but rather one trying to come to life.

John took the poker and spread the ashes apart. Then he did something he had never done in a hearth fire before. He filled up a Coke bottle with water and sprinkled it over flames and embers. When he was satisfied the fire was out, he turned off the lights and headed to the bedroom. He didn't bother to put the fire screen back in place.

With the ribbed skeleton of what would be a domed structure rising behind him, Makwamacatawa sat before the small fire at his place atop the knoll. The bear's head weighed heavily on his own, and his neck ached from holding his head erect. More than anything, it was the lack of food. He had found the two jugs of water someone had left for him on the side of the hill, but he hadn't eaten anything now in thirty-six hours. The hunger was intense at times, but more and more the pain seemed to be giving way just to weakness.

Makwamacatawa suddenly threw his shoulders back and looked at the heavens. He had to keep himself awake. He had to work at making himself ready. The sweatlodge wasn't complete, but the Ancient Ones had tried to cross the line last night. They could try again tonight.

He lowered his eyes to the lively scene of dancing yellow in front of him. It made sense that they chose to speak to him through the flames. That's how they had apparently chosen to answer the sacrilege. That's how they would let him know what he was to do.

Race—the great divider in life—is to the archaeologist in most applications a matter of little consequence in death. What is important to him are the acts and works, the accomplishments and failures, of man. As for the skeleton the physical anthropologist has to work with, it is the great leveler of racial distinction. Underneath, man is the same. Except in one respect.

When the mandible and maxilla of Native American peoples are closed together, the incisors usually occlude edge to edge. In Caucasians, generally there is an overbite. Of the nine skulls Fielding had fitted together, each one occluded in the same fashion. In each, there was a distinct overbite. Based on that, it was evident to him, as he knew it was to Jean Shawshequay, that the people massacred in the Cave of Bones were European in origin.

Why she refused to accept the obvious he wasn't sure. She didn't strike him as someone who would be concerned about appearances, worried that the local Ojibwa who appointed her their representative would not believe her. But then again, there were lots of things he didn't understand. Was her behavior just one aspect of the pattern?

Lying in bed, staring at the ceiling, Fielding reviewed that pattern of events. Bog-iron manufacture at a pre-contact site. Indian pictographs at the entrance to a chamber that was the site of a massacre of a Europe-derived people. The incineration of two men in proximity to the site, one of them leaving finger marks as if dragged back toward the fire. The burning punctures of his hand in the bottom of the pit. And the blue flame that seemed to envelop Jean in the cave, that, in what he decided was an illusion, seemed to enter her.

But was the blue flame, Jean's fangs of fire, an illusion? He had concluded that it was by analyzing the effect of his panic, his fears, the suggestion already planted in his mind. Could his conclusion that it was not real have been the result of a similar process? One in which the varying elements of logic and reason and what he knew to be impossible combined to yield the only conclusion science would allow: that he had been mistaken?

Fielding kicked the sheet lower. His skin was moist and clammy, and he was increasingly uncomfortable, because of the heat, because of the dead ends his line of thinking led him to.

Perhaps that was his problem, he thought. He consciously created the dead ends. He was conditioned to accept certain parameters of what was possible and what was not. Was it time to consider answers that fell beyond those parameters? And there *were* answers, if he did not restrict himself to the world of reason and science. There were connections between all the events and circumstances he had been mentally reviewing.

Fielding flung the sheet completely to the side and swung his feet to the floor. He sat there on the edge of the bed, hot and sweaty, gripping the mattress with both hands. It didn't make sense, he told himself. What he was thinking. Connections forged by concepts foreign to the world as it is were not connections at all.

A few minutes passed, and gradually the heated feeling that had driven him up from the mattress began to change. He began to cool off, but it was not a return to comfort. Instead he felt chilled.

He no longer was thinking about the burning deaths or the iron or any of the other events. He was thinking about Jean. Not about something he wasn't sure had actually happened, but something which very definitely had occurred.

Sitting half-nude on the edge of his bed, wide awake in the middle of the night, he was thinking about how Jean had clutched the small backpack when he tried to help her with it. He thought about her taking it with her when he dropped her off at Miriam Goodmedicine's. He hadn't even questioned her about it when she climbed out of the truck. Instead, he just sat there and watched her walk up the steps and into the house.

It had occurred to him then—as it did now—what the pack might conceal. But like all the other questions, he felt he knew the answer, and yet he didn't. He didn't because it didn't make sense.

He could think of no reason within the parameters of his logic that explained why she had taken the pack. Or what she was going to do with what it concealed.

Chapter 14

SHE WAS TIRED, but couldn't sleep. She was awake, but seemed to be dreaming. She remembered the cave, but thought it really hadn't happened.

It was a contrary world she had drifted into, and in this realm of paradoxes there seemed to be only one certainty. She was weak. Sick. Feverish. Miriam Goodmedicine had noticed it when Jean came in, and Miriam had brought her up some tea and food on a tray. The tea eventually cooled, and the food went untouched. And Jean's weakness seemed to deepen.

She was vaguely aware—in this interstice between dream and conscious thought—that she should do something about her condition. She should eat, she should take medicine, she should go to the hospital. Something, anything, to get stronger. It shouldn't have been such a difficult decision, but in her world of paradox she could not decide. She could not concentrate. She could not focus on what she wanted. Instead, her mind drifted over the events of the evening. Most of everything that had happened replayed in her mind like a silent film, but a film that was not in any particular order. The bats, the lantern, the rocks blocking the entrance, the sinkhole. The strange thing though—strange to her even in her state of drift—was that none of the major happenings and discoveries—locating the cave itself, the pictographs, the sudden flash of the propane lantern, the bones—seemed to have left any lasting impact. For some reason, her thoughts kept coming back to something decidedly minor, something she had barely noticed. Indeed, something she must have seen a half dozen times and never paid any attention to.

On the drive back into town, Jean had been quiet, resting her head against the glass, staring out the side window. A short distance after they turned onto the highway, they passed another dirt road cutoff. Next to it was an eighteen-inch wooden sign hung from a post. On the sign in routered letters written in flowing script was a single word. It was a name, a family name.

It was the sight of this sign that her mind kept coming back to. Not the cave, not the excavation, not Christopher Fielding. But the sign. She didn't understand why, and it was so much easier not to try to understand. It was easier not to concentrate. It was easier to let herself drift. For after all, she was weak. She needed strength. *They all needed strength.*

Jean Shawshequay was in bed, but she wasn't. She was trying to sleep, but she was getting dressed. She was aware of what was happening, but it didn't seem real.

When the tone sounded, John Verhoven didn't react. Maggie had to reach across his chest and hit the bar on top of the clock, then shake him awake. He got up early every day in the city without any trouble, but four A.M. was even too early for those biorhythms to kick into effect. In less than twenty seconds he was sound asleep again.

He stayed asleep until he felt himself being gently nudged again. His eyes cracked open. Lindsey.

"Come on, Dad. It's four-fifteen."

He let his eyes shut with a groan.

"Come on," Lindsey said, grabbing his arm. "We're going to wake up the fish, remember?"

"Yeah, I remember." Slowly he sat up in bed, swinging his legs to the floor. Lindsey was all dressed. Probably it had taken her all of sixty seconds.

"We'll catch so many trout we won't be able to carry them all, if we get out there early. Like you said."

"I said that?"

"Yes." She had a grip on his wrist and leaned back, pulling him to his feet.

"Okay, okay."

She wouldn't let go. Tugging on his arm, she pulled him to the bathroom. "Hurry up."

John leaned over the sink as Lindsey turned on the light. "Oh," he grunted, recoiling from the sudden glare. Gradually, he got used to it, until at last he looked over at her and said, "All right. I'm up. It'll be just a few minutes."

Lindsey watched him skeptically for a moment. "Can I trust you?"

That made him laugh, which in turn made him more awake.

"I'm fine. You go on." As she was turning away, he called, "Oh Lindz?" She paused. "Go wake up your brother. Tell him to get ready."

"Jimmy? Why?"

"He's going with us."

Her face paled. For her brother to invade what she shared exclusively with her father was a world change for her. And it all arrived with the suddenness of a slap to the face.

"That's okay, isn't it?"

Lindsey managed a smile. "Sure, Dad. I'll go wake him."

John started to get ready, and a few minutes later there was a weak knock at the door. It was Lindsey again. "I tried, but he won't get up," she whispered.

"You didn't have any trouble with me."

"Jimmy's different."

John said all right, he'd get him up. He went to his son's room and shook his shoulder. Jimmy rolled over, as if annoyed. "Jimmy. You said you wanted to go fishing." The boy didn't say anything.

"See," Lindsey said. "I told you."

John shook him again. "If you want to go, you have to get up." The boy mumbled this time and his lids rose and he gave his dad a glassy look. "We're going now, Jimmy. Get up, if you want to come."

"I want to come," he said in a thick voice. Then with his eyes barely open, he started to rise out of bed.

John left him and went back to his room to finish getting ready himself. Dressed, he bent over to kiss Maggie on the cheek. The touch of his lips roused her slightly. "Goo-luh," she murmured.

"Thanks."

She opened her eyes a little wider. "No more stories about temptation. I expect some fish."

John grinned, then left the bedroom. At Jimmy's room it was quiet. He looked inside, and the boy was sound asleep, curled under a sheet. A predawn rising wasn't the way to get started anyway, he thought. He'd take him out in the afternoon.

Downstairs, Lindsey didn't even ask about her brother. She already had her waders on and was standing by the door with her new rod. "Come on, Dad. Let's go."

"You're eating breakfast first."

"We're having trout for breakfast. When we get back. Remember?"

He had said that, hadn't he? "Well, a bowl of cereal won't spoil your appetite."

She rolled her eyes but relented, figuring it was best to hurry up and get it over with rather than argue. She spooned the cereal down in record time, then left her bowl on the table and went toward the front door. "I'll be down at the river," she said.

"Wait on the bank," he called after her, his voice rising in volume as she disappeared out the door. He finished a minute later, then got his own waders and slipped on his vest. His tackle box was on the stone ledge by the hearth.

Bending over for the molded plastic box, he hesitated, then reached instead for the poker and raked the ashes. He wouldn't be able to explain why he had done that. He wasn't sure why he was so concerned. But for whatever reason, as he left the cabin and headed toward the river, he was not thinking about trout or Lindsey or the river at all. He was thinking about the fire. As he thought more about it, as he neared the watery course shiny black in the dark, he realized why he had doused it before he went to bed. It was crazy, but it seemed as if there were something more to the fire, something more to the flames that danced nervously across the wood surface. Something that made it not want to die.

It became almost like a haunting. The picture in her mind of the eighteen-inch wooden sign. It wouldn't leave her alone. She kept coming back to it in her thoughts as if it were a scene of paramount importance. As if she should know what it meant. As if something had happened at that site she should remember. Or something that would happen.

She wanted to sleep, to force her mind into a neutral state where unwanted visions could not intrude. She closed her eyes, but her sight did not go black. It was dark, but that was because of the night. She tried to look away to escape, but all she saw were trees. Movement. The sense of rushing forward. Or was it falling?

And then the haunting returned. She saw the sign dangling from its post just as before, except that this time, it was clearer. Set more carefully in its surroundings, by the side of the highway, next to the private road. The picture in her mind was so vivid this time, it was as if she were actually there. As if it were not a dream but was really happening. As if she were turning past the sign and driving up the road it marked.

It was suddenly much darker. She was in the woods, and the sense of rushing or falling lifted. More importantly, the haunting at last left her alone. No longer did she have to fight to keep the vision of the sign from dominating her thoughts. That was past her. Now she could concentrate on the thin passage through the trees. She could concentrate on getting stronger.

John Verhoven and his daughter padded along a narrow path that paralleled the river. The soil was soft, black, and mushy, and the vegetation was lush. It was less than an hour to sunrise and it should have been getting lighter. Instead, the cloud cover was thickening, forestalling the forces of dawn, allowing the darkness to linger on amid the deep thicket of the woods.

The trail passed into a stand of cedars, and they veered off to the left. It was just a few steps to the river. The bank was low, and it was there that they would enter, a half mile upstream from the cabin.

"Are the brownies awake yet?" Lindsey whispered, as if not to disturb the fish.

"They'll be nice and hungry. Don't you worry."

Lindsey had been quiet most of the way up the trail. She felt the kind of anticipation that was excitement and nervousness at the same time. Heading out before the crack of dawn, having her own bamboo rod, slipping silently into the deep forest—it was as if she were ascending to the final ranks of the trout fishermen.

They prepared their lines, then eased into the water. They separated enough not to get tangled, then began to cast into the dark, moving slowly downstream.

This was what fly fishing was meant to be, John thought. Alone. On a wilderness stream. The only sounds the sounds of the water, the swish of the line, the splash of a trout rising.

He looked over toward his daughter. Such a small thing, waist-deep in water, her line snaking above her, once, twice, drying in the air, then flicking forward with the speed of a flying insect. Set against the lingering dark, half-hidden by the water, against the backdrop of the towering pines, she seemed—they both seemed—an insignificant intrusion in the vast canvas of the wilderness. And that's the way it should be, he thought.

They were minor players. Center stage was for the trees and the animals and the flowing conveyor of water.

It was a comforting outlook he felt settling over himself, but at the same time the sense of insignificance and solitude made him feel small. And isolated. And vulnerable.

How could it be a dream when it seemed so real? How could it be real when she knew it was a dream?

The dirt road disappeared under her vehicle. Trees slid by slowly to either side of the car. It was like the narrow trail into the excavation site. Was her memory replaying the trip over that road? It was similar, and yet it was very different. Was the difference because of the dark?

It suddenly became darker still. In her dream, the lights that pushed back the forest went out. But the sense of motion did not cease. The car continued to creep forward. Or was it that the vision that came to her mind kept slipping past?

In the next instant—or what seemed like the next instant— she was out of the car and moving into the trees. She could hear the crunch of dead leaves under her feet, the swish of branches brushed back from her face. And in the distance, if she listened carefully, she heard the rushing sound of moving water.

She continued moving forward, maintaining a steady course. She didn't know where she was going, and yet she moved purposefully. She couldn't fight it. She wasn't strong enough to fight. She could only let herself drift.

Drifting ahead in time, the scenes in her mind changed. She was shooting forward. As when she came out of the cave, there were gaps in her memory of what she had just done. Also as when she came out of the cave, draped from her hand by the shoulder straps, she carried the small pack.

A city boy's fears, he told himself. Vulnerability associated with isolation. John almost laughed out loud. This is what he had sought. This is what he needed. Danger came from other people, not the wilderness. And there was no one around for miles.

Dawn finally began to show an effect in the sky, but then with the decisiveness of a final curtain, whatever manner of lightening the sky exhibited was lost to the clouds. Swirling, deep black clouds.

John watched them assemble with only marginal concern.

But Lindsey didn't pay the clouds any attention at all. She was intent on her mission. Drawing out a little line with her left hand, bringing the rod straight back with a snap, then flicking it forward with full arm extension, guiding her hooked missile with increasing accuracy toward the deep holes or protected waters or other places the trout would likely favor.

With the clouds came an air change. There was a fresh smell of rain. It would be good for the forest, John thought, for the most part unconcerned about being caught in the rain himself. If anything, it would encourage the trout to rise.

The lack of concern vanished in an instant at the distant crack of thunder. He felt it inside, as if it were plucking a single cord of his nerves.

In her contrary world of muffled sounds and dim images, the thunder and lightning were just one more paradox. She was afloat in her dream when the echoing blasts from the sky swept away all pretense of dream. She was in the dark world of subconscious thought when bright flashes silhouetted the forest in stark relief. She was flotsam caught in the wash of waves, a willow branch in a gale, thrust forward and back by forces over which she had no control.

All the while she was moving forward, slipping past trees, ducking under branches. All the while responding to whispery suggestions that slowly swirled in her ears like milky water caught in the outer vortex of a whirlpool. At all costs she must get closer. She must get stronger. *We all have to get stronger.*

A bolt of lightning cracked overhead with the sound of an ax splitting her bedroom door. Maggie sprang awake, jerking from the waist straight up on the mattress. She flung the sheet back and jumped out of bed. She thought for sure the house had been hit, it sounded so close.

She rushed to the window and looked out. The trees flashed with the uneven strobe of the storm, bringing day into night and then snatching it away.

Maggie grabbed her cotton robe and flung it around behind her as she hurried toward the door. She half ran toward the staircase.

"Mommy!" Sharon whimpered from her bedroom.

"It's okay, honey," Maggie called as she began taking the stairs. "It'll pass."

She hit the lights and moved toward the front door. As she did, her eyes flashed across the table, taking in the two empty bowls, each with a residue of milk and soggy cereal at the bottom. She was powered only by one thought: Members of her family caught in the storm.

She swung open the door, stepped onto the porch, and went to the edge of the steps. Her eyes scanned the woods toward the river. "John!" she cried out. "Lindsey!"

She walked to the end of the porch at the corner of the cabin. Rain spraying under the overhang spotted her robe, but she was oblivious to the water. She was oblivious to the blown mist that began to collect across her forehead and on her cheeks. She leaned over the rail and called into the woods, "Jimmy!"

Her voice lost to the torment of the storm, no one heard. No one responded.

The river in darkness had a textureless flow, an inky, glistening surface movement that seemed more a reflection of motion around it than its own current. Even the river's folds and bulges over submerged obstructions were smooth like molten glass. It was a scene of peace and tranquillity. But the rain changed all that.

Individual drops shattered the glassy calm like miniature bombs striking the surface, sending up shrapnel which in turn added to the disruption. It was war between chaos and order, and with this storm, with these fishermen, the forces of chaos were winning.

John yelled at Lindsey to pull in her line; then they climbed out of the river into a stand of cedars. The lush, conical crowns of the trees broke the direct onslaught of the rain, and for a time they would remain relatively dry. But only for a time, John knew.

They were protected from the lightning by high banks on both sides of the river, on which grew red pines higher than the cedars that sheltered them. They could wait it out, John thought, or they could head back. "How you doing, Sport?" he said to Lindsey.

A flash of lightning and a crack of thunder came almost simultaneously, and Lindsey flinched. She looked up at her dad. "Fine."

She was scared. *He* was scared. They would head back. "Think Mom'll be mad if we don't bring home dinner?"

Lindsey actually smiled, and with that look, that expression of innocence, she seemed again suddenly so very young. She tried so hard to act older, and because she didn't complain and whine so much like her brother and sister, John had come to accept her as a mature young woman. But she wasn't an adult. She was still a little girl, and with that realization, with the look in her face, he felt a sudden pang in his heart.

It was more than mere nostalgia. It was an actual ache, as he might feel over something lost that could not be regained. As they started back on the trail toward the cabin, whether because of the thunder, or because walking in front of him she seemed so small and vulnerable, the feeling began to change. The ache became like a sickness in his stomach. He began to worry that it wasn't just her youth he had lost. He was worried he would lose her.

"Mo-om-my!" Sharon was in her nightgown, shivering, standing in the open doorway to the cabin.

Maggie looked at her, then glanced back at the woods. As she did, another crack of thunder sounded and lightning split the dark. The thunder was so loud it took a few seconds for her to hear that her daughter was now crying. She turned.

Sharon's fists were clenched in tight little balls up by her shoulders, and she was wailing in fright, her eyes wrinkled shut and tears streaming down her face. Maggie left the corner of the porch and strode toward her. She was going to turn Sharon around and usher her inside, but as soon as she touched her, the girl latched both arms around her thighs. Another explosion from the storm, and she clenched her even tighter.

"Inside," Maggie yelled, but her daughter didn't budge. "Get inside!" It was hard to break the hold, but Maggie did, and finally she managed to turn Sharon around, and both of them stumbled back into the living room. Maggie slammed the door behind her.

Sharon turned toward her mother and wailed anew. "Mommy!"

Maggie sat on a pine chair at the table and hugged her daughter's head to her breast. The girl was wracked by sobs, and she clung so tightly to her mother that Maggie had trouble taking full breaths. Slowly, though, the pressure eased, the sobs became less wrenching. Just as Maggie felt her daughter coming under control, a new bolt of lightning struck. The thunder was

louder, closer, than anything so far, and the flash was blinding.
Though Maggie shut her eyes, she could not escape the glare. It
was as if the jagged streak of electrified discharge had not restricted itself to a brief life of seconds, but instead had frozen its
existence, refusing to die.

Maggie's eyes remained closed, but the flash of sky fire
wouldn't relinquish its pursuit. She could see it still, a burst of
light etched into the black. She clenched her eyes tighter, her
entire body seeming to constrict, and without realizing it, she
was clutching Sharon with a fear even stronger than her daughter had shown.

The force of the blast knocked Jean down. She was deafened,
but she could still hear. She was blinded, but she could still see.
She could see the cabin. It was just another of the paradoxes, a
cabin where there had been only wilderness, and it drifted into
her vision on wisps of unspoken suggestion. But it was suggestion of such commanding strength that it eclipsed the glare of
the lightning strike, keeping the sight of the cabin in focus. As
with the eighteen-inch sign by the side of the road, she didn't
know why it appeared in her dream. And as with the sign that
had haunted her sleep, she came to feel that she could actually
see the cabin.

As the glare of the lightning subsided, as she could begin to
distinguish trunks of trees and the lacy fabric of vegetation, her
vision seemed to become reality. The cabin was there, through
the woods, lights beaming through the windows. And as sight
merged with dream-vision, she felt she was again in motion,
acting out a series of functions she could not explain, all done
because of the whispery suggestion that powered her will.

The deafness from the blast took longer to subside, but in
time it did lift. What she heard first sounded like rain, but it was
not rain. It carried the same frantic disorder, but there was a
crackling, explosive sound as well. It was the sound of forest
debris being consumed. It was the sound of sudden drafts and
leaves disintegrating into dust. It was the sound of destruction.
The sound of fire.

She pushed herself slowly to her feet. The lightning had split
an oak from branch to ground, and in the cleavage and at the
base of the trunk flames were sucking life from the forest. She
watched as the fire grew from a wild display of yellow tongues

violently slapping at the air, to a cohesive force of power and energy.

Standing before this phenomenon of heat and light, for the first time she felt no subconscious call to action. Reality remained suspect, but dream or not, at least it was *her* dream. *Her* thoughts. Yet despite this new mental freedom, she was still trapped in a world of paradox. She could not move. She could only stand and stare. And in her dream, the fire stared back.

The flash of lightning lingered as an afterimage in Maggie's eyes as if it had been burned into her optic nerve. She remained sitting on the pine chair clutching her daughter, still trying to shield her eyes from the glare, for a good sixty seconds after the blast. It could have been only a few moments, given how unable she was to measure time. It seemed to have stopped for her, like the lightning bolt itself.

Sharon relaxed her grip first, as if her mother's fear had acted as a powerful vacuum, leaching her own fear from her chest. "Mommy. Look."

Maggie let her eyes unclench. Her grip around her daughter eased. She looked where Sharon pointed, toward the window. The glare of lightning seemed to still be there. Was the afterimage scorched so deeply in her eyes?

Maggie let her arms drop from her daughter; then she eased her back as she stood. Slowly, she began to walk toward the window that seemed to glow with the flash of the storm. It was bright outside, but it wasn't the blinding glare of a lightning bolt striking close. It was an uneven source, yet it had continuity, a flickering, wavy light that glinted off the varnished logs just inside the glass.

At the window, Maggie peered toward the woods. She expected to see the fire, so when she confirmed that expectation, she didn't react with any surprise. Her nerves were actually held in check at first, because it was not a wild conflagration, but a localized blaze. It seemed well into the trees, and as she watched, it was getting smaller. But brighter. More intense.

Maggie moved quickly to the other window. "What is it, Mommy?" her daughter asked, but Maggie did not respond. It was as if she didn't hear her, so intent was she on the fire. On what she thought she saw.

From the other perspective, the fire seemed to have changed. Was it even more intense? Or simply closer? Maggie began to feel her stomach tighten. The fire seemed to be moving, toward the cabin, on a direct line. She went to the first window. It *was* closer. She was sure of it. And it was moving. Faster. Toward the cabin. As if it were . . . running.

Maggie spun away from the window. "Sharon! Get your coat. From the closet. And your rubber boots."

"But Mom—"

"Do it!" she shouted. "Now!"

As her daughter turned, Maggie stood as though paralyzed for a moment. Paralyzed by indecision. By thoughts that came at her from every angle. The phone, she thought, and actually started looking for it on the kitchen wall, where it was at home. But there was no phone. Of course there wasn't. The lines didn't come out this far.

Another crack of thunder split the sky overhead, and Maggie jumped. As though energized by the electrical discharge, she began moving, around the end of the table. Another atmospheric blast, and she stopped. She was shaking, uncertain whether to move or stand still. If the fire came, was there anything she could do? What should she save?

"Mommy? Could you help me?" Sharon was trying to put on her yellow raincoat, but a snap at the bottom was already fixed. She had one arm in a sleeve, the other bent awkwardly behind her, trying to force the jacket open.

"Of course, darling." At last, a clear focus to her mind. What she should do. She took a step, but then noticed the two bowls on the table. She stopped, staring. Again the indecision.

"Mom—my!"

"Just a second." Something about the bowls froze her to the spot. She tried to think, to analyze, but everything was happening so fast. So many ideas were flashing in her head at once, she couldn't figure out what they meant. Without realizing what she was doing, she was picking up the bowls, carrying them to the counter, about to place them in the sink.

"Mom-my!" her daughter screamed and the lightning exploded and Maggie dropped the bowls, both of them shattering on the stainless steel. She spun toward Sharon. She was twisting, fighting the raincoat, crying.

Maggie dashed across the room and tried to open the bottom snap. It was snagged, or else she had lost her dexterity, her patience. She pulled again, but it was stuck solid. Her daughter's wails suddenly rose in pitch. Maggie grabbed each side of the coat and ripped it open. "Get your boots on!"

Sharon dropped to the floor, still crying, and started to pull on her bright red rubber boots. Maggie pulled her own rain parka from a hook at the side of the closet, flinging it over her back. As she reached for her own boots, thick green ones still flecked with black muck from the riverbank, there was another blast. Not the sharp sound of thunder and a lightning bolt crashing into the woods, but a deeper concussion. As if something heavy had fallen into soft earth. As if something of substance but no mass had thrust against the cabin. Against the side wall. Maggie turned, then screamed. Fire raged against the side windows.

She seemed to be at the center of the fire, but she was not burning. There was no pain, no external heat. Only the sensation of being enveloped by fire.

She seemed to be moving away, and yet the cabin grew closer. As before, she had no control over what appeared in her mind, and what appeared in her mind were competing visions of reality. She could see the trees and the vegetation, and in a few moments she imagined her car was just ahead. But at the same time she could see the cabin, the individual logs piled horizontally, the paned windows. It was as if she was peering out a black hole rimmed by fire, fire that did not burn. Then she was at the window, of her car, of the cabin.

She looked inside, and as she did, her chest heaved. The weakness came back in a rush. She felt fatigued, feverish, ready to collapse. Her mind began to spin in a dizzying whirl. It was as it had been before, except that the confusion was worse. Actual sight and mental suggestion were not merging into one, but were growing more distinct. She was moving in opposite directions. She was trying to get away. She was trying to get closer. She was clawing at bare glass. She was fumbling with the latch. Nothing seemed to make sense. It was dark and she was alone. It was bright and she could see faces. She threw her head back in anger, in frustration. That which was dream seemed real, and that which was real could only be dream. The competing visions spiraled together, spawning mental incoherence. There was no order, no direction. Except for one thing. One imperative: She had to regain her strength. She had to get inside.

• • •

The fire sprayed against the windows as if blown by a gas torch. It spread out flat against the glass, billowing toward the edges, building up along the panes. The narrow strips of wood that crisscrossed the windows became linear concentrations of white-hot light. The fire was searching the wood, seeking a way inside.

Maggie watched in horror the action of the fire. It seemed to have method to its attack, and Maggie found herself trying to analyze the fire, guessing what it was going to do. It was like watching a rabid dog rather than an element of no substance. She stood there with one boot on, the other still in her hand as if afraid to move, as if afraid to incite it to further madness. And yet its designs were obvious. It was going to come through.

Maggie quickly scanned the room, and suddenly it looked like a tinder box. Newspaper on the side table. Books on a shelf. Paper in the baskets. Firewood by the hearth. Pine furniture layered with varnish. And fabric everywhere, curtains, rugs, upholstery. Clothing!

"Hurry, Sharon," she shouted, pulling on her boot. The place would flash fire in an instant. They had to get outside to the rain.

Maggie grabbed Sharon by the shoulder, but the girl was stiffened by terror. She couldn't seem to move on her own, and as Maggie pulled, her small knees locked. "We're going outside. Hurry, honey."

Sharon's eyes suddenly widened. Maggie spun toward the window. Flickers of flame were penetrating into the interior. One of the panes was blackened and charred and ready to give way. Maggie grabbed her daughter and hoisted her in her arms and started toward the front door. She took two steps, three steps, and then she was traveling backward. Thrust backward by the force of a blast. The window imploded into the house, spraying tiny shards of heated glass and flame throughout the room.

The force knocked Maggie against the wall, and she was momentarily stunned. It took a few seconds for her to realize what had actually happened. A few more to realize that she no longer had Sharon. Her daughter was stumbling backward, moving away from the front door, toward the far corner of the room.

Maggie lunged toward her, tripped, and fell, her knee jabbing into broken glass. Knots of flame had struck throughout the room, and a hundred fires were beginning to form. "Come here, baby," she said, holding out her hand.

The second window burst, and a new torrent of fire flared inside on a rush of superheated air. Sharon shrieked in terror, pulling farther away from the fire, farther away from her mother.

Ribbons of small flames slashed across the rug between Maggie and her daughter. It was only a matter of time before they took hold, before the entire place was an inferno. Maggie pushed herself to her feet, the glass cutting into the palms of her hands. She stepped through the lines of fire toward the back corner of the room. When she reached Sharon, she tried to grab her to hoist her off the floor. But the girl resisted, pressing herself back against the wood. Her eyes seemed like blank plates; her face was chalky white despite the heat building in the cabin. She was shrieking at the top of her lungs.

Maggie forced her arms around behind her daughter, then hefted her to her chest. She turned and started running as best she could toward the front door. The sound of fire ripping through the cabin, the sound of her daughter's screams in her ears, combined to form a secondary assault on her, penetrating deep inside her skull, pounding, hammering, seemingly ready to split her head wide open.

At the door she twisted the knob and swung it open. Outside was the rain, the cool, forgiving rain.

"Mommy!"

Maggie started outside. "It's okay, darling. We're safe."

"Mommy!" The call was more distant this time, almost lost amid the building rage of the fire.

Maggie thrust Sharon away from her chest so she could see her face. She was crying still, tears sheeting across her cheeks. And as she stared at her daughter, fresh horror began to creep into her consciousness. She wheeled around back, toward the interior.

Jagged spikes of flames were rising from the couch. The lit lines across the rugs were rising higher as they spread. The curtains were already blazing. The wood of the stairway was beginning to char.

The stairway! At the very top. "Jimmy!"

In the woods it was as dark as midnight. The clouds were that thick, the storm was that intense.

John Verhoven wanted to hurry his daughter along. But she could only go so fast. *He* could only go so fast, restricted by the bulky canvas waders that billowed up to his chest, fixed over his shoulders by suspenders.

They were following the trail that ran alongside the river back toward the cabin. The tree cover had protected them from the rain for a while, but that was now well saturated, and water from the leaves fell in large drops down upon them. A bolt of lightning crackled in the sky, and for a strobelike moment the forest flickered between day and night, their environment of spiked pine needles and soggy oak leaves alternating between harsh silhouette and a kind of negative image. Lindsey was halted by the flash, but John didn't see her stop. He banged right into her.

Lindsey cried out and turned abruptly around. She stared at her father with something different from innocence. It was fear, childlike and unrestricted. Because of the dark, the intermittent light, the storm.

John went down to one knee. "It's okay, honey. We're almost home. We'll be there in a few minutes. Look around you. You remember the trail, don't you? Where we are?"

Lindsey forced a gulp, but she still couldn't speak. Looking around at the trees, at the drooping branches, she nodded.

"All right then," he said. "Let's go."

He walked next to her now, holding her hand, his legs brushing through the ferns and bushes because he was forced off the trail. As they continued forward, as he concentrated on avoiding low-hanging branches, he began to become aware of a change. Up ahead, through the trees. It was light, out of direct eyesight, but enough to form a glow some indeterminate distance ahead. It must be the cabin, he thought. Mags had been awakened by the storm. She had the lights on. She would be there on the porch, worried, waiting for them.

He tried to pick up the pace, but now it was he who held them back, because of the brush. His concentration alternated between his path and the glow ahead, and the brighter the light grew, the more he came to notice that it was not a steady source. Rather, it was a wavering, glimmering light. Not the even illumination of electricity. But the flickering radiance of fire.

"My God." John had come to a halt.

"What is it, Daddy?" Lindsey said.

He tore his eyes away from the distant fire and turned his daughter toward him. His hands on both shoulders, his face bent down near hers, he said, "You can follow the trail back to the cabin, can't you?"

"Y-yes. But why? Where are you going?"

"I have to hurry ahead. I'm afraid your mother might be in trouble."

Lindsey's eyes opened wider. She began to tremble as she looked from her dad toward the wavering light through the trees.

"Just stay on the trail. Hear me?" She nodded absently. John lingered for another long second, staring at young Lindsey, sweet Lindsey; then he dropped his rod, broke away from her, and started to run toward the cabin, leaving her behind. Leaving her alone and scared. And vulnerable.

"Oh, dear God. Dear sweet Jesus. No!"

Maggie was besieged by confusion, by disbelief. He wasn't here. He wasn't supposed to be here. He was fishing. With his father.

Suddenly, the whole early morning scene convulsed in confused images in her mind, and she was struck by a new horror: Was John up there too? Lindsey?

"Mo—" Jimmy started to call out again, but broke off in a fit of coughing. Smoke that had collected in the peaked ceiling was billowing downward like violent thunderheads. Jimmy gripped the rail and bent over at his stomach.

Maggie pushed Sharon onto the porch. "Get outside. Run!" she shouted. Then, without seeing if her daughter heeded the command, without determining if Sharon possessed the ability to overcome her paralysis of terror, Maggie started back into the cabin.

A sudden ball of flame boiled upward, and she raised her coat reflexively, trying to shield her face. The fire seemed to have a force of its own, and it threw her back, against the side wall. Flattened against the wood, Maggie couldn't help but take a moment to survey the scene, the hellish spectacle of blue-tinged flames slashing violently at the air within the cabin, seeking to grow higher, delving deeper into the plentiful tinder of the room. She looked toward the top of the staircase. Jimmy was staring at her as if in a trance, gasping for breath. She pushed off the wall, slipping along the outer perimeter of the room. Just a few more steps and she'd be at the bottom of the stairs.

A roar of wind more than fire seemed to pull Maggie back. She staggered against the force, but couldn't make much headway. She turned toward the center of the cabin, shielding her face from the blast of heat. Fire swirled toward a central focus in great long plumes, spiraling together in a maelstrom of color and smoke, shadow and glare. The fire created a centrifugal force that sucked each of the room's individual flames into a single mass, a solitary column that spun faster, hotter, feeding on itself.

The column blossomed upward, its golden-corded helix becoming denser, brighter, all the while increasing its spiraled flow. It seemed to be stealing the oxygen from the room, from Maggie's lungs. She gasped for breath, forcing her eyes to look up toward her son. He was still hanging on, still waiting for her. With her arms stiff against the side wall, she started toward him again. As she took her first step, one of the flaming cords of yellow twined around the central core broke free and was flung toward the wall below the upper balcony. Before it hit, this narrow stretch of fire suddenly reared back, as if coiling; then near the tip it began to split apart into five separate flames, five distinct spikes of light, five sharp-lined tongues of yellow that began to arc in synchrony, five—

Maggie screamed. Her hands clutched the side of her head in horror and disbelief. The flaming appendage had split into five claws, and it slashed forward, raking across the back wall just below where Jimmy stood on the balcony.

Powered by her terror, by instincts beyond self-preservation, Maggie lunged toward the staircase. Nearly there, she heard a slashing sound, the sound of a whip cutting through the air. She shouted out in surprise, in pain, and then she crashed to the floor. She was pulled to the floor. Her ankles suffered a burning, razored feeling, and when she looked down, a coil of fire was just beginning to loosen from her legs. It reared back, splitting into five separate flames.

Maggie watched them rise, then forced herself to look away, toward the staircase. The top of the staircase. Then she turned toward the door. She could never make it. She lacked the will even to try. She just wanted it to be over. But then she noticed her. Sharon. Still standing there, paralyzed on the threshold, watching her, watching the fire.

"Go," Maggie yelled, trying to rise. "Run!"

John Verhoven felt as if he were going in slow motion. The loose, heavy fabric of the waders shortened his stride, the soft earth seemed to grab at every step, and the extra effort required increasingly robbed his lungs of the capacity to provide oxygen to his body.

Each pounding footfall resonated dully in the center of his chest, a weak counterpoint to the frantic rush of his heart. Fatigue wasn't a factor, powered as he was by his fear, his anguish, his frustration at not moving faster. Working against him was the conspiracy of the woods. His arms flailed wildly in front of him, sweeping branches out of the way, but still, pointed twigs and prickly needles left their marks on him, stabbing his cheeks, slashing across the side of his neck.

The fire was there; he could see the signs of it for sure. And then he heard the scream, a high-pitched shriek that was beyond fear, beyond terror. It was a continuing wail of agony, and as that sound wavered above all else in the lively atmosphere of the storm, it was as if he could feel the pain, as if he shared the torment, as if he suffered the same torture that powered that cry.

He burst from the trail into the cleared area in front of the cabin. He paused only long enough to scan the expanse of grass tufts that sloped down toward the river, hoping that he would see his family, hoping they had made it out. But the lot was vacant, bathed only in a sickly orange glow from the flames inside the cabin.

John rushed toward the front door, and as soon as it came into full view, he halted again. He was stopped dead not because he searched for something that wasn't there, but rather because of what he saw: a small figure, black in silhouette because of the fire behind her, the fire around her.

"Sharon!" he screamed and bolted forward in the same instant. He seemed again to be dropped into a world of slow motion where the activity of his mind far outpaced the action of his body. Even what he witnessed seemed to grow sluggish; the flames holding back their billowing arches; the tiny, blackened arms of his daughter pinwheeling around her head. His vision narrowed, until it was as if he were peering into a cone. All he could see was his little girl. All he could visualize was her futile battle against the fire. And everything went strangely, deathly silent. There was no sound of the blaze, no sound of his daughter's voice, no sound even of his own heart. So focused was his concern that he had not noticed what the fire had done. He didn't realize that he was no longer running. He didn't realize that it was happening to him.

Before he fell to his knees, he turned toward the trees, toward the trail. He wanted to cry out in warning, to yell at Lindsey to stay away, but in his vacuum of sound and feeling he couldn't hear if he had made a sound. For all he could tell, his voice was nothing more than a mere puff of fire.

Lindsey struggled through the woods. She had picked up her father's rod, and, together, both eight-foot bamboo lengths continually snagged the leafy borders of the trail.

Through it all—the minor struggles, the untangling of the narrow tips—she tried to keep her eyes on the wavering glow of reflected firelight through the trees. As she got closer, when she could finally see brief flashes of the flames themselves, she noticed that it was not one fire but two. There was a smaller one, well away from the house, in the front yard.

The rods slipped from her hands. She stepped beyond the last of the alders blocking her view. Slowly, her head began to shake from side to side. Gradually, recognition began to take shape in her mind, and her voice became a staccato monotone as she tried to deny what she was seeing. "No, no, no," she whimpered over and over, the tiny gasps of breath nothing more than defiance stillborn.

As if carried on legs not her own, she progressed out into the clearing, circling in front of the vertical column of fire in the yard. Her words of denial changed, but the repetitive cadence remained the same. "Daddy," she breathed, as if everything she valued in life was tied up in that one word. "Daddy, Daddy, Daddy," she continued, as if every wish she'd ever wished were combined into a single word, a single cry, a single desire.

She wanted to rush up to her father, to let him wrap his arms around her, and she almost did just that. She almost ran into the flames. But it was not her father. Not all of it, anyway. Where his eyes should have been were red-hot coals of fire, and rather than moving with his usual ease, his body was stiff and vibrating, as if electrified. She couldn't tell if it was clothes or skin, but whatever it was turned black and cracked into surface ash, covering ember as on a log in a camp fire. Then the blackened shape fell away, collapsing in a heap on the ground. But the other thing did not.

Lindsey's monotone of denial, then hope, fell silent. It was as if she had been transported to a land of fantasy, and in this foreign landscape she tried to explain what she was seeing. Fortunately for her understanding, this world of fantasy was not ruled by logic. And children, by their nature, are not burdened by the need for rational explanation. To them, monsters are real. And that's what she saw, rising above what had once been a man. And it saw her.

Though Lindsey could not have isolated the internal commands that caused one foot to slide backward, followed by the other in an awkward back step, she was indeed moving. It was as though her nervous system operated at one level, while her mind was on another. Her mind remained focused on the flames that had come to approximate a bipedal form, a creature of shifting physique with shoots of fire like devil's horns growing then leaping free from every section of its frame. At least that's how it appeared in her eyes, her twelve-year-old eyes steeped in juvenile imagination. She couldn't be sure exactly what it resembled, because it seemed to change. Like a fire in the grate, it flashed and snapped and gyrated in infinite variations. Except in one regard. In the middle of the uppermost aspect of the fire-being, there were changeless shadows—deep, sunken eye sockets with single red embers afloat in the very center of the black holes. Embers that seemed trained on her eyes.

A jagged tear suddenly opened below the twin shadows in the face of flame, and as it gapped wider, narrowing spikes of white-hot light tapered until they separated in the middle, revealing daggered fangs of fire. The field of what was pure energy threw its head back and began to imitate what Lindsey would have described as the thrashing motion of a werewolf howling at the night sky. It resembled that act, except that the noise emitted was not a growl, but a throaty rush of heated air like the sound of a blast furnace given sudden vent through an opened flue. It seemed a display of triumph. Or was it anticipation?

The cohesive conflagration that was the mass of flames began to move. As it did, the separation within Lindsey of nervous commands and conscious thought began to disintegrate. She began to realize what she was doing, what was happening, what was going to happen.

The thing was fast coming closer. She stumbled backward, her booted heels tripping over roots, on tufts of grass, on any manner of forest obstruction. The fire raced as though propelled by the wind. Lindsey's hearing became suddenly acute, infected with the adrenal tension that had been released in her system. She could hear the rush of flames, the throaty brush of hot air, the individual puffs of vapor from raindrops reduced to steam as they came near the sharp-pointed spikes of light. And she could feel the heat, getting closer, hotter. Then suddenly there was the sound of wind by her ears. Not the heated rush of the fire, but the cool air of the dawn storm.

She was falling, reeling backward, sailing off the last hump of the bank, and for a moment she was weightless and free and distracted from the horror that pursued her. Then she hit the surface of the river hard, and at first she floated, drifting backward on the icy wetness, her hands flailing behind her for support. But quickly the water breached the top of her waders, and she began to sink. She was flat on her back, and the water rushed over her chest, submerging her neck, and the sides of both her cheeks. She tried to thrust her head upward, but the weight of the water filling the canvas garment was too much to resist. Her mouth dipped below the surface, and she gagged. One final buck upward and she was able to gasp a bit of air. Then she was back under, sinking to the bottom.

The river was only two or three feet deep, and suddenly she thought of countless warnings from her father. All it took was two inches, he would say, if you can't get up.

Her thumbs hooked under the suspenders, and she snapped them off her shoulders. Letting the current roll her like a log, she came over to her knees. Grabbing the tops of the waders, she peeled them down to the middle of her stomach, to her waist. Then with a muscular surge she shot her head above the surface and air rushed into her chest. She sucked in deeply, inhaling nearly equal parts oxygen and water, which caused her to gag and spit and wretch for more air.

Below her waist the pressure had flattened the waders to her legs, preventing the inflow of any water, but the same pressure prevented her from taking them off completely. On her knees, neck-deep in the river, she seemed trapped. And above her, on the bank, the bipedal column of fire lifted a clawed appendage, slinging it forward.

Lindsey turned her head, and the daggered claws cut across her neck, over her cheek and across her chin. She screamed, falling backward, underwater. The current rolled her again, onto her back, and with her eyes open, she could see the fire, magnified into something even larger than it was. She pushed off the bottom and broke the surface, gasping for more air, and instantly the creature struck again. She could feel it across her scalp; she could hear the sizzle as it touched the water, and then she slipped under again.

Viewing the lighted form through the crystal liquid, it seemed strangely clearer, crisper, brighter, like sunlight reflected through a diamond. She could see it rear back, wolflike, but this time neither in triumph nor in anticipation. It thrashed from side to side in frustration, in anger, and then it was coming toward her, slicing through the air, then the water itself.

Oh my God, she thought. It was coming underwater, after her. The light penetrated the depths, coming down to her chest, wrapping around her arm. She could hear the hiss of the water; she could see the rise of bubbles; she could feel the feathery pressure on her skin. But it did not burn! The burning was only in her chest, in her lungs. She needed air!

The appendage retracted, and Lindsey broke the surface, convulsing in great heaves of breath. She needed to stand up, to let her lungs adjust, to bring some manner of normalcy back to the act of breathing. But she could not. It was coming for her. The claws, the fire, the slashing reach of the beast.

She went down again, and again she was pursued by the light. She rolled so she faced the bottom; then she began to stroke the pebbled subsurface, grabbing rocks, wavy strands of river grass, sinking her fingers into the sand, whatever she could use to propel herself downstream. And each time she broke the surface, there was the light, the fire, the burning. Each time she went under, there was the cold, the silence, the darkness. She was drifting, falling, in the river, in her mind. It was cold, so cold, and numbing. The deadness of feeling seemed to deepen, penetrating into her chest, stealing the power of her heart. It seeped higher, into her skull, behind the orbs of her eyes, bringing blackness as it advanced.

She was tired of fighting, tired of the pain. The burning, the freezing, the lack of air. Then against this black-scape that her mind was becoming, she saw her father. He seemed to be beckoning to her. Telling her to join them. It was so much easier that way, just to give up. As he had. As they all had.

Lindsey could sense that she was slackening her muscles. She was losing her resolve. She was giving up the battle. She was drifting, just drifting, deeper into the black. Until at last, she slipped totally into darkness.

• • •

Her body seemed at rest, but her mind was active. She had retreated to a realm of silence, but she could hear the screams. She felt the chill of rain, but she could also feel the fire.

Her contrary world was a world of extremes, a hundred battles being waged at the same time, all with the same goal. Control of her mind.

The lines of engagement were growing closer. She was visited again by the haunting, the eighteen-inch sign that was so real in her dreams it seemed actually to come into existence. She could sense the darkness, the hurried rush through the trees, and then her entire body tensed as the cracks of lightning exploded above her, in front of her, inside of her. She could feel the energy of the fire, and she could feel the confusion. The confusion of the battle. The confusion of whether reality had lost its hold, or her subconscious had forged a new reality. She was caught between the two, a witness to the violence, a victim of the extremes. She was being thrashed back and forth, weakened by the assaults, and all the while she could hear the voices. The torment. The sounds of death. The screams.

The screams! They entered her. They took control of her nerves. They sparked throughout her system, sending vibrant signals into her legs, her arms, the very center of her chest. Awake or asleep, it no longer mattered. The paradoxes were collapsing in on themselves. Turmoil reigned within her. She was failing, dying, the individual threads of neurons ready to ignite and flare in one final, incandescent expulsion of energy. One final end to the contradictions.

The screams took on a power and a force of their own. They began to solidify. They filled her lungs with a mass that constricted her breathing. They grew in volume, dominating every attempt at independent thought. She could hear them in her mind. She could hear them in her ears. *The screams!*

Jean was sitting up in bed, the screams echoing in the room. They were her screams, her torment. Her entire body was like a single clenched fist. And then she was moving, swaying from side to side. Someone was on the bed with her, sitting next to her, wrapping an arm around her shoulders, gently rocking her back and forth.

"It's okay, it's okay," Miriam Goodmedicine was saying, over and over, and gradually her voice had an effect. The screaming came to an end. "You've had a bad dream," she said, continuing to rock her, "but everything's all right now. You're awake. You're going to be fine."

She *was* awake. She was in bed, in the upstairs dormer room of Mrs. Goodmedicine's house.

"No wonder you had a bad dream," Miriam said, feeling her forehead. "You're burning up. And your hair. It's soaking wet."

Jean was slowly becoming aware of things. Who she was. Where she was. And where she was not. She recalled the haunting, as well as the rest of the contrary world of continuing paradox, and though sitting there in bed seemed incontrovertible proof that none of it had been real, she nonetheless felt certain it had not been a dream.

Chapter 15

It seemed as if he had just fallen asleep when the knock came at the door. It had been a fitful night, not because of anything he dreamt, but because of real visions worse than any nightmare.

Slowly, Fielding got out of bed and pulled on a pair of pants. It was the proprietor of the motel at the door. "I got a call from Miriam Goodmedicine," he said. "She wants to see you at her place right away."

"Did she say why?"

"No. But by the sound of her voice, I wouldn't waste any time."

Fielding retreated back into the cabin, and as he did, he retreated back into the wakeful nightmare. The knot of sick tension was there in the pit of his stomach, but worse than that was the uncertainty, over what had happened, what *was* happening. And what was going to happen.

It had to do with Jean Shawshequay. He was sure of it. He had chosen last night not to press the issue of the small backpack, but as he got dressed, he realized he should have.

The flash of the propane lantern had changed her. Was it shock from being suddenly engulfed in flames? Did she hit her head when she fell? Was it a concussion? Was the injury to her head affecting her now?

Whatever questions he posed to himself, they were all framed within the context of some manner of physical malady affecting her. As a man of science, he had no other way of approaching things. He had no other option but to look for the bits of rationality that surely were there. As his thoughts continued to turn over in his mind, he came to feel that searching for answers was a premature exercise. Conclusions based on incomplete data were not conclusions at all, but guesses. So, as he would at an excavation, Fielding knew he must first acquire all relevant information. Only then would he be in a position to analyze the data and formulate an opinion.

As he drove to Miriam Goodmedicine's, this simple review
of the scientific process lessened his state of tension, lifting the
anxiety that had kept him awake so much of the night. But for
all his control, he sensed it was merely a state of induced calm,
one that could unravel in a hurry.

Miriam Goodmedicine looked drawn and tired when she
opened the door, but Fielding didn't ask about her. He asked
about Jean. "How is she?" he said simply.

Miriam only shook her head as she ushered Fielding inside.

"What's wrong with her?"

"I don't know," Miriam said. "And neither does the doctor,
near as I can tell."

"Doctor?"

"He left a little bit ago. She seems like she's got a fever or
something, but the doctor said no. There's no temperature. He
thinks she's got herself all worked up because of stress, or anxiety. He left a prescription for something to settle her down, and
Ray's out picking that up right now."

There was a bang from upstairs, like a furniture leg hitting
the floor, followed by a moan. Fielding looked up the staircase.

"There's something more," Miriam said, and Fielding turned
back toward her. "She didn't talk much when the doctor was
with her, but before that . . ."

Fielding had to prompt her. "What did she say?"

"I'm not sure exactly. She had had a bad dream, and maybe it
was just the fever—the stress, rather—but whatever got her
talking, to me she wasn't making much sense."

None of it made much sense, Fielding thought. From the invisible jaws in Buck Billings's dead camp fire to the blue flame
in the cave.

"You'd better get up there," Miriam said. "Maybe you'll be
able to understand her."

Fielding's eyes strayed away from hers, eventually returning
to the stairs. He started up, then paused on the third step. "Did
you see a small backpack in her room?"

Miriam was momentarily puzzled, more by the question itself than her memory. "A gray one? REI?"

"Yes."

"I think it's on the side chair. In the corner."

Fielding continued up the stairs. He knocked, opening the
door a crack to announce himself. As he did, he could hear the

sound of heavy breathing, a snorting sound almost, and the rapid thrashing of sheets and covers. He stepped inside.

What he saw was almost as inexplicable as what he had imagined he saw inside the cave. Jean gripped both bedposts at the head of the bed, and was throwing herself back and forth on the mattress, breathing violently. Fielding just stood there and watched, until suddenly, she sat straight up in bed and stared at him.

She maintained her rigid posture for a few moments, then in a voice devoid of all emotion, she whispered, "They're dead." Her eyes drifted away from his, looking past him, as if locking on some invisible point on the wall. "They're all dead."

Fielding blinked once, twice. Though his face was suddenly as drained as Jean's, inside his mind worked furiously. Was she referring to the deputy and the poacher? The people massacred in the cave? Or somebody else?

Jean's shoulders slumped; then her entire body seemed to sag and she slowly collapsed back to the mattress. Fielding strode to her bedside. She was lying almost peacefully, and for a moment he was frozen by indecision. He wanted to pursue his questions, but he could see she needed rest. Then he thought of last night and the questions he should have asked but hadn't, and he reached his hand to her shoulder and touched it lightly. She looked up at him. "Who's dead?" he asked.

Jean's eyes shut as if fatigue were overcoming her. When she gathered her strength, she looked at him again, saying, "I don't know."

As Miriam had warned, she wasn't making sense. Fielding eased himself onto the edge of the bed.

"But I saw it happen," Jean said as if she knew what he was about to say. "I saw them die."

"Was this last night?"

She nodded.

"But you were with me last night. I dropped you off right here and you came inside."

"It wasn't here. It was back there, in the woods."

"Are you saying you went out to the woods by yourself? Later?"

"No. I mean, I must have. I saw it, didn't I?" She rolled to her side, away from him. Then in the next moment she dropped back flat again, bringing her hands to the sides of her head. "Oh,

I don't know, I don't know. I must have been out there. How else could I have seen it?"

Fielding watched her silently for a few moments, allowing her time to consider the alternatives herself. "It was a dream," he said at last. "That's all."

"It wasn't a dream," she said angrily.

Again a pause, then, "Miriam said you had a bad dream."

Jean looked away. She remembered waking up screaming, Miriam comforting her. But the rest? "It couldn't have been a dream," she said, but this time in a tone clearly expressing her own doubt. She looked at Fielding. "It was so real."

It *was* so real, Fielding repeated in his mind. He looked toward the chair in the corner. His small gray backpack rested on the wicker seat, the handle of his folding shovel protruding from the top.

"There was a road," Jean continued, "like the one out to the sinkhole—"

"It *was* the sinkhole road, as you pictured it in your dream."

"No. At least I don't think so. It was different. And there was a—" Jean broke off, her eyes suddenly clenching as if a headache had sliced full-blown into her cranium.

"What is it?"

She waved him off, forcing herself up to one elbow, forcing herself to remember. "There was a cabin, through the trees. I could see a cabin, and a fire. I'm sure I didn't walk toward the cabin, and yet . . ." Jean's face became contorted with the effort to remember. As it had been the first time, there was confusion. As if two different things were happening at once. "I . . . I'm sure I was moving away . . ." She gasped.

"Don't force yourself," Fielding said.

She wasn't looking at him. She wasn't listening to him. "I was walking back to my car, and yet I was getting closer to the cabin." Jean suddenly sat full upright, gasping heavily. She bent at the waist, holding her stomach.

"Lie down," Fielding said, wrapping his arm around her shoulders, trying to pull her down to the mattress. "This isn't helping anything."

She resisted him. "Inside, I could see faces." She lifted her eyes to Fielding. "I can still see them," she continued, growing stronger, "and then I saw—"

"You didn't *see* anything. You were tired. You had a bad experience at the cave. You were thinking about the lantern exploding, the two men who have died. It all mixed together in your dream. The same thing as happened—" Fielding caught himself.

Jean leaned closer. "To you?"

Fielding let his hand slip off her shoulder. He shook his head. "You dreamed it too?"

"No."

Jean studied his face, thinking. "What was it you saw in the cave?"

"You know what happened. You were there."

Jean swung her legs rapidly underneath her, raising herself to her knees. "What was it that happened to me?"

"The propane canister pulled loose. The gas flashed . . ."

"That wasn't all of it. You saw something. You said we'd talk about it later."

Fielding stood, turning his back to her, walking aimlessly toward the corner. Toward his gray pack on the chair.

"Chris! *What did you see?*"

Slowly, he turned, then shrugged. "It was an illusion. There was the propane flash, the darkness, the flashlight on the ground. And, uh, for a second . . ." He swallowed, then took a breath. "For a second, it seemed like the blue fire was inside of you."

Jean settled back on her calves, absorbing the information.

"But it was an illusion. Weaved from strands of things that had been happening. Just like happened with you, in your dream."

Jean flung the sheets from the bed and swung her feet quickly to the floor. "I'm going out there."

"Going out where?"

"To the cabin."

"You can't go anywhere. Not how you're feeling."

Jean was still wearing what she had had on last night, and as she collected her shoes, she said, "I feel fine."

Fielding was about to protest further, but then he hesitated. He knew there was nothing he could do that would stop her. As she started putting on her shoes, he turned to the chair in the corner. He looked again at the handle of his folding shovel as it protruded from the top corner of the gray pack. He reached tentatively to the handle, nudging it with one finger. Then he opened the pack. Besides the shovel, inside were the remains of the lantern, a flashlight, and a coil of rope. Just what he had put in it last night. He turned back to Jean. She was nearly ready. "Mind if I take this?"

As she looked at the pack, her brows came together in an expression that was hard to read. At first it appeared to Fielding as if she were surprised to see it there. As if she had no idea why it was there. But as they left the room, as they walked down the stairs, Fielding couldn't help but sense that in her expression had been the spark of a memory. It was as if for the briefest flash of an instant, she had remembered.

At the head of the stairs leading to Jean's bedroom, a short hallway branched off to the left. It led to a walk-in closet. In front of the closet there was three feet of space, just enough to allow the door to be opened and not interfere with the bedroom entrance.

After Jean Shawshequay and the archaeologist passed, Ray Goodmedicine emerged from that space. He had returned with the medicine for Jean, but as he came up the stairs, he couldn't help but overhear the conversation. As he lingered in the shadows by the linen closet, he listened to the talk of illusions that both of them suffered. And he couldn't help but think of what he thought he had witnessed in the fire in front of Makwamacatawa.

Fielding hadn't thought they would find a road marked with a wooden sign before the sinkhole cutoff, but as soon as he saw it, he remembered seeing it before. It was just such an insignificant detail that it hadn't made an impression.

The sign hung from a cut section of unfinished tree limb that extended out from a post. Inscribed in flowing script was the family name, Verhoven's.

"This is it," Jean said.

As the Jeep truck turned then slipped deeper into the woods, Jean studied the curves of the road, the banks of vegetation, the slanting trunk of a dead tree caught in mid-fall in the yoke of another. What she saw seemed familiar, and yet it wasn't. The diversity of the woodlands blended together into a kind of sameness, and they could just as easily have been on the road to the excavation or any of a dozen other dirt trails near Watersdrop.

When they first caught a glimpse of the cabin through the trees, neither was surprised. It was a private road, after all, marked by a sign on the highway. They expected a river cabin at the end of it.

The canopy acted as a barrier to airborne scents, but the closer the truck came to the open area around the log structure, the more they could notice the odor. It was a strong smell, the heavy odor of charred wood doused with water.

As the truck slipped between the last of the trees and the cabin came into full view, Jean suffered a deadening pang of weakness. She couldn't speak. She could barely breathe.

The sheriff's car was in the driveway, parked behind another patrol vehicle. Next to the two police cars was an ambulance, angled off the gravel drive onto the grass. And around the side of the cabin was an emergency step-van from the fire department. None of the vehicles had their emergency lights on. Apparently, there was no more urgency.

When they stopped and got out of the Jeep, Deputy Sheriff Kinsey appeared around the front corner of the cabin. Instead of coming toward them, he went back for the sheriff.

Walking slowly, unsteadily, Fielding moved along the north wall, Jean a few steps behind. Parts of the log wall seemed barely touched by the fire, but around the two windows that flanked the stone chimney the charring was deep, as it would be if an interior fire had flashed to the outside.

Sheriff Halstead came around the corner of the building. "Word travels fast," he said.

Fielding looked at him blankly for a moment. "We didn't hear anything. We just—" We just what? Came out to check because Jean dreamed all this? He turned suddenly, looking for her. She was there, her face as whitish gray as the sky.

"Kinsey was the one who saw the smoke," Halstead continued. "By the time he got here, the flames were mostly out. Strange fire. It burned fast and hot, but then it seems to have gone out on its own."

"The rain?" Fielding suggested.

"It didn't rain inside." Halstead's gaze narrowed as he briefly eyed Jean Shawshequay. "How did you know about it?"

Fielding shrugged. "We were just on our way to the excavation, and we . . ."

"We smelled it," Jean said.

"Uh-huh," the sheriff grunted noncommittally. Then to Fielding, he said, "I'm glad you're here, though. I was going to send for you."

"Why's that?"

Halstead jerked his head toward the front. "Come on. I want to show you something."

Fielding glanced at Jean. He had so much he wanted to ask her, but he had no choice but to follow the sheriff. As they walked around the corner of the porch, Jean gasped and came to a halt. In the front yard, two paramedics were hunched over a black body bag. One of them was zipping it shut.

Halstead looked back at her, then said to Fielding, "Maybe she'd better wait in the car."

He nodded, then took her arm and turned her around. Leading her back around the side wall, he whispered, "Is this it? Is this what you saw?"

Jean looked at the window, then the other one. "I don't know," she breathed. She had to stop to steady herself. Her eyes fluttered shut for a moment. "I can't be sure."

Fielding glanced back toward Halstead. He was standing at the corner, eyeing them. "You wait by the truck," he said to her. "I'll be back."

As Fielding came back to the sheriff and they walked toward the front steps, Halstead said, "She wouldn't be able to take what's inside. They got three more."

"They?"

Halstead stopped dead and stared at Fielding. "You saw the burn pattern at the side. Don't tell me that was natural."

"It wasn't?"

The sheriff gazed harshly at Fielding, then turned toward the front. "You'll see. Inside."

There was another body bag just outside the front door. At first Fielding thought it was empty, but as he passed it, he could tell it was not.

"The experts won't be here until this afternoon," Halstead said just inside the door, "but with the way the fire spread, or rather didn't spread, my guess is somebody came in here with a flamethrower."

Everything inside was burned to some degree or blackened by smoke. But the sheriff was right, Fielding could see. Distinct scoring marks were apparent in various places, on the floor and the walls, as if an intense source of fire had slashed about the room.

"A fire begins in one place and spreads," Halstead pointed out. "This, it looks like fire was thrown all over."

Fielding studied the pattern of charring. "Somebody could have splashed gas around."

"Could be, but do you notice the smell?"

Fielding sniffed. "No."

"That's right. No smell of gas, or kerosene, or anything else." Halstead stepped over some debris. "Come over here. I want to show you something."

Fielding followed. Beyond the remains of what had been a couch was another body. An adult incinerated in the fashion of Buck Billings and Deputy Cole. Male or female, Fielding couldn't tell.

"Over here." Halstead had continued to the back wall and was waiting for him underneath the balcony. "What do you make of this?"

Fielding approached slowly. At first the marks were hard to distinguish because of the smoke damage. But as he drew closer, he could see an unmistakable series of deep striations, slanting downward from left to right. There were five of them, all more or less parallel. Fielding knew what they looked like, but he couldn't bring himself to say it. He couldn't say aloud that the black scoring on the wall looked like claw marks.

She felt like climbing in the truck, but instead she was moving in the opposite direction. She wanted to be away from the cabin, but something drew her closer. She seemed to be dreaming, but she was very much awake.

Jean Shawshequay wandered past the porch, then by the black plastic body bag in the front yard. One of the paramedics said something to her, and if she responded, she didn't know what she said. She felt as though she were drifting, carried forward on an impulse she could not yet identify. She seemed drawn toward the river, and when she reached the bank, she stopped and stared down into the water. She saw the submerged waves of river grass, the rocks and sand on the bottom, and most of all, she saw the constant motion of the current carrying everything downstream. She turned and followed the flow with her eyes as the river curved and was swallowed by the forest.

No longer questioning herself—asking if this was the cabin she had dreamed, were these the people she had seen die—her mind was probing other matters. Questions posed by an uncertainty not her own. An uncertainty she could not decipher.

Though she couldn't say exactly what it was, she nonetheless had the feeling that she should know. Standing there on the bank, staring downstream, it was as if she were trying to remember something. As if she were looking for something.

"I got a brother in Alaska who's got a hunting cabin on Kodiak Island," Sheriff Halstead told Fielding as the archaeologist studied the five parallel gouges on the wall. "He doesn't get over there much, and it seems the bears use his cabin as much as he does. It's a problem for a lot of the people over there. The bears just splinter the doors and go inside. Some of the people try pounding spikes through the doors, but my brother, he just leaves his door open. I was up there once, and he showed me the claw marks the bears have left, and you know what? They look just like that," he said, pointing to the scorch marks, "except that these are larger."

What manner of creature could have left these? Fielding thought. A creature large enough to scar an entire wall, yet small enough to survive in the embers of a dying camp fire. A creature born of mythology and nurtured by continuing strands of belief. A creature of little substance that drew energy from foreign sources. A creature of fire.

"Crazy, ain't it?" Halstead said.

Crazy, it was. What he was thinking. What he allowed to course through his mind. Fielding stood back from the wall. "So what do you make of it?"

"That's what I want you to tell me."

"Well, I can't deny it looks like somebody caused it. Deliberately."

"This Three Fires thing with the tribes around here," Halstead said. "Is this some kind of mark of theirs?"

"What do you mean?"

"You know, like a sign they'd leave to show they were here. Their cult signature, so to speak."

Fielding shook his head. "The Three Fires wasn't a religious thing. It was a loose confederation of sorts. That's all. They held fire in high regard, maybe even worshiped it, like most hunting societies. For that matter, like almost any early society you can think of. From the Egyptians to the Aztecs, worship of the sun—and its equivalent on earth, fire—was common."

"I realize that. But what I'm getting at is, if a bunch of Indians steeped in the old hocus-pocus came out and torched this place and they wanted to make sure we knew who did it, would they have left marks like those?"

"I've never seen anything like that associated with the Ojibwa, or any of the other Great Lakes Indians."

"Never seen five marks like that before, like on a cave wall or something?"

"No, and I think you're sniffing in the wrong place. If there are some radical elements bent on violence, why would they come out and get these people? What could they possibly have to do with the excavation?"

"They built a cabin out there on sacred ground," the sheriff said. "With the Indians all riled up, that may have been enough by itself. Or maybe it's simply a warning against the white man to get out. And this family was a convenient target."

Fielding exhaled a deep breath and turned away, taking his time to survey the entire room, the ceiling, the heavy beams crisscrossing the open space above. He couldn't explain a great many things, but of one thing he felt certain: There wasn't a mad group of Indian terrorists on the loose. He couldn't explain why he felt certain of that, or perhaps it was more accurate to say he didn't want to try to explain why he felt that way. Perhaps he feared slipping back into the irrational.

Could the five parallel gouges have been there before the fire? Could a spiked rafter have swung loose and fell to the floor?

"Sheriff!" The call came from outside. It sounded urgent. "We got something!"

There was motion there, amid the leaves. She was sure of it.

Everything else around her went suddenly silent. The shuffling and sifting of the investigators up by the cabin, the splash of the river near the bank, the gentle brush of leaves overhead. It was as if she had retreated into a parallel world where all other objects and events became secondary to her solitary focus. Unlike the duality of last night's unfolding events, which had seemed to coexist, she was decidedly cast into a single universe. All she could hear was the rapid rush of blood through her temples. All she could think about was the motion she had noticed. All she could feel was the impulse to move forward. Downstream. Along the bank. Into the woods.

● ● ●

Fielding followed Halstead out the door then around the side of
the cabin and toward the woods. Kinsey was standing at the
edge of the tree line, and he waved them toward him. "This
way."

Fielding looked ahead. There was movement deeper in the
woods, about a hundred feet in.

"What is it?" Halstead called out to his deputy.

"Looks like another fryer."

They followed Kinsey as he led them through the trees. They
walked fast, stepping over ground litter and leaving a wake of
broken three-stemmed ferns in their path. As they neared, the
first thing that drew Fielding's attention was a tree trunk blackened and split by lightning. A short distance beyond it, another
deputy crouched over a spot on the ground.

Kinsey circled around behind the other deputy, allowing
Halstead and Fielding to see it clearly for themselves. The sheriff stared at the ground for a few moments, then slowly went
down to one knee. It wasn't what he had been expecting. It
wasn't like the others.

As Fielding looked at the ground, he suffered an involuntary
chill. It was the same creeping uneasiness that had gripped him
back in the cave, or more accurately, when they were leaving
the cave. When Jean had climbed out of the narrow entrance to
the inner chamber. When she insisted on controlling the small
gray backpack.

"Still think your Indian friends aren't behind this?" Halstead
said to Fielding.

It wasn't another "fryer," as Kinsey had suggested. There
was a skull and a few other assorted bones, all in a pile, but certainly not the remains of a complete skeleton. And it didn't take
an archaeologist to see that the bones were aged. And that they
had been blackened by an ancient fire.

Why she was walking along the bank downstream she wasn't
sure. But despite the uncertain nature of her behavior, she was
nonetheless moving purposefully, as if whatever motives
guided her were grounded in logic that would be revealed to
her, in time. There was a sense of expectation, but with that
feeling there was also a nervousness, a sense that something
was missing. As if something had been left undone.

The motion Jean Shawshequay had noticed a few moments
before proved to be a shifting phenomenon, staying just out of

sight, retreating as she advanced. And within her mind the very same drama was being played out. Mental images remained just out of reach. Memories of last night brightened momentarily then faded before sparking full recall. Logic that would explain her behavior continued to elude her understanding. She was drifting, falling, in the forest, in her command of reason. No matter how close she thought she was, sightlines remained blocked, and inner vision remained unclear.

She tried to remember, she *wanted* to remember, but the memories did not come. She tried to see, she *wanted* to see, but whatever drew her into the woods remained hidden.

She picked up her pace, trying to catch up. Her mind began to work faster. Her breathing brought a new rawness to her throat. The needles of a spruce branch stabbed like a thousand pinpricks as she waved it aside. She was working harder to remember, to see. Her eyes were darting in every direction; her thoughts were tumbling out of control. Everything seemed to be moving. In a hundred directions all at once.

And then it stopped. Jean came to a halt and stared straight ahead at the fallen trunk of a huge white pine. It was rotten and the bark was peeling, and mostly hidden by ferns was a long cavity in the side of the trunk. As her chest continued to rise and fall rapidly, as she stared at the hidden cavity, her attention was drawn not by any movement. But by the stillness.

"These bones have anything to do with your dig?" Halstead asked Fielding.

The archaeologist forced his eyes from the ancient human remains to the sheriff, who was still below him, kneeling on one knee. Fielding's throat had gone so dry, his chest so tight, that he wasn't sure he could speak if he tried. So he shook his head, no.

Halstead was skeptical. "You telling me you don't know anything about these things?"

Fielding crouched next to Halstead and picked up a long bone to study. Turning it over, evaluating it, he said, "It's old, but I'll have to get it to the lab to say how old. Same thing with this ash residue. It'll take some study to determine if the fire was contemporaneous with death." He looked over at Halstead. "But I can say one thing. These bones didn't come out of the ground." In other words, they didn't come from his excavation on the lip of the sinkhole.

The sheriff took the bone from Fielding and examined it himself. There was no soil discoloration. No residue of dirt sticking to its surface. "That's all very interesting, and as far as I'm concerned, you can study these things from now until the next century. But the important question I'd like to get at is, what do you suppose they're doing here?"

That was the question in Fielding's mind as well. What were they doing here? Why were they here? Fielding shook his head. "I don't know, Sheriff."

Halstead gave Fielding a sour look. The man still refused to make the obvious connections.

"Uh, Sheriff?" It was Kinsey. "There's something else. Over there."

Halstead stood and looked toward the fire-blackened ground at the base of the tree. "Yeah. I saw that. Looks like a lightning strike."

"Not that," Kinsey said. "Just up there."

The sheriff took a few steps. He looked, but he didn't notice anything. He turned his head back toward Kinsey, his brows furrowed.

"The ground," Kinsey said, stepping past Halstead and Fielding. "The burn marks."

Fielding followed him past the tree. He wasn't sure what the deputy meant. Kinsey was standing by a patch of scorched ground, pointing at it. Was that all?

"So?" Halstead said. "I said I saw the fire."

"But this is different. Look how it goes."

The patch of ground at Kinsey's feet was blackened in a roughly circular shape. It wasn't connected to the larger fire mark around the base of the tree, but that seemed of little consequence. It could have been started by a spark.

As Fielding came up to Kinsey, an unsteady feeling began to churn in his stomach. He figured Kinsey must be referring to some tangible bit of evidence left by whoever had dumped the bones there. He expected to see something of Jean's.

But there wasn't anything like that at Kinsey's feet. There were only the filaments of incinerated leaves, the charcoallike ash of twigs, the blackened remains of hemlock needles. Fielding widened his visual search, and a few feet away he saw another blackened patch. It took a moment for him to realize that that was what Kinsey meant.

Fielding stepped toward it, and as he did, he noticed a third patch. Circular like the first two, and in a line leading away from the tree. Beyond the third was a fourth, and he and the sheriff began to follow the progression: a somewhat staggered line of circular patches of scorched earth a few feet apart, leading in the direction of the cabin.

At the edge of the tree line, Fielding could see where the trail of blackened patches continued toward the cabin. Leading directly to the window that showed the heaviest scorching.

Looking down at the closest patch of burnt earth, gazing at the pattern as it led from the trees to the cabin, Fielding had no ready explanation for what it was. What it meant. How it was caused. But he did know one thing. He knew what the pattern looked like. It looked like footprints.

The stillness of the woods enveloped her, yet within her mind the noise seemed deafening. She could hear the cracks of thunder, the thrashing of vegetation, the frantic splashing in the river, and overall was the sound of fire. The crackling, snapping sound of tinder engulfed by flames, the rush of heated air, raindrops vaporized with a sound like the angry hiss of a viper's nest.

Underlying the tumult of the imagined storm and fire, she became aware of a haltingly rhythmic sound. The sound of her own unsteady heart? Or the sound of breathing? Scared, uncontrolled breathing.

Jean Shawshequay reached into the ferns and began to part them. As she did, the images from her dream became more vibrant. She remembered being in her car in the woods, driving away from where the lightning had struck. But she couldn't see the trees on either side of the car. It was like looking down a tunnel, a long, narrow tube with darkness at the end and rimmed by fire. And then she saw—in this replay of images torn from her contrary world of competing visions—the face of a woman. A girl. A child. And the child was moving backward, stumbling awkwardly, trying to distance herself from the tunnel of fire.

Hitting the highway, swinging onto the black ribbon of asphalt, Jean sensed a flutter of weakness, a dissatisfaction arising from a feeling of matters left unresolved. She had to regain strength. She had to complete her task.

As had happened last night, conflicting visions interfered with her sight. What she saw was obscured not only by ferns, but inexplicably, also by water. She was looking into brush. She was staring into a river. They were contrasting scenes, and yet they were the same. It was the same face, staring up at her from underwater, staring at her from the protective hollow of the white pine. The only difference was the expression. In one version was a look of hot fear, in the other a dull look of old terrors that had exhausted all nervous energy.

Jean Shawshequay hovered in place, caught in the confused swirl of relived nightmare and present reality. Through it all she felt the same impulses of last night, and she heard the same sounds. They were the sounds of terror and pain, the sounds of panic and escape, the sounds of fire and water. And most piercing of all were the screams. The screams that filled her ears, that took command of her thoughts, that exerted pressure within the entire expanse of her skull.

It was a pressure that hurt, in her dream, at the present moment. It was a pressure that urged her to answer the impulse. That grew with each second ticked off the clock, building in intensity, pushing harder, faster. Louder. Seeking release.

"I think this makes everything pretty clear," Halstead said.

To Fielding, nothing was clear. In fact, as he stared at the scorched footprints, he was doing all he could to deny the irrationality that threatened to take possession of his thoughts. Events that are inherently unbelievable can never be accepted as fact, no matter the circumstantial evidence, unless they are witnessed firsthand. That's what he told himself anyway. That's what he tried to make himself believe.

"Wouldn't you say?" Halstead added.

"What's that, Sheriff?"

Halstead regarded Fielding closely. He wasn't sure if the man was toying with him or really was that dense. "This trail of burn marks makes it clear who dumped the bones out there. And why. And who is behind the torching of the cabin."

"I don't see how these marks can possibly lead to a conclusion of any kind."

"To me, it couldn't be any plainer if they had left a note. They wanted us to find the bones so they made this trail from the cabin to the woods. To the lightning strike."

"And the message is?"

"The message, God damn it, is quit fucking with our burial grounds or we'll sic the ancient fire demons on every last one of you." Halstead sucked in a long, wavering breath then exhaled slowly in an effort to control his temper. It didn't work. "For Christ's sake, Fielding. Don't you get it now? There's a group of fanatics out there as crazy about their so-called religion as the craziest Iranian is about his ayatollahs. They think what you're doing violates their sacred trust with their ancestors, and they mean to stop you using the old voodoo."

"I don't believe that. And even if this fire was deliberately set, I don't see how you can assume that Indians opposed to the excavation are responsible for it."

"Then what the hell you think those bones are there for? How the hell this trail of fire get from there to the cabin? Who made those claw marks on the wall of the living room?"

Fielding didn't answer. He couldn't answer. He couldn't phrase the building illogic within the privacy of his own thoughts, much less speak it aloud.

Halstead continued to press. "Don't you think there's the vaguest connection between those masked lunatics who danced their magic dance on you and your truck, the fact the Indians around here have a thing about fire, and the fact six people now have been incinerated?"

There were connections, Fielding thought. But were they the connections Halstead wanted him to see? He was about to speak when he was cut off. Not by the sheriff, but by a scream. A scream muffled by distance and the heavy vegetation, but a scream as piercing as cold steel driven through the core of his spine.

It came from beyond the cabin. Fielding broke toward the front, dashing around the corner of the porch. Kinsey and Halstead trailed behind. The two paramedics who had been near the body bag in front were moving more cautiously toward the far tree line, but nonetheless were well ahead of Fielding.

The scream rose and fell in pitch, gathering strength with each new rise. It was the scream of a woman. It was Jean Shawshequay.

There was movement in the woods, Fielding could see. Beyond the paramedics. A frantic, rushing effort to escape the thicket of branches and leaves, of ferns and cluttered ground. Fielding ran harder, until he caught up to the two men in front of him, until he saw the person charging toward them. It wasn't Jean Shawshequay, but rather a young girl. She was pinwheeling her arms through the branches and breathing in terrified gasps. She didn't even seem to see the men in front of her until she ran straight into them.

The two paramedics caught her between them, and she continued to struggle as if they were just another obstacle of the forest. "Hold on, hold on," one of them said to her, but to little effect. She continued to fight, trying to wriggle free, to escape the woods.

She was wearing a pair of waders, and her hair was stringy and matted as if she had gotten soaked in the rain and let it dry. But most significant were the burn marks across her scalp, on the side of her face, over her chin, and across her neck. To Fielding it looked as though she had been lashed with a burning strap.

"Jesus," Halstead breathed, having come up behind Fielding.

There was the sound of cracking vegetation, and Fielding looked up. It was Jean, making her way out of the woods. For the first time the child stopped fighting the paramedics. She turned to face Jean.

Halstead went down on one knee next to the girl. He took her shoulders in his hands and tried to turn her toward him. She was panting, her face blotched with patches of red, and her eyes were active, darting in terrified glances from the sheriff to Jean and back again.

"The fire," she said, and tried to pull away.

"I know, I know," Halstead soothed. "It was a bad fire."

She started to shake her head, then glanced into the woods, toward Jean Shawshequay. "The fire," she said again, as if she feared it still. As if she expected it to flare anew at any second.

"Yes, we know," Halstead said again. "We saw where the fire was. But you're all right now."

The girl looked at the sheriff, her eyes wide. Her entire body began to tremble, and her head began to shake in tight spasms, back and forth. She tried to pull away.

"It's okay," the paramedic said. "You're safe now."

She looked at him, then back toward the woods. Jean had stopped, holding back about five paces.

"What's your name?" Halstead asked.

She practically shouted, "The fire!"

"We know all about the fire, but it's out now."

Her head shook violently.

"Sheriff," the paramedic said. "We better get her out of here. To the hospital."

Halstead looked up at him, then back at the girl. "Did you see anybody last night?"

The girl stared at him for a moment, her eyes still wild. Then she turned away as her chest convulsed and she heaved a great gasp of air.

"Did you see who started the fire?" Halstead asked.

"It's *alive*," she breathed.

Halstead glanced up at Fielding. "She saw them!"

"It's alive," she repeated, her fear welling up to the surface.

"Sheriff," the paramedic insisted. "We've got to take her."

Halstead eased his grip on her, then nodded toward the cabin. "The fire isn't alive anymore. It's dead out. And you're going to be all right. You have nothing more to fear."

As the paramedics eased her away and started toward the front yard, leading her toward their vehicle parked around back, Halstead spoke, as much to himself as to Fielding. "She saw who it was," he said. "I just hope to God she'll be able to tell us who it was she saw."

Fielding listened in silence. He couldn't help but feel that the sheriff was misreading things again. When she'd said the fire was alive, she hadn't been looking in the direction of the cabin. She'd been staring straight at Jean Shawshequay.

Chapter 16

THE SHERIFF WAS driving alone in the car. He wanted it that way, to give himself time to think.

The kid didn't make much sense, but it was clear to him she had seen somebody. And whoever it was must have seen her, the way she was burned. She was lucky though, Halstead thought. She got away. Kids are like that. Elusive. Once she'd broken into the woods, the killers hadn't had a prayer of finding her. If she was like most kids, she knew the woods around her cabin like the back of her hand.

She had lapsed into shock, that was obvious, and who could blame her, after what she must have witnessed. And then she was scared shitless by that Indian anthropologist screaming like a hyena. But she would come out of it, Halstead felt certain. Any kid who could survive what had happened last night had enough spine to pull herself out of any hysteria. At the very least she'd be able to point somebody out in a lineup. And that's all he needed, for right now.

The deerskin mask had linked the son of Wes Goodmedicine to the assault on Fielding, proving that he was a part of the radical group Halstead suspected of using terror to stop the excavation. But until now—until the girl—he hadn't had anything to tie Ray Goodmedicine or Blackbear or Johnny Penay to the fire deaths, except his suspicions. That was going to change, as soon as he picked up Ray Goodmedicine. As soon as the girl was calm enough to pick him out of a lineup.

Once he had Ray, Halstead was convinced, the rest would fall into line. He had checked police records through the LIEN and come up empty on Johnny Penay. But he hadn't checked the military. If a flamethrower had been used on the cabin, chances are it would have been by someone with military training. Knowledge of that kind of a weapon was not something you picked up at the local hunt club.

Halstead had a feeling Penay was hiding something in his

past. Had his criminal history been while he was in the service? Had he been court-martialed? It was an area of investigation he would have to cover, as soon as he had the man behind the deer-skin mask.

The darkness of the basement usually offered him a degree of peace. It was a place to which he could escape, a place where he felt safe. But this time, having heard the conversation between Jean Shawshequay and the archaeologist, having seen the shapes in Makwamacatawa's fire, the solitude offered little comfort.

For a second, Fielding had said, *the fire was inside of you.*

Shivering, Ray shut his eyes and hunched forward, clasping his hands together between his knees, recalling his night visit to Makwamacatawa's vigil. *For a second, something was inside the fire.*

Ray threw his head back, exhaling a wavering breath. He didn't know what he should believe. He didn't know what he should do. His life was a conflicting boil of past injustices brought to the fore by Blackbear, and a young man's uncertainties about his future.

Ray suddenly felt cheated and abandoned and angry all at the same moment. He came to his feet and kicked a chair, sending it crashing against the wall. "You goddamn drunk," he screamed. "You were supposed to be here. You said the vision quest would provide answers. It'd provide me with a guide for the rest of my life. But where were you?" he said, his voice weakening. Sinking slowly to his knees at the foot of the steps, he added almost plaintively, "Where were you?"

"He was there all along," Miriam said, and her son looked up quickly. He hadn't heard her open the door. "He's here right now. Inside of you." She came down and sat on the last step and brought her hand to the back of Ray's head, caressing his hair.

"He told me he learned from the spirits. The ones who visited him in his dreams. He said they would come to me too, when it was time. But he left before it was time for me, and now they'll never come."

"Ray, the vision quest he spoke of is a matter of your own inner strength. A matter of calling upon the pride in your heritage and using that to help you in the decisions you have to make. Life is not as easy as asking questions and being told answers. You have to make your own way. The spirits aren't real. They're only what your own convictions and character make of them."

"But they are."

"They are what?"

"They are real."

Miriam let her hand slip slowly from the back of her son's head. She leaned away, studying him, not sure what he meant.

"I saw them. I saw them in the fire."

"You saw what in the fire? Where?"

"I saw the spirits coming to Makwamacatawa. In his fire."

Miriam for the first time noticed the dank chill of the basement. It seemed to creep up the back of her neck.

"But they didn't seem to be the kinds of spirits Dad described," Ray continued. "They didn't seem . . ." he broke off, not sure how to describe what he meant. And then suddenly, his expression changed. He looked past his mother. Toward the window.

Miriam spun around. She heard something. *He* had heard something. Looking up at the window, a shadow passed by it. She turned back to Ray, afraid.

He strode quickly to the wall then took a high step onto a table, raising his head to the level of the window. He peered outside. "It's a deputy," he whispered. "He's watching the back door."

As Miriam's fear took on a new focus, there was a knock upstairs. At the front door.

"You'd better answer that."

He spoke with the voice of an adult. He spoke with the voice of his father. Miriam turned and went up the steps. When she opened the door, she saw Sheriff Halstead standing there. He didn't say anything right away. He didn't have to. She knew by the look on his face that Jean's ravings were true. People had died.

"May I come in, Miriam?" he said at last.

She nodded, then stood to the side, holding the door for him. As he passed, she noticed for the first time what he held in his hand. She saw the mask.

Halstead laid the deer-hide mask on the coffee table; then standing behind it, he faced Miriam. She looked at the mask, then back at him. "You should have told me," he said.

Miriam turned and closed the door, lingering with her back to him as she collected her nerve. When she looked at him again, her expression was strong. "I don't know what you mean."

Halstead regarded her for a long moment. He couldn't blame her. What mother wouldn't lie to protect her son? Slowly, he retracted a folded piece of paper from his shirt pocket and opened it, holding it out for her. "This is a Xerox copy I made from an obituary in the *Newsfall*. It's from twenty-eight years ago. The photo didn't come out too well in the copy, but I think you can tell who it is." When she didn't reach for the sheet, Halstead set it on the table next to the mask, facing her.

Miriam didn't make a move to pick it up. But she couldn't stop herself from lowering her eyes, looking at it from a distance.

"It's Wes, Miriam. With his mask. The one Ray wore in the assault on Fielding."

"There were many members of the deer clan. There were many masks."

"No, Miriam. This one is his."

She glanced down at it on the table. "If I can't be sure, how can you be?"

"Perhaps you can show me Wes's then." He paused as a flicker of discomfort passed across Miriam's face. "You wouldn't have thrown it out, would you?"

"Things get lost. Or stolen."

"Miriam," the sheriff said firmly. "You can't protect him from what he's already done. It'll be worse for both of you if you try."

"I haven't heard what he's done. I don't see any evidence. What are you accusing him of? Where is your proof? Do you have any witnesses?"

Halstead took a deep breath and stepped to the rear window. Outside he could see Deputy Kinsey keeping an eye on the back door. He turned back to Miriam and nodded, speaking more reasonably now, almost as if he hated to say what he did. "Yes. I have a witness. A witness to the murders of four people. Last night."

Miriam went light-headed, her eyelids fluttering shut for a moment. "They're dead," Jean Shawshequay had said coming out of her dream. She talked about drifting, about a cabin, about a fire. How had she known?

Stepping toward her, Halstead continued. "I know how a young kid can get wrapped up in a group and do things he wouldn't normally do on his own. Especially when the others he is involved with are older men. I know whatever Ray did was not his idea. He did it because of the pressure of the group."

Miriam was watching the sheriff closely, listening to his evaluation of things, picking up the hints. "If he's not to blame," she said carefully, "then why are you after him? Why aren't you after the 'older' ones?"

"I am after the older ones. And if Ray can help us, things will work out okay for him."

Miriam wanted to press him on what he meant. What did "okay for him" mean? What did the sheriff want from him? What would happen if he didn't cooperate? But she resisted. She thought it more prudent not to reveal anything. "I'll ask Ray if he knows anything about what has happened," she said. "And we'll both think about what you said."

Halstead's lips grew taut. "I'm afraid, Miriam, I'm going to have to take him in now."

Miriam's eyes grew suddenly wider. She was scared.

Looking around the room, glancing toward the staircase, Halstead asked, "Is he home?"

Reflexively, Miriam's eyes darted in the direction of the basement door. She caught herself, but the sheriff followed the drift. "I'm not sure where he is," she said, a trifle too forced. "He doesn't always tell me of his comings and goings."

"Is he in there?" he asked, indicating the basement door.

Miriam shook her head no.

Halstead began walking toward the door. "Do you mind if I look?"

She didn't say anything until he reached the door. Until he opened it. "Sheriff." He stopped. "Let me go down first."

Halstead considered this, then took a step back and waited for her to walk in front of him. The lights were off, and Miriam flicked the switch at the head of the stairs. At the bottom they stopped, and Miriam scanned the room. She didn't see him. "Ray?" There was no response. "Ray. Where are you?"

Halstead stepped past her and conducted a quick search. The basement was empty. He opened a door, revealing a half flight of stairs. "Where do these lead?"

"Out the side," Miriam said.

Halstead climbed the stairs to the slanting fruit-cellar door. It was unlocked, and a sock had been wadded up and placed over the latch, silencing any metallic noise as it was shut. Halstead pushed the door up and open, then stepped outside.

He looked toward the back. His deputy was not in view. "Kinsey!"

The deputy appeared around the corner. "Sheriff?" he said, perplexed at seeing him there. Then he noticed the open metal door, the closeness of the woods, and instantly the situation came clear. "Oh, shit."

"You didn't hear a thing?"

Kinsey shook his head. "But he couldn't have gotten too far. I can go after him."

"You won't find him out there," Halstead said. He'd know those woods like the back of his hand. "But he'll turn up." Miriam had followed the sheriff up the fruit-cellar stairs and now stood behind him. He turned to her. "There's not many places he can hide."

What did the young girl see in Jean Shawshequay? What made her think the fire was alive?

The sheriff had given permission to Fielding to gather for study the bones found in the woods. They couldn't lift prints from that kind of surface, and "Besides," Halstead had said, "if I gave them to the State Police, they'd just give them to an expert like you to examine."

The sheriff and the EMS vehicle were already gone when Fielding came back to his truck. Jean Shawshequay was inside, waiting listlessly. Fielding paused with the door open, staring over at her. She gave no indication at all that he was even there. Fielding put the bones behind his seat and climbed behind the wheel.

He looked at her a second time before firing the engine and shifting into reverse. As the truck slipped deeper into the woods, as the new imponderables discovered at this isolated cabin on the river began to stack one atop the other in his mind, for a second Halstead's explanation suddenly seemed to offer an attractive solution. Attractive because it would lift the weight in his head.

But that would be too easy, Fielding realized. The sheriff hadn't felt the bite of the fangs from the dead camp fire. He hadn't seen the fangs of fire in Jean's mouth. But had *he* seen the fire? Fielding asked himself. What had happened to his conclusion that what had occurred in the cave had been an illusion, a trick of lighting and suggestion already planted in his mind?

Fielding rolled down the window. He was getting warm. He arched his back against the seat. How long could he keep denying things? At what point did his denials of nonscientific explanations become more unreasonable than acceptance of those explanations?

He glanced over at Jean. She was sitting there, drained and forlorn, probably in need of the hospital's care as much as the young girl was. But she had seen something. She had *known*.

Fielding turned the truck into a grassy opening and hit the brakes. Jean lurched forward, almost hitting the dash. As she dropped back, she looked over at him, startled. Fielding stared hard at her face as if in the creases of her forehead and the lines of anxiety the answers he sought could be revealed. But as the seconds drew out, he could read nothing. She offered nothing. "How did you know?" he said at last.

She continued to stare at him, as if she didn't understand.

"Jean. How did you know?"

Her mouth parted as if she were about to speak, but then her lips seized in a circle of indecision. She didn't know what to say. She shook her head slightly.

"You described the road, the cabin. You said the people were dead. How could you have known all that?"

Jean looked away from him, settling back in her seat, looking out through the windshield, into the woods. "I saw it. Or I dreamed it. Now, I don't know which."

"What made you go off into the woods?"

Her eyebrows lifted. She shook her head.

"You knew the girl was out there, didn't you?"

She looked at him, her eyes scared. "I didn't know. I only had a feeling."

"A feeling about what?"

She took a short, quick breath. "I felt there was something in the water, drifting. I felt it falling away from me." She gasped, then leaned back. "I felt I was falling with it, getting weaker. The farther I went, the weaker I felt." Her chest convulsed, and she slumped forward, breathing heavily. The weakness was affecting her again. "I had to stop it. I had to stop . . . the weakness." As she spoke, a dizzy incoherence came to her thoughts. She was describing last night. She was describing this morning. The distinction between the two had become blurred.

"What's going on with you?" Fielding said. "What are you seeing right now?"

Shaking her head, she said, "I don't know."

"You have to know, damn it. You were here. You saw the fire."

Jean's head rolled back and forth against the headrest. Fielding wasn't sure if it expressed denial or simply a wish that he would stop. But he couldn't stop. Not now. "I'm trying to understand things. But you have to help. You have to tell me what's happening."

She looked at him, her eyes practically swimming in their sockets. The tempo in her breathing increased.

He tried a new tack. "When you were in the cave, you shouted out, 'Let go.' Then 'Get away.' What did you feel? What did you see?"

Her features sharpened, and she stared at him with a touch of disbelief. "I don't remember that."

"You remember the flare of the lantern, don't you?" he practically shouted.

She reeled back. "Yes."

Fielding leaned closer, his voice even louder. "You remember the soot on the walls of the cave. You remember what we found."

Her eyes closed. "Yes."

"Then think," he said, grabbing her by the shoulders, turning her toward him. "What happened after the flash? What did you see?"

She grimaced, shaking her head in a tight spasm, her entire torso clenching tight. She could hear him, but his voice seemed more distant. As if she were drifting away. Back to how it was, in the cave, in the car last night. It was almost as if she could remember. It was almost as if she could see the fire. The blue flame against the black of the cavern. The column of fire at the foot of the tree. They were different, yet the same. The same patterns.

She could feel Fielding's grip on her shoulders, the concussion of his voice. But other sensations overpowered her. She felt hot. And feverish. As if she were burning up. Her head lolled back and she let out a moan.

"Why did you take the bones out of the cave?"

Her eyes snapped open. The question suggested a wisp of

recollection. But that's all it was. A hazy, nonmaterial thought. As insubstantial as a hot flash passing across her forehead.

"Don't you remember?" Fielding said, his voice easing, his grip slackening.

She managed a swallow. "No. I don't remember. I don't remember." Her eyes closed again. "I just don't."

Maybe she didn't take them, Fielding thought. Maybe it was something else entirely.

Fielding took a deep breath and sat back in his seat. He had come full circle. Back to the irrational. Back to his denials. But it wasn't just denial, he knew. Even if he were ready to accept a supernatural explanation, there was still nothing within that realm he could conceive of that would explain what had been happening. So, as before, like the scientist he was, he continued to think of his task as one of acquiring information. Assembling the data. And the data in part was history. And history was a thing that was remembered. It was passed down through the generations.

"There are people here who do know things," he said simply, and Jean looked up. "It's time they told us."

Miriam sat nervously in her living room after the sheriff left. Not too often was she at a loss to know what should be done. But she was now. All she could think about was Ray. What the sheriff thought he had done. What was going to happen to him. Worst of all, she was concerned about what Ray was going to do.

When Christopher Fielding and Jean Shawshequay arrived, she couldn't help but continue her preoccupation. They sat on the couch in front of the coffee table, and she perched on the edge of a hard-backed chair across from them, her fingers knitting and unknitting together in her lap.

As Fielding outlined for Miriam what had been discovered at the cabin in the woods, Jean avoided looking at her. The headache had lifted, and she felt as well as she had since before entering the cave, and perhaps it was because of feeling more normal that she wanted to avoid Miriam's gaze. She imagined what the woman must be thinking of her.

Jean's eyes wandered over the table in front of her, catching on an unfolded piece of paper. It was the Xerox of the obituary left by Sheriff Halstead.

"You have to help us," Fielding concluded.

"Help you? How?"

"By telling us what you know."

"If there was something I could do to help, I'd surely do it. You know that."

Fielding eyed her for a second or two, then shook his head. "You haven't told us everything."

Miriam's eyes opened wide. Her cheeks turned pallid.

"You know something," Fielding continued. "Something that might help explain the burnings."

"You mean you want to hear about evil Indian spirits," Miriam said, the color returning to her cheeks, the anger rising in her voice. "About our pagan beliefs, our savage practices. Our secret societies of fetishes and black magic."

"That's not what I meant," Fielding said.

Miriam came to her feet. "You may think you're not like the rest, but at the first hint of uncertainty, you come looking for explanations that reflect your true prejudices."

"Miriam, I don't know what I'm looking for. All I know is that nothing seems to fit. I've tried to understand, but there are things that have happened that I just can't explain. And I need help."

"Ask her," Miriam said, pointing to Jean. "She's the one who knew about the fire at the cabin."

Fielding glanced at Jean, then back at Miriam. "She can't explain things either."

"It all started after she came. After both of you came."

"That's not true," Jean said, and Fielding looked at her in surprise. She held Halstead's Xerox so it faced Miriam. "It's happened before, hasn't it?"

Miriam went suddenly blank. She stared at the photocopy Jean displayed for her.

"What's that?" Fielding asked.

Miriam's eyes drifted nervously to Jean's, then she began to ease away, back toward the chair.

"It's a story about a young Ojibwa boy," Jean said, "who was found burned to death by his camp fire, out near the sinkhole. Twenty-eight years ago."

"That was an accident," Miriam said. "A tragedy. The same thing could have happened anywhere."

"Why were these men in traditional garb?" Jean asked.

Miriam shifted uncomfortably in her seat, her hands coming again to her lap. "I don't know."

"It wasn't an ordinary funeral. What was the magic they were doing? And why?"

Miriam didn't speak this time. She just shook her head.

"You do know, Miriam," Fielding said.

"No. I really don't." Her voice was steady but resigned. "And neither did they," she said, referring to the photo of her husband, with his deerskin mask, and the others.

"It's happened other times as well," Fielding probed. "Over the years."

Miriam nodded. "There have been stories. Nothing that seemed important, or that I thought was even true. Just another false historical invention." She looked up quickly. "There have been so many slanderous things written about the native peoples, why help to perpetuate the lies?" She said that almost plaintively, waiting for some sign of understanding. Neither of her guests wished to interrupt, so she took a breath and continued. "So the people of my generation never spoke about the old stories connected to the Cave of Bones. We just hoped to let them die."

"Can you tell us now?"

Miriam shrugged. "There isn't much to tell. Oh, there have been other burnings, as you guessed, from my grandfather's time, and from the time before him. Those stories are not much different from what is happening now, or what happened twenty-eight years ago. I suspect what you want to hear is how the Ancient Ones were said to have fought people from the underworld. A people who, it was said, came out only at night, whose skin was pale because it was never reddened by the sun. They called them the Awshkoute, 'they that make fire.' To save themselves, the Ancient Ones were forced to do a horrible thing. They had no choice, it is said."

"What did they do?"

Miriam shook her head. "A generation sometime before my grandfather's made a decision similar to the one we made. So we don't know what they did. Except that it stopped the Awshkoute."

The massacre, Fielding thought. In the cave. But Miriam was wrong. It hadn't stopped them.

Fielding wasn't sure if he was ready to make the connections between the past and the present. But there was one thought that began to settle with a disquieting weight within his mind.

The one undeniable fact amid everything else was the proximity of the bones to the fires. And the uncomfortable knowledge that as fire consumes its fuel, it grows stronger.

Chapter 17

JOHNNY PENAY WAS older than Blackbear by only a few years, but from appearances the age difference could easily have been thought a decade or more. Whether it was the short but deeply cut lines at the corners of his eyes, the rough, weathered texture of his skin, or the cold calculation in his stare, there was something about Penay that made him appear more mature than his years. It was not a maturity of wisdom, but rather one of cunning. It was an impression that was conveyed especially when news of his enemies' betrayal stimulated his cool passions.

To the nineteen-year-old William Quilltail and the twenty-one-year-old Rene Wawatessi, at this moment Johnny Penay appeared the picture of shrewd control. But as the silence lengthened, neither young man could avoid the unease. So Quilltail spoke. "Maybe we should go get Blackbear. Tell him what's happened."

"No," Penay said, his eyes never shifting from an indeterminate point at the far side of the room.

Quilltail glanced at his friend for support, and Wawatessi said, "I know we shouldn't disturb him during his vision quest, but this is important. He would want to know."

Penay turned slowly to Wawatessi. He couldn't have cared less about disturbing Blackbear's meditations. But he did care about bringing back a voice that had lost its clarity of purpose. Blackbear's sojourn to the spirit world could only muddy the situation, which was something Penay wanted to avoid. Especially now. Especially after hearing the news the two young men had brought to him.

Quilltail's sister was a nurse at the hospital, and she had heard from her friend in Admitting what had happened at the cabin fire in the woods. Her friend had heard it from the EMS paramedics who had brought in the twelve-year-old girl. After Bill Quilltail talked to his sister, he got Rene and they drove straight to Johnny Penay. They told him about the fire, the girl in the woods, Jean Shawshequay being there. And they told him about the disinterred bones of the Ancient Ones found near the cabin.

"They lied," was the obvious conclusion, drawn for Penay by Wawatessi. "They said they wouldn't disturb any graves, and they did."

"And the woman," Bill added, referring to Shawshequay, "had promised to prevent that from happening, and she didn't."

Penay was angry, but at the same time he felt a kind of perverse satisfaction. It was what he had expected of them. It would put more weight behind his more confrontational approach. What tack that would take from this point on, he was unsure, and as he debated those alternatives privately, Quilltail suggested contacting Blackbear.

It was when he looked at the young men, showing a smile they could not decipher, that the phone rang. If they wanted to think his reluctance to go after Blackbear came from respect for the man's vision quest, then let them think that, Penay thought.

He lifted the receiver. It was Ray Goodmedicine. The sheriff was after him, Ray told him. "I think he's got a witness who's going to say I started the fire that killed the family."

Penay covered the mouthpiece and asked Quilltail about the young girl who was brought into the hospital.

"She's pretty spooky right now," Quilltail said. "But my sister said there's nothing seriously wrong with her. Physically. So she'll probably come out of it, sooner or later."

To Goodmedicine, Penay said, "You weren't at the cabin, were you?"

"No!"

"Then you have nothing to be afraid of."

"But the sheriff. He's got that mask. He'll get her to say whatever he wants."

Penay's initial reaction was to stay clear of Ray Goodmedicine. After all, he was the magnet drawing the sheriff's attention. But as he talked to him on the phone, as his overall assessment of all the new information continued to percolate in his mind, he started to feel that maybe the kid could be useful. After all, the main problem was the archaeologist and the woman from Oklahoma. And none of them had as direct access to Jean Shawshequay as the son of Miriam Goodmedicine.

● ● ●

Ojibwa Village was at the farthest extent of Watersdrop, three-quarters of a mile from the Lake Superior shore. In between was Clearcurrent River, one of the four nearby streams that passed over the dolomite ridge on their way to feed the big lake. Where it cut the ridge, Clearcurrent River had been an easy descent for Ray Goodmedicine.

The lakeshore was mostly owned by people from Detroit or Chicago, who built expensive cottages they used no more than a month or so a year. It wasn't hard for Ray to find an isolated cottage that was unoccupied. He broke in and called Johnny Penay.

When Penay arrived with the others, he didn't say much at first to Ray. Instead, he strolled casually through the cathedral-ceilinged front room, eyeing the expensive Indian-motif prints on the wall, the designer furniture, the Navaho rugs worth more than his car. The decorating scheme made him smile. "You chose the home of a cousin," he said, and they laughed. Penay opened the refrigerator and took out four cans of beer. "I'm sure he wouldn't mind."

As they took seats around the kitchen table, Penay asked about the sheriff's visit. Ray told him what he had heard from the basement before he left by the fruit-cellar door. Then Penay asked about Jean Shawshequay, and Ray told how she had awakened in terror and that he had been sent for sedatives. He also told them that she seemed to know about the fire at the cabin before anyone else.

Penay's interest was piqued by Jean's foreknowledge, and he questioned Ray closely. Then they told Ray about her treachery, about the disinterred bones discovered at the cabin fire. Penay couldn't explain Jean's part in all this, but he was sure of one thing. "She is not there to protect our people's interests."

"What are we going to do?" Ray asked.

"What are we going to do?" Penay repeated, looking at all of them in turn. "The same as we decided to do before. We stop the desecration."

The answer begged the question. Ray looked at Quilltail, then Wawatessi, for further explanation. But if they knew anything, they were not saying.

Reading his uncertainty, his vulnerability, Penay continued. "These men are your brothers. I am your brother," he said, extending his arm, clasping Ray's, wrist to wrist. "We are your family. Whatever has to be done, we will do it together."

"What do you want me to do?"

"When we're ready, I'll get in touch with you. Be ready, and be careful. No one else is to know you're here." Penay released his grip on Ray's arm. "And that includes your mother." He let the concern register in Ray's face, then he continued, "She had her way of dealing with things, and she was wrong. It's our turn now."

Ray licked his upper lip. He glanced at Bill and Rene, then back at Penay. "What about Makwamacatawa?"

"Forget about Blackbear. He's looking for his own personal guidance. He's looking for visions."

Ray almost blurted out that he had seen the visions too, but the harshness of Penay's tone made him hesitate. Forget Blackbear, Penay was saying. Forget what you saw.

Superstition at one time was science, and to some today, science was superstition. And in some inexact disciplines the line had never been drawn clearly.

Fielding was sitting nervously at the desk in Miriam's attic bedroom. Jean Shawshequay was lying on the bed, trying to rest. Fielding had stopped checking to see if she was actually asleep, because he was being consumed by other thoughts and other concerns.

Was there such a clear distinction in his own discipline, Fielding considered, when the study of hard artifacts turned to the interpretation of the spiritual life of the people who had used them? There was much that science could not explain. Was it so blasphemous to say there were things that could never be understood within the parameters of his science?

The sheriff's working theory was that the deaths had resulted from a deliberate attempt to recreate some manner of native supernatural vengeance. Was the answer somewhere in between? Could acts envisioned by supernatural beliefs have been brought to life by an unwitting accomplice, someone steeped in the old beliefs, someone whose mental dysfunction kept separate twin personalities that had only dim recollections of each other's behavior?

Fielding looked over at Jean Shawshequay. Her eyes were closed; she seemed at rest now. And in this state she offered a neutral facade, one which hid her thoughts and feelings. And memories.

How much did he really know about her? Rather than her gaps in memory and her prescient dreams being a new phenomenon, did she have a history of like episodes? Fielding began to review her whereabouts at the times of the incinerations. As he did, his own eyes lightly closed. It wasn't her, he told himself. There were too many other things that she could not control. It wasn't Jean Shawshequay who felt the bite of invisible fangs from a pile of ashes. It wasn't Jean Shawshequay who saw a blue fire inside herself. It wasn't Jean Shawshequay who planted evidence of archaic iron manufacture on the lip of the sinkhole.

Fielding massaged his forehead with his fingertips. Was the bog-iron part of the mystery, or was it simply an anomaly that had little to do with the current phenomena of fire?

As he thought about their discovery of iron, the European bones in the cave, and Miriam's legend, he realized there were connections, if the method by which the iron was manufactured had not been archaic to those who manufactured it. There were beliefs, Fielding knew, that were not the beliefs of the early Christian explorers, but beliefs of people who far preceded them in their own lands, that could have given rise to the horrors of Miriam's story. It was conceivable, if the history of European contact in America were incomplete; there were connections, if he were willing to look beyond the parameters of his world of science and logic.

But was it necessary to cast his gaze so far afield at this time? It was still a matter of acquiring the information, testing the facts against theory, examining critically every possible alternative. That was the scientific way, after all. Wasn't it?

The phone on the desk was a trimline, with the buttons in the handle. He picked up the receiver and punched out Curtis Heath's office number at the Great Lakes Natural History Museum in Detroit. He wasn't in his office, but in the lab. The secretary would switch him over. As Fielding waited, he felt comfortable that he had not taken any leaps into fancy. He wasn't looking for supernatural explanations. But if he were honest with himself, he'd realize he no longer ruled them out.

If someone had told Christopher Fielding one month ago that before the French explorers, before Jamestown, before Columbus, there had been a European settlement near the shores of Lake Superior, he would have reacted the same as if he had been asked to believe in the supernatural. But that's exactly what Curtis Heath was telling him. Carbon dating of the charcoal residue on the bog-iron remnants placed their manufacture at 1410 +/– 25 years.

Fielding remained quiet as he considered the implications. European penetration into the interior still wasn't conclusive, he considered, until the bones were dated as well.

As if reading his thoughts, Heath added, "It's about the same for the skeletal remains."

Fielding came forward in his chair. The receiver pressed flush against his ear. "What are you talking about?"

"Chris, Chris, Chris," Heath said sadly. "You never intended to tell me about the cave."

"How . . . ?" Fielding's voice trailed off as his mind groped for how Heath could have known.

"Does it matter?" Heath paused a second before allowing himself a brief laugh. "As it happens, I followed you down. Do you think I didn't realize she had found something?"

Fielding's mind began working fast. Jumping ahead. "Did you go inside?"

"What do you think?"

"The skeletal remains you examined. They were from the cave?"

Heath laughed, amused by the panic building in Fielding's voice.

"Damn it. Answer me. Did they come from the cave?"

"An interesting mystery, isn't it? We've had some very odd deaths by incineration out there in the woods, and come to find out, there was a mass immolation almost six centures ago at the very same site. Do you make anything of that?"

"You've got to bring them back," Fielding said evenly.

"Is it just coincidence?" Heath continued, ignoring him. "If it's not coincidence, how could there possibly be a connection between what happened then and now? What could an ancient massacre have to do with a series of strange killings?"

"Dr. Heath. You didn't hear me. I said you have to bring the remains back."

"Oh, I heard you, Chris. But frankly, that's not what's important. Aren't you curious about the questions I've raised?"

"Yes, I am. But—"

"So what do you think?" he interrupted. "Is there a connection between what happened to a fifteenth-century European settlcment, and what is happening now?"

"I don't know. All I know is that there's a connection between the proximity of the bones and the fires." The words were propelled by the speed of his thoughts. Fielding wasn't sure where they were leading him. He was only sure what had to be done.

"I see. And what does that mean?"

"It means, damn it, you don't realize what you're dealing with there. You don't realize the danger you're in."

Heath bellowed with laughter. "Professor Fielding. You sound as if you believe there's some sort of magic at work here."

"I don't know what's at work." With the events near the sinkhole, or within the labyrinth of his mind. He wasn't analyzing his own feelings. He wasn't questioning whether he was ready to step beyond the parameters of his scientific world. He only knew that it was imperative the bones be returned.

"You don't know what's at work," Heath prodded, "except that the power—the evil—is derived from the skeletal remains of those who were massacred. Is that what you're saying?"

"I'm saying you have to return what you stole from the cave."

"Nothing was stolen," Heath barked. "And don't you dare even intimate to anyone that it was."

"You're making a serious mistake. And you're the one who's going to pay for it."

"By suffering the ancient curse? Come on, Fielding. Get a grip on yourself."

Fielding took a deep breath, running his hand through his hair. That's exactly what he tried to do. Get a grip on things. But things were moving too fast. It was as if he were speeding toward a conclusion already formed, yet scrupulously denied.

"You've either gone off the edge," Heath continued, "or you're making a piss-poor case for reestablishing control over the discovery. Which by the way, you can forget about. The museum is withdrawing its sponsorship."

"Damn it, Curtis. You still don't get it. This isn't about sponsorship, or money, or credit. It's about the fiery deaths of six people. And the danger of a great many more dying."

"I'm beginning to sense you actually believe it's about myths come to life. About spirits and manitous or some sort of haunting from the past."

"I'm not sure what I believe anymore," Fielding answered. His equivocations were making it easy for Heath. "You're right when you say it's not about sponsorship. It's about you. Simply stated, Professor Fielding, you're not fit to run any archaeological dig. And when I speak to the dean at the university, I'm sure he'll agree. And quite frankly, I wouldn't be surprised at all if he might feel you're not fit to teach, either."

Heath wouldn't listen, Fielding thought. There was nothing more to say.

After he replaced the receiver in its cradle, he turned to look at Jean. She was wide awake and staring at him.

"What can we do?" she said.

What can we do? Fielding echoed to himself. The question touched off a tremulous chord within him, and carried on its quavering notes, a thought resonated that had come with uncomfortable certainty to his mind earlier: *As fire consumes its fuel, it grows stronger.*

Fielding couldn't answer Jean's question. And he didn't know how much time he'd have to try.

The time was coming. Tonight. He was sure of it. Life would rise from the flames.

Sensing the excitement, Makwamacatawa rose quickly to his feet. But he moved too fast. He had forgotten the dizziness. The blood rushed from his head, and he stumbled backward, falling against the scaly bark of a red pine. He closed his eyes for a moment, but that only caused the whirling sensation to worsen.

Makwamacatawa lifted his face upward and looked at the sky. Tonight would be the third night of his vision quest, the third night he had been without food. The hunger was a constant, almost throbbing, pain in his stomach, but that kind of pain he could put up with. It was the dizziness that incapacitated him. When he moved too fast, it felt as though a scythe were set in motion, revolving around a fixed point in the center of his skull. There was nothing he could do to stop the motion of the blade but wait.

As he stood slumped against the tree, staring skyward, staring at the long needles and bunches of pinecones, all intermingled with leafy intrusions from a nearby beech, the motion he felt inside left his mind and spiraled on high. The leaves and needles, cones and twigs, began to move in synchrony, not with the wind, but with some other force. He began to see—he thought he saw—the upper canopy coming together into a recognizable shape. A face, a symbol, he wasn't quite sure. All he could be sure of was that the shape coalescing above him was not a natural form. It was an attempt at making contact.

He pushed himself away from the tree, not noticing that the pain in his head had subsided. He took his eyes off the scene above him for a second as he glanced at his footing; then as he looked upward again, the shapes, the motion, the attempt at communication, were gone.

A hallucination? The doubt blipped only momentarily in his mind. They had appeared in the fire. And on other occasions, he had thought they were attempting other links. Each time, he questioned whether what he witnessed was genuine or only his imagination, but increasingly, he lacked the ability to differentiate between the two. Increasingly, the difference between the two seemed to lack significance.

Makwamacatawa looked at the clumps of moss in the towel tucked into his waist like an apron. This would finish it, he decided. What he had just collected would be the last of the insulation for the sweatlodge.

Tonight he would enter the chamber of heat and purification. Tonight he would cleanse himself of all his earthly impurities and at last become a vessel receptive to the messages of the Ancient Ones. Tonight the continuum of past and present would be fused.

Chapter 18

THE LIGHTS FLASHED overhead, signaling that the library was closing in five minutes. Fielding regarded them with frustration. There was so much to learn. So much he didn't know.

A theory had begun to take shape in his mind. Who the people of the cave were. Why they died. And what was happening now. Northern European anthropology was not his field, but through the course of his studies, he had been exposed to it. That's why he could only sketch the outer limits of an explanation. That's why he had rushed to Michigan Tech in Houghton to get access to the university library.

He had found plenty of material on the subject, which helped fill in the blanks, but in the final analysis, these were scientific works. They were not manuals of lost ritual. But could he have reasonably expected anything more? So, like the Late Woodland people who had first encountered the Europeans, Fielding would have to determine what to do on his own. He would have to figure out his own way to battle the legacy of the Awshkoute.

Though he remained uncertain about a lot of things, the connection between the skeletal remains of the people in the cave and the fires was undeniable. It was for that reason he had urged Curtis Heath to return what he stole. It was for that reason he had to return to the site of the excavation the assortment of bones recovered from the vicinity of the cabin fire.

The sweatlodge was a small, domed structure about seven feet in diameter and no more than five feet high. Makwamacatawa had cut and stripped fifteen maple saplings and sunk them in a circle at the top of the knoll. The poles had been bent over and lashed together, then covered with rectangular swatches of cedar bark and insulated with dried bunches of moss.

In the center of the hut was a scooped-out depression for the stones, and from there a sacred path led out the narrow door to Makwamacatawa's fire pit. He had prepared a grid of wood to support the rocks once the coals had taken well. At the moment, the rocks that would become his messenger stones circled the pit.

Makwamacatawa eyed the rocks. Then he studied the lodge. Everything was ready. The sky was darkening. It was time to light the fire.

He was nervous, and unexpectedly, he sensed a growing fear. He feared he would lack the strength to carry everything to its conclusion. He feared he would fail his people. And he feared the shapes in the fire.

As if to deny the anxieties, Makwamacatawa hefted a plastic jug and poured himself a large cup of water. He gulped it down, letting it spill out the corners of his mouth and run down his chin onto his neck. The water had sustained him, but it did not nourish him. It seemed to intensify the emptiness in his stomach, heightening the pain he felt. But the hunger would soon recede. He would soon glimpse the open-time. He would soon learn what to do about the spiritual sickness that had gripped the land.

Makwamacatawa slowly went down to his knees, and speaking into the frozen features of the black bear, he recited his litany of respect and pleas for guidance and strength. When he finished, he lifted the cloak from the bush and draped it over his back, fixing the head of the black bear over his own. The anxieties he had felt were already dissipating, partly due to his activity, partly due to a conscious effort to leave all worldly thoughts behind.

In this latter regard, he was succeeding. His twentieth-century self increasingly seemed but a dim memory. He was moving back along the continuum, as the ancients, he was certain, were moving forward. He felt one pace from the open-time, and tonight that step would be taken. Of that he was confident. He had seen them struggle to take shape in the fire the last two nights, and he could sense the frustration. He was sure they sensed it too. They wanted to come out of the fire. They wanted to enter him.

Makwamacatawa knelt at the circle of rocks, lit a match, then began to ignite the kindling.

By the time Fielding had retraced the sixty-five miles from Houghton to Watersdrop, then another seven to the dirt cutoff that led to the sinkhole, it was dark and he couldn't help but feel a simmering sense of danger. He glanced at the small gray back-pack on the seat next to him. It was almost laughable that he, a man of science, a chronicler of past histories, would fear the centuries-old reach of these fire-blackened remains. But despite the illogic of it all, the fact was he had felt its reach once. He had seen it. And six people had died.

As he entered the tunnel of trees, the dusk sky darkened all the more. It seemed as though the woods were closing in, the branches were reaching lower, the narrow gap behind him coming together after he passed. It was as though he were being swallowed by the forest, as though the trees and brush, the woody stems and grasses, all conspired to absorb him into the seamless fabric of this wild place. It was drawing him in, deeper, cutting him off from all contact with the outer world, erecting barriers behind him, seeking to prevent his escape.

Fielding's hands grew slippery on the wheel. He watched the road and the forest to either side of the road. It was as if he expected something to emerge at any time. It was as if he expected to see the return of the representatives of the Ancient Ones.

He drove slower as he neared the dig, the truck easing through the potholes and ruts, and over the embedded stones and scuffed roots. As the surroundings became increasingly familiar, he could not hold himself back from glancing ahead, trying to see through the trees, to view the site of the excavation.

Something was different, he could tell. Instinctively, he hit the lights. Following the sudden deepening of the pall, the difference was all the more noticeable. There was an uneven texture to the night, a glimmering, glowing quality to the space beyond the last rows of trees.

Fielding let the truck glide to a halt, then cut the engine, looped his hand through the shoulder straps of the gray pack, and climbed out of the vehicle. He listened for a moment before moving on, following the dirt trail toward the clearing ahead.

As he neared the site, he could see the flickering reflection against the bank of trees above him. He could see the orange glow wavering in the night sky. He could see the fire.

The flames had leapt high, but that's not what Makwamacatawa was waiting for. He continued to add eighteen-inch lengths of one-to-two-inch diameter sticks, laying them carefully over the burning wood, renewing the grid as it burned down. When there was a thick bed of coals, when the grid was still substantial enough to support the weight, Makwamacatawa began to roll some of the rocks onto the fire.

When each rock dropped onto the grid, a splash of sparks flew off into the air. They were mini-tracers, leaving yellowish streaks of afterimage around the periphery of his eyesight. As he worked, as more rocks were shoveled onto the pile, as more streamers were ejected from the fire, the afterimages began to overtake each other. They seemed to be combining into linear patterns. Into another attempt to reach him. And why shouldn't another attempt be made now? he thought. It had been happening all day. The white pine needles that prickled his back with no wind, the nuthatch that clung upside down to the bark, eyeing him, and the motion in the trees above him when he gathered the last bit of moss.

The Ancient Ones were here. He could sense them. And soon, he would see them.

Fielding could see the frantic activity of the sparks. And he could feel it. Inside. The same heated tempo of activity had entered his body, touching off a series of electrical discharges that sparked throughout every nerve in his system.

It was an eerie sight he witnessed, a fur-cloaked figure awkwardly moving about the fire, framed by a semicircular mound of earthen materials behind him. Watching the scene, witnessing the action of the fire, Fielding began to fall victim to an indecipherable dread. It was irrational, he knew, but in past days the rational world had yielded its control on events to the power of the fire.

Could this man resist it? Could he control it? Why was he spared when six others had died?

Peering through the cover of leaves on the edge of the clearing, Fielding studied the terrain he would have to cross. He checked the sightlines, the potential cover, and based on his observations, made his decision. He had planned to revisit the cave with his gray pack, but because of the time, the darkness, he could not go that far. At least, those were the reasons he allowed himself to admit.

Pushing through the leaves, he began to creep forward, all the while keeping his eyes trained on the knoll, on the bear-cowled figure in front of the dark hut, on the streamers that erupted out of the fire. He couldn't explain why stealth was so important. Under critical examination, he would have been hard-pressed to explain why he was afraid. All he knew was that he could not deny the sensations generated by his fear. He could not deny the urgent command not to be seen.

It was the eyes that startled him, the glass eyes set in the head of the white-tailed deer. They reflected the beam of his flashlight.

Curtis Heath turned on the overhead lights, revealing a ceremonial deer hide draped over a brace in front of a light blue background. The museum photographer was in the middle of a shoot, part of his current task of photographing the institution's holdings for the new catalogue. The photographer wasn't there now, which was why Heath had come. The entire studio was deserted at this hour.

Photography was a tool as important as any in an archaeologist's toolbox, and Heath had mastered the techniques in far more difficult surroundings. Just as he had done the carbon dating on his own, he would create the photographic record by himself. It was bad enough that that hopeless soul Christopher Fielding was part of the picture. He didn't want to risk bringing anyone else into the loop of information.

As he laid out white sheeting on a bench, he couldn't help but think about his conversation with Fielding. After he had gotten off the phone with him earlier, he felt certain that the man was trying a desperate ruse to salvage his professional stake in the discovery. But the more he thought about it, the more that just didn't make sense, even for a man as pathetic as Fielding. So Heath came to the only logical conclusion. The man really had broken. Like a schoolkid who hears noises in a cemetery, he panicked, ascribing what he did not understand to ghosts.

Heath smiled as he lifted the lid on the cardboard box. Carefully, he extracted the blackened skull and jawbone of a fifteenth-century European he had recovered from the Cave of Bones. He joined the two pieces together, bringing the mandible up against the maxilla, then positioned the skull on the bench so the first set of photographs would show clearly how the teeth occluded.

With the skull set in place, he began to work on placement of the lights and camera. The last thing he had to do before he was ready was to connect the flash heads of the strobes to the condenser. The condenser included the flash generator, and together they formed an electronic box the size and weight of a car battery. Its function was to augment the power of the normal electrical current, to as much as two thousand volts.

When the insulated cords were plugged in, he was ready for the first shot.

The sharp crack split the night air with the resounding effect of a rifle shot. Makwamacatawa staggered back, as much from the sound as the shower of sparks that spat out of the pit. The bits of flaming debris struck him in the face, the chest, and in the fur along his arms. Instead of reacting to the pinpoints of pain, he reared back and bellowed at the sky in the voice of the black bear. The Ancient Ones were present. They were communicating with him. The messenger stones were ready.

Makwamacatawa picked up a four-foot stake he had readied for the next aspect of the ritual. Jabbing it into the pit, he began to maneuver the rocks. The one that had cracked from the heat fell into two sharp-edged chunks. He levered them to the side, then selected a stone from the center of the heap of red ash. Wedging the stick under it, he rolled it out of the fire, then maneuvered it along the sacred path, through the entrance of the sweatlodge, and into the depression under the peak of the dome. Retracing his steps, he selected a second stone.

As his stake again delved amid the flames and embers, the fire seemed to react to his interference. It began to jump and dance, gorging on the infusion of oxygen, greedily seeking out more. Flares bulged and spiked, chasing back the dark, snapping at the wind, reaching out toward the cowled figure. And Makwamacatawa began to react to the fire.

He began to feel it inside of him. Hot fluids flowed through his veins, capillaries carrying the heat to the surface of his skin. As he worked, as he drew more stones out of the fire and maneuvered them into the sweatlodge, the heated feel of exertion and excitement merged with the heat of the fire. He was at the confluence of these rivers of heat, their combined flow increasing in degree and current, moving faster, hotter, making everything about him faster, hotter. Leaves and ferns near the summit of the knoll seemed to roil in a wind. The minute pits and pebbles of the sacred path lost their distinction. The ribs of the interior of the sweatlodge and its earthen smell came and went rapidly with each entrance and exit. And the fire . . . it seemed little more than a yellow-white blur flashing in the dark, spearing the night air with sharp, pointed lobes that frantically curled back inward on themselves as if reaching for something, as if trying to snare more fuel, as if in a desperate effort to hook and draw into its furnace the stuff of its life.

The fire pulsated with energy, its long flickers of light stretching out tortuously, like the fingers on an arthritic hand, like the claws of an anguished carnivore. As Makwamacatawa bent over the pit, as his stake raked the rocks and glowing ashes, the fingers, the claws, the many-tentacled fire reached out around him as if seeking a hold, as if trying to grasp and draw him down. But the flames of course were of one elemental nature, and he another. They lacked the substance to affect him directly. But the flames did affect the febrile flow in his veins. He was hot and sick and his mind a cycloning firestorm, spinning faster, hotter, stealing his equilibrium as it stole his independent thought.

Makwamacatawa stabbed the stake into the heap of ash and leaned heavily upon it, hovering directly over the pit, staring straight down into the fire, into the coals, into the red-hot heart of the beast of flames.

From his position flat on the ground, Fielding watched the half man, half bear balanced over the fire. He watched as the flames shot up, practically engulfing him. His first urge was to shout out in warning, to clamber up the knoll and pull Blackbear out of the fire, but instead he remained prone, his head cocked awkwardly above the earth.

Fear restricted him, to be sure, but there was something else that made him hold back. The fire seemed to be having little effect on the bear-man. He was encased in a glowing cocoon, the tongues of yellow heat lapping up, around and over him, but not igniting what he wore. Was he fooled by his own perspective? Fielding asked himself.

He didn't have time to consider the answer before there was another crack. He had dived to the ground earlier, before he realized that the sound was not a weapon but a stone splitting in the heat. This time, the effect on him of the sharp report was the reverse. Fielding pushed himself to his feet and dashed toward the V-shaped trench that cut to the lip of the sinkhole.

He dove to the ground, then rolled to the bottom of the trench. Without stopping, he scrambled on his hands and knees toward the brink of the sinkhole, and at the edge he dropped down to the first ledge. Searching frantically, he dislodged some rubble, wedged his gray day pack into a crevice, then covered it as best he could with the stone debris.

He climbed back up to the surface and glanced once toward the knoll before breaking across the open field. In the brief instant he had allowed himself to look, he had seen that Blackbear was standing straight now, having pulled back out of the fire. As for the fire itself, it seemed even larger than before.

As his feet pounded over the hard surface, as shafts of chilled night air rushed through his throat, Fielding thought of the circular burn scars that had led from the lightning strike to the cabin. He visualized them being formed. He wondered how fast *it* could run.

Powered by his fear, by the vision of horror that came uninvited into his mind, he pushed himself harder, faster, until the twigs and brush of the surrounding cover slashed at his face, until the bank of vegetation thrashed at his arms, around his legs, threatening to ensnare him. The leafy, crinkling sound for a moment seemed the noise of fire, pursuing him, coming closer, about to overtake him.

Fielding crooked an elbow around a sapling and spun back toward the clearing. There was no fire near him, nothing at all in pursuit. But the flames atop the knoll had lost none of their energy. Through the brush he could see them flashing and flickering and gyrating in front of the bear-cowled figure. Was he still stirring the coals? Was he adding new tinder? Almost involuntarily, Fielding found himself pushing back to the edge of the clearing, bending aside the last branches for a clearer view.

Blackbear was highlighted by the flickering brightness, and though Fielding was too far away to see his face, partially covered by the upper jaw of the bear head, he could see that the man was staring into the flames. And he could hear him. From across the clearing Fielding could hear words of English and syllables of a near-dead language mixed into a rhythmic chant.

As he watched, the fire seemed to take on the same rhythm. It boiled upward on the rise of Blackbear's voice, individual lobes snapping and breaking free at the height of the shouts, then receding to the embers as Blackbear began again. The fire was an active, excited display of primal energy, and though Fielding was also too far away to distinguish its details, it did seem to generate a continuing pattern. Light and shadow seemed to appear in the same places, over and over.

Fielding tried to swallow, but his mouth had gone dry. It was as if the fire had indeed touched him during his mad run, as if it had come into his chest and now lingered inside him, producing a raw, burning feeling down his throat, in his lungs, in the delicate membrane of his eyes.

He scrunched his eyes tightly closed to dispel the dry sensation, to chase the image of a fire controlling its own release of energy, but when he opened them, nothing had changed. In fact, the pattern seemed to be holding. The flames seemed to be growing. And Blackbear was unhitching the strap across his chest, lifting the cowl off his head, removing the cloak of the bear hide from his shoulders.

Though Fielding couldn't discern his features, for a second, for one awful moment, it seemed as though Blackbear could see him. It seemed as though his gaze locked directly on Fielding's position in the brush.

Fielding let the branches snap out of his hands, and he began to retreat, sinking farther into the woods, into the darkness, into the conspiracy of this wild place.

He lifted the black cowl off his head and looked at the light. Heath thought he discerned a burnt odor, but nothing appeared out of the ordinary. Perhaps it was just the heat of the strobe burning off collected dust.

The camera he used was a Deardorff, a wooden-box studio camera that used four-by-five transparencies. Sliding the thin metal sheeting over the exposed transparency, he lifted the entire frame out of the camera and replaced it with another.

He was about to raise the focusing cloth over his head again, when he thought better of it. Looking through the lens on the earlier shots, it had seemed as though the flash of the two strobes on either side of the bench was too bright. He couldn't be sure, it wasn't his equipment after all, but it just did not seem right. So he decided to expose the next transparency with his head out from under the focusing cloth and concentrate instead on the lighting.

He plunged the cable release and instantly recoiled. He grabbed his eyes and squeezed, but the glare, the burning feel, only seemed to pulse brighter. "What the hell—?"

Settling on a stool behind him, he arched his neck back, then opened his eyes wide. At first there was no change, but gradually the imprinted glare began to shrink and he started to recover his vision. As he did, he stared at the silver-hooded flash heads, each of them standing quiet and dark, their flat quartz faces directed toward the skull on the bench.

Heath hadn't been staring at them directly when he shot the picture, so he couldn't be certain, but as he replayed the sudden and brilliant flash, it seemed that it had been something more than an electronic burst of light. It seemed as though, for just a second, the electricity had yielded to a more primitive form of energy, as though the light it emitted had some manner of substance to it. It seemed as though an arc of true flame had bulged outward from the strobes.

He had seen them, in the heart of the fire. He had heard them, in the crack of the stone. And now they reached for him, in the waver of the flames.

Rearing back his head, the black bear growled at the stars in a voice of pain and pleading. Then in the next instant the voice of man erupted with the same emotion, the same pleas. "Ancient spirits—*Kewaze maw-neto*—soul of our people, we need your guidance. We need your wisdom. We need your courage. *Nossimog, Nomeshawmesemog, kenaw wob kene-tchawnog. Kenaw wob keweyaw.* Come to us!"

A crackling, snapping tumult of wood being twisted and broken by the heat almost deafened him to his own voice. *"Nawdo pone-getaytaw-we mawtchi kegeto,"* he was saying, pleading for forgiveness in allowing the desecration; *"Nawdo dawmaw tchawn mawtchi kegeto,"* calling for help in ending the desecration: *"Wekau Nomeshawmesemog pesaw nin,"* inviting his grandfathers to enter him. He repeated the lines, the prayer becoming a mantra. As he chanted, as he stared straight ahead, the bank of light and dark shimmered like a stage curtain dipped in luminescent paint. The brightness blinded him to everything else, blacking out the clearing, the woods, even the stars. He was encased in a black envelope, and his sole focus became the fire, the flames, the mad flashing movement of its arms.

Arms they were, he was sure of it. The frantically flailing limbs of his people, grasping desperately for substance, for a chance to communicate. They were seeking contact with their descendant on the continuum, a vessel pure enough to receive their godly presence. They were seeking him!

Makwamacatawa ripped open the chest strap, pulled his head from under the cowl and raised the hide of the black bear from his body. He turned and strode with a new steadiness to the sweatlodge and fixed his cloak to the top of the doorframe, draping the bear fur so it completely covered the opening. He stood back and pulled his shirt open at the front, snapping off most of the buttons. In a few seconds all his clothes were strewn to the side, and in the custom of his people, he entered the sweatlodge bare-skinned and totally unconnected to the temporal world.

Makwamacatawa crawled to the far side of the pile of heated rocks and sat on the ground, folding his legs in front of him. The heat made him breathe harder, but the temperature was only beginning to rise. Next to his position was a wooden bowl of water, and cupping his hands together, he ladled some of it onto the rocks. The water hissed, turning instantly to steam, and as it rose, it carried with it a wall of heat. The wall was a solid thing, and it rocked Makwamacatawa back on his haunches. He gasped for breath, but the hot air offered no relief. It scorched his throat and collapsed his lungs. It was burning away the impurities. It was cleansing his soul. It was carrying him back on the continuum.

Makwamacatawa reached again for the bowl of water, but it seemed to be in motion. A storm brewed on its surface, the clear liquid seeming to bulge and settle as if it were an entity possessed of life on its own. Makwamacatawa's eyelids closed briefly, and as they did, he felt adrift in the storm, rising and falling with the waves, subject to its currents, spinning into its whirling action.

He felt sick and dizzy and afloat in another world, falling away from this one, drifting back in time. "Grandfathers," he breathed. "I am here. Come."

Forcing himself forward, relying on touch rather than sight, he dipped his hands into the water again and sprinkled it on the rocks. A second assault smacked into his chest, his face, engulfing his entire body. His skin seemed afire, his mind seemed awash, but through it all he felt a kind of happy delirium. The visions would come, he was sure. The Ancient Ones were coming. The desecrations would end. The spiritual sickness that gripped the land would cease.

"Carry my message to the soul villages," he said into the steam as it rose above the rocks. "Come."

The fire in the pit outside the domed hut breached its enclosure and began to move. Whether reacting to the entreaties of the man inside the sweatlodge, or guided by its own designs, the fire was answering his prayer. It was coming.

Ground litter turned brilliant red, flared briefly into flame, then turned to cinder as the fire progressed. It progressed as a fire does, by following its fuel and leaving the combustibles consumed in its wake. And yet it advanced not as a random movement of nature, but in a disciplined fashion, along narrow parameters, choosing which tinder to engulf, ignoring dry grasses all around. Its advance carried the appearance of deliberate motion. It suggested the reactions of a thinking organism. It displayed the behavior of a predator that knows its prey has nowhere to run.

Makwamacatawa's journey had begun in fourth grade, suffering the insults of his schoolmates after seeing the skeleton of his grandfather in the glass case at the museum. He sensed that his journey had reached a crossroads. A new signpost lay just ahead.

Along the way, there had been other defining moments. At present, his vision quest was one. But despite the demanding nature of all he was enduring, despite being buffeted between a conscious world of deprivation and his hoped-for world of liberating visions, what came so forcefully into his mind was a time when he had sat alone at a desk in a lecture room of desks. As quiet exists at the heart of a storm, Makwamacatawa would—for this brief moment—see and remember everything about that day in class at the university. He remembered the professor describing the excavation of the Indian cemetery, how the bodies were carefully exposed to the air, how the skeletons were disjointed bone by bone. He remembered the details of the lecture as if he had witnessed the desecration himself: They pulled jewelry off fingers, beads from around necks; they separated medicine pouches from the bodies, emptying them of the otter and fisher skulls, thus destroying the magic they contained. They pulled hair from the skull with dried skin still attached, to analyze with acids and chemicals, and where the hair was threaded through tinkling cones, they removed the cones, taking them, and other artifacts given to the dead for their use in the next world, and placing them in the dusty recesses of laboratories or in glass cases on public display. Makwamacatawa remembered sitting there in class after everyone had left, and thinking about the souls cast into eternal suffering because they no longer had the power or the implements to feed and protect themselves. He remembered the sick feeling that permeated his soul. He remembered the despair. And he remembered the anger.

The anger of that time revisited him, bringing with it its own manner of heat. It was an internal warmth that combined with the dry heat of the stones, the oppressive atmosphere of the tiny hut, to push him closer to the limits of reality.

He sprinkled more water on the rocks, and as the steam boiled upward, he began to imagine he could see facial contour in the rising clouds. He thought he could see the tentative first foray into this world from the other. He looked hard for his vision. He wanted desperately to see the vision. And soon, he felt certain, he would see it.

The line of yellow and blue flames hugged tight to the ground, but the colors and brightness were intense. And the flames were active, flickering madly as if in a continuing crosswind. But rather than reacting to the currents of air and spreading in every direction, the fire kept close to its core. Whatever new energy it absorbed went into its intensity and its singular advance. If indeed guided by a sentient force, it could be imagined as marshaling its power, waiting until the moment was ripe; seeking out selected tinder. Then finally, it was there.

The line of fire touched the bottom edge of the barken wall, and as it did, it flared suddenly upward. As if sucked by a powerful draft, the flame raced up across the side of the sweatlodge, hugging tight to its surface, following the twisting, striated grooves of the patches of cedar bark. Instantly, the curving side wall of the hut was transformed in appearance to an expanse of living tissue, exposed veins pulsing with yellow fluids. The fire followed the grooves, it flowed through the veins, it greedily snatched new fuel from the woody material. It burned into the bark, gouging at the weakest points, seeking to bore its way through to the cavity inside.

All the while, the pulsing action of the ribbons of flame throbbed faster. They became whiter, hotter. Tiny spikes of fire leapt free of the hut, snapping excitedly at the night air. An anxious expectancy had come to the fire. It was growing stronger. More powerful. It seemed as though it were reacting to the new tension atop the knoll. It seemed to sense the tension inside the sweatlodge.

• • •

He could hear them. Scratching and clawing at the outer surface of the lodge. They had heard his prayer. They were coming.

Makwamacatawa's heart pounded in his chest. Sweat glistened on his naked skin, and where it touched his lips he could taste the salt. Where it seeped into his eyes, he could feel the sting. His vision was clouded by the sweat, by the steam, by the fervor of his religious zeal. But through the blur the interior of the lodge was changing. It was growing brighter. To his left, the arched wall was beginning to glow.

It was a patterned glow, a network of snaking lines of brightness, and as he watched, as he waited, linear scars of red light began to appear on the inside of the bark. Moss stuffed into the cracks began to drop, and on occasion, the red light spread like a lit fuse through its veins and tiny sprigs.

It was a bright, glorious light. The light of the heavens, the light of the sun. The light of fire.

They had tried for two nights to speak to him through the fire, and now the frustrations would end. He was a pure vessel, a worthy conduit of their knowledge and power. He was their descendant. He was part of them. The continuum was a single line. There was no end and no beginning. Who existed before existed now. Who lived today carried the spirits of the past.

Rocking from side to side, Makwamacatawa accidentally dropped his hand on the wood bowl, and it tipped, throwing the last of its water onto the rocks. A serpent's hiss filled the hut, and a new wall of heat and steam exploded into his chest. As it pushed him back, there was another eruption, coming so fast he would have thought it part of the action of the steam, an integrated maneuver in response to the message of the stones.

Along the network of glowing lines, at the edges of the rectangular slabs of overlaid cedar bark, the fire of the ancients burst into the chamber. Makwamacatawa could only look on in wonder, for suddenly, he was not alone.

The fire flared again. This time, there was no mistake. Heath circled to the far side of the bench, staring at the strobes as he kept them at a distance. They stood mutely, undamaged and unchanged.

Noises in the graveyard, he thought. That's all it was. And damned if he was going to be like Fielding and leap to absurd conclusions. There had to be an explanation for what seemed a flash of flame from the strobes.

Heath stepped back around the bench, walking to the condenser. He wasn't used to this kind of studio equipment. Was it set too high? He checked the gauges, the switches, making minor adjustments. He double-checked the wiring to the flash heads, then looked into the face of the lights themselves. He could see the quartz-glass shell filaments, the carefully lined seals, the precision hardware. All specially selected to resist and control the incredible surge of energy. For just the fraction of a second, the heat produced in each flash neared one thousand degrees Fahrenheit.

After rotating the skull a quarter turn, Heath stepped back to the camera. This time, he pulled the focusing cloth over his head. Peering through the lens, staring into the empty sockets of a man who had burned to death six hundred years before, he hesitated. He couldn't help but feel that he was not alone. He couldn't help but feel that there was life within that dead gaze.

His voice was an indecipherable sound, a tangled blend of terror and awe. And answering him came a throaty rush of heated air. It was the sound of fire drafted through a vent, the sound of a windstorm blowing through the slats of an old hill house. It was the voice of the ancients.

Illusion had become real; reality had blended with illusion. Whatever was happening, Makwamacatawa was part of it. He was part of his own vision, or the hallucination had absorbed him into its false images. It was all the same.

The fire had crept inward along the edges of the bark slabs like water seeping through rotten floorboards. Gradually it had come together, forming a flat expanse of light. It was light that moved, both with the natural motion of fire and the deliberate motion of something seeking its own order. The flames followed the contour of the bark, but they also displayed a contour of their own. It was an uneven outline, a shape with ephemeral borders that expanded and retreated with the flickering of the flames, with the blackening of the wood. But despite the shifting nature of his vision, Makwamacatawa could recognize the shape for what it was. It was a visage come to him from the end of the continuum.

"Grandfather," he breathed, "come to me. Teach me. Show me the open-time."

In the center of the two-dimensional representation of a face, a black crevice began to part. It was an approximation of a carnivore's jaw slowly opening, revealing narrow spikes that gleamed not with internal moisture, but with white-hot heat. The creature hissed, and its breath carried into Makwamacatawa's face a wall of heated air like the hot blow released earlier by the messenger stones. The Ancient Ones were trying to reach him. They were trying to speak.

From along the edge of the wavering curtain of light, a round hump of flame began to take the shape of an appendage. Slowly, it pulled free of its flat expanse, extending outward from the wall of the lodge, reaching out toward Makwamacatawa. And he reached his arm toward it.

Fielding's foot came down hard on the brake, then a fraction of a second later, on the clutch. The dirt trail had yielded first to grassy ruts, and now it disappeared completely in front of him. All he could see was a tangle of vegetation and small trees. The conspiracy of this wild place had reclaimed the old lumber trail, and it threatened to engulf him.

Fielding looked quickly over his shoulder, then shifted into reverse and gunned the engine. He had to drive backward a good hundred feet before there was a clear enough spot off the road for him to turn around. As the truck lurched forward, the wheels dropping heavily into the ruts, he edged forward in the seat for a better view of the ground he was covering.

He hadn't noticed where he had gone wrong. So many of the intersecting trails looked alike, and he hadn't been concentrating on what he was doing. He had been thinking about the fire. He had been thinking about the man who stood like a sorcerer almost engulfed by the flames, chanting in the language of the people who had lived on this land half a millennium ago.

The fire had seemingly come alive, reacting to Blackbear's voice, billowing skyward with the same excitement and energy as its enchanter. Or was it Blackbear who was under the thrall of the fire? They were acting together, the rising shoots of flame a visual display to match the frenetic cries of the man. It was a vision Blackbear had been seeking, and it was a vision that Fielding had seen. But a vision of what he wasn't sure.

If it was a manifestation of the people in the cave, how could it join with the descendant of those who had massacred them? What was the man's power over the fire? Or was his a power of a different sort entirely, conjured out of the magic of his own people's past?

Fielding let an unsteady breath escape from his lungs. What was happening to him? A man of science so easily falling prey to the foolish prattle of the superstitious. Had his fear reduced him to such a state so fast?

For a second the reflection from the woods on either side went to black, and Fielding hit the brakes again hard. It was an intersecting road. He looked out his side window, then turned onto the new path. It was the road to the highway. He was sure of it.

As he made the turn, he immediately began to question himself again. About the road, about what he believed was happening. The simple truth was, he didn't know what he believed anymore. And it was the lack of knowing that affected him the most. Though he couldn't say how or why, he did feel certain that he had seen the root of something evil back at the site of the excavation. And he felt he had to get away as fast as possible.

He wasn't sure what he was seeing. Even in his dreamlike state he could not interpret all that was happening. But he was certain that whatever it was, it signified his acceptance into the eternal order. It told him his journey that had begun at that museum was about to end. It marked his near-arrival in the open-time.

Makwamacatawa's fingers neared the fiery appendage that extended from the wall of flame. It was the arm of his grandfather, the hand of their protective spirits; it was his link to his people's visionary past.

The claws of the fire-thing touched his fingertips, and Makwamacatawa stiffened with the sensation. It was a sharp feel that penetrated the length of his fingers, converging in his wrist, rushing up the length of his arm. As a jolt of electricity both packs a heavy force and burns, the surging power held Makwamacatawa fast and inflamed him with its spread. His whole body seemed to vibrate, and his neck straightened, throwing back his head.

He cast his eyes directly forward at the burning wall of light, and he could see that the creature of the flames was developing new contours. Along the edges it was rounding, coming out of the wall, developing three-dimensional form. Deepening hues of yellow and red framed the blackening orifices of the beast.

Shadows became more distinct. Features more defined. It was coming alive!

And Makwamacatawa was weakening. The heat-fever threatened to steal his consciousness. He gasped, seeking sustaining gulps of oxygen to hold on. For his people, he needed strength. For his own vision, he needed to keep his mind receptive. He needed to communicate. He needed to hear. He needed to meld with the being on the continuum. He needed all of these things, and yet despite his efforts, he could not stem his growing feebleness, which corresponded with the increasing activity and depth of definition coming to the beast of light. The connection between the two was lost on him. In his half world of dream and illusion, he did not understand that the flames were gaining vitality while he was losing his. And the process only accelerated.

The creeping electricity passed through his chest. It bled upward through the narrow isthmus of his neck. The surging advance touched his brain. It entered the very center of his skull. As it did, Makwamacatawa's thoughts came wondrously alive in a shower of sparks and tracers of light that rocketed across his closed eyelids. It was the end of his journey. He had passed the temporal boundaries. He had entered the realm of the never dead and touched the soul of his people.

Makwamacatawa shouted out in triumph. The tendons in his neck stretched taut as he bellowed in jubilation at his achievement. His voice shrieked in recognition of the contact. He cried out in pleasure at his ascendancy. He cried out at the culmination of his sacrifices. He cried out . . . in pain.

Makwamacatawa's body went suddenly limp, and he slumped at the waist. Forcing his chin up, opening his eyes, he saw that the being had broken off its touch. And it was standing on twin pillars of fire directly atop the messenger stones, tethered at its back by stringy lobes of flame to the combustible tinder of the lodge wall. The fire itself had spread throughout the domed hut, entombing its two occupants in a glowing web of support poles and beams. Bits of the incandescent being broke off from itself and snapped at Makwamacatawa, burning lesions in his chest, his stomach, his thighs. Barely aware of the pain, Makwamacatawa concentrated on keeping consciousness, on keeping his eyes open.

The spectral representation of his visionary image raised a limb. As it rose in front of him, at its extremity the fire split into a lineal pattern of projections, an array of clawlike firelets too numerous to count. They spread wider, rearing back, all the while holding Makwamacatawa under his visionary spell. Then suddenly, with the swiftness of a windblown blaze, the appendage lashed forward, cupping its palm across Makwamacatawa's face, spreading its lineal projections around his head, sinking its claws into the back of his skull. The flame entered his nostrils, his aural cavities, it forced its way between his teeth, sucked inward as if responding to an internal draft.

Blinded, deafened, mute, Makwamacatawa silently mouthed the words, "Come, Grandfathers," and the fire that was not his grandfather came inside.

Fielding let the rise of the hill slow the truck, until at the top he came to a full halt. He was at the ridge that presented a view over the trees toward the Cave of Bones, where, a seeming eternity ago, he had seen the smoke hovering in the sinkhole from Buck Billings's last camp fire. Now, of course, because of the dark he couldn't see the circular imprint like an elephant's track, but he could see a glowing smudge. A distant light. A fire.

Fielding climbed out of the truck and ran to the brink of the ridge. He stared at the distant light, trying to judge its shape, its size. But fire is not a constant thing, rather a series of advances and retreats. It doesn't offer exact boundaries. The intensity of the light varies. For these reasons, it took a few seconds for Fielding to get a fix on what had happened back there atop the knoll. It took a few seconds for him to realize what had changed.

No longer a camp fire restricted to the confines of Blackbear's pit, it was a raging blaze the shape of a half dome. The shape of the sweatlodge.

As Fielding watched, as his pupils dilated and expanded with each subtle movement of his eyes between the pinpoint of light and the black, the fire changed suddenly, and he flinched. Squinting, he stared at a great upwelling of the flames, the skyward thrust of a yellow saber. It was an explosion without sound, an angry, slashing display that pierced the night.

Fielding staggered, suddenly unsteady. Momentarily blinded by the light, he couldn't distinguish ground from air. His heels began to grope backward, seeking to move away from the edge of the ridge. Loose stones rolled under the soles of his shoes, contributing to his dizzy instability. Fielding kept his eyes away from the brightness, and slowly some manner of vision returned. He knew he shouldn't look back, at least until he was on safer ground, but the temptation to understand what was happening was strong. He turned and saw a pillar of fire, and for one awful moment he was frozen again by the glare. By chords of fear resonating throughout his nerves. By the fact that the fire was changing again.

It was spraying forward like a lava spurt in a storm, its flaming detritus blown away from its source, landing on new tinder, setting it afire, advancing at first slowly, then picking up speed as it fed on itself. The fire spread outward, but not in a growing circle. It was more like a wave channeled through a narrow chute, flowing only in one direction. In the direction of the ridge.

The fire surged with new energy, blasting skyward through the roof of the hut, spitting streamers into the black air, flailing, snapping, rippling with a display of violence and primal forces no longer held dormant. There was a directionless madness at first to the flames, then very quickly, some manner of order came to the fire. It began to arch forward in a single direction, as if responding to an unfelt breeze. It threw fingers of flame out toward the upper crowns of the trees, as if seeking to touch them with its destruction, as if seeking to add their fuel to its growth, as if seeking to breach the clearing at the foot of the knoll and progress into the forest.

Isolated bits and bolts of fire snapped free from the furthest reach of the flames and were carried across the gulf of open air, some flaring out, some striking the leaves of oaks, the needles of pines, flashing anew, regenerating itself, renewing its energy. The fire in the trees became a draft for the fire from the knoll, pulling it across the open space. The flames ignited new tinder, and within moments the new conflagration began to move, setting out across the upper canopy, expanding neither right nor left, but advancing in a straight line, flashing over the trees, moving increasingly faster with each passing moment. The trail it left, the course it took, were evidence of a force at odds with the laws of nature. It was the action of a deliberative entity guiding its own fate. It was an action that suggested the fire had an ultimate aim.

• • •

Fielding turned and started to run toward the truck. But in that first instant, before his eyes could adjust from the intense source of light to darkness, he ran blind. He managed just a few steps before he tripped, sailing head-first, scraping the heels of his hands on the ground. Scrambling forward, pushing himself up, he lost barely a second in his dash to the vehicle.

Inside, he released the brake and floored the accelerator. The thickly veined lugs of the tires bit into the roadbed, and the truck leapt forward. He was again into the narrow canyon of trees, racing to escape this place of dried wood and windless firestorms. It was like his earlier mad drive, after hitting his head, after being attacked by the representatives of the Ancient Ones, except that this time he wasn't running from men in disguises or from his own hallucinations. He was running from something as real as the skeletal remains in the cave.

Fielding thought of the circular imprints burned into the ground that led to the river cabin. He thought of the claw scorch marks on the wall inside. And he thought of the spearhead of light he had just seen from the brink of the ridge, delivered through the black of night with an accuracy he felt certain could not be far off.

He took his eyes off the road long enough to glance in the mirror. Then out the side window. He envisioned the forest alive with fire, and as he did, the heat of his imagination flared across his skin. He fought the feeling. He resisted the creeping fear. He struggled to retain control.

Outside his windows the trees flashed by in a blur. Massive pillars of aged bark came into view, then disappeared in an instant. Fielding was working hard, and the sweat was collecting above his eyebrows, beginning to run downward, following the curve of the bridge of his nose, seeping into the corners of his eyes. He took one hand off the wheel long enough to pinch his forefinger and thumb together between his eyes to try to stop the sting. As he did, there was a flash of light. Or what he thought was a flash of light.

Leaning forward, he glanced up through the windshield. It came and went so fast he couldn't be sure what he had seen. He couldn't be sure if it was the reflection of his own lights, or the glow of fire in the sky.

It was the sound of wind. It was the sound of brittle things crinkling and collapsing inward. The fire sucked the life from the leaves and needles dried by drought and left them ashen skeletons that only resembled their former shape. There were no slow fades from red to black, no lingering coals amid the twigs. Nothing was missed. Nothing was wasted. The fire consumed everything as it raced across the nearly seemless canopy of the forest.

The phalanx of flame near the knoll that had become a spear point, had narrowed even more as it advanced. It seemed more concentrated. More focused. More precise in its aim. It was a fiery missile streaking across the black, gaining speed as it grew more streamlined. Causing the branches to sway in its draft. Creating its own thrashing tumult. Spraying the forest floor with a rain of ash.

Still at odds with the laws of nature, the fire changed again, as if reinventing its own physics. From a racing column of visible heat, the fire blossomed outward, sprouting flames in a widening arc like a prairie fire in a sudden gust. Night became day, and shadowy objects gained substance from the light. And it began to turn downward, descending through the canopy, sinking toward the ground, toward the level of the dirt road.

Fielding hit the brakes. He had no choice, so blinding was the sudden glare of light.

Fire fell like water over Niagara. He was behind the falls, within the falls, surrounded by the falls. The fire had a cohesive facade, and yet at the same time it was composed of individual flares and bulges of flame, distinct edges and deep shadows, opaque yellows and wispy sheens of pale white. The fire was a flowing, continuous thing; it was a complex of shapes and shades; it was a shimmering canvas that hinted at bestial form hidden within the folds and curves, the colors and tints.

Wherever Fielding looked, the shapes appeared to be emerging. Flames bent in approximation of limbs. Dual shadow flickered like negative images of animals' eyes spotlighted at night. Daggered spikes of linear light appeared to slash at the air. But every image was short-lived. Over all was the boiling billowing curtain of flames. It was as if he had been cast into furnace, as if he had suddenly appeared whole in the center of the sun, as if he had fallen into hell.

Fielding shifted into first. He tried to see where the road continued beyond the curtain, but it was no use. His vision could not penetrate the fire.

His foot came off the clutch and the truck bolted forward. As it did, a hundred souls grew round in the flames as if emerging from the sheet of fire. Then just as fast, as an inhale follows an exhale, the emerging shapes drew back into the curtain. And the curtain began to change. Fielding's envelope began to collapse.

The Jeep hit the wall of fire, the flames flashed momentarily against the windshield, and then he was through. But the glow did not fade. The fire was instantly above him, in front of him, raining down in a new firefall that lit the woods like an incendiary charge. Flames flashed to life in the trees, the brush, the ground litter, the strips of grass in the center of the dirt tracks. Each flame shot skyward, then began to whirl together in a hurricane of heat.

The truck was grazed by a tree, and Fielding fought to bring the Jeep back into line. He could see the twin shadows of the dirt tracks. He could follow the burning center strip. He just had to keep moving. He had to outrace the fire.

But the fire had its own propulsion. It stayed with him. It continued to flash new tinder all around. It continued to spin together in a swirling mass of flame and smoke and vivid color. And then a new change came to the firestorm. Streaks of flame began to react to the centrifugal force, spinning outward in long, swirling tentacles of fire. Appendages of fire. Claws of fire.

The multiple limbs suddenly flashed against the windshield, billowing against the glass like a dozen flamethrowers all trained on Fielding's position. The front wheels of the truck hit the side embankment, and Fielding was off the road and into the woods. His foot came off the accelerator, but he continued forward. All he could see was the fire through the glass, rushing against the window, spraying around to the other side.

Driving blind, Fielding pulled the wheel to the left, hoping to drop back into the ruts. But instead the truck crashed into a tree. He slid forward into the wheel, then dropped back in his seat. With barely a pause, he shifted into reverse and the Jeep jerked backward. He steered left, easing forward, seeking the trail.

The billowing flames at the windshield took on a distinct shape. The outward curves outlined the overall form. Pits and cavities began to give facial definition to the form. Features emerged, and Fielding was suddenly staring straight into black holes that approximated the visual organs of a beast conjured from the imagination of a soul damned for eternity. As Fielding stared, as the truck continued to brush through ferns, snapping saplings at the bumper, deep in the black sockets he could see a tiny glare of red fire, the color of hate, the color of madness, the color of blood.

The wheels dropped into the ruts, and Fielding screamed and stomped on the accelerator at the same time. The fire continued to blow, but it began to change. Not in shape, but in color. The deep hues of yellow and orange began to fade. Fielding didn't notice the color change as much as he noticed that he could begin to see through the fire. He could see the outline of the forest. He could see the road. The truck began to speed faster.

The beast of fire reared back its representation of a head and opened its jaws, shaking its fangs back and forth. They were the fangs of a carnivore, the fangs of a killer, the fangs that had sunk deep into Fielding's hand from the remnants of Buck Billings's fire.

Fielding gripped the wheel tight. He looked past the thing of fire, beyond the fangs, through the ocular pinpoints of fading red. He was winning. He was escaping. The creature of the flames was losing its substance. From a curtain of fire it had become little more than a sheer fabric. A diaphanous haze. Only the barest suggestion of light. It retained a ghostlike image for a few more seconds, and then it was gone.

The fire was out. The night had returned. The forest had become again a quiet place of tempered passions.

It was a quiet place, except for the engine of the truck. It was a temperate place, except for the heat that coursed through the driver's veins. His passions would not cool, because the beast was still alive. And with the certainty that comes from near-death, he knew he would look again into its eyes.

Chapter 19

"BECAUSE I SAW it," Fielding said. "I looked into the fire and I saw its eyes."

Indeed, it was as if Fielding could see them now, pinpoints of red in the shadow of the hallway that branched off from Miriam's living room.

Earlier, after he first arrived, he had tried to outline the results of his findings at the library. They wouldn't believe him, he felt, without the same understanding he had acquired.

But as he spoke, he knew he wasn't making much sense. The adrenaline rush still cycled his thoughts through his mind. Images of the fire and his escape interfered with the ideas and story he was trying to tell. But the more he was pushed by the two women to detail the results of his research and his theory, the more organized his presentation became.

He told them of a civilization transformed by twin invaders, the first conquering by political means, and the second more slowly, through religious conversion. But as with most conquered peoples, he said, ideas survived. Customs were preserved. And along the fringes or in remote pockets, the conquest was never complete.

Their roots were in the great Indo-European valleys of the Asian steppes, and they first emerged as a distinct people half a millennium before Christ. They were an independent and fierce lot, a collection of related tribes that spread their civilization across all of northern Europe. The Parisii, the Bretons, the Belgae, the Teutons, the Norse, were just a few of the separate tribes, whose names survived as cities, regions, or countries. There was no Caesar among them to unify them under a single government, but they were a related people nonetheless. Related by culture. And by religion. A religion that practiced human sacrifice. That worshiped fire.

Caesar called them collectively the Gauls. His legions called them *furor celticus*. The fire warriors.

"Sometimes they threw off their garments and fought without clothes," Fielding said, "because of the heat of exertion. Because they believed they were possessed of their fire gods." But in the end neither their fierceness nor their faith could stave off Caesar's conquest. The Roman bureaucracy divided them into countylike districts they called *pagi*. This administrative term became the generic word that described the conquered peoples, and subsequently, these *pagans* were subject to another invasion. Their religion came under attack by a spreading Christianity that neutralized their beliefs by either destroying their gods or assimilating them into the pantheon of Christian saints.

This secondary assault on the first northern European civilization worked slowly over time, and in stages. The customs most offensive to the early Christians were targeted first, and gradually, actual human sacrifice by fire yielded to burning effigies. But despite Christian successes, the process of conversion lasted for centuries, and to this day traces of the old fire rituals remained, in midsummer celebrations, the maypole, the Yule log.

"Who—or what—was the fire god of these people?" Since morning, Jean Shawshequay had spent most of the day in her room. Though the rest had not wiped away earlier events, it had given her strength. She had been sick. The dreams were a function of the illness. She felt much better now, and more in control of her own thoughts. There's nothing like the irrationality of someone else, she thought ruefully, to slap a person back to reality.

Listening to Fielding's history, she felt more and more uncomfortable with his seeming readiness to accept the irrational. It wasn't a dispassionate review of history he was reciting, but rather a statement of belief. For her own part, she tiptoed around that impression, probing him with questions, seeking information, hoping to uncover a hint of rational explanation.

"There was no one fire god," Fielding answered. "There were hundreds of them. Nearly four hundred deities have been catalogued as having been worshiped by the northern European peoples. Over three hundred of those existed in only one place. Rituals were similar, but there was no Vatican to issue encyclicals, forcing believers to conform to a single dogma. Instead, there was great diversity. Variations revolving around a single theme."

"And you believe that today," Jean said, "on the shores of

Lake Superior, we are confronted by one of those ancient fire gods?"

"The god. The people. All of it." Fielding stared for a moment into the blank faces of Jean and Miriam. "You see, they believed their souls did not die, but became part of the same whole. Merging in a sense with their god. That's why some of them chose to sacrifice themselves in the flames. That's why they had communal cemeteries. Bones of the dead were disarticulated and stacked together in single ossuaries. Merging themselves with the spiritual entity they worshiped made this entity or power or god stronger." Fielding took a breath, searching their faces for comprehension. For acceptance. For understanding. "Don't you see? When the people Miriam's ancestors called the Awshkoute were massacred, they became one with their god. Enlarging it. Empowering it. Able to come to life in its only physical manifestation. Fire!"

Jean settled back, stealing a glance at Miriam. The woman didn't look at her, keeping her eyes focused on Fielding and her thoughts well concealed. "It just seems so . . . fantastic," Jean said. "Granted, a lot has happened we can't explain. I've felt things that I can't explain. But to say that some ancient fire god, filled with the souls of a massacred people, is able to take command of the properties of fire, is going too far." She raised her hands in frustration. "Without . . . proof, it's saying simply too much."

"Something like this can never be proven with scientific certainty," Fielding said. "All we can do is gather the evidence. Add it up. Test it against what we know has been happening. And then come to a conclusion based on the totality of the circumstances."

"Mr. Fielding," Miriam said, "when my people speak of the Ancient Ones, it is more an expression of belief in our heritage than a testament of actual belief in ancient spirits. In coming to any conclusion based on your evidence, it seems to me to be one thing to say one sort of pagan sect managed to arrive here before the French explorers, and that these people—and my ancestors—may have believed in the old powers. But it is something else entirely to say that the old powers were genuine. That the beliefs are real. That they are what's controlling events today."

"It *is* happening," Fielding said. "And it happened twenty-eight years ago. And you said it's happened before that."

"People have died by fire. That cannot be denied. But I have heard of no one who was witness to the kind of apparition you describe. How can you be so sure it exists?"

That's when Fielding said he saw it. That's when he told of looking into the fire and seeing its eyes.

The two women, an Ojibwa and a Potawatomi, looked at each other silently as Fielding glanced off into the shadows of the hall.

"If the Awshkoute were the people of your research," Miriam asked, "why would they have ended up here?"

"To escape religious persecution," Fielding said. "From the Pilgrims to Jim Jones, dozens of other sects have done the same thing. Like I said before, pockets of the old pagan ways survived well beyond the collapse of the civilization that nurtured them. Human sacrifice was reported in Scotland as late as the eighteenth century. It's not hard to imagine one such remote sect, driven from their home, coming to a new world seeking religious freedom."

"But in the time before the age of exploration, before Columbus, how would they have known?"

"The Vikings were here. They settled at L'Anse aux Meadows in Newfoundland around the year 1000. And they had been plying the northeastern seaboard before that. And where they went, they wrote about, their sagas detailing their voyages in prose that was part myth, part history. For someone seeking an escape, the sagas could well have provided a way out."

"Assuming a small band did cross the ocean," Jean said, "assuming they managed to arrive where the Vikings once did, how could they possibly have found their way so far inland?"

"Out of necessity. And secondly, because of a continuing sense of pilgrimage." Fielding looked from one woman to the other to gauge how his rationale was being received, before continuing. "You see, the Algonquins who lived at the mouth of the St. Lawrence congregated there in the summer, for fishing. During the winter, they'd break into smaller groups and follow the waterway inland to family hunting grounds. It was how they survived, making use of the available food. If an outside group settled in the outer reaches of their range, it stands to reason eventually they would have had to adopt the same proven methods of survival."

"And the . . . pilgrimage you mentioned?" Jean prompted.

Fielding leaned back, casting his eyes up at the ceiling as he tried to organize a theory he had not fully formed. "The Celtic people," he began, "believed in the sanctity of certain natural formations. They felt that depressions in the earth, that springs, were sanctuaries, sacred places where the boundary between the spiritual world and this one was narrow. And it was at these places that they practiced their religion. It's where they performed their sacrifices.

"When they heard about this geological curiosity the Algonquin called the Cave of Bones," Fielding continued, "sunk in an area of four rivers, it's not hard to imagine how they would have thought it a holy place. And to get here, all they had to do was follow the natural waterways. As the French explorers later did, penetrating deep into the Great Lakes region well before other coastal areas were settled."

Miriam Goodmedicine slowly pushed herself to her feet. She felt tired and old and worn down by the toll it was all taking on her. Sometimes it seemed that the entire weight of her people's destiny fell on her shoulders. Her people expected so much of her, and she had always given whatever she could, despite the fact there were always some who fought her on every issue. She had been president of the Ojibwa Association for a long time, and suddenly it didn't seem fair. It didn't seem fair that she was expected to give so much. It didn't seem fair that she had to make the sacrifices. It didn't seem fair that she was confronted with Fielding's theory as if it were up to her to decide what to do. It wasn't fair that all this was happening while her son was God knows where needing all of her energies.

Miriam rubbed her forehead, her eyes lightly coming together. "If this is all true, if what you have pieced together really explains why people have died, what can possibly be done to stop it?" She let her hand drop heavily to her side. She stared at Fielding without rancor, without emotion of any kind. "This . . . presence, if you are right, has been here for nearly six centuries. Maybe all there is to do is isolate it. Stay away from its power. Make sure no one can even come close to the Cave of Bones."

Fielding didn't answer her right away. He sensed the real reason behind her resignation, her fatigue, and he waited, hoping what she suggested would collapse in her mind under the weight of its own faulty logic. When her expression didn't change, he said simply, "You can't close off the woods. How would you possibly explain the necessity?"

"We've lived with it for all these years. We can survive with it in the future."

"It's different now," Fielding said.

"What's different?"

"Something has happened that has changed it all."

"Nothing's changed. People have died before. People will die in the future."

Fielding sensed his building hesitancy. He suddenly became very aware that he was doing all he could to keep from looking at Jean. "It's changed because the power is stronger now," he said. "It's no longer simply reacting to opportunity."

"What do you mean?" Miriam asked.

"It's seeking a way to control things more directly."

"More directly?" Miriam said, still perplexed. "How?"

Fielding glanced down at the floor nervously, then back at the Ojibwa matriarch. "It's seeking to control a living human being."

Miriam grew quieter. Pensively, she considered his statement carefully before saying, "And does this person know?"

"She knows something's not right."

Though the archaeologist still resisted turning his gaze, Miriam had no such reservation. She looked toward Jean. "They're dead," she had said, coming out of her dream. *She had known.*

Jean Shawshequay thrust herself angrily to her feet. "This is absurd." She took two steps away, then spun back toward Fielding. "So you not only suddenly believe in evil spirits, you believe the devil has possessed me?"

"I wouldn't phrase it like that."

"But that's what it boils down to. You can't disguise it behind a lot of historical discussion."

"I'm not trying to disguise anything."

Jean Shawshequay breathed heavily in disgust. "You go from a man of science to somebody quaking in the face of something he doesn't understand. Tell me, what has happened to you?"

"It's because I'm a man of science that I've come to these conclusions."

"Why? What does this have to do with science?"

"Because there's no other way it makes sense."

"No other way a series of burning deaths make sense, other than to believe in ghosts?"

"Not just the deaths. But the other things as well."

"What other things?"

"The fire I saw inside of you, at the cave." Fielding paused as a bit of the anger visibly lifted from Jean. Then he continued. "You placed some of the bones in the gray pack and brought them out with you. Then you took them to the Verhoven cabin. You don't remember, because you were not controlling things. But you have memories of what happened. Things you cannot understand. Things that terrify you."

Jean felt herself drifting back, half sitting, half collapsing in her chair. She suddenly felt hot and weak and feverish all over. As she had before. As she had the other times. But it was just the sickness, she cried out angrily in her mind. It would pass. She would recover. Things would return to normal.

"They're trying to come back to life," Fielding said. "They're trying to come back to life through you."

"Dreams. That's all they were, you said. You both said." Jean looked anxiously from one to the other, waiting for the same words of comfort they had offered earlier. But at this moment she saw no comfort, only pity. "Miriam?"

Slowly, Miriam Goodmedicine got up and walked to the hallway leading to her bedroom. At least this was one issue in which she didn't have to take the lead. She turned to Fielding. "There're blankets and pillows in the closet left at the head of the stairs," she said, if he felt he had to stay. Clearly, she felt he should.

After she left, Jean turned on Fielding. "You weren't even sure what you saw in the cave. You said so yourself."

"I know what I saw. I just couldn't believe it, at the time."

"You called it an illusion. Formed by a continuation of different things, all coming together in a moment of fear."

"It was no illusion. I've seen the thing in the fire now. I've looked into its face. And for a second, it was the same I saw in you in the cave."

Jean felt the heat again, but this time it was from anger, not fever. The nails of her fingers dug into her palms, and her knuckles turned white. How could logic persuade the irrational? And that was the source of her frustration, she told herself. Trying to deal rationally with an absurd assertion.

Jean Shawshequay turned without another word and stalked up the stairs to the attic bedroom, slamming the door. It remained noisy upstairs for a while, but eventually, the house quieted down. Eventually, the toll of the day took fuller effect, and Fielding found it harder to resist his body's demand for rest.

He sat on the couch for a long time, thinking, until he realized there were some things that couldn't be thought through. He went outside for a while, then came back in and turned on the radio; he tried to read a magazine. But nothing helped him rest. More than anything, what churned in his stomach was the guilt.

Would it have all started if he hadn't come here to dig? Yes, of course it would have, he told himself. He didn't guide Buck Billings to the sinkhole. He wasn't here twenty-eight years ago. Or six hundred years ago.

That measure of solace proved only temporary, because Fielding realized that he had led Deputy Jerry Cole to the site of the excavation. He had engineered Jean Shawshequay's participation in his project. And she had taken the fire to new sources of energy for the creature of the flames. Without his interference, would the Buck Billings death have been just one more isolated occurrence, followed by another twenty-eight years of calm?

Fielding turned the volume up on the radio, but the music offered little reprieve from his continuing sense of guilt. And because he felt responsible for the people who had died, and for the woman from Oklahoma who had been merged in part with the entity of the cave, he couldn't avoid the feeling that it was up to him to bring it all to an end. He had looked into the face of evil, and he knew he could not turn away.

Fielding turned suddenly toward the stairway. Upstairs, there was a muffled thump. It was the sound of something heavy falling on the floor or being thrust against the wall. Fielding listened, waiting for it to come again. Slowly, he rose from the couch and walked toward the foot of the steps.

In sleep, there was no anger to black out the accusations. There was no anger to black out the memories.

In sleep, her mind was undefended prey to the suggestions of the others. And her intentional repression of memory proved but a chimerical barrier, as she was led in her dream back to the cave, to the lighting of the lantern. She saw the sudden flash of light, the blue flame coming toward her. "No!" she cried, in her dream, spinning and falling in what seemed a black void. Everything came rushing back from that moment—the shock, the dizziness, the terror—except that it was worse. Dreams isolate and heighten emotions, bypassing conscious restraints. And that's what was happening now, in her sleep. Every aspect of her mind focused on the terror, on the outline of the blue flame, coming closer. Her body stiffened. She grabbed the bedposts above her, and the headboard banged against the wall. "Get away!" she shouted in her dream, the echo of her cry passing across her lips as a garbled sound of panic. But as it had back then, the plea had no effect. The apparition approached.

She tried to retreat, and though she experienced a weightless, falling sensation, the thing of the fire fell with her. It became more distinct, its features sharpening, its appendage rearing back. In the fashion of dreams, it was all happening slowly, each measure of terror a separate increment of time by itself. She could see the narrow column of fire coming toward her, frozen in the black like a bolt of lightning captured on film, and then it was striking her, penetrating her, sinking deep inside.

She screamed a soundless scream as the flame cut like a blade through her chest. She collapsed in on herself, gasping for breath, grasping for a hold to pull away. But in the void there was nothing. There was no help. There was no hope.

Neither was there any visible wound or any blood. But she could feel the hot invasion. She could feel the fire. She *was* the fire.

Was it a voice he heard? Fielding placed a foot on the first step, his hand on the banister; he was ready to dash up the stairs. He strained to hear, listening for the murmured sound of distress. But the music was too loud, or the voice too soft. He edged up another step. What was it he had heard? *Get away?*

As he tried to replay the muffled sound in his head, there was a distraction, other voices, clear and distinct. They were from the radio. The music had gone to news. At first he tried to block it out so he could focus on Jean Shawshequay upstairs, but the voices on the radio carried a sense of excitement, a note of urgency.

The lead story shifted to a reporter in the field. He was at the scene of a fire, and suddenly, Fielding turned toward the radio. Finally, it registered. There had been a fire at the Great Lakes Natural History Museum. And at least one death. A voice clip of a photographer was playing. "The studio was set for a shot of a ceremonial robe," he was saying, "but everything was disconnected. I'm sure of it."

"Curator Curtis Heath has not yet been located for comment," the reporter said, "and so the extent of damage has not been released. But it's hoped the fire was confined to the nondisplay area of the photographic studio, sparing the many priceless and irreplaceable artifacts in the museum's collection." The reporter then introduced a voice clip recorded earlier, from one of the first firefighters to enter the burning building. He described the intensity of the blaze and finished by saying, "We tried, but we just couldn't go any farther. It just . . . flashed up in our faces. It . . ."

The firefighter broke off, unable to describe what he had seen. And listening to his inability, Fielding knew why the man couldn't describe it. He knew why he wasn't sure what he had seen.

Back at the studio, the radio announcer concluded by saying the one body that had been recovered was burned beyond recognition.

"Please!" Fielding heard, coming from upstairs. "Let me go."

She was the fire. And yet she wasn't. The fire was all around her. *They* were all around her. Suggestions of faces, black shadows pitting bulging contours of flames, oral cavities opening in screams that carried only the heated rush of the conflagration.

They approached from every direction, but she managed to maintain her distance. They appeared to get no closer because she was shrinking. She was getting smaller. Weaker. Yielding more of the space to the creatures of the fire.

They were reaching out to her, beckoning to her, and at the very core of her resistance, a suggestion nipped. It's easier this way, the thought whispered. It's better for all of us. You will be stronger. We will all be stronger.

A trident-lobed projection of flame suddenly flared over the gulf of distance that separated her from the fire and hooked around her arm just above the elbow. She pulled back, terrified, and the new terror welled up in her throat. She could feel it; she could hear it. She gave voice to the terror, to her weakness, to her wish to flee.

Fielding thrust the door open and looked in. Moonlight squared by the window cast a dim glow that crossed diagonally over the lower half of Jean's bed. The lineal mound of her legs under the covers shifted as she curled in on herself, and Fielding heard a whimpering rush of unintelligible syllables.

He crossed the oval rug toward her, not sure if calling her from her dreams would be worse than letting it run its course. The top half of the bed was in shadow, but closing to within a step of her, Fielding could see that her arms were tucked in close to her chest and her right hand gripped her left wrist tightly. Her face he couldn't read, but it looked as if she were forcing her head deep into the pillow.

Fielding went down to one knee, leaning close. "Jean," he whispered, hoping to gently lift her from the dream.

He whispered her name again, but it had no effect. Instead, she rolled suddenly to her back and thrust her arms out to the sides. Reflexively, Fielding stood up and leaned back half a step. As he watched, her whimper became a series of hot breaths. The covers rose and fell. Her head thrashed one way then back the other. Though he couldn't see the sweat on her face, he could smell her heat, the oil of her skin, the fear.

"Jean," he said more loudly, coming closer, reaching out for her.

From the moment the thing of the fire touched her arm, visions of past events that had been shrouded in confusion had come suddenly clear. The contrary world of her earlier experience became but a single existence. She could see the cabin, she could feel the fire, and this time, there was no secondary interference. There was no car in the woods, no drive through the trees, no return to the attic bedroom of the small frame house. There was only the cabin in the woods near the stream.

In that instant of contact, their memory became hers, and she saw the interior of the cabin clearly, she saw the face of the woman, the face of a child, and she heard the screams. There was terror and panic, and it felt good. She was ravenous, and she ate of the fear, she absorbed the energy, drinking it down, gorging on the life force of the woman, siphoning it into her own, into the fire, into the collective soul of them all. It was easier this way, as they said. She was stronger. In her dream, this suddenly clear recollection of that night of continuing paradox, she could feel again the influx of energy, she could feel the power, the nourishment, the pleasure of long-dormant desire being fulfilled. And there would be more, atop the stairs on the balcony, at the doorway in the front.

She wanted more, but inexplicably her free-fall into the flames was arrested. The flashing yellow white lobes began to dim, the flow of stolen energy diminished, and with this deprivation she sensed a growing anger. Quickly, the anger became rage. Why was she being drawn away? Why was the vision fading? She struggled to see again, to open her eyes, to confront this new interference with the fire of her rage. She struggled to confront it with the fire.

Fielding had his hand on her side, and he was shaking her. "Wake up," he said.

Jean rolled forcefully to the other side of the bed, pulling away from him. Her body was taut with tension, and she exhaled a heavy blow of air, like a hiss.

Fielding sat on the edge of the bed and reached over her, using more force now, trying to bring her out of it. "Jean, come on. Wake up." He got a grip on her arm and pulled in an attempt to roll her back toward him.

She resisted, tightening her muscles, and then in an instant she changed. No longer fighting him, she was moving in the direction he sought. And she moved fast, spinning toward him, rising from the mattress, her hot breath hissing between her teeth.

Coming out of the shadow into the moonlight, her oily sweat caught the reflection and her face flashed brighter. Fielding flinched, the breath seizing in his throat. At the same moment, Jean froze in the patch of dim light; she froze on the threshold between dream and conscious thought. Her eyes opened wide in terror, or anger, Fielding couldn't be sure. Then in the next instant, the spell was broken and she was coming up toward him again, circling her arms behind his back, preventing his escape.

She lifted her face toward his as she pulled his toward hers. Fielding didn't have the strength to resist, even if he wanted to, so fast was her action, so forceful was the maneuver.

Her cheek pressed against his chest and her arms tightened around his back. The hiss of her breath had become a wheeze, and her body convulsed with a series of tight spasms. And then she spoke, her speech a halting exercise timed to the convulsions. "They're coming," she said. "Oh God, they're coming for me."

"They're not coming," Fielding said. "Not anymore."

"They're coming!" she insisted, hugging him tighter.

"You're awake now. You're okay. No one is coming."

Jeans's grip eased a fraction, and her cheek slipped against his chest. "They're inside," she said. "Like you said. They're taking me. They're coming . . ." Her voice trailed off, overcome by tears.

Cupping his hand behind her head, caressing her hair, his other arm wrapped around her back, he said, "I won't let them take you." She eased her head back and looked up at him. "I promise. I won't let them take you."

Slowly her head sank back to his chest. Her muscles slackened, and the spasm of her lungs gradually evened into a steady rhythm.

From that first day in court, Jean Shawshequay had struck Fielding as an individual of rock-hard beliefs and unshakable personal strength. Though that impression he felt certain was still valid, at this moment, as he held her to his chest, she suddenly seemed so slight and powerless. And vulnerable.

I won't let them take you, he had promised. But even as he said it, he had known she was right. They were coming. They were coming for all of them.

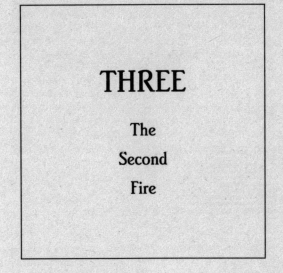

THREE

The
Second
Fire

Chapter 20

SHE WAS BEAUTIFUL in sleep. Free from the kinds of concerns that had come to dominate her, her face struck a neutral expression. There were no furrows in her brow, no tight wrinkles webbing from the corners of her mouth, and within this placid facade was a look of innocence. An innocence he had put at risk, Fielding thought.

Her face was smooth and dry now, Fielding having dabbed her cheeks and her forehead with a towel. He had held her for a long while, and then had laid with her until her grip around him had relaxed completely and the rhythm of her body acquired the evenness of sleep. In one respect he felt he should go back downstairs, but instead he stayed in Jean's bedroom, taking one of the other beds, closer to the window.

The moonlight carried across him and into her face, and with her skin emanating this celestial purity, he began to wonder how it could be possible this woman of intellect and beauty harbored such ancient evils. Was her nightmare tonight a derivative of his historical ramblings? Had he led her to believe they were coming for her?

These questions were actually a derivative of his own suggestion, or rather, what he would prefer to believe. And near sleep himself, it was easy for him to believe what he wanted. But even in this state of wanting, all he had to do was see the gauze he had wrapped around Jean's arm just above her left elbow to realize no amount of wishing could explain the burn marks on her arm. "That's where they took hold of me," she had said. "That's where they were pulling me toward them."

Fielding had accepted it as true when she said it, and as he lay in the dark trying to fall asleep, he had no reason to doubt its truth now. The people of the cave had taken hold of her arm. They were pulling her closer to them.

• • •

The Awshkoute had been dealt with once before. It hadn't been a permanent solution, but for six hundred years their black acts had been restricted to the area of a remote sinkhole in the woods. For Fielding, the only way to understand what must be done now was to understand what exactly had transpired back then.

The logic of this approach was the sum result of an entire night of fitful lunges between sleep and active concern over what would have to be done. By morning, he had begun making plans to return to the only possible place where the story of that early confrontation would be recorded.

Jean said she was better when she got up, but she looked worse. There were dark rings under her eyes and she looked sick, but she insisted on going with him to the sinkhole. Fielding didn't try too hard to stop her because she was in command of herself again, and because he would need her.

When they arrived at the site of the excavation, in some ways it was like a replay of past events: the sheriff's cars, the medical examiner's van, the smell of fire.

"Getting to be a habit," Halstead said. "Meeting like this."

"This is where I work," Fielding said, his eyes steady and unblinking.

"Hey, don't take offense. Nothing suspicious about this one anyway," the sheriff said, gesturing toward the charred skeleton of the sweatlodge atop the knoll. "Accidental all the way."

Fielding listened without comment, then asked if he could take a closer look.

"Be my guest," the sheriff told him, then walked with him up the hill. Jean Shawshequay stayed behind, at the truck.

The bark covering and moss insulation were all gone, at least from about a foot off the ground all the way around. Most of the sapling ribs remained, bowed curiously over even though they were burned through at the top. The other curious thing was the bear hide. It had been spared from the flames.

"You can take it if you want," Halstead said to Fielding. "For the museum."

"Lucky thing it survived."

"That ain't the only lucky thing," Halstead said. "I suppose you saw the scorching on the way out here?"

Where the fire had enveloped his truck, Fielding thought. "Yeah, I saw that."

"It's a miracle the whole damn forest didn't burn down, dry as it is."

"Why do you say this one was accidental?" Fielding asked.

"The thing was a firetrap," Halstead said, as if it were obvious. "And this idiot lights a fire in the middle of it. What do you think he expected would happen?"

The bear-hide-covered entrance came about up to his waist, and standing in front of it, Fielding could see the pile of rocks in the small depression in the center of the sweatlodge. Those were the messenger stones, Fielding knew, heated in the fire outside the lodge as he had seen last night. It was a distinction Fielding didn't think necessary to draw for the sheriff. He was right in a way, though. It was accidental. Makwamacatawa thought he was calling the spirits of his people, and instead he got something else entirely.

"I can't say what he expected, Sheriff," Fielding said. "In his own way, he was probably trying to do just what you're doing."

"Yeah? And what's that?"

"Put an end to all this."

Halstead frowned. The guy refused to accept the obvious about Blackbear and the rest of his group. At least, the right person was burned this time. As Fielding was turning away to retreat down the slope, Halstead said, "By the way. You're around the Goodmedicine place a lot. You know anything about where the hell that kid of hers is?"

"No. Sorry."

"Haven't heard anything?"

Fielding shook his head. He had started to turn away again when he was stopped a second time by Halstead.

"It's important we find him, you know," Halstead continued. "We got that little girl who survived the cabin fire. Lindsey Verhoven. We got her and would sure like to see if she can recognize him."

"How is the— How is Lindsey?"

"She seems okay to me. Still keeps saying that the fire was alive, though. Just like yesterday at the river. All I can figure is, she saw somebody against the blaze. And I'd sure as hell like to see if she can identify who that was."

"I understand," Fielding said.

"So you'll tell me if you hear anything from Miriam," Halstead said, not as a question but as a statement of fact.

Fielding nodded in a fashion that could have been read either as agreement, or as simply an acknowledgment of the request. "You've got work to do," he said, "and so do I."

"Fielding," Halstead said after Fielding had taken a few steps away from him. As Fielding turned back for the third time, the sheriff nodded at the lodge. "You forgot the skin."

Fielding looked at the ceremonial cloak draped over the door frame. He looked at the head of the bear, into the glassy eyes, the same face that had seemed so alive that day it confronted him in the woods. Now it was lifeless and as inanimate as the rocks and charred wood of the sweatlodge itself.

Fielding unhitched the hide and carried it down to his truck, folded it carefully and placed it in the back bed. The magnetometer was there amid his tools, and he retrieved it, slinging the nylon web strap over his shoulder. Taking his leather-covered field book, he walked toward where Jean was standing, by the V-cut on the edge of the sinkhole.

"You ready?" he said to her.

Jean didn't respond. She continued gazing out over the tops of the trees, scanning the rim of the circular depression.

Fielding hopped down to the first ledge, then began to remove the stones he had piled to cover the gray pack. It was still there, and he pulled it from the crevice. He stood straight, then paused, looking up at Jean Shawshequay. "Jean?"

She glanced down, then back across the treetops. "You know, there are other cuts, like this one."

At first Fielding didn't catch on to what she was referring to. "You mean this drainage ravine?" he asked.

"Yes," she said. "Just like this one. I saw them when I checked out the rim, that first time I was out here with you. I didn't think much of them at the time. They were overgrown, and indeed showed the erosion of rain drainage, like this one. And then, of course, I saw the bats and everything else suddenly became inconsequential."

Fielding began to understand the drift of her thinking. "You think these cuts could be man-made?"

She turned and pointed. "East is that way, isn't it?"

"Yes."

She looked at him, and Fielding looked at the cut in the rock, then at an imaginary rising sun. "At the summer solstice perhaps," Jean said, and Fielding turned as if sighting the sunlight down the vee toward the bottom of the sinkhole.

"And the others," Jean continued, "I expect were cut to catch the first solar rise of the other seasons."

It was another hint, another clue, another point of verification. And he needed to understand them all, if he was to be sure what he was up against. If he was to have a chance at deciphering the six-hundred-year-old record in the cave. "Let's go," Fielding said, and this time he didn't wait for Jean. He began to follow the downward path into the quiet, near-subterranean world of the pit.

Jean followed, and at the bottom they made their way to the central clearing where Buck Billings had set his emergency camp, where the sun during solstice or equinox, given a treeless path, would shine directly onto the ground. Fielding unfolded his entrenching tool and began to dig, not with the care of an archaeologist beginning an excavation, but with the speed and tension of a homicide investigator seeking evidence of a murder.

The dirt turned a different kind of black about twelve inches deep. No longer the moist humus of organic soil, it was a woody, charcoallike residue. It was the remnant of ancient fires.

Fielding locked the blade at a ninety-degree angle and began carefully to scrape the soil to the side. Eventually he put the shovel down altogether and began to brush at the dirt with his fingers, the ash residue discoloring his skin. He came to a fragment of man-made design, a crosshatched weave of half-inch strips. It was flimsy and black, little more than an ashen fossil of what it once was. With great delicacy, Fielding lifted the fragment from the ground and cupped it in his palm. Holding it, he was cradling not only evidence of an act of murder six hundred years old, he was staring even further back in history, back toward a forgotten ritual written about by the Romans.

"Caesar was the first to describe it in any detail," Fielding said. "The barbarians to the north would take their conquered foes—or even their own people—and burn them in wicker effigies." He raised the crosshatched fossil so Jean could better see it. "I imagine the effigies were woven of reeds, just like these."

Jean began to back away as someone would in a cemetery, realizing she was standing on a grave. But that feeling for her, for both of them was even more intense, for this was a place of human sacrifice.

Archaeologists piece history together based on fragments of information. And that's what Fielding did.

The bog-iron remnants, the massacred Europeans, the Celtic-like henge in reverse, the residue of a sacrificial fire altar. What was theory before was now fact, as far as Fielding was concerned.

A European band had come here, bringing what was once the common northern European religion with them. It was a religion that spanned national boundaries, controlled by pre-Christian priests whose power superceded political leaders and who preached a religion that worshiped fire, that practiced human sacrifice by immolation in wicker effigies. That much was certain in Fielding's mind. The question was, What had the Late Woodland proto-Ojibwa done to the fire warriors?

They made their way carefully over the matted earth that had filled in between rock debris on the sinkhole floor. When they reached the cleft between the boulders that partially concealed the entrance to the cave, Fielding went down to his knees and stuffed his head and shoulders through the semicircular opening. From daylight to darkness, even with his flashlight it took several seconds for his eyes to adjust. Capillary roots still dangled from the ceiling, old spiderwebs brown with collected dust were overlaid with new ones, and over all was the pungent smell of bat guano.

Fielding slid the magnetometer in ahead of him, then pulled himself out so he could go in feet-first. One last look at Jean showed she was tense. The circles under her eyes seemed to have darkened, and her face was tight. "You okay on this?"

She nodded, tight-lipped.

Fielding edged backward into the opening, sliding his feet ahead of himself. Sand dislodged from the roots showered down upon him, and he felt the gritty rain across his back, then on his neck and down his shirt. Bats interrupted by his intrusion brushed by him, seeking escape to the outside. Other bats held their position, baring their teeth at him in silent snarls, their wings cupped open around their bodies.

Carrying the magneto, his pack, and his light, Fielding eased himself down the first drop, his hands gripping stone edges rounded by generations of early men. When he reached the flat section, he called up to Jean, telling her he was clear. He waited, but he didn't hear a thing. "Jean?"

Jean Shawshequay hovered in the entrance above him in the world between light and dark. She was drifting, hearing distant echoes, of what she wasn't sure. And there were smells she couldn't identify. Moist, rich odors so thick she could almost taste them on her tongue. Everything was black; either her eyes had not yet grown used to the abrupt change, or her vision had become secondary to her other senses. She listened to the distant clamor reverberating out at her as if from the depths of a tunnel. Voices, she decided, and she leaned forward, trying to hear what was being said. But it was too garbled or too remote or too weak to understand clearly. Or was it a different language?

An electric tingle rose up the back of her neck, spreading across her scalp. Her eyes were wide open, and yet her sole concern was her sense of hearing. As she strained to hear, the hollow dissonance changed suddenly. Like a kaleidoscope focusing on a single image, the voices came together.

"Jean!" It was Fielding. "What's wrong?"

"Nothing," she said, and with the clarity of voice came clarity of vision. She could see the root particles, the embedded rocks, the eyes of angry bats. "I'm right behind you."

"You sure you're okay?" came his voice from the bottom of the first drop.

"Yes," she said in a tone that rang not with confidence, but indecision.

"Let me come back up," Fielding said.

"No. I'm okay, really. I'll be right there." And the next thing she knew, she was right there, standing next to Fielding amid the network of passages. She turned and shined her light back up the rock descent, where she had just come from. But she had no memory of that climb, just as she hadn't the first time she was in the cave, inside the inner chamber, the site of the ancient massacre. When they had left the last time, she had watched Fielding climb into the narrow aperture, then found herself entering, then standing next to him. She had shot forward in time back then, and the same thing had just happened.

Jean tried to breathe in steadily through her nostrils to still the trembling unsteadiness that arose inside of her. It was fear she felt, and with it came a hot blush that flushed across her skin. It was fear not so much of the black episode she had just experienced, but of it coming alive again, in her dreams. As it had last night.

Fielding was shining his light, getting his bearings. Cracks in the walls led in every direction, and perhaps because of the distraction of the bats, he was momentarily undecided as to which path to take. Before he recognized the right direction, Jean stepped past him. "This way," she said and began to lead, as if she was trodding over old and familiar ground.

They descended the next drop, entering the long passage that led to the narrow entrance into the large, inner cavern. Training their lights on the ceiling, they came to the twenty-inch-tall pictograph of a man standing in the lineally paired lines representing a log fire. Next to it, visible under a thin coating of lime, was the better part of a triangle. And beyond that would be the rest of the story, recording what Fielding hoped would be the history of the Ojibwa encounter with the people they called the Awshkoute.

"Let's get started," he said.

They twisted the heads of their flashlights to wide beam, then propped them so they were directed on the ceiling. Jean began to sketch the first pictograph in the field book as Fielding readied the magnetometer.

The reddish pigment of the paint used on the ceiling was ocher, a mix of iron hematite and fish or animal fat that caused the earthen dye to bond to the rock. An idea that had come to Fielding during his early morning sleeplessness was to read the traces of iron ore through the encrusted lime with the magnetometer.

He adjusted the settings downward, then activated the audio aspect of the indicator. Using the ground probe as a wand, he raised it to the visible pictograph of the figure in the fire. As he passed it across one of the ocher lines, there was a single tick from the speaker and the needle bobbed a fraction in the meter display. "A little higher," he said, keeping the probe close to the ceiling.

Jean started to reach for the machine on the ground, then pulled up short, sucking in an abbreviated, sibilant breath. Above her elbow on her left arm, the burn had suddenly flared hotter.

"What's wrong?"

She grabbed the burn, but that only made it worse. She let go, holding her arm out from her body. "I moved too fast," she said. "I brushed it against my side."

"Let me do it," Fielding said, lowering the probe.

"No. I'm fine. It'll take all day, you jumping back and forth." She knelt next to the mag and adjusted the dials as Fielding passed the probe over the visible markings.

The crackle of the tiny speaker varied little in tone, only in frequency, but as the static ebbed and waned, as the probe passed over the traces of metal streaked on the stone ceiling, Jean began to hear something in the abbreviated dots and scratches of the machine's voice. As the static increased, it became increasingly an excited sound, an impatient, urging call that began to touch a resonant nervousness within her. Each blip of electrical discharge, each rash of the mag's wider output, became a separate sound, a distinct noise. An individual voice.

As in the entrance to the cave, she could hear the voices in the distance. Except this time, there was a heightened tempo to their calls. They were clamoring, shouting, raising their volume. Becoming more insistent. Coming closer.

"Jean!" Fielding almost shouted. "The chalk."

Of course, the chalk. He had been asking her for it. The machine was tuned so both the audio and visual indicator gave a good recognition signal as the sensor passed over the iron pigment. She had helped him with it, hadn't she?

"Right along here," he said, and Jean traced behind the sensor, drawing a chalk line on the ceiling. It was the triangle, to the right of the figure in the fire, that was partially observable through the lime. It was an equilateral triangle set on its base, and the angle farthest right was completely covered with the stony residue. Fielding traced the lines out as they appeared likely to go, and the machine's staticy voice verified the shape. Jean outlined it with the chalk on the ceiling.

"Like at Agawa," Fielding observed, "the triangle calling on the beings of the spirit world to bear witness to events."

To witness, Jean thought, and she could witness. She could see the triangle on the ceiling, not in shades of chalk, but in the full richness of the red ocher. And she could smell it, the wet earthen odor of the paint, the thickly rancid odor of the animal fat. It seemed so strong and so fresh she could taste it on her tongue, the same mineral-rich taste as water from a country well. Involuntarily, she gathered saliva in her mouth and spit on the floor.

Fielding only gave her a glance before he moved on. He moved the wand carefully back and forth, but the magnetometer remained silent. Were the encrustations too thick? He checked the meter to see if the needle wavered a bit. It did not.

"Keep going," Jean said.

He looked at her a few ticks longer this time, but did as she said. Past a space at least the equal of either of the first two pictographs, the speaker came suddenly to life. With broad strokes, Fielding squared off the extent of the hidden drawing and Jean marked the corners. Then he began to pass the sensor methodically across the surface, searching for patterns, being guided by the machine, sweeping in and out of flurries of static. As he zeroed the probe in on what he could not see, the static became more prolonged. As a line began to become evident, he would continue in the same direction until there was a change.

Jean kept pace, etching the same pattern with her chalk on the ceiling. It was an exercise that required communication and cooperation, and though she reacted as she should, it seemed more instinct than conscious effort. As before—as so many times before—there were competing sights and sounds in her mind. She was speaking with Fielding and yet what she heard was an echo. She was listening to the echo and it wasn't his voice. But the voices of others. And what kept flashing into her vision was not a dark tunnel, but a place of flickering lights and motion and earthen smells.

The pattern taking shape on the ceiling resembled the first pictograph, except that there was no figure rising out of the fire. There appeared to be only the lineal representation of logs, radiating from a central point. But as Fielding worked the probe, as he charted the bends and twists of the hidden lines, he recognized a new pattern taking shape atop the logs. Moving faster as recognition overtook false starts and stops, a figure of a man did begin to appear in the chalk tracing of Jean Shawshequay. It was a simple figure, similar to the first, except that it was lying on its side, across the logs. Consumed by the fire.

The fire! She could hear the crackling of the logs. She could see the flickering glow cast against the ceiling. She could feel the heat.

The static of the mag had taken on the character of a fire, its signal the snapping and cracking of twigs, the fracturing of the surface of the logs into squares, then their curling at the edges. The sweat was running down her sides. It was turning the chalk in her hand to paste. But still the dichotomy of her natures continued. She continued to draw out the figure on the ceiling. She continued to trace the outline of a man consumed by the flames.

"The sacrifice begins," Fielding said, pointing to the first pictograph. "They're calling the spirits—the triangle—to witness what evil was performed upon them, to explain why they had to do what they did. And here, the sacrifice is complete."

She could hear the fire, and she could hear the echoes. Not voices, but screams. Distant yet distinct. The cries of people in their death's agony; the shouts of others in celebratory ritual.

Fielding was moving on, passing the probe along the surface of the ceiling. There was another gap, the same width as the one between the triangle and the third pictograph, and then the static erupted again, the fire roared anew.

Jean drew the palm of her hand across her forehead, bringing it down across her face in an attempt to wipe away the sweat, in an attempt to brush away the competing visions. But the fire was too hot. The screams were too loud. And the vision was too intense. She could see them! She could see them by the fire.

Fielding outlined the parameters of the fourth pictograph. It was only a narrow horizontal band that caused the machine to register. He went back to the beginning and began to zero in on the precise shape. It was a line, not straight like another geometric shape, but rising in a gentle arc, then falling. He waited for Jean to trace the new figure, but she didn't move. He looked over at her. "You okay?"

She didn't respond. Instead, she raised her arm to the ceiling and began to scratch the chalk across the lime, not where Fielding's machine had just indicated, but in the gap between that space and the last pictograph. "What are you doing?" Fielding said.

She ignored him, continuing to draw. It was a crude figure, the representation of a man. And then below him, she began to draw another.

Fielding lowered the probe. "What the hell's going on?"

"They're here," she breathed, finishing the second figure, then beginning another. "They're all around."

Fielding looked at her closely, noticing that her face was glistening with moisture. He had to force a swallow as he studied her, then the figures she was drawing. With each one she worked faster, slashing them out on the rock. Each one was like the last, a crude stick figure of a man, circling the sacrificial fire he had traced with the magnetometer. "There's nothing there," he said at last, trying to break her spell. "I checked with the mag," he said, holding up the sensor as if to prove the irrefutability of his science.

"They're here," she repeated. "Watching."

Fielding raised the probe to the figures she had drawn. The

speaker was silent. The display meter didn't budge. "Look at this," he challenged. "Nothing registers."

"They weren't painted in ocher."

Fielding felt a heated sensation begin to radiate out from the marrow of his bones. What did she mean?

Jean dropped her arm and turned to face him. "They were drawn on with chalk." She raised her own piece of pale whitish material, shaking it in front of him in her fist. "Ground with fat to make it bond, but without the metallic content, it doesn't register."

Fielding could find no wind to power his speech. He could only stare at her, then at the ceiling, at the circle of figures around the sacrificial fire, at the pale impressions she had traced on the stone. The pale devils from the underworld. The Awshkoute. The refugees from northern Europe.

"They're gathered around the fire," Jean said, "watching and celebrating the sacrifice of the Indian."

Fielding looked again at her, incredulous. "How could you know?"

"I can *see* them," she cried. "I can feel the fire."

Fielding's chest rose and fell. He took a wavering breath as he tried to steady himself. "We're getting out of here."

"No."

"*You're* getting out of here."

"I can't, Chris. You know that. This is my only chance."

Fielding's eyes darted rapidly across her face, then up at the chalk figures on the ceiling. He wasn't sure what to do.

"We have to go on," she said. Then, pushing him forward, she added, "We have to hurry."

Fielding turned and raised the probe to where he had already begun to reveal the next sign. It was a wavy line, left to right, with another one paralleling the same course just below it. The dual lines were open at both ends.

"It signifies a passage, or journey," Jean said, not because of any preternatural insight, but because of her knowledge of similar pictographs in other locations.

Fielding concurred, moving on. He squared off the next site, then began to pass the sensor across the defined space. The speaker crackled intermittently, and for Jean the static was only the sound of the machine. She remained hot, but from the exertion and stress, not from the fire. She was focused on what she was doing, on what Fielding was doing. But there was a problem. He couldn't seem to get a fix on the hidden diagram. The magneto cracked and spit, then broke off. There was no pattern. Just a random series of positive indications, as if there were no design at all. An unfinished message?

As he continued across the squared-in space, seeking connections, Jean sensed the growing heat. She could hear the echoes. Her eyes fluttered shut and she was cast into darkness. Into night. She was staring at the night sky.

"That's all they are," she blurted out. "Single spots of paint. Points of light."

Fielding looked at her, thinking.

Jean reached to the ceiling and started stabbing her chalk against the rock. She turned to Fielding. "The night sky!"

Fielding looked at her representation of the stars and then back at the prone Indian in the sacrificial fire. It made sense. "After death, his spirit travels to the soul villages in the sky."

The next pictograph came easily. Another triangle, but balanced on one point, with a flat side rising vertically on the left and another point aimed to the right. "Focusing the power of their spirits," Fielding said.

"Yes," Jean agreed, but the effort to mouth the single word fatigued her. Her chest heaved, her shoulders slumped, as she fought to stay in command of herself. As she struggled to hold off the sights and sounds of *the others*. But they were inside of her and they had their own voices. Voices that echoed over the years. Voices that cried louder in her mind. Voices that threatened to become her own.

Jean slashed out the chalk lines as indicated by Fielding's detection. At first it seemed that there were two more triangles, nearly point to point, one above the other. But there was no corresponding line in either design opposite the points. Soon it became apparent that the narrowing lines represented the passage through the stone wall, and as Jean continued her strokes, she could see how it was, the horizontal chalk figures, one before the narrow chasm, the other just beyond.

Her breath wavered in her throat. She could see what was happening. She could sense what was happening. She could feel her arms secured behind her back, her wrists tied together. She could feel the rough surface of the stone as she was pushed into the opening, then the spear point jabbing at her feet.

Fielding had identified a closed circle as the next pictograph, and Jean rapidly traced it out. "Get back," she said, grabbing his shoulder, pushing him aside. In her vision the red paint was fresh and the chalky residue still wet. She could see the pictograph as the artist had rendered it, and she could see the cave the drawing represented.

The motif of the burning logs was repeated at the bottom of the circle, and stacked like so much firewood atop it were chalk figures. She traced them out as she saw them, and as the crude picture became more complete, the interior of the cavern became clearer in her mind. The floor was strewn with dry grasses and atop that was a veritable latticework of split lengths of wood and shavings of birch bark, and larger logs tented in upward-pointing cones. As she saw the layout, the fear she felt inside threatened to tumble out of control. It worsened, because she knew what was going to happen to her. Because she knew what was going to happen to all of them.

"Jean!" Fielding shouted. "Stop!"

"No!" she cried.

"We have to get out."

A little more, she thought. It's almost done. Just a little more. Fielding was trying to grasp her by the arm, but she twisted free. The chalk she held looped in a wide arc across the ceiling. The next pictograph, another circle. But the inside of the circle she left blank. Fielding was shouting at her, but now what he said was the echo, and the distant cries were what she heard. Whatever the language, she could understand the meaning. They were pleas for mercy, bellowing shouts of panic, frantic cries of conflicting demands.

She began to draw on the next blank space of encrusted lime. It was the last of the series, and it came quickly. Two wavy lines like those that indicated the journey of the fire victims' spirits, except that the lines were vertical, and they were connected at either end, closing off whatever passage there may have been.

The chalk dropped from her hand, and she stumbled backward, grasping both sides of her head. She tried to block the screams, but it was no use. They were inside of her, loud and shrill and commanding her back in time. She looked up at the pictograph of the cavern with the log fire and the Awshkoute stacked atop it, and she could see it. She could *remember* it. And suddenly, she was reliving it.

They were all around her, arms still secured behind their backs, running and pushing and shouting out in panic. Men were knocking down women with their shoulders, women were biting the clothes of children and pulling them back. All of them, scrambling over rock, climbing into the cavities, seeking another way out. And then at the entrance appeared the fire, flaming bundles of tied sticks. The first was heaved far to the right, near the wall, then came another, toward the opposite side. Toward her! With the appearance of the fire, the screams rose to a new crescendo of panic and terror. The shrill calls crackled against the stark stone barriers, resounding louder with each echoed refrain. The screams were like steel needles driven into her ears, and this time she couldn't even try to block their piercing effect with her hands. Her movement was restricted. Her arms were bound behind her back. The screams magnified in volume, usurping the full awareness of her thoughts, filling her own lungs, then being expelled from her throat.

Fielding shouted at her, but her screams eclipsed his voice even in his own ears. He was gripping her tightly on the biceps, trying to bring her out of her spasm, her fit, her dream—whatever the hell it was—but she only slipped away from him faster. And she was growing stronger. With a powerful tug, she twisted her shoulders free, stumbling backward, falling to the floor, pushing with her feet and clawing with her fingers as if to burrow into the rock itself.

The fire raged from a dozen points all around. The grasses flared like paper, the split kindling and the birch bark only a degree less combustible. And then the logs themselves were taking hold of the fire, accepting it onto their surface, pulling it into their pulpy cores, giving to it all the power and heat of their stored energy.

She screamed from the pain, the burning, the searing heat. She tried to roll away from it, but whichever direction she moved, she was closer to the flames. They were billowing upward, following the curve of the rock wall, lapping into every crevice and hidden enclosure. The others were still scrambling, but through the smoke they were little more than shadows. And the sound of the fire overtook the sound of their cries.

The heat on her skin, the fever in her veins, grew more intense. She was suffering, she was choking, she was dying. Rolling over on her back, she gasped for breath, but inhaled instead a smoky ball of heat. She coughed, her eyes bulged, and then within the din of roaring flames there was a cracking, crashing explosion and a shower of sparks that billowed above her head, then spiraled downward, sprinkling across her chest, landing on the exposed flesh of her face.

At last, the fire had touched her directly. A matted mass of burning vegetation had landed on her cheek, and she instinctively tried to raise her hand to brush it away, but she couldn't move her arm. The pain, the terror, gave new vigor to her screams, and she shrieked with the power and the voice of the damned souls that were inside her.

Fielding could do nothing to protect himself from her screams. He could only try to protect her. She was clawing at her face, and he grabbed her wrists and fought to pull her hands away. She had a strength that belied her physique, and Fielding had to get on top of her, using his weight to leverage her arms back from her face. As he did, he saw the fresh mark of fire on her cheek. "Jesus," he whispered, his strength wavering.

Her hands bound with hemp behind her, somehow unable even to roll to her side, she began to thrash back and forth in an attempt to break free, in an attempt to rid herself of the flaming debris stuck to her face. She screamed again in panic and pain. In frustration. And in anger. She couldn't move, she was being restrained; the anger became hate, then transformed rapidly to one last desperate expression of malice, directed against what was happening to her, against the bonds that tied her wrists, against the people who had done this!

Fielding's grip had eased involuntarily as he stared at the burn, but it wouldn't have mattered if it hadn't, so swift was her motion, so strong was the upward thrust of her body. She rose at the waist and her jaws snapped open, exposing needlelike fangs of fire.

Fielding shouted and tried to pull back at the same time, but she was too fast. Her face rose quickly to his, and she buried her fangs into his shoulder, at the base of his neck. He screamed and fell to the side, but she rolled with him, maintaining her hold. Fielding grimaced as he wedged his fingers under her throat. He pushed, but his left arm was nearly useless from the pain of the multiple punctures. The burning feel of the fire radiated the entire length of his limb. It streaked down his side, and following the stretch of his neck muscles, it stabbed into his skull.

The sound of her voice was the pressurized rush of concentrated fire, and she began to wrench her head back and forth. Fielding grunted with the renewed waves of pain, with a new effort to break free. Pulling his right forearm into his chest, he pushed hard, and her grip was finally broken and she fell away from him.

She fell into the fire. Into the hot yellow wall of energy and motion. It was all around her, it was consuming her, she was joining the flames. She could feel it stealing her energy, melding it with its own, trading light and heat for her weakness. She screamed in agony, and whether because of her last strength or the action of the fire, her arms were free. She slashed out in desperation for a hold to pull herself away, for a last assault at her tormentors.

Fielding looked on in abject helplessness. She appeared barely conscious. They were taking her. He could see the smoke rising from her body, the charring of her clothes. He could smell the fire!

As he started to come down to her, her arm suddenly reared back and her fingers emitted narrow daggers of light. Claws of fire. She slashed at him and raked his chest. Fielding didn't recoil. Instead, he grabbed her arm and twisted it quickly behind her back. Then, half lifting her, he pushed her toward the end of the tunnel. "You've got to climb," he shouted into her ear. "Jean! Hear me!"

He let go of her arm and twisted her around. "We've got to get out of here." Her body seemed to go limp, her head lolled back and her eyes rolled up into her skull. But where there should be white there was a glimmer of red, a flickering heart-colored tongue of flame.

Fielding put his shoulder into her stomach and hoisted her at the waist over his back. He reached his foot to the first rock protrusion and stepped upward, grasping the ledge above him. He struggled with his load, bringing his other foot up a bit higher, getting a better hold with his hands, then moving fractionally up the rock. It was a rise of about eight feet to level surface, and when he could place Jean's backside on the ledge, he leaned forward, carefully letting her down. Her legs bent at the knees over the edge, and she lay there, moaning.

Fielding let himself catch his breath, then eased himself back down to the tunnel floor. He went back for one of the lights, turning the other one off and leaving it along with the rest of his gear behind.

He turned and began to race back toward the far end. His thoughts were on escape, Jean Shawshequay, getting her out of here fast. The beam of light slashed crazily ahead of him as he ran, and whether it was because he was already looking ahead, or because of the unsteady source of light, he didn't notice the change until he reached the rock ascent. She was gone.

"Jean!" he screamed. Then, without waiting to hear if she'd reply, he slid the tube of his light into his belt and scaled the wall. At the top he drew his light as if drawing a saber and pointed its beam into the narrow black crevice.

He called her again, but there was no response, and he could hear no sound of movement. No scraping of soles over hard rock, no grunts of exertion as she pulled herself up the next rise. Only silence as deep as the black just beyond the tapered cone of his light.

He began to ease himself into the network of sharp-edged crevices. Peering around the first edge, he was greeted with the angry faces of dozens—hundreds—of bats, their wings unfolding, ready to take flight. He pulled his arm back and continued following the main passage but pausing to check with the light a second, then a third, intersecting crevice.

Fielding stood still and listened, and as he did, as he fought to control the noisy rush of his own breath, he began to discern the sound of breathing that was not his own. At least it carried the cadence of breathing. The sound itself was an intermittent whoosh, almost a hiss.

"I'm here," he said. "I want to help you."

Just ahead a seepage fissure crossed the one he was in at an angle. Carefully, Fielding leaned beyond the closest crevice and quickly scanned the bare rock cavities, the shadows, the guano-streaked floor. Nothing. "I know you can hear me," he said, edging forward. He turned toward the fissure's extension on the other side. He saw the bats, and as he did, he realized something was wrong. Not in front of him, but where he had just looked. There were no bats!

At the moment of realization he heard what sounded like the sudden venting of air. But it wasn't air, he knew. It was fire.

He spun in place, and out of the dark, like a spectral vision of hell, came blood-red eyes, glowing fangs of fire, and to either side daggered claws honed to pinpoints of white-hot light. The vision had the appearance of an incandescent horror from the deep sea, and as his fright registered, it swam, it flew, out of the black toward him.

Fielding lunged to the side, and the thing of light and fire fell past him. He turned as the creature opened its jaws wide in roar that was half animal, half the sound of a blazing inferno. It swung a limb toward him, the claws swishing forward with the sound of a sword slashing empty air. Fielding reacted fast, attacking. He swung the barrel of his light and connected squarely across the creature's forehead.

It was a creature of fire, the repositor of the souls of the Awshkoute. And it was the body of Jean Shawshequay, frail and weakened and injured. And it was this latter manifestation that suffered the blow to the head.

The internal fire flamed out and Jean collapsed to the floor. Fielding sheathed his light again, and grabbing her arm, he hoisted her up and over his shoulder. She moaned as he did, as he carried her to the rise that led through a hole to the entrance to the cave.

"You've got to help," he said, putting her chest up against the wall, pushing her higher. "Grab on and pull." He struggled to raise her, and then it became easier. She was grabbing and guiding herself, if not using her own muscles to lift. "Good," Fielding said. "Keep it up. Just a little more."

She half crawled, half fell into the earthen cavity at the mouth of the cave. Fielding climbed up and over her, then, pulling from the front, dragged her outside by the arms.

Jean moaned and shivered at the same time, trying to open her eyes, to look up at Fielding. "It's okay now," he said. "We're out."

He looped her arm over his shoulder, then with his shoulder in her armpit, he began to walk her out. "Can you help me?"

"Yes," she breathed, and as they moved over the matted trail under the oaks, she gradually asserted more of her own power. When they reached the path to the surface, she started to make her own way, slowly edging up the trail, pausing frequently to rest. Fielding helped where he could, but much of the climb required individual effort.

By the time they reached the rim, she had expended her energy, and Fielding carried her to his truck. She tried to protest, but lacked the strength even to do that. So she relented, allowing herself to be placed in the seat, to have the harness stretched over her lap.

As Fielding got behind the wheel, he took a moment to look over at Jean. Her cheek was blistered from a burn, her lips were raw and cracked, and she held her fingers curled and upraised in her lap. The tips of her fingers were the color of a severe sunburn.

She saw him watching her and she tried to talk, but her throat was too dry. She ran her tongue over her lips, but that brought no moisture.

"Don't try to say anything," Fielding urged.

She shook her head in her first display of vigor. "No," she managed to say.

"You'll have time to talk later. After you've regained your strength."

Her head sank back against the seat, and her eyes fluttered shut in frustration. She turned her face back toward him. "The pictographs," she breathed.

He looked at her, and this time he did not urge silence.

"I know what they mean."

Fielding watched her struggle to maintain consciousness, and he waited, almost reaching to shake her alert, tempted to get her to explain what she meant. But he held back, realizing he could not push her. Realizing it would be better to let her go. And within seconds, her eyes fluttered shut again, this time not in frustration but in surrender.

Fielding shifted into first and steered into the trail leading back toward the highway. He would get her home and safe, he would listen to what she said, and then he would come back to discover what she knew. What it was she had *seen*.

Chapter 21

JOHNNY PENAY SAT quietly by the phone, thinking about Jean Shawshequay. First she had betrayed her people, permitting the desecration. And now Blackbear was dead.

It was time to stop the insult and end the treachery, and do it in a way that both avenged and sent a message. That's what he had decided. That's what he had told Rene Wawatessi and William Quilltail. And that's what they had told the rest to be ready for.

When the phone rang, Quilltail picked it up on the first ring. He covered the mouthpiece as he said to Penay, "She's there." He continued listening a few moments, then said into the receiver, "Okay, hang on. I'll give it to Johnny." He passed the phone to Penay, saying, "He said there's a problem."

"What's wrong, Rene?" Penay asked.

"Kinsey's parked down the street," Rene said.

"Alan Kinsey? The deputy?"

"Yes. He's in his own car, but it's him. I'm sure of it. I got a real good look as I drove by. It looks like he's keeping an eye on the house."

Penay paused, thinking. He was conscious of Quilltail staring at him, and of the silence on the phone. They would all be waiting on him now, he knew. And watching. "Is anybody else at the house, besides her and Miriam?"

"The archaeologist. He brought her in. She didn't look too good."

The archaeologist, Penay thought. They could deal with him, if he were still there when they were ready. The police were a different matter. But after getting off the phone and thinking about the situation, he grew thankful he had trusted his instincts earlier regarding Ray Goodmedicine. Despite the risks of maintaining contact with the person attracting the sheriff's attention, he had felt the kid would be useful. Now at last he could see how.

• • •

Deputy Sheriff Alan Kinsey was parked up the street and around the corner from Miriam Goodmedicine's. Where he had set up surveillance, he could easily see the front, and more importantly, if a car left her house, it would pass directly in front of him.

When the black Comanche pickup truck pulled up, Kinsey radioed the sheriff. "Something funny's going on," he said. "Fielding just carried Jean Shawshequay into the house. Didn't you say they were out at the site?"

"Yes, but they climbed down into the sinkhole. They were still there when we left."

"Think she fell?"

"Don't worry about her," Sheriff Halstead said. "Just keep your eyes on Miriam."

Kinsey acknowledged and broke the connection. Then he sat back, continuing his vigil.

Ray Goodmedicine sat in the shadows in the corner of the front room overlooking the big lake. The house had been designed to shed the sun, and it was cool inside. He hadn't touched any of the thermostat settings or turned on any lights since he arrived yesterday, and he tried to remember to stay out of view of the windows, just in case a stroller on the beach would catch sight of him.

He hadn't had anything fresh or cooked to eat, surviving off crackers, stale potato chips, and coffee. Lots of coffee.

He wanted to call Penay. He could trust him, he told himself, despite the uneasy feeling the man always seemed to convey. He wished Blackbear were around, and alternating with his desire to call Penay was an idea to leave the house and make his way to Makwamacatawa's sweatlodge. Perhaps he could join Blackbear in his quest.

It was a fanciful notion, he realized each time the idea occurred to him. How would he get there? How could he elude the police? Would Makwamacatawa welcome him? Though practical realities had so far turned him away from the attempt, at least the idea was still there, in the back of his mind, if things became desperate.

With the thought of the situation becoming desperate, in his almost constant cycle of mental turmoil, he returned to worrying about the sheriff. Could he get a twelve-year-old kid to identify him as an arsonist responsible for four deaths? The answer in his mind was certain: Of course he could.

Propelled by his nerves, clouded by indecision, Ray stood suddenly and began to pace across the room, in front of the floor-to-ceiling picture window. As he turned at the wall and began to come back, he caught sight of a figure outside. On the beach. Two figures. A man and a young boy, both wearing brightly patterned Gore-Tex jackets. And they were pointing, at the house.

Ray spun to the corner, bracing his back against the wall. Had they seen him? Were they neighbors? Would they know the house was supposedly vacant? The questions came rapidly, welling up under his paranoia, pushing him closer to panic. They couldn't see through the glass, he tried to convince himself. The reflection of the afternoon sun would be too much. It was too bright outside.

Peering around the edge, he saw the pair walking away. There was no hurry to their gait. No urgency to their retreat. But that was little consolation because he couldn't be sure exactly what the two of them had seen. He couldn't be sure how long it would take for them to piece things together. He couldn't be sure what he should do. He couldn't be sure how long Penay was going to make him wait.

Ray thrust his head back against the wall, staring at the ceiling, unable to stifle the rapid call of his lungs for air. He felt so alone, so terribly alone, and in the pit of his stomach he ached. He let out a wavering sigh, almost a whimper, and his tension began to yield to self-pity. He slumped slowly to the floor, his back sliding down against the wall, but when he reached the surface, his progression of emotion seized suddenly. The tension spiked anew with a tremulous intrusion. The phone!

He listened, deathly still, to the first ring; then halfway through the second, the connection was broken. It was his signal, what he had been waiting for.

He punched out the number Penay had given him, and Bill Quilltail answered on the first ring. After verifying who it was, he passed the phone to Johnny. "How have you been?" came Penay's voice through the line.

"Fine," Ray said, trying to match Penay's casual tone. "I just been waiting, you know. For you."

"And here I am." Penay paused, letting the imbalance he sensed build. "Right, Ray?"

"Yeah, Johnny. You're right."

"I'm your brother. We're all your brothers, and we don't forget each other. Right?"

"Right."

"And we don't let each other down, when we need each other."

Ray swallowed hard. "I know that, Johnny. I knew you were going to call, as soon as you decided what to do."

"That's right, Ray. And you know what?"

Ray was still off balance, not knowing whether to answer Penay's question or let him go on. When the silence continued, Ray felt himself responding, "What?"

"We've decided. The desecration is going to stop. It's gone on too long, and if we hope to make any claim as the new leaders of our people, as the protectors of our past and the guides of the future, we have to act. We *must* act."

"That's good," Ray agreed. "That's what I want too." It was, wasn't it?

"We must act to show others in our midst, like her, that we have to stand together. We must act to show the outsiders that we are prepared to defend our dignity and our culture against those who have tried to destroy us."

Ray's sense of imbalance, his uncertainty, worsened. "Wh-what is it?" he stammered. His mouth had gone dry and he had to try again. "What are we—"

Penay cut him off. "The interloper, the betrayer, the bringer of bad spirits, must be removed."

Removed? Ray tried to swallow, but he lacked the moisture in his mouth.

"It was she who said she would watch the desecrator," Penay continued, "but in fact became the desecrator herself."

"You mean to kill her," Ray blurted.

"The Ancient Ones will deal with her in the manner they have chosen themselves."

"But is she . . . Are you sure?" Ray couldn't form the thought fast enough or clear enough to say. It was a feeling more than anything he was trying to express. A feeling of fear at being involved in a murder.

"She betrayed us," Penay said angrily, his anger calculated. "She has carried to us a spiritual sickness that has infected the land. She knew about the fire at the cabin, you told us that yourself."

He was right, Ray thought. And there was more he hadn't told them. "The fire was inside of you," Fielding had said. Ray gripped his forehead with his free hand. The words of Penay, his own thoughts, were swimming in his mind. She had known!

"Her spirits are strong," Penay continued. "Unless she is consumed herself, she will consume us all, as she has with Blackbear."

Ray went suddenly light-headed. "What's happened to Blackbear?"

"Blackbear is dead. Seeking his visions for the benefit of us all, he was consumed in flames by the spirits she has brought to the land."

"At the sweatlodge?"

"Yes," Penay practically hissed.

A feverish rush filled Ray's cheeks. He was hot and chilled, frantic and numb, all at the same time. Makwamacatawa dead? Consumed by the flames? He didn't know whether to stand or sit, to pace or remain still. The sense of imbalance, or not knowing what to think or do, increased. Blackbear had inspired them all. His father had never been there for him, but Blackbear had seemed to know the things Ray should know. He had taught him. He had guided him. And even in the past twenty-four hours, he had held out the last alternative for Ray, the last refuge.

"He fought for us, and now we will fight for him and the Ancient Ones he hopes to join. And you will help us," Penay said, not as a question, but as a command.

Ray asked, "What do you want me to do?"

"You're going to make a call," Penay said. "You're going to call your mother and tell her where you're at. You can't risk coming home, but you need her to come to you. To talk. To bring food. To help decide what to do. Do you understand?"

The knot of tension had tightened again as he listened. His mother? Draw her into this? "What do you want with her?"

"We want her out of the way. So she won't get hurt." Penay listened to the sound of breathing on the line, the scared silence of indecision. His voice softened. "Ray, there are others who say Miriam is the same as Jean Shawshequay. She brought her here. She housed her. And she placed her in position to join the desecration. They say she should be treated no differently. But I don't agree with that, and I don't think any harm should come to her. Do you?"

Ray shook his head, not thinking that Penay couldn't see him. *"Do you?"* Penay repeated.

"No," Ray said quickly.

"Then you'll call her. Tell her you need to see her tonight. That's all you have to do. We'll do the rest."

That's all you have to do. The thought stayed with him after he hung up the phone, as he stood in the shadows of the big house that was not his own. And then what?

He had thought things were bad earlier, being alone and not knowing the first thing to do. But now it was worse, knowing what was going to happen. And what had already happened to Blackbear.

Jean accepted the glass of water from Miriam, cupping it with both palms. Balancing the rim carefully on her lips, she sipped slowly.

Miriam couldn't help but stand above her and stare at the lips cracked and reddened, at the burned fingertips, at the fiery blisters on her cheek. "They're trying to come back to life through you," Fielding had said last night. And *she had known*, Miriam thought, about the people in the cabin.

Miriam could not begin to imagine what was happening, but she was an experienced enough leader to know when to lead and when to get out of the way. She had brought it on the girl herself, after all. Jean hadn't wanted to stay, but Miriam talked her into it that day in the judge's chambers and then upstairs in her daughters' room, giving her the mink carved by Wes. Jean was older than her daughters, but she could just as easily be one of them. One of her daughters could have just as easily been the one they had chosen. Miriam had to turn away, because of the sense of responsibility for what had happened, because of her shame.

Fielding had his own wounds, but when she offered to tend to them, he said he was all right. As Jean handed Miriam the half-empty glass, Fielding said he wanted to get her upstairs.

"I'll bring some cream," Miriam said. "For the burns."

Fielding carried Jean to the dormer, and Miriam followed a minute later with a tube of antibacterial salve and cotton balls.

"I'll do it," Fielding said, and though Miriam assented, Fielding could see the concern—the fear?—in her eyes as she looked at Jean. He followed her to the door and on the landing tried to assure her Jean wasn't a danger, so far from the cave. At least for now.

Miriam nodded, but as she closed the bedroom door behind her and walked down the stairs, it was not herself she was worried about. She was worried about Jean. And she was worried about Ray.

As Quilltail hung up the phone Penay had handed him, he couldn't help but feel a disturbing sense of unease. He had grown up with Ray and had known him all his life. And because of that, he could not hold back, no matter how intimidating Penay was. "You know, that's just going to get him caught."

"We all have to do our part," Penay said.

"Miriam's going to lead the sheriff right to him."

"And away from the house. That's the point, isn't it?"

"Who knows what Ray'll do when he sees he's trapped? Who knows what the sheriff will do? He thinks he's a killer, after all."

"We're all taking risks."

"We could at least warn him."

Penay rose slowly to his feet and stood before Quilltail. As the younger man tried to rise too, Penay pushed him back in the chair with a rough hand to the shoulder. "It's too late to back out, Billy," Penay said. "Things are already in motion, so don't even think of betraying us."

Don't betray us like Jean Shawshequay, Quilltail thought. Penay's message was clear.

I know what they mean, she had said. The series of images painted in ocher and chalk compounds on the ceiling of the cave told the history of how the native peoples of this region had dealt with the pagan outcasts from northern Europe. And she knew what they meant.

But so did he, Fielding thought, sitting on the chair in the corner of the three-bed attic room, watching Jean Shawshequay sleep. He had understood the progression of events, from the first pictographic representation of the sacrificial fire, to the barren circle and vertical wavy bands, signifying the end of the proto-Ojibwa's ordeal. What else could there be to it, he wondered. What else had she seen?

Fielding stood and walked over by her bed. Her breathing was steady and relaxed, a result of the sedatives. When they first arrived back at Miriam's, she had seemed in a fog, outwardly aware of what was happening, but at the same time somehow distant. It hadn't seemed a preoccupation with the pain, but rather as if she didn't care. As if she were sinking farther away. As if they were pulling her away.

Fielding turned from her bed and walked back to the chair. He was anxious to hear what she read into the pictographs, but more than anything, she needed her strength, continued rest. And he needed his.

He tried to stay awake, but he had had little sleep, if any, the night before, and much had happened to him as well in the cave. It wasn't long before he dropped off. He was out for an hour, ninety minutes maybe, when he came out of his sleep with the suddenness of waking from a nightmare.

Jean Shawshequay was sitting up in bed, staring at him. "We don't have much time," she said, her voice tired. "We're going to have to move now."

Fielding exhaled, breathing deeply. "What do we have to do?"

"We have to finish what was started back then."

Finish? Fielding edged forward in the chair. "What was started?"

"It was there, on the ceiling. Didn't you see it?"

"No, I didn't. I mean yes," he said quickly, "but I don't understand the significance you see in it."

"The last pictographs," she said. "That's what was significant."

"The empty circle? The closed journey?"

"But was it empty?"

"You're the one who saw it. You traced it that way in chalk on the ceiling."

"The cavern the painting was supposed to represent," she corrected. "Was that empty?"

Fielding felt himself shifting back in the chair. "The bones?"

"Their remains exist," she said. "And where they exist, their power exists."

Undeniably, the burning deaths over the last few days, over the years, had occurred only in proximity to the skeletal remains. Were the bones themselves the reservoir of the evil that Fielding had witnessed so graphically?

"We have to finish what my people started," she said.

"We have to destroy the skeletal remains?"

"We have to incinerate the bones," she said. "We have to reduce them to ash."

"It's been said the native people believed that existence in the soul villages was similar to life in this world, with the same challenges to prove your goodness. They believed the spirits would rest only when their bones on earth turned to dust. And that's what they thought they were doing at the fire in the cave. They thought they were destroying the spirits of the Awshkoute. They thought they were reducing them to dust."

Was the belief in the lingering presence of the soul in physical remains Jean talked about all that dissimilar from the beliefs of the northern European people who had settled there? They had communal cemeteries, Fielding considered, stacking the bones together in ossuaries in the belief they were joining themselves to the entity they worshiped.

He got up and began to pace. He was no longer tired. His mind was alert and anxious and gripped with the excited tension that builds on the verge of a discovery. It was similar to the sensation he felt when sitting in an excavated trench, brushing off the last dirt from a mud-encased artifact, knowing what it probably was, but holding back so as not to let emotion cloud judgment. It was always difficult to stifle that sort of soaring anticipation, and at this moment, he was having little success. The power he had seen, and had felt in Buck Billings's camp fire and in Jean's assault, was immense, and yet if she were right, they had a means to fight back.

If she is right, Fielding thought. Given the parameters he had already crossed, in the realm now of non-science, what she proposed had a certain basic logic in it. All the manifestations of the living fire that had led to people dying had been in proximity to the bones, and in the case of the cabin fire, the bones had been carried to it. Last night, when the fire had engulfed his truck and he continued driving, Fielding saw how the intensity of the flames diminished until it faded to nothing. If the entity that took possession of the fire needed to be close to its source, it followed that if the source were destroyed, then the power would be destroyed as well.

Fielding turned to face Jean. Not only was it simple logic, she was convinced. And after all, she had *seen*. She had *remembered*. She was part of them.

Jean turned the sheet back and brought her feet to the floor. "I have to go back to the cave."

"You're not going anywhere," Fielding said. "This is something I'm going to handle by myself."

"No. It's something I have to do," she said, a toneless quality to her voice.

"You can't go," he said, almost in exasperation. "You can barely walk. And after last time, you might not survive another trip."

"Whoever goes will not come back."

Fielding's energy began to do a slow fade. "What do you mean?" Then more insistent, "What else have you seen?"

"It's not anything I've seen or felt or been told. It's just simple logic."

Simple logic. And as soon as Fielding began to consider the problem, he understood what she meant. Indeed, it was elementary: How to use fire, when fire is the agent of that which he's trying to destroy. Like putting a match to fuseless dynamite, the igniter would suffer the blast as well.

"Which is why I have to go," Jean continued in the same somber tone. "By myself. You know, you were right. They are inside of me. And to destroy them all, there can be no haven left for them."

"They're not inside you at this moment."

"I can see them every time I close my eyes. I can hear the whispers, the subtle demands. Each time it gets a little worse. Each time the hold is a little stronger."

"Which is why you can't go anywhere near that cave. They'd never let you destroy them. You know that. They can control you there, like they did this morning."

He was right again, Jean thought. They'd never let her destroy them. Indeed, her presence could only make it worse. As it had for the family in the river cabin.

Fielding recognized her surrender, and he eased himself down onto the bed next to her, bringing his hands gently to her arms. "There'll be a way," he said. "I'm sure of it. I'm sure I can think of a way."

Fielding kissed her, and though she offered no resistance, he felt little warmth. As if she knew there would not be another embrace. And as Fielding left her and walked down the stairs, he couldn't help but share that same resignation. Despite what he had told her, he couldn't imagine how it would be possible for him to incinerate the skeletal remains in the cave without the creature of the fire using the flames of the pyre against him.

Whatever was going to happen, Fielding knew he didn't have much time. *Each time it gets a little worse,* she had said. *Each time the hold is a little stronger.*

Miriam was waiting for Fielding as he came into the living room. "How is she?"

"As long as she remains where she is," Fielding said, "she'll be all right. But you'll have to stay with her, and above all, make sure she doesn't leave."

"Where are you going?"

Fielding paused at the door. "I'm going back to the cave."

Miriam prepared dinner even though she knew she couldn't eat. It was mainly for Jean's sake anyway, she told herself. She readied it on a tray, but before she could take it upstairs, the phone rang. It was Ray. "Why did you have to run?"

"I couldn't help it," Ray said. "I had to get away. I heard what the sheriff was saying."

"Don't you realize what it looks like, running away? It makes him think he's right about you."

"He's already convinced. What difference does it make if he has another reason to believe?"

Miriam steadied herself. "We can worry about him later, Ray. Where are you now? Are you all right?"

"I need help, Mom," he said.

His voice to her suddenly seemed so small and weak and so very young. "I know you do, Ray. And I'm here to help you. But you have to come home for me to be able to do anything."

"No," he said quickly. "I can't. But you can come to me."

Miriam noticed the change in his voice. "Where are you?"

"You won't tell anybody?" he said. "You won't tell the sheriff?"

"No, I won't tell anybody."

"I'm in one of the cottages on the lake," he said, giving the three-digit Lakeshore Drive address.

"You broke in?"

"No one was here. I was careful about that. You'll come, won't you?" he added quickly, fearfully. "If you don't, I'm going to have to leave."

"Where would you go?"

"I . . . I don't know."

"I'll come, if you promise to leave there with me."

The phone was silent for a long moment before his voice came, sounding again weak and young. "I'm not sure what I'll do. What I should do. I . . . I just don't know."

He didn't know what he'd do, Miriam thought after getting off the phone. What was he capable of?

She parted the curtains, looking out toward the road, hoping to see Fielding's truck returning. He didn't appear, though, and she knew he wouldn't be coming back for a long while. She glanced at her watch. It was almost seven.

She went to the bottom of the stairs and looked up at the closed door. Some battles were more important than others, she thought. Sometimes, risks had to be taken.

Jean was drifting again, not so much back over events as away from them. Where she drifted it was dark and quiet and absolutely still. It was as if she were in a cave.

Her conversation with Fielding was but a distant echo, and though she was vaguely aware of Miriam placing something on a chair next to the bed, it wasn't enough to draw her back from her world of darkness. She remained there, in this passive state, even after she heard the click of the bolt in her bedroom door lock.

Chapter 22

THE DEPUTY TURNED the key in the ignition with little force, as if deliberately trying to silence the sound of the engine. It turned over, caught, and then he rested his hand on the wheel-mounted gearshift.

When the old blue Toyota station wagon drove by in front of him, he shifted into gear and eased around the corner. At the same time, he reached for the radio and called in to the sheriff. "She's left the house," Kinsey said, "heading out of Ojibwa Village."

Halstead's voice spat out of the tinny speaker. "She alone?"

"Yeah. She's by herself. Think this is it?"

"We'll find out," the sheriff said. "Stay back and keep her in sight. Remember, there's no reason to get too close to her."

"Okay, Sheriff."

"Good. We're on our way."

Johnny Penay was leaning back in the driver's seat, his face hidden in the shadows of the solid panel van. As the Toyota, then Deputy Kinsey in his own car, passed by, he leaned forward, watching them in the sideview mirror until they turned out of sight.

Penay looked over his shoulder into the back. "We're ready, boys."

It was a ten-year-old Ford Econoline, a utility vehicle with a ribbed metal floor splotched with various colors of paint spilled by the first owner. Quilltail was there, sitting on the floor with his back against the windowless side wall, as was Rene Wawatessi. Penay had brought along others, Jim Leveque and Peter Migisi, but from the looks of it, there wouldn't be any problem at all. Inside the house, the woman from Oklahoma was alone.

Quilltail slipped between seats up front and sat across from Penay. As the old, battered van rolled down the street, he said,

"The cellar door is on this side. You can back into the driveway, then edge onto the grass. We should be blocked from the road over there."

Penay backed the van up the drive as he'd been told, then partly around the front corner of the house so the tailgate fronted the fruit-cellar entrance. He pulled up the parking brake and turned off the ignition, then climbed between the seats into the back. "You stay here and watch," he said to Quilltail, and the young man nodded almost in relief. Penay made eye contact with the other three, then grabbed the rear latch and opened the back doors.

Leveque hopped out first and ran with a crowbar to the slanting metal door. He checked the hinged latch, then looked back, smiling. "It's not even locked."

One by one, Penay, Wawatessi, and Migisi jumped onto the ground and made their way to the door. Leveque had it swung up and open, and all four of them followed the half flight of stairs into the basement.

"Ray said her room's upstairs," Penay said, "but we can't be sure where she's at now."

"I told you," Rene said, "the archaeologist had to carry her in. She's not going to be anywhere but in bed."

"Just the same," Penay whispered, "let me go first." Taking the crowbar from Leveque, he walked silently up the stairs and very slowly cracked the door. He didn't see her; he didn't hear any movement.

Quickly, Penay checked the first floor, then signaled the others to come up.

"It seems so damn quiet," Migisi said to Rene. "You sure she's here?"

"She's here," Penay said, answering for Wawatessi. "Up there," he added, indicating the stairway to the attic dormer.

Leading the way, Penay stepped quietly up to the landing in front of the closed bedroom door. When they were all there, Penay gripped the doorknob and began to twist it slowly. He pushed, but it was locked. Then, just as slowly, he let the knob uncoil in his hand. Backing off, he looked at Migisi and jerked his head toward the door. "Kick it in."

There were voices in the cave. Faint, but the harsh acoustics of the cavern amplified the sound. She had been adrift in the void, floating, seeing muted flashes in the dark, like heat lightning, over the lake. If the people of the fire were there, the fatigue, or perhaps the sedatives, had kept them beyond the horizon. But things were changing. First came the voices, then the sound of movement in the dark, like night creatures closing in on a woodland camp. She peered anxiously into the blackness, looking for the things that moved, watching for the glint of eyes, the gleam of fangs. She turned—in bed and in her dream—but the darkness was just as deep, her vision just as ineffectual.

In the distance the light flashed again, and she flinched. It was brighter, closer, and for one brief flicker of a heartbeat, the distant flare had pushed back the dark. She rolled over again, murmuring in her sleep, calling out in her dream. She wanted the light to stay; she wanted the things of the darkness to leave her alone.

She felt the effect of the fire inside of her, its heat causing her blood to flow faster, her skin to begin to sweat. The flash came again, but it was no longer distant and it was no longer a muted flare. It was a distinct source of yellow light. It was the fire. And the voices were closer too. The sources of movement.

In her dream, in the bed, she called out for the safety the fire offered. She wanted it to be closer. She needed the fire. She needed *them*.

Fielding's tension had become a thing of substance, a hard knot of muscle and tissue that contracted tightly in the center of his stomach. He cursed its effects not because of the fear it nurtured, but because of how it interfered with his thinking. He had to be able to concentrate, to follow new lines of inquiry, to qualitatively analyze the surge of ideas that lit then flickered out, like fireflies in his mind.

It was the tension that inhibited his faculties, contributing to a confused swirl of idea and hope and urgency. Urgency, because he knew that regardless of where Jean was, eventually she would succumb. The fire was inside of her and would destroy her. She would be absorbed into the whole.

Since he'd left the Goodmedicine house, he had been preparing to complete what had been begun nearly six hundred years ago. The bones themselves were old and dry and would burn easily, given the right combustible. He decided on kerosene, as safer for him than gas. But would that distinction really matter? In thinking about safety, he couldn't help but come back to the simple logistical problem presented: how to use fire when the striking of the match would give life to what he sought to destroy. Was he so willing to die along with them?

As he poured the single-gallon containers of kerosene into the two five-gallon rectangular cans in the parking lot of the hardware store, he tried to think of ways to avoid exposing himself to the flames. It wasn't a structured pattern of logical thought he was able to follow, but rather a continuing swirl of ideas begetting hope followed by dismissal, only to have the cycle renewed by his tension. There seemed no escape from his circuitous thinking, and so he tried to ignore the problem. Any technical solution was flawed because time was crucial. He couldn't wait. Jean couldn't wait. He had to do it tonight. He had to incinerate them in the cave, as the early Ojibwa had decided.

Though he tried not to think about what was going to happen, the images of all those charred bodies were too vivid to shut out of his mind completely. Hefting the five-gallon cans into the back bed of his truck, he saw the blackened form of Buck Billings with his fingers crooked like claws in the dirt. He saw Deputy Jerry Cole, the Verhoven family. Blackbear in his sweatlodge.

As past observation melded with images of future fire, Fielding was transported back to the night clearing, looking up at Makwamacatawa hovering over his fire. He was half man, half bear, and as Fielding remembered the sight, he felt the same sense of awe. And the same wonder. How did he resist the flames?

Fielding slammed the tailgate shut. Blackbear had been up there for three nights, chanting into the flames. Why did the fire not take him earlier? Why was he spared until the sweatlodge was complete?

As the questions joined the cyclical pattern of hope and analysis, a renewed sense of excitement began to percolate in his mind. A new possibility began to emerge, and as it did, he fought his fear for control of his reason. The mental battle carried a physical price, and Fielding sensed his own fatigue as he tried to think, as he tried to focus his thoughts.

He leaned against the door, his forehead coming into contact with the glass. Makwamacatawa had been spared until he went inside the lodge, until he entered the hot and closed confines of the bark hut in a pure state unfettered with the trappings of the material world. He had been spared until he entered the sweatlodge in the custom of the rite.

Fielding pushed himself away from the door and peered through the narrow window into the back bed of his truck. With the stark clarity of sudden understanding, he realized the difference between Makwamacatawa's tempting of the fire and all the others. He stood still, testing the logic of his latest hope, and as he did, he could think of no other way to explain what had happened, and more importantly, what had not.

In her dream solitary lobes of fire wavered in the black like the beckoning arms of her saviors. In turn, she reached out toward them, toward the light, toward the protection. But as it is with dreams, distances were not finite. They existed as barriers between imagination and reality, teasing with promise by holding out unattainable goals.

She could feel the heat of the fire, but she couldn't touch it. There was light, but the glare only served to heighten the darkness that concealed the *things* that were out there. She could hear them, the voices and the movement, and she was afraid. She was moving, in her dream and in the bed, from side to side. Struggling to see. To get away. She was hot and cold at the same time. Sweat poured off her, dampening the sheets, which in turn contributed to the chill.

She called on the fire to help her. She could feel it inside of her, growing hotter. She wanted it to come closer, to fill her, to extend out of her.

The cave exploded with sound, and the delineation between dream and reality was shattered. Yanked forcefully back across the line, Jean sat up in bed, suddenly thrust into a world of light and movement. And strangers.

Peter Migisi stumbled backward as the doorjamb splintered, and Penay burst through first, half falling, turning with the sweep of the door. Rene, Leveque, and then Migisi rushed past him. They were to get to the woman on the bed before she could scream, but instead they halted just inside the door.

"Go!" Penay shouted, spinning toward the bed. And then he too froze in mid-step.

She was sitting up, her arms braced behind her, absolutely silent. All she was doing was staring at them.

"What the fuck is this?" Leveque said.

Her eyes were open, but they weren't eyes. They were deep sockets of red, a wavering, flickering light. Her eyes were pinpoints of fire.

Rene took a half step back, but Penay grabbed his arm. "She's what we said she was." He turned back to her, and her eyes, her fire, trained on him. "Damn you to hell," he rasped and then broke toward the bed.

She flung the sheet to the side and tried to jump to the floor, but Penay was too fast. He grabbed her, pulling her back, throwing her down flat on the mattress. And then Migisi was there, and Leveque, on the other side holding her.

She let out a spitting, hissing snarl as her neck, her entire back, arched against the mattress. "Her feet, damn it," Penay shouted at Rene, and he came forward, grabbing her by the ankles.

Her head twisted violently, and she reached it toward Migisi's hand. He felt a sudden blast of heat and recoiled.

Using her lunge to his advantage, Penay rolled her over, turning her in the sheet. Leveque continued the motion, rolling her facedown. Her arms were pinned close to her body, and they spun her again, wrapping her tightly in the sheet.

Her mouth opened wide in a scream that could have been the roar of a blast furnace. Penay smothered it with a pillow and, leaning his entire weight over her face, shouted to Migisi, "Rip a sheet from the other bed, for her mouth."

Migisi did, and they gagged her. Then Penay yanked the pillow from its case and pulled the case over her head, knotting it at her neck. "Let's go."

They carried her down the steps, then into the basement. Rene went out the fruit-cellar door first and opened the back doors of the van. Penay ran to the driver's door as the others hustled their captive into the back, sliding her onto the metal floor, jumping in after her, and slamming the doors.

Penay had to grab the wheel to steady his hands. He didn't move; he was afraid to try. Instead he remained fixed where he was, gripping tighter, pushing himself back harder into the seat, breathing heavily.

Quilltail watched him, then looked in the back. In their own way, the others were the same, sitting on the floor, their backs braced against the wall, staring at the cocoon stretched along the far side of the van. It wasn't moving. She was completely still. "What went wrong?" Quilltail said.

Migisi looked slowly toward him. "My hand," he said. "She burned it."

Quilltail stared at him, puzzled. He didn't know what Migisi meant, or how it could have happened. But he could sense the fear.

The engine roared and the van lurched forward, gouging twin ruts in the dirt until the rear wheels caught the pavement of the driveway. The van fishtailed, then spun out into the road, the right side wheels coming down hard over the curb.

Sand ground in the disc brakes as the blue station wagon jerked to a halt. Miriam looked over at the grand house, the multi-angled roof, the natural stain of the wood, the double entrance doors. And in the foyer window, a face. It startled her, but it was gone in a second, and she realized it must be Ray.

She got out of the car and looked around self-consciously. There were other houses along this strand of beach, but they were well spread out and set among hardy stands of white pine and cedar. She could see why he had chosen this one to break into.

The entrance was recessed between the garage on one side and a back wing of the house on the other. When Miriam neared the doors, one of them opened for her. She stopped where she was and waited. "Ray?"

Slowly, his head appeared around the edge of the door. "Come in."

She shook her head. "I'm not going in there." Not because she was afraid, but because it was wrong.

"You just going to stand out there?"

"I want you to come out and talk to me."

"Somebody might see us."

"They might, and believe me, I don't want any harm to come to you. But no matter how much I fear that, that's no excuse for me to violate the law."

Ray edged more fully into the opening, looking beyond her toward the lane. "You didn't tell anyone you were coming, did you?"

"No." She waited, then said, "If you're not coming out, then I'm going back home."

"No. Don't do that," he said quickly.

"Well?"

Ray bit his upper lip, then eased out onto the porch. It was the first time in twenty-eight hours he had been outside, and he re-acted as an animal might, flushed from its lair. He squinted and looked around nervously.

"Is this how you intend to spend the rest of your life?" she asked. "Hiding? Afraid to step out into the light?"

Ray blinked once, twice. He had done what Penay told him to do, and she was here. But things were no less clear to him than before. Makwamacatawa's death, the sheriff's suspicions, Penay's plan for ending the desecration, it all combined again to rekindle the confusion. His fear. *The rest of your life,* she had said. He couldn't think into the next minute, much less the rest of his life.

As the heat of uncertainty began to rise within him, there was a sudden uptick of fear. He had heard something. He looked at his mother and her expression confirmed it. She had heard it too.

Ray stepped past her and looked out toward the road. He listened, and the sound came again. It was a car door opening, then very carefully being closed. There were other people who lived on this lane. But what he heard was different from a normal exit from a car. It was an attempt to silence the noise.

He spun toward his mother. "You told them!"

She started to shake her head, but he was past her already, closing the door. "Ray," she called. "No!"

The voices were shouting in his head. Why couldn't he hear them?

Nearing the edge of town, Fielding was still testing the logic of his explanation why Makwamacatawa had been spared for three nights by the fire. Was it conceivable that his magic was as strong as theirs? Was the power of the Ancient Ones a match for the beings of the fire?

They were questions Fielding was ill-equipped to answer. After all, Makwamacatawa and his ancestors were on equal footing with the Awshkoute. They existed in a similar world of spirits and magic, while Fielding's world was one of science, and in his science, he needed confirmation of his theory. If the striking of the match gave birth to the power, could it not thwart the very act he sought to accomplish? Without certainty, it was a risk he could not afford to take.

The circuitous pattern was holding true to form, casting doubt over seeds of hope, and that's when the voices were loudest. Each thought had its own voice, carrying its own disruptive demand to be heard. He tried to think things through, to continue his analysis, but it was only as he passed the last commercial outpost beyond the town limits that one thought alighted with singularity in his mind. Like the others, it had its own voice, but it was not an echo of something he had said. It had been disruptive when he first heard it, as it was now. He had been standing at the base of the steps, listening to Jean upstairs.

It was the radio report of the fire at the museum, and what came back to him at this moment was an isolated statement. The photographer quoted had said the studio was set for a shot of a ceremonial robe.

Fielding swerved to the right onto the shoulder and did a quick U-turn. He drove back to a gas station, jumped out of his truck, and raced to a phone booth set off from the garage. He fumbled for his telephone credit card, then began to punch out the numbers. He stopped in mid-dial. It was too late. No one would be at the museum, if indeed the offices could be reached. He fumbled again through his pockets and pulled out his address book. Lynch. Joe Lynch, the deputy director, in charge of native field exhibits. He called him at home, and his kid answered. Hurry, he said to himself, waiting for Lynch to come to the phone.

"Hello?"

"Joe? This is Chris Fielding, up north."

"I wondered when I was going to hear from you."

"It's been crazy down there, I know, but it's been crazy up here too."

"You heard about Heath?"

Fielding wasn't sure. "What about him?"

"It was his body, in the fire. As we figured it must be. They confirmed it today by dental records."

Fielding tried to dispel the trembling urgency. "Was anything destroyed?"

Lynch paused, thrown slightly off guard. "You mean the exhibits?"

"Yes."

"Fortunately, it didn't spread beyond the studio."

"I mean in the studio," Fielding said. "Was everything destroyed in there?"

"Yeah," Lynch drawled uncertainly, trying to figure out his friend. "It was scorched."

"I heard on the news it was set for a shot."

"Oh yeah. A deer-hide cloak of a Midewiwin, I guess. That was saved. A miracle it survived the flames."

It wasn't a miracle, Fielding thought. It was magic.

Miriam spun toward the road. "He heard us," she heard someone shout, and at that the sounds of stealth ended. There were the sounds of people running, and at the corner of the garage a uniformed officer glanced around the edge, then came into fuller view. "Okay," he said, and another deputy ran past him, across the opening, to the back of the house extension. Both had rifles with large clips. Assault rifles.

Miriam turned back toward the house and ran to the door. It was locked. "Ray," she shouted. "You've got to come out. You'll be hurt!" She pounded on the wood frame. "Ray!"

"Get her out of here," she heard from behind her, and then she was moving back. Being pulled back. It was all happening so fast. It was unreal: the men, the guns. Her son inside the house. "Ray!" she shouted.

"Does he have any firearms?"

Miriam looked at the officer. His voice was like an echo. This couldn't be happening.

"Does he have any guns?" he repeated, louder.

Miriam's head began to shake. "No," she managed to say. "He's just . . . he's . . ." She was gasping so hard she couldn't catch her breath to speak.

"He armed?"

Miriam looked. She was behind the garage, and it was the sheriff, speaking to the man who had pulled her back.

"Can't be sure," the deputy said.

"He's not," Miriam said, going toward Halstead. "He doesn't have a gun. You can't hurt him."

"I told you, Miriam, it would have been easier if you had helped us. Now, we have to go in and take him."

"No, Sheriff. He's afraid. He ran because he was afraid, and he's afraid now. He won't do anything. Let me talk to him. I'll bring him out."

"Too late for that. I'm sorry, Miriam, but it'll be better for us and for Ray if we act before he has a chance to do something stupid."

"Ready, Sheriff," another voice called.

Halstead looked over to Kinsey, still in plainclothes. "Take her, Alan. Keep her out of the way."

She felt Kinsey's hands on her arm, and she was moving again back toward the road. "Sheriff! Don't hurt him. Please! Don't hurt my boy!"

She tried to jerk her arm free, but Kinsey was ready for that. "Don't be doing that, Mrs. Goodmedicine. You don't want any more trouble than we already have."

"But you don't understand," she said. "None of you understand. He's just a boy, a scared young boy. He did nothing wrong, and he's afraid."

"It's too bad this has got to happen, but he torched Cole, and he's got to pay for that. Now or later."

Miriam sensed the air escaping from her chest. He didn't *torch* anybody. He's just a young man grasping for the kind of meaning that all young people search for on the verge of adulthood. The events of the fire had complicated things for him, and he had been led into some wrong conclusions. Just as the sheriff had been.

From around the garage there was the sound of wood and glass being shattered. They had kicked in the door. They were going in.

The sound of the headlight breaking was like the snapping of sticks being prepared for the fire. She was in the cave and she couldn't see and she couldn't move. She had been sensing motion, but it had come to a sudden stop with the sound of breaking twigs. The sound of crunching metal. The excited cries of men in a language she found harder to comprehend.

How long she hovered in space she couldn't tell. Time for her had lost its dimension. Eventually, however, the sensation of movement resumed. As for her own ability to move, she still could not walk or stand or even raise her arms. She was bound tightly, around her mouth, around her entire body. She had fought at first, reaching for the flames, but then the fire dimmed as her strength ebbed. She had sensed the need to rest, that the fire would return. And as the motion continued, as the timeless scape drew itself out longer, she began to see again the brief flashes beyond the horizon. She was being carried to the fire. It was waiting for her. And she was waiting for them.

• • •

For Miriam, it was as if every faculty she possessed had seized with the sound of the door breaking. She couldn't sense her own breathing, every joint seemed locked, her sight was but a narrow tunnel. All that counted was what she heard. The shouts from inside the house, the heavy stamping of feet, doors slamming with such force she could hear them clear back by the road.

It was what she didn't hear that kept her from collapse. She expected it, she waited for it, she dreaded it. The sound of gunshots. The death of her boy.

But the rifles never rang out. The commotion died down, and it wasn't until she saw Ray being led away from the house that her emotion and feeling and relief all came gushing out. "Oh dear God," she gasped, the words escaping on a rush of air. "It's Ray. Ray!" she called, starting forward.

Her son hadn't heard. He looked dazed and scared and was being guided hurriedly by two deputies with a grip on each arm. His hands were cuffed behind his back, and his eyes were cast on the pavement in front of him.

Miriam angled to cut them off. "Ray!"

At the sound of her voice, he changed suddenly. He turned rigid and his face jerked in her direction.

Miriam came to an abrupt halt.

A single question shot from Ray's mouth with the force of a slap to the face. "Why?"

Miriam was staggered. Her head began to shake back and forth. "I didn't know."

The deputies pulled him by the arms, resuming their walk to the patrol car. Ray turned his head, speaking over his shoulder. "You wanted me outside. Where it would be easier. Where they could see me."

"That's not true," Miriam said, keeping pace. "All I wanted was for you to come home. I didn't want you to be hurt."

The deputies turned him around and guided him onto the backseat. Ray paused and looked back, a strange smile coming to his lips. "I didn't really need you here, you know."

Miriam was perplexed. "What do you mean?"

"What I said on the phone. It wasn't true."

"What are you talking about?"

Ray shrugged; then one of the deputies put his hand on his head, and he ducked inside the car.

"Wait," Miriam said, leaning forward.

"Come on, Mrs. Goodmedicine," Kinsey said. "You have to let him go."

"It doesn't matter anyway," Ray said to his mother. "It's too late for her now."

Miriam's face paled. She started to sway back.

"I didn't need you at all," Ray added. "The Ancient Ones have shown us the way."

Miriam was as still and drained as a winter birch. Standing in the lane, she watched as the car with her son in the back pulled away. But it wasn't her son she was thinking about. She was thinking about Jean Shawshequay.

"Fortunately, no one got hurt," the sheriff said. "He came easily enough. Maybe you should go home and call a lawyer."

Miriam didn't move. She was supposed to stay with her. It had been her responsibility. But was this the danger Fielding had foreseen?

"Alan," Halstead said to his deputy. "Maybe you'd better take her home."

"No," Miriam said, stepping toward her car. "I'm all right."

"Maybe you can call that attorney who helped you on the injunction," the sheriff suggested as she was getting into her car. "Or I can give you some names, if you need them."

She only nodded as she closed the door. Ray was safe for now. Some battles were more important than others. Sometimes, sacrifices had to be made.

Chapter 23

It was a place of history. It was a place of death. It was a place of passage where the spiritual power of a different age transformed flesh into fire. It was a place where man had conspired with nature to create a wilderness temple of sacrifice, and where nature had conspired with man to conceal the massacre of a people from a distant continent.

The pit, the sinkhole, the geological curiosity called the Cave of Bones, was a place that attracted ancient habitation, and in turn it was a place that attracted the interest of archaeologist Christopher Fielding. He had come to uncover the secrets of those ancient peoples, and now he came to bury those secrets.

His truck came to a halt near the brink of the descent. Fielding climbed out of the cab and went to the back to open the tailgate. He pulled out what he would need and piled it near the edge of the pit. It would take two trips, he had already decided, and so he began, taking one of the five-gallon cans of kerosene, a wool blanket, and his flashlight. He left them near the entrance to the cave, then ascended back to the rim.

At the top, Fielding paused to rest before heading down again. He looked at the V-shaped cut in the rock covered with his peaked tarp, where the grinding bowl had been found and where he had begun his excavation. He had thought it was merely a storm drainage ravine, but that was only the first of his mistakes.

Fielding turned and saw the skeleton of the sweatlodge atop the knoll, and then he turned again, looking out over the tops of trees rising from the floor of the sinkhole. All these things—the rock cuts chiseled at the critical points of solar acclination by religious outcasts from northern Europe, a charred replica of a native chamber of purification, and trees probably as old as the dramatic events that transpired here—for Fielding made this a timeless place, a place where the continuum of past and present was not a line but a circle. It was a lost world of spirituality for gotten by the modern creeds of science and technology. It was a lost world he was about to enter.

Fielding hefted the second can of kerosene and the folded black-bear cloak worn by Makwamacatawa, and he began his retreat, back down into that lost world.

Miriam could tell the house was empty as soon as she came inside. She paused at the bottom of the steps, where she could see that the bedroom door was open. She climbed the stairs rapidly, and when she saw the splintered doorjamb, she did not react with surprise.

The Ancient Ones have shown us the way, her son had said. In Blackbear's and now Penay's distorted interpretation of things, the fire was retribution for the desecration they perceived was being inflicted on the spirits of their ancestors. Following their logic, it was clear that they intended to bring the fire directly to the desecrators. And Miriam was convinced that they intended to bring their own fire to Jean Shawshequay.

Penay feared Miriam's influence over the others enough to have arranged for her to be out of the picture when they took Jean. Because of that, Miriam was confident she would be able to stop them, as long as she got to them in time. As long as she knew where to find them.

It took little deductive reasoning to decide where they planned to carry out their own act of desecration.

At the bottom of the sinkhole, between the boulders that helped conceal the subterranean passages, Fielding shoved one of the cans into the earthen hole. Most of the bats had already taken flight, but the usual stragglers cupped their wings angrily, and some dropped from their perches, darting over his head and out the exit. Fielding maneuvered the kerosene to the first drop, and with a three-inch-wide canvas belt looped through the handle, he lowered it in the dark the eight feet until it touched solid ground.

He repeated the procedure with the second can, then, after dropping the blanket and the robe, he followed, passing through the familiar border of constant dank chill. He had been sweating from the exertion, and now the moisture from his pores became a weapon against him, setting off a tremble that gave texture to his skin. It was a creeping sensation that found a secondary source in the simmering fears he harbored. He was cold and hot, scared and determined, all at the same time. He was on the brink of facing undead spirits, and to this combat he was bringing his own mortality.

It was unavoidable that the doubts would come, and as he labored through the narrow crevices, bringing his implements to the edge of the descent into the tunnel of pictographs, Fielding thought again of Makwamacatawa and his sweatlodge. From the beginning Blackbear had seen the spirituality in what was happening, and as Fielding was now, he had tried to deal with the fire on its own terms. He had sought answers in his vision quest, and he had failed. And it was in his failure that Fielding saw his own answers?

Fielding set the second can down hard. Blackbear's quest for guidance from the Ancient Ones had proven ultimately successful, Fielding argued, facing down the doubts. By his death he showed how to resist the power of the flames. And he would resist them as well, Fielding thought, in the same fashion.

When he reached the floor of the arching tunnel, Fielding carried his gear to the narrow aperture that led to the inner chamber. He moved fast, barely glancing at the painted ceiling, but when he went back for Blackbear's cloak, he found Jean's flashlight lying next to the magnetometer. Using its beam he flashed it across the series of pictographs, the ocher representation of the man in the stylistic log fire, followed by the chalk tracings.

Jean had seen more than his machine had revealed, and standing below the whitish representations of the Awshkoute, for a few seconds it was as if it all had come to life for him too. It was as if he could hear the screams, as if he could sense the frantic scramble for life, as if in the passage of his light over the uneven surface he could see the flicker of the fire.

Firelight played off the edges and cavities of the rock, shimmering with the movement of the torches. She sensed the anxiety she had felt back then, and she could sense it in the men who forced her movements through the narrow vaulted chamber. They were silent and somber, as if reluctant participants in a distasteful operation. She felt sympathy for them, for she was also of their blood. She floated between two worlds and, as a result, existed in neither. Despite the apprehensions, it was almost a peaceful state in which she drifted. The light, the silence, the touch of hands moving her along. But even as she drifted, she knew the respite of calm would end soon. And it did. With a metallic grating sound she was jerked from the silence and felt herself being hauled into the open air.

The door of the van swung wide on rusted hinges, and the men slid the woman wrapped in sheets out the back and laid her on the ground. They were parked near Fielding's Jeep, but the archaeologist was nowhere to be seen.

"What are we going to do about him?" Quilltail said.

Penay was studying the charred sweatlodge atop the knoll and didn't answer.

"Johnny?"

Penay turned. "We'll deal with him, if we have to."

Quilltail sensed a disquieting flutter. One step follows another. There was no turning back.

"Pick her up," Penay said, stepping toward the drop.

Rene looked at Migisi and Migisi at Leveque. None of them wanted to touch the woman again. From the lip of the sinkhole, Penay slowly turned back. He saw the hesitation, and he recognized the fear. "What you saw in the bedroom is why she must be destroyed. It's the reason Blackbear died," he said, gesturing toward the burned frame of the sweatlodge, "and it's the reason I chose you to do honor to our people."

Rene glanced again at Migisi; then the two of them hoisted the shrouded woman between them. Leveque took the first step down, then turned back to help with the burden. As they worked her down the first drop, Quilltail came to the edge. Penay stopped him with a hand on his arm. "He's as much a part of the desecration as she is," he said, fixing him with his eyes.

Quilltail didn't say anything. He couldn't find the words to speak. So he joined the others, and together, the five men carried Jean Shawshequay to the floor of the pit.

The heavy metal can ground against the rock as it was pushed forward. Fielding was on his belly in the narrow slit that led into the inner chamber. It was hard enough for him to get through on his own, much less maneuver a forty-pound can of kerosene in front of him.

When it reached the end, Fielding let it teeter over the edge, allowing gravity to do the work. Slowly, he eased the can down with the canvas strap. When it rested securely in the chamber,

Fielding allowed himself a few moments rest before working himself back out, fraction by fraction.

He brought the second can through, then the robe and blanket, and finally came through himself, lowering himself headfirst down to the rock ledge. He opened Jean's flashlight up to wide beam and positioned it in the aperture, casting a diminishing glow throughout the entire chamber. Flashing his own beam, he surveyed the cavern.

It was familiar and yet it was all new. The vaulted ceiling with shadowy recesses was the same as he remembered, as was the floor of the cavern sweeping lower below his position, strewn with broken boulders from above. His perception of it was what was different. Fielding viewed it not as a geological feature, but as an execution chamber. This was how he had to view it, since he had become the executioner.

Beyond the center of the bowl, closer to the far side, there seemed to be a relatively flat space, an easy collection point, and one that should give him clear access back to the exit. It would be there he would assemble the remains of the Awshkoute. He made his way across the chamber, and folding the blanket in half, he laid it flat on the floor. Then he began to collect the bones.

They were dry and light and very brittle, and where they had once been held together by cartilage and sinew and muscle, they had come apart and lay in crude representations of human bodies. They seemed to be so much harmless calcified matter, little different in substance from the chunks of stone that also littered the floor. But despite the inanimate feel of everything he touched, Fielding sensed he was not alone. He felt as if he were being watched. As if they were waiting for him to bring them to life.

Fielding didn't gather the remains with the care of an anthropologist, carefully mapping locations and seeking to keep the bones with their constituent parts. Instead he picked them up in armfuls and dumped them in a pile in the center of the blanket. As he worked, the remains became progressively harder to recover. In places he had to lie on the floor and reach down into narrow spaces where some bones had slipped. Where he couldn't reach to the bottom, he used a long bone from a leg as a tool to grapple and raise the skeletal pieces.

He began to sense the terror they must have felt, the flames rising, the smoke billowing, the screams resounding off th walls. They would have been scrambling, fighting, clawing to escape the heat. To escape one another. To escape!

Fielding began to think as they must have. He began to sense the heat, coming from within. He imagined the scene of panic, and he felt the urge to escape. He stabbed his beam through the dark, looking for possible places to retreat. A niche, a crack, a black hole. Any place, if it would buy a few seconds. If it offered a few more gasps of air. A chance to extend life.

At the side of the chamber, a jagged extension of rock bowed out from the wall. Viewed from the entrance, it would have appeared just an outward bulge, but from his angle now, he could see the shadow behind it, the cavity it concealed.

Fielding crossed to the rock extension. He went around the edge, moving quickly, as if escaping the flames himself. He shined his light and felt a sudden expansion of fear in his chest. His first thought was *They are alive.* Staring at him. Waiting for him. But of course mere skeletons were not alive. People dead for six hundred years could not move. The motion came from him, from the movement of the light, casting shadows through the rib cages of the people who had died here.

There were six, maybe seven skeletons, piled and mixed together, little different from what they were like when they died, crushing against one another into the shallow niche, all fighting to escape. Fielding followed in their footsteps and began to cart them out, lifting the remnants of their existence from the rough-hewn catacomb, picking up fingers still locked into claws, staring into empty sockets and almost seeing the horror and panic in their eyes.

Fielding dumped them all onto the blanket, onto the rising pile of blackened remains. He turned, flashing his light back around, looking for avenues of escape. Where would he have gone?

Against the far wall the rock was jagged, a natural stairway. Was there a ledge or a shadow? He crossed quickly to the base of the rise, then ascended to the dark slash. Coming up over the top, he found another of them. Two more. A child, lying on its back, its head cocked toward the wall where an adult lay cowering in the corner. Fielding could feel the child's fears, and he could feel the panic of the adult. They were the same fears, the same panic, and they were inside of him now, an infection that bridged the centuries, a debilitating scramble of nerves and rushing blood and untempered thoughts.

Fielding grabbed the skull of the child and heaved it toward the mound of its kin. He climbed the rest of the way to the ledge and began to toss the bones, singly and in bunches, toward his chosen place of cremation.

When he was done, he climbed partway down the rise, then jumped the rest of the way. He did another survey, another full loop of the cavern. There were places in the cracks that he just couldn't reach, and there he would douse the stray skeletal piece where it lay. There was nothing more to collect. Nothing more to do, but to resume the ritual destruction of the spiritual presence that lingered in this place, that emanated from the remains of the bodies, that still harbored the demand for sacrifice, for power, for the flesh and souls of new victims.

Fielding rushed to the entrance aperture. He hefted both cans of kerosene and brought them across the cave. Until now he had only sensed what the terror must have been like. He had only imagined the fire. But he was close to reigniting the inferno. He was close to bringing back the fire. He was close to reliving the terror.

Penay sunk the blade of the shovel into the dirt. He needed three shallow holes, and he began digging near a hole that someone else had dug recently. He and Quilltail were in the small clearing where the poacher's charred corpse had been found, and Penay assumed the twelve-inch hole had been a result of the investigation. It did not occur to him that the archaeologist had dug it, searching for confirmation of an entirely different interpretation of what had been occurring.

Migisi, Leveque, and Wawatessi had dragged over three logs and now were scavenging firewood from the floor of the sinkhole. When Penay finished with the third hole, he looked over at Quilltail. "You done?"

Quilltail was notching the tops of the three logs with a hatchet. "You want to check?"

Penay came over, and ran his hand in the rough-hewn depressions carved into the wood. "That's good enough," he said. "Let's get started."

Quilltail swung his hatchet into the ground and stood. Together, he and Penay raised the three logs, planting them into the holes and bracing them against each other at the top where they were notched.

"Firm them up with the dirt," Penay said. "I'll tie them at the top."

Quilltail used the shovel at first, scraping the soil back into the holes, burying the posts. Then he went down to his knees to finish. As he touched the black material with his hands, molding it into shape around the wood, he noticed that it had a fine, almost greasy feel to it. He rubbed it between his fingers, then tried to brush it off on his pants. The stain did not clear. The carbon of the ancient fires had marked him.

Penay saw Quilltail resting on his haunches, smelling his fingers. "What are you doing?"

Quilltail looked up slowly. "It's ash," he said.

Penay's expression didn't change, but as he looked at the thick black residue, as he considered the implications, he suffered an interior chill. He had always thought Blackbear too soft to be a good leader, that he was unable to decide when to stop preaching and start using the belief he instilled to establish real political power. But at this moment, as he struggled to contain his nervous uncertainty, for the first time since Blackbear had left on his vision quest, he wished he were here.

"They've said it's happened before," Quilltail added.

"People like her have been here before," Penay said. "And we will deal with her as we've been told. As they did before."

Quilltail looked down at the carbon stain on his fingers. What Penay said made sense, and for the first time, the doubts he had had about what they were going to do began to recede.

Miriam kept telling herself that she would stop them. If not Penay, then the others, whom she had known since they were children. They would listen, she was sure of it. The only uncertainty was time.

She risked pressing harder on the gas pedal. The road through the trees was a winding affair, but the stretch that had just opened up ahead was straight. As the car picked up speed, she saw a shadow, a depression in the ruts. Before she could react, the car dipped into the hole, its low clearance causing it to crash on the center strip of hardened mud and embedded stone. Miriam dropped forward, her hands coming off the wheel, and the car bounded up and veered off course, into the woods. Her foot came down on the clutch first, but her speed didn't change. Indeed it seemed to increase, the linkage having been disengaged. She came down with her right foot on the brake, and the car skidded through the dirt, then conked out.

Miriam fell back in the seat. Her forearms were like steel rods, her hands clenched in a death grip around the wheel. In front of her, to either side, was the forest, and glancing in the mirror, she found it too dark to distinguish much of anything behind her. She had to get out. She had to stop them.

She tried the key and the car jerked forward. The clutch. She stomped on it hard and turned the ignition, but the engine only grinded without starting. She tried again and the headlights fluttered and the engine missed. The battery! She turned off the lights, and as she did, the deepening pall of dusk for a second seemed transformed into midnight. But that was only a second, as her eyes adjusted. As the leafy outlines of brush and tree came into hazy focus. As the effects of half light began to work on her fear.

Miriam twisted the key hard, and the old car grumbled to life. She pulled the light switch, then began to back up. The square back of the station wagon allowed tall ground cover to come right to the window before falling back out of sight, and for Miriam it made the reverse trek an exercise in driving blind.

Her neck hurt and her back was sore, from the hard hit on the bottom, from the driving itself. She had never worked a car so strenuously. But she had never been in this kind of a race. A race against time. Against wild misinterpretations. Against the fire.

The car seemed to waver from side to side as she drove. It hadn't seemed that she had traveled this far into the woods. Could she have turned and not realized it? Could she be backing away from the trail?

Miriam's foot involuntarily pressed harder. The car increased its speed incrementally. The engine began to whine in the low gear. And then the rear wheels dropped into the ruts. She felt them before she saw the road.

Pulling on the steering wheel, she came straight in the ruts, then shifted into first. Just in the few minutes she had left the trail, the forest had darkened. Even with the headlights, she was losing sight of her surroundings. Night was falling rapidly.

She started slowly, but now was not a time for caution. It was only a few miles to the Cave of Bones. She just had to concentrate. Drive under control. Keep her eyes on the road, the trees, the obstacles. There were so many things to keep track of, she didn't notice the change in the sound of the motor. She didn't notice the sluggish feel to the engine, maybe because of the natural rise and fall of the car through the ruts. She didn't notice the smell of gas, or if she did, it didn't strike her as something to be concerned about, especially now, when time was so crucial. She had smelled the odor of gas before. The carburetor was out of whack, Ray had said. He'd fix it, he had told her. When he had a chance.

The smell of kerosene had a thickness to it he could taste. And the fumes stung his eyes, blurring his vision. Fielding had to pull back, righting the can. He was dizzy from the vapors, almost sick from the odor. He put the can down and stepped away, stumbling over the uneven surface. He gripped his forehead and rubbed his eyes, then turned and went back to the pile of bones.

It was a macabre mix of skulls and ribs and broken skeletal matter that defied description. It was the assembled remains of an outcast tribe that had sought freedom by bringing their peculiar brand of homicide to a new land.

Fielding chose one of the leg bones to maneuver the entire stack, making sure it was all exposed to the flammable liquid. He turned over arms that had fashioned iron with peat drawn from the bogs; he maneuvered barren fingers from hands that had ignited fires that tortured and incinerated unsuspecting natives who had welcomed the strangers to their land. They had acted in the name of their religion. In the name of their god. And now they would perish with the force they nurtured with such effort.

Fielding hoisted the kerosene and resumed splashing it over the pile. All moisture and resistance to fire in the bones had long since evaporated. The marrow was now a network of tiny cavities that sucked up the fuel like a sponge. And underlying the pile was the wool blanket, now soaked with the kerosene.

The last bit of liquid drained from the first can, and Fielding heaved it to the side. He opened the second, moving away from the primary location. There were three crevices where stray bones had slipped that he couldn't reach. He went to each one in turn, dousing the former bits of life, then splashing kerosene on the rock around the cracks. It would all ignite at once, from the flash of the primary fire.

He started back to the central pile, scuffing over rock stubble. In the clattering of pebbles dislodged by his feet, he could hear

the nervous chant of priests. In the hard clank of the metal can
banged off a rock, he could hear the sudden bellow of a man
about to die. In the brush of his clothes, the shortness of his
breath, the animal grunts of his effort, he could hear the growing panic of the people. They were here, with him in this place,
watching and waiting, ready to come alive, ready to snatch back
what they had lost, ready to resist their destruction by the element that was their power.

Fielding tired to shake the images from his mind. He tried to
deny what he imagined the sounds around him to be. But it was
no use. They were here. And to destroy them he had to first
bring them to life.

It had happened before, and she wouldn't let it happen again.
None of them would let it happen again.

She could hear noises in the cave, the clatter of stones, the
brushing of people against each other, the winded grunts of
growing fear, and she knew the time was coming. Inside her
chest she could feel the heat rising, and in the distance the flash
of fire returned, except that it came faster, brighter, and it was
moving closer. On every horizon she could see the fire. She
spun in place, and with each arc of movement the flares increased in intensity. She had the sensation of being in a whirlpool, but it was as if the world of lightning flashes were
revolving around her. She was near the vortex and the hold on
her was strong. *Their* hold was strong. She sensed that they
were moving closer, and she was moving toward them. Her
aimless drift had taken on a definite direction. No longer caught
between two worlds, she was about to leave one and enter the
other.

She could hear the noises, she sensed the heat, and she could
feel the touch of the hands.

Penay ripped the sheet open from neck to waist. "Take her
arms," he yelled, and Rene and Leveque grabbed her from each
side.

She had lain silent in her white shroud as if mocking them
with her compliance, as if daring them to release her, as if confident in her powers to defeat them. It was an impression that
preyed on Penay's mind as he finished the triangular posts and
laid the tinder under them. His eyes kept coming back to the
white shroud, motionless on the ground. Why didn't she strug-

gle? Why didn't she try to scream? What was it that guided her heart?

Though he could cover his fears outwardly with a raised voice and commanding manner, he could not deny them to himself. He could not deny what he had glimpsed in her eyes in the attic bedroom at Ray's house. He feared her power, and it was this fear that powered him to swifter action. She would be destroyed. She *must* be destroyed. Though he lacked Blackbear's insight and could not in his own mind explain all the connections, it was supremely evident to him that the evil she commanded was at the root of the desecration. It was at the root of Blackbear's death. And it was her evil that would perish in the flames with her.

Dead leaves and twigs had been spread under the posts and extended outward a few feet all around. On top were laid sticks and dead branches and larger lengths of dried oak logs scavenged from the surrounding area.

Having ripped the sheet off her, Penay directed them to drag her to the triangular stanchions. He took her left hand and lashed her wrist above her head, to one of the posts, then stepping behind her over the wood debris, he seized her other hand. Still, she did not resist. She *could* not resist, he told himself. The nervous tension that churned within him began to percolate upward. It was almost time. She was about to die. And he was about to take his place among the heroes of his people. He had stopped the desecration; he had thwarted another attempt to steal a bit of their heritage; he had taken the lead in asserting control over their own destiny.

With both of her hands strapped to the wood logs above her, Jean Shawshequay was stretched out in rigid bondage. Penay ducked under her right arm and turned to face her. The pillowcase that shrouded her head was still in place, as was the gag that silenced her. But those restraints were needed no longer. Penay wanted to see her eyes now; he wanted her to see what was happening; he wanted to watch the evil inside of her consumed by the flames.

Her head jerked and her eyesight returned in a rush. A face hovered a few inches in front of hers, and she recoiled. The wrap around her mouth was released next, and she tried to scream in newfound terror. Her throat burned with the effort, the tendons in her neck stretched taut, but in her own ears her cry was silent.

All she could hear was a rushing sound like that of pressurized air.

She could see the hate in the expression of the man before her, and penetrating faintly through the rush of air, she could hear his voice. She couldn't understand him, though, because he spoke in a tongue that was foreign to her. All she could understand were the voices that called to her across the centuries. They spoke to her on whispers of fire, a haunting, fluttering sound that promised new life. And that is what she sought. Their life. Their strength. She called for it. She felt it inside, the heated rush of blood, the burning feeling of energy through muscular tissue. It was a powerful feeling, one of anger and need at the same time.

The shell she occupied was losing its significance. She was immobilized, as she had been the last time, as she had been the night she was forced into the cave, but it didn't matter. The old world didn't matter. She was a being of the timeless dimension, existing now, existing then. And she would exist forever, once she was released from the confines of her shell, once she crossed the last threshold, giving up the substance of this existence for the collective survival of them all. She would float forever through time, the voice of fire said to her, as soon as she surrendered herself. As soon as she accepted the flames.

And she would accept them, she shouted within the confines of her timeless world, and they would accept her. They would absorb her into the whole and she would be stronger for it. They would all be stronger for it.

The thick black of the woods increased her isolation. And it was that growing sense of isolation that emphasized to Miriam that she was the only one who could stop it. She was the only one who could save the visitor from Oklahoma.

The trail road seemed to drag on forever. It was only a few miles, but her speed was deceptive. Each time she glanced at the dash, the speedometer was only hovering around the twenty-five-mile mark. And yet she couldn't go much faster. The closeness of the trees, the curves of the road, wouldn't permit it.

Miriam ached physically from the strain, but the psychological torment was even worse. If only she had agreed in the judge's chambers to watch over the archaeological dig. If only she hadn't dragged Jean into the affair. If only Ray had confided in her about Penay's intent. If only Wes had been there when his son needed him most. It was a despairing cycle of regrets that clouded her judgment. It threatened to eclipse the clarity of purpose that drove her, that she would have to have to display to Penay and the others.

Miriam fought to escape the trap of despair. She fought to control the car. It was firing erratically, the engine spitting and bucking under the hood. She figured this was due to the heaves and rolls of the uneven trail, to the acceleration and braking as she drove to her limits.

She couldn't see the spurts of gas escaping from under the carburetor, leaking through the gasket that long ago had lost its elasticity. She couldn't see the explosive puffs of vapor as droplets touched the manifold. She didn't understand the forces that were at work seeking to capture those brief flashes of fire, trying to draw out their existence, seeking to bring them to life. She didn't realize how close she was to the timeless strand that breached the generations, connecting her to the many grandfathers who had walked this land before her. She couldn't foresee the rupture of the rubber seal and the spillage of the gasoline.

Fielding maneuvered the half can of kerosene out the narrow aperture, then slid back into the interior cavern. The relative purity of air for just a few moments made the sickly stink inside all the more severe. Fielding resisted the involuntary impulse to disgorge the heavy taste of the fumes. There was too much to do to allow himself to be distracted. He had to act fast. There was no time for physical weakness. There was no time for doubts. He would live or die on the whim of forces beyond his understanding. All he could do was follow the course his logic decreed, and logic, whether based on science or on something else, followed certain fundamental rules that could not be ignored.

Makwamacatawa had taken on the representation of his people's ancient spirits when he donned the sacred cloak of the great bear. It was the repositor of magic of a different sort from what was unleashed by the fire. It had protected him those nights he sat on the ground atop the knoll chanting for guidance, and he became a victim of the timeless breath of the Awshkoute only when he disrobed to enter his chamber of purification. The sweatlodge and everything it contained were destroyed, except for the ceremonial animal pelt that served as its door.

Fielding slid the fingers on his left hand into the ringlets sewn into the underside of the bear's paw. He dipped his shoulder and flung the hide over his back, catching the other foreleg and securing it to his right hand with the loops. Grasping the head and upper jaw of the bear with both hands, he pulled it up and over the back of his head, setting it onto his scalp. Lastly, he secured the chest strap.

Looking out through the teeth of the sometime carnivore, he became the same creature of mixed design that he had seen that day after the court hearing, rising out of the woods, coming toward him, bellowing its otherworldly curses in a blend of human speech and animal sounds meant for no man to understand. But at this moment, he began to understand, not the actual message Makwamacatawa had delivered to the guiding spirits, but the linkage the robe conveyed to the power of the spirits, the power of the bear. In one respect, except for the weight of the garb itself, he felt no different. But in another respect he could not identify, he felt a kinship to the people and the events that had transpired here.

Fielding reached down and grasped the two-foot length of wood swathed at one end in cloth he had soaked in kerosene. He was ready.

Stepping carefully, the thick fur of the dead bear restricting his movement, Fielding edged along the side of the cave, coming no closer than fifteen feet to the assembled mass of the Awshkoute remains. He wanted to remain at a safe distance from the flash.

Raising the torch above his head, he ignited a small butane lighter and touched it to the base of the cloth. Instantly, a wavering curtain of flame shot up the torch head, rolling over the top, coming to a single point, a curving dagger of fire, a scimitar of visible heat slashing frantically at the dead air.

The torch in his hand left a tracing glow in the night blackness as he waved it back and forth. "Burn!" Penay shouted, turning toward the others. "Bring her the fire!"

Quilltail held his own unlit torch at his waist. He looked anxiously at Rene. Wawatessi's face was contorted with fear, of Penay, of taking part in this barbarism, of the fire he had seen in the woman's eyes in the bedroom.

The five men stood equidistant in a circle around the tristaked pyre. The anthropologist from Oklahoma, the bringer of the spiritual sickness that had infected the land, the desecrator and betrayer, was fixed helplessly to the posts, her arms spread wide high above her head. Her eyes were active and bulging with terror. But strangely, she remained silent. It was as if she had already retreated into a maze of trauma, as if in body she showed that she understood the horror of the moment but had somehow pulled back from it all psychologically. It was as if, Quilltail thought, she were only partially there.

Rene lit his torch; then to either side of him, Leveque and Migisi lit theirs. Through the pyramid of logs Quilltail could see his friend Rene, and as with the woman, there was something indefinable embedded in the contours of his face. It was as if he too were a being of split existence, a man little more than a boy showing fear, and yet he was stepping forward, as they were all stepping forward. All except for Quilltail. The unlit torch slipped from his fingers and dropped to the ground. He staggered backward, first one step, then another.

Penay stabbed his torch skyward, and looking up at it, at the black sky beyond, he cried, "Deliver the people from treachery. Deliver this land from her evil." Then lowering the torch, he finished his prayer. "Deliver us from the flames."

Johnny Penay went first, touching his torch to the outer ring of tinder. He exhorted the others to add theirs to his, and they did, in a four-point circle around the pyramid.

The fire caught slowly, spreading, as fire does, in the natural combustibles of leaves and pine needles and broken twigs. The pyre had been designed to catch slowly, allowing the heat of the kindling to build over enough time to bring deep fire to the stacks of heftier wood. It would build to a great conflagration, a source of immense heat, and that was what was needed to consume the flesh and blood and bones of the desecrator.

A muffled whoomph was accompanied by a lightninglike flash Miriam glimpsed reflecting in the trees to either side of the car. It was gone so fast she couldn't identify where it had come from. Her thoughts were tumbling so rapidly in her mind, she didn't make the connection between the flash, the muffled explosion, and the fact that the car itself had shuddered.

It was just one more obstacle to ignore. She was almost there. What happened to the car didn't matter. As long as it held together long enough to take her to the pit.

The engine seemed to misfire, practically stalling. But instead of relieving the strain, Miriam pushed harder on the accelerator, increasing the flow of gas to a carburetor already choked with fuel, sending a sudden flood through the gasket and onto the manifold.

The second explosion buckled the hood and sent the car off the road into a tree. Miriam was thrown forward, her head cracking against the windshield. She fell back with almost as much force, her head whipping against the seat. She tried immediately to reach for the wheel, to get the car going again, but her arms wouldn't respond to her commands. She was dizzy and reeling, and her eyes couldn't focus. It seemed as if everything were moving around her. As if it had come to life. There was a shimmering quality to the woods beyond the windows of the car, a flowing movement that rose in waves from bottom to top, that rose in flashes and flickers and excited bursts of light. It rose on the rapid currents of fire.

Miriam grabbed the sides of her head with both hands. The fire was in front of the car. It was on both sides, having billowed out from the engine below the chassis. Miriam turned, and the flames were there too, lapping up the back of the tailgate, playing off the window, slapping at the glass in a growing frenzy. Miriam screamed, the sound of her own voice adding to the terror. But it was her voice, her scream, that provided the only release. And it was release she sought, from the flames, from the entire ordeal. *Please, sweet Jesus,* she wanted to pray, but the words were lost in her panic, in her terror, in the inarticulate volume of her scream.

The scream burst forth in her mind with the incendiary effect of pine sap exploding in green wood. Tracers of sparks arced high on the rising call of terror. She could see the flames all around her, and she could hear the screams. Horrifying screams, wrenched from the primal soul, filled with the realization of failing survival and ringed with futile protestations against mortality.

She could hear the screams, and she could see the people scrambling over the stacked tinder, the arms of all but the children bound behind their backs. But the children were still at a disadvantage, being shouldered aside, some of the people using their teeth to drag them out of the way. It was a result of the panic, an unthinking rage, powered solely by fear of the flames, the very element they had used on the *skraelings*, the savages they had found infesting this place. Every bit of terror and agony they had witnessed in their victims' death throes became theirs, and they fought to escape that fate.

Her arms were tied and she couldn't move. All she could do was wait for the flames to come to her. And watch as her people struggled. Because she couldn't move, because all she could do was watch, she began to notice that not everyone was there to suffer. She began to see the others, the ones who had shoved them through the narrow hole into the cave. They were out there, staring in on them, and she could see them. She could see through the solid rock of the cave and see the men who had done this to them. Their features were distorted by the flames that surrounded her, but she could recognize the look of satisfaction. The look of pleasure.

It was a senseless, timeless world where vision penetrated stone and feelings were absorbed through the senses of all her new people. She felt their terror, and she could feel the heat. As the fire spit its sparks, she could feel each one that landed on a child's neck, that showered onto the hair of an older man. It was her baptism into the whole, the last step in her union with the people of the fire. She sensed it coming. She could feel the conflagration growing inside her skull. And she could feel the pain.

Her neck stretched taut, the ligaments of her arms straining at the hemp ligatures that fixed her to the posts, her voice joining those of her people, and she screamed. She screamed their primal scream. She gave voice to their agony, their struggle, their panic. She gave voice to their anger.

The half bear, half man Fielding had become was imprisoned by the fire.

It had started at the torch head as the kerosene-soaked rag was rapidly sheathed in flame, drawing the fuel upward into a single point, a gyrating, peaked tongue that lashed at the black, dead air of the cavern. It was a source of bald, unfocused light, and the contrast at first made Fielding squint. He held it above his head and away from him as his eyes adjusted. He looked toward the waiting pile of skeletons, now bathed in a wash of dancing colors, then back at the curving, peaked bulb of flame. Each thrust of the fire bulged outward before snapping free, slashing at the black. It was a blade of fire, and in the few seconds Fielding allowed himself to watch, the sharp yellow instrument swung an edge downward. It came with the surprise of a pendulum breaking free from an unseen corner, and Fielding stretched the torch higher, as high as he could reach. But the flame—the pendulum—stroked lower. And other blades began to drop.

The curved lobes changed as they drooped below the peak of the torch. They stretched into narrowing funnels, siphoning bits of themselves lower, sending out shoots of corded flame in front of Fielding's face, behind his back, all around. In a matter of moments he was enclosed in a ribbed cage of fire.

Fielding could feel the power emanating from the head of the torch. It threatened to overtake his own strength, pulling the length of wood from his grasp. But Fielding also sensed the power of the black bear. As it had protected Makwamacatawa, it protected him. He was protected by the many offerings breathed into the nostrils of the beast, by the residual power of the Ancient Ones, by his own act of becoming their representative, surrendering part of his humanity for the claws and fangs of the bear.

The cocoon of stringed fire pulsed with the motion of a breathing organism. Staring at the narrow tendrils of yellow, at the pale white of nearly translucent flares sheeting between the fiery ribs, Fielding sensed again the kinship with those who had begun this task. He had become part of the continuum, as much a member of the whole as the men who laid the logs in the cave six hundred years earlier. He was invigorated with the strength and courage of those who passed before him, and he took a step into the strings of fire.

The fire parted like the dangling hemp it resembled, and then it began to change, the narrow tendrils becoming fingers, each curving tip a claw. It reached for the rock, snagging on the sharp edges, seeking to forestall Fielding's advance, to wrest the torch free from his grasp, to keep him from closing in on the remains.

Fielding struggled to control the torch. He began to rotate his body, twisting away from the wall, breaking the grip of the clawed fire one hooked tip at a time. As each released its grip, he could hear a snap like a metal strip pushed past its tensile limits. And with each break of the stringed fire, the energy flowed into the rest of it, making it all stronger, more difficult to overcome. The fire was a thing of substance, a corporeal entity that could affect its surroundings in ways wholly divorced from its natural properties. It could touch and feel and exhibit strength. And yet it could not affect him directly.

Fielding wasn't analyzing the beast. He was reacting, accepting things as they were, fighting it with all the strength he possessed. It became a test of endurance, a physical battle, and Fielding could feel the strain. He continued to twist his body, pulling on the torch with both hands, circling almost directionlessly away from the wall until the hold had become a single grip, one hooked tip of flame snagged on the black rock of the cave.

Fielding called on his reserves, the weight of his body, and wrenched the claw free. He stumbled backward a few steps before catching his balance, then immediately spun toward the pile of bones, no more than five feet in front of him. He was closer than he had planned, but he had to act fast. There was no time to think, to maneuver to a safer location. There was only time to act.

The torch left his hands, and for a moment time seemed frozen. The burning length of dead wood, swathed in cloth at one end, did one half revolution before it came over the pile. It seemed to hover there—in Fielding's mind—tip end down, pointed toward the remains of the Awshkoute. It was like a comet against the night sky, and it was that image—because of the blast—that froze in Fielding's mind.

The kerosene ignited while the torch was still in midair. The explosion lifted Fielding off his feet and threw him against the rock wall. His head, his back, his entire body, cracked hard against the stone, and the bear-man he had become was stunned.

As the fire billowed to life, all the man and the bear could see was the frozen tumble of the torch, the comet against the night sky. And even that was fading.

The fire had spread from the four points along the perimeter until each of the separate flames joined the next, forming an unbroken circle. Leaves and pine needles yielded their stored energy, igniting the larger tinder of twigs and broken branches. Slowly, the fire curled around the larger logs, dipping into the striated patterns of bark, digging with a thousand hungry tongues deeper into the pulpy fuel.

The circle grew in height, and as it did, the flames increased the tempo of their action, snapping faster at the night air, stretching for every bit of new altitude, flickering, shimmering in an excited curtain. The light reflected in the faces of the men, showing their own rise in tension. They were excited and scared and a roiling blend of a dozen other emotions they would never be able to identify.

As Penay fell under the spell of the flames, he wasn't taking satisfaction in the message he was sending or in his paean to lost heritage. His excitement was on a simpler plane. He was enthralled with the visible spectrum of energy coming to life before him. And he was intoxicated with the prospect of watching the woman die.

The smoke from the leaves was thick, and even after it yielded to the cleaner source of the wood, the rising heat, the waving bands of yellow, hid and distorted the woman lashed to the triangular posts. Penay could only see a suggestion of her form, and it was more in his imagination than in actual sight that he saw the rise and fall of her breasts, the terror in her eyes, the writhing of her torso against the bonds that held her defenseless against the coming assault. He was hypnotized by what he could see and what he imagined, and because of that he didn't notice the peculiar action of the fire. He didn't notice that it did not react to what could be described as the dictates of physics.

But the others recognized the contrary motion of the flames. Quilltail was long beyond direct sight, having reached the base of the cliff and begun his ascent, but his friend Wawatessi, along with Leveque and Migisi all saw how the fire resisted advancing into the center of the pyre. They saw how it seemed to suck its fuel from the perimeter, billowing outward in curving sheets that broke and danced and snapped at the air, but always growing higher, brighter, hotter.

"What's happening?" Rene shouted, but over the roar of the fire he could barely hear his own voice. To his left Migisi seemed in a trance, transfixed by the rapid action of the flames. To the other side, Leveque's sweaty face gleamed with the colors of the fire, highlighting his growing fright. And through the circle, beyond the silhouette of Jean Shawshequay, Penay still stood in rapt observation.

Rene left his position and came around to Penay. "Johnny," he shouted. Then again he called his name, practically in his ear. "We've got to get out of here."

Penay swiped his forearm at the distraction, clubbing Rene across the chest. Wawatessi leaned toward him, grabbing Penay by the arm. "The fire! It's coming!"

Penay turned suddenly and grabbed Rene by the chest, lifting and pushing at the same time. He flung him toward the fire, and Rene landed hard, rolling to his side, his face mere inches from the flames. And the flames reacted, billowing outward, sending a curving sheet of fire toward Rene's position.

Penay didn't move to help the man he called his brother. He hadn't even turned to watch as Rene rolled close to the circle. He kept his attention on the pyre, on the sudden rupture in the wall of flames. Penay stepped closer, peering into the breach. There was light and shadow, fire and flesh, all at the same locus. He could see the woman, and he could see the fire. It was inside of her. It emanated from her mouth, her nostrils, and most distinctly, from her eyes. They had become pits of red flame, intense points of burning energy that drew on the lives and blood of the people who had died, the people who existed in the flames, the people who gave life to the fire.

Her mouth opened wide, but it was Penay who screamed. He screamed in terror, in panic, in complete hysteria. And yet he couldn't back away. He couldn't run. All he could do was stare into her eyes of fire.

Miriam teetered on the twin brinks of consciousness and insanity. Her head throbbed, her world had become a waving, shifting inferno, and in the middle of the fire she sensed life, she sensed intelligence, she sensed she was being watched. She could see the eyes!

Miriam allowed her lids to cover her own eyes. Even in her delirium she knew it must be hallucination. Things like that weren't real. They didn't happen. They didn't happen to her.

When she looked again, the eyes she had seen just beyond the windshield were gone. But the fire was still there. It was all around, playing out its natural rhythms, rising in shifting currents of color and shadow. She turned and looked out the back. How long would she have before the tank exploded? Could she break through the wall of flame and escape?

She turned again and reached for the door latch. As she squeezed it, as she eased the door open a fraction, the sheet of fire suddenly spread outward toward the cracks. It concentrated at the opening, and like quicksilver on cracked glass, it began to leak through. Miriam started to recoil without thinking, and the thin wisps of flame pursued. The door, she thought, and with that realization she lunged back, grabbing the handle, pulling it shut hard.

The wisps of fire died, but Miriam could still feel the heat. The fire had reacted as if it had seen. Gripping the wheel, she found she was pushing herself back into the seat, as if trying to escape the flames that rose over the hood and sent fingers of fire toward the windshield.

She began to watch the fire, its advances and retreats, its forays against the glass. As she did, she realized it was not acting strictly on its natural rhythms. It was acting deliberately, as if following a plan. It was probing the glass, the edges of the windows, the narrow cracks between hood and fender. My God, she thought, it was searching for a way in.

Miriam's hand went to her forehead. She looked frantically all around. It was the same wherever she looked. The fire wasn't advancing into the woods around her. It remained at her car, probing, seeking a path inside. "Oh, no," her voice wavered, "please, no." It was a descent into panic she was following, and her body reacted, her heart pumping faster, her lungs seeking to keep pace. The dizziness returned in a rush. Her voice continued to whimper, but the syllables of her pleas were inarticulate to her own ears.

The fire flowed like water over the hood. But it wasn't fire. There were arms, splitting into fingers. Claws! Miriam cupped both hands over her eyes, her nails jabbing into her forehead. She couldn't be seeing this. It couldn't be happening. Like the eyes of fire, it was not real.

Miriam pulled her hands from her face, but unlike the last time, the hallucination remained. The claws were testing the cracks between the hood and the car's firewall. They were reaching closer to the glass. They were sinking into the pattern of tiny openings at the base of the windshield. They were flowing into the air intake!

As observation blended with comprehension, Miriam lunged for the vents. The fire reacted even faster. It streamed through the intake, and in the next second it was inside. From below the dash, from every opening for air flow, the fire flared with explosive force into the closed confines of the car.

Miriam covered her face with her arms and slumped toward the side. She didn't want to see. She didn't want to hear. All she could do was pray. She prayed it wouldn't take long.

The inside of the car was like a furnace, the streamers of fire swirling in frenzied circles. Outside, the body of fire reacted in a similar way, an excited, mad, flickering display of billowing heat and color. It was a celebratory dance. It was a bacchanalian display. It was new life stolen from the old. And in addition all of these things, it was an answer to Miriam Goodmedicine's last prayer.

As fire consumes its fuel, it grows stronger.

At the site of the ancient sacrificial altar, the circle of fire flared upward in a sudden flash. Penay staggered backward, propelled by the rush of heat.

Inside the cave, the kerosene fire flared suddenly brighter. The image of the comet against the night sky was overcome by the greater flash of white light. The semiconscious creature of mixed design braced against the rock wall felt the rush of heat and opened his eyes.

He was aching and stiff, deafened and nearly blind, and what gradually came into focus in front of him did little to rush his return to lucid thought. It was a dream vision he saw, because only in a dream could the pattern of the fire make sense.

Fielding had become a creature of myth, a foil for the greater powers that rose in fiery grandeur from the remains of the people who had served and later joined themselves to their god. He was experiencing the archaic world of his academic discipline, not through the broken and discarded relics of ancient times, but as an actor in the drama scripted for the beings of those times. Their mythology was his reality, but it was a reality explicable only in the free-form of subconscious thought.

Fielding struggled to leave the nightmarish landscape of what he was witnessing, but when he reached for the soreness on the back of his hand, he felt fur. He pulled his hand back and looked at it, and he saw the claws of a bear. He felt suddenly lost in his own body, and he pushed off from the wall and started to free himself from the cloak of his hallucination. He had to get it off. He had to reclaim his humanity. He wrenched his fingers from the ringlets under one paw, and the foreleg of the bear hide swung to his side. He groped for the other paw, but he was distracted by the light. By the excited urgency of the light. All he wanted was to be free, to escape the nightmare, to release himself from the cloak that kept him in this world, that fogged his brain, the spun illusion in three dimensions in front of his eyes.

He reached again for the paw that smothered his own hand, but as he did, the light was upon him. It was a narrow band of fire and it had wrapped around his forearm. Fielding yelled in pain, in anger, and finally, in recognition of what was happening.

Dream was reality, and his attempt to deny the dream had laid him open to the dangers of what was real. Fielding buried his arm against his stomach, smothering it with his cloaked limb. The tendril of fire flared out, and he quickly became again the creature he had been, sliding his hand back into the underside of the bear's paw.

As Fielding tried to shake off the effects of the concussion and the counterfeit hallucination it had inspired, at the site of the three-posted pyre, Penay was falling further into the realm of the unreal. The fire had been invigorated with new tinder, and yet it had not progressed beyond the outer perimeter. He was aware of the men screaming, of Rene Wawatessi somewhere near him scrambling in the dirt, trying to get away from the circle. Vaguely he could see that the fire was bursting out of its confined area with spears of light, slashing at the other men as they scattered, twisting in vinelike tendrils around the curves of their bodies, seeking a hold, seeking to pull them back.

He did not react to these happenings, because of the intensity of the blood-red flames that burned in the orbs of the thing he had tied to the posts. He didn't react—he couldn't react—because of his terror, because of her power.

In the eyes that burned even through the excited curtain of yellow flames, Penay understood the message they conveyed. She was coming for him. She was going to kill him.

Whatever humanity had existed before was gone, eclipsed by the pull of the people of the fire, by the call for vengeance. It wasn't a collective vengeance, but a very personal one, and upon that she would act.

Her sight was no longer distorted by the flames. Instead, the fire made her vision all the more penetrating. Its light carried her sight wherever it shined. She could see her tormentor standing in front of her, watching her in her struggles. She could see him, and she could hear the screams in the cave, and she could feel the fire licking at her own skin, at all of her people's skins. The fire was inside her, it was part of her, and she was part of it. She gave body to the fire. She could feel the energy. The power. She listened as the others called for new strength. And she heard her own call for vengeance.

Her head snapped toward the random shoots of yellow heat flickering beyond her protected cove, and she willed them to coalesce around a single core. She willed the core to rise, and a effortlessly as raising her arm, the appendage of fire rose at her command. It swirled into a tighter coil, rearing back.

She was a being of pure energy, a creature of the timeless void, a part of an entity whose spiritual dictates were torn from the blackest pages of the world's religions. She felt one with the whole, and she focused her energy, she focused all their energy, as well as their hate and needs and calls for vengeance, at the furthest extremity of her limb, at the very tip of the column of fire, and with the concentration of power complete, she willed the fire to uncoil.

Penay had read the message in her eyes, but despite his descent into the quaking realm of abject terror, he could not visualize how she would deliver on the threat. She was tied to the stakes, engulfed by flames. She would be destroyed in minutes. She should have already taken on the flames. And yet she stood in a dark cocoon surrounded by the light. Surrounded by flames that refused to seek their inner tinder. Flames that instead spun out of the circle in arcing shoots like a spiral galaxy come to earth.

Penay staggered backward. She was doing this. He looked into her eyes, those pinpoints of red in the center of her face, and where they focused, the fire responded. It coiled together, it reared back. Penay screamed, holding his arms protectively in front of himself.

The pike of fire shot forward, piercing his chest. It delved deep inside the core of his body, and Penay took on a stunned look of pain and helplessness. And then he began to rise. Impaled by the fire, he was lifted off his feet.

Penay reacted with numbed disbelief. He wrapped his hands around the fiery substance, but there was no substance to touch. There was nothing to grasp except his own hands. They joined together in the fire. The fire! He grimaced in pain, and it was the burning feeling on his hands that finally overpowered his astonishment, that caused his eyes to widen in panic. Yet no manner of sound escaped from his lips. Instead all that was emitted between his teeth was a pale yellow glow. His entire face began to glow, creased only by shadowed lines of his contorted expression, an expression of terror, of pain, of one witnessing his own extinction.

ielding shielded his eyes from the sudden intensity of light. It as a circular brightness the size of a plate, but more oval in shape. As Fielding watched, as his eyes adjusted, shadowed lines began to lend contour to the light. It began to take on recognizable form. Flames billowed in and out, holding the upward flow of their energy in a stable position. Cavities appeared, rounded edges looped together, protrusions extended from the living substance.

Fielding let his hands fall from his eyes. There could be no mistaking that he was looking into the contorted representation of a human face. As he stared, as the contours grew more distinct, the face itself became recognizable. It was one of Blackbear's group who had opposed any accommodation with him. It was the face of Johnny Penay.

Penay's voice was the sound of a blaze gorging on new fuel. Aloft on the fiery pike, he was consumed by the flames from the inside. The fire was coming out his mouth; it dripped like blood from his ears, and his eyes had taken on the same deep red pinpoints of color as the flaming sockets of the woman tied to the stakes. It was as if he had been touched with the same vision, except that in her, it was a controlled fire, and in him, the deep red quickly evolved from the color of smoldering embers to the bright, hot flare of molten rock newly disgorged from the earth. Then within seconds the fire was released from his eyes, erupting in twin geysers of molten froth. Penay shrieked, and on the hot winds of his breath was carried the sound of agony, the sound of tortured death. He shook involuntarily with the energy coursing through his system, his arms outstretched, his fingers hooked like claws. His skin grew brighter until pockets of flame like pustules erupted all over his body, burning holes in his clothes, shooting outward from his extremities, bursting forth through his skin.

In a matter of moments, the figure held aloft was reduced to a charred resemblance of a human form. And then the mass of blackened carbon dropped to the ground.

The face of Johnny Penay disappeared in a bright flash of white light that forced Fielding to protect his eyes. When he opened them again, he was staring into the representation of another face. It didn't appear gradually, as the last one had, but rather seemed fully formed. Neither was it a bright flare, but rather it blended in with the contour of the flames. And it was not a face torn by torment, but rather one with an expression of serenity. ▶

was almost as if the fire were stone and this visage were chiseled into its surface. It was a face of strength and composure. The same strength and composure that had struck Fielding that first day in the courtroom when he watched her on the witness stand.

It was a face of beauty, the same beauty that had driven him into the cave.

They were trying to come back to life, he had said. *They were trying to come back to life through her.*

Christopher Fielding stared into the glowing representation of the face of Jean Shawshequay. And the thing in the fire stared back.

Chapter 24

HE SAW A facial representation of a human being consumed by the fire, and he saw a second face appear then fade gradually, blending the substance of its form back into the greater whole of the flames.

By all conventions of reality, it should have been a dream. But it wasn't. His body ached, his head throbbed, and it was all made worse by the heat, by the invisible currents of energy that rolled over him in waves. It was all made worse by the fire.

The fire! It roiled out of the mass of bones with expanding swells of yellow-orange light marked at the edges by twisting black lines of soot. Where Fielding had splashed kerosene into crevices, sheets of flames rose from cracks in the rock in a primordial scene lifted from the birth of the planet. Or the end. At the final judgment. With souls cast into the eternity of their own making.

Entombed in the black rock and confronted with a spectacle lifted from Dante's verse, Fielding knew which eternity awaited him. And there was no mistaking the fate divined for the people of the fire. He could see anxious bands of Hell's element lapping inside the rib cages of stacked skeletons, the action of the fire creating an illusion of movement. And at the edge of the pyre a single skull lay balanced flat on its upper jaw, staring at his position, a deep-red flickering through its open sockets as if the fire had found its visual organs and were watching its tormentor, its executioner, its adversary on this plane of the supernatural.

Fielding pushed off from the wall, and as he did, the fire bulged toward him. It had a fast, flickering quality to its surface, a nervous expectancy, and as the dull-witted disability from the blow to his head eased by a fraction, Fielding began to pick up a bit of the same tension and activity as the fire. He looked around anxiously. The place seemed transformed. It was hard to get his bearings. He looked for the exit aperture, but it seemed lo

amid the crags and shadows and wavy reflections of the fire. He
turned again, covering the same space with his eyes, and it
wasn't the hole he noticed, but the dot of light. Almost lost in
the glare imprinted on his retinae was the flashlight he had left
balanced on the rock in the exit.

Fielding swung toward the light, the weight of the robe slowing his movement, making him feel all the more cumbersome.
And then the whole room seemed to move with him. It appeared
that the fire was still in front of him. The dizziness returned in a
rush. He reached his clawed appendage out to the rock wall to
steady himself, and as he touched solid stone, he realized it was
neither the room nor himself that had lost equilibrium. The fire
had reacted to his movement, sending a streamer of flame to
block his path. He turned back toward the pyre, and the
streamer retreated into the core of billowing heat. It added to the
body of fire, sending it higher, pushing it toward the ceiling of
the cavern.

The fire should have diminished as the kerosene was expended. But instead it was growing. It was as if it had discovered new sources of fuel, as if the life force of the souls it
consumed were being metamorphosed into its own life. Johnny
Penay was gone. Would others of his group be giving up bits of
their own lives? As if in answer to his deliberation, the fire
surged higher, lapping in sharp-tongued frenzy at the stone.

Fielding sensed a growing dread. Was she part of them now?
Would she die with them?

The flames soared, billowing outward against the roof of
the cavern, following the curve of the ceiling toward the walls.
Fielding turned again toward the only way out, and again a
yellow-white streamer of disembodied flame erupted in front of
his passage.

Fielding spun back angrily. He was one with the people of the
bear. He was kin with the spirits of their land. He was part of
the continuum, linked if not by blood then by deed to those who
had ignited the first fire. He was master of the second fire.
There was nothing it could do to stop him. Their connection to
his world was failing with each upward boil of flame, with
each bit of disintegration of the skeletal remains.

Fielding's defiant gaze fell on the single skull at the base of
the pyre, and though its empty sockets were devoid of the powers of sight, its vision seemed to come alive in the sudden
tightening of the colors, the flare of heat. It came alive in a pair

of pointed spikes that erupted from the orblike black holes of the six-hundred-year-old head and were propelled across the gap of stale air. The bolt of fire came so fast Fielding didn't even have time to flinch. It came directly at his face, then flattened and sprayed to the sides inches in front of his eyes as if it had struck a plate of glass. But the light nonetheless caused pain. It tore all shadow and contour from his sight leaving only a field of white.

Fielding was rocked back by the blast, and cast into the world of no shadows, he stood unsteadily, his arms groping for balance. Whether his eyes were open or closed, he couldn't tell. The white veil was so complete it filled his entire brain, leaving not a single vestige of contrast to give shape to his world.

He was awash in a colorless void. He was a creature of mixed form in a formless place. He was adrift in a stellar cloud. It could have been any of these things, given the blinding glare, but it was the force like the wind wrapping around his head, trying to pull him forward, that was the medium of truth: He was inside the fire.

They were dying. And yet they were coming alive. It was a world of paradox, and somewhere between the opposing truths she could feel the pain of dying as well as the vibrancy of birth. She could hear the screams and she could hear the calls for more strength. And she could see the fire.

At either end of the spectrum the only constant was the fire. It spun in great spears of light out of the circle of flame that surrounded her, slashing at the *skraelings* that had helped fix her in bondage, stabbing into their backs as they tried to escape, whipping around their ankles, searing their flesh black, stealing the stuff of their lives and feeding it into the furnace that powered the lives that were coming back into being on the currents of visible energy.

The fire was also in the cave, rising from the stacked logs and scattering her people into the nooks and niches of the black chamber. Time had become a dimension without barriers, an open-sided expanse where what existed before existed now. She could feel the fire ripping into her body, into all of their bodies, and she suffered the agony of her flesh being devoured. She felt the desperation, the struggle for survival, and most of all, in her stasis between the two worlds of contrary design, she could feel the anger. The anger was a fire of its own making, and on its ris ing currents she allowed herself to be carried higher. The anger and the pain and the call for survival became a single command taking control of the power that had been unleashed, guiding its action, focusing its fury.

As before, she could see through the rock walls of the cavern, and in her world of past and present, amid the screams and the pain, the dying and the birthing, she could see the heathen garbed in the hide of an animal, and she sensed the creature's weakness. She sensed its vulnerability. She sensed its surrender.

In a world without shadow in the center of a flame, all Fielding could do was maintain his balance. He fought the pull of the hot wind as he shielded his eyes in the crook of his elbow. His vision would come back gradually, and until then he had to rely on the magic of the masters of the first fire. He had to rely on the same forces that had bested the Awshkoute once before, that had protected Makwamacatawa as he sat for three nights atop the knoll looking into the flames for his vision.

The sound of the wind by his ears was the sound of centuries, and on that steady rush of heated air he imagined he could hear whispers urging him forward, urging him to give up the battle. It would be easier, they were telling him. But Fielding recognized that the whispers were his own, rising out of his fatigue and fear. He swung his arm out blindly to fight the mental weakness. He spun in place. He staggered without direction. Anything to gain some movement, to pick up the challenge.

For whatever reason, the wind changed. And so did the voices. He could hear the fire building in intensity, and on the snaps and violent cracks of the peaked lobes of flame, he could hear the screams.

They were the collective cry of a lost tribe, suffering the agony of the first fire. And in their voices Fielding heard the wrenching anguish of failing life. He heard the pain and panic that must have transpired as the fires spread inside the closed confines. And most of all, he heard the feeble protests against the manifestation of their own god. It was a justice they refused to acknowledge. It was a sacrilege of inestimable outrage. And the terrible bitterness and anger and hate of that time were coming alive again, in the furious onslaught of the blaze against the ceiling, in the explosive nature of the combustible eruption, in the rapid uptick in the motion of the flames. It was alive again in the second fire.

Fielding wanted to get away. He had to get away. But still he couldn't see. Then, slowly, grays began to settle in the colorless void. Shape and shadow began to return to his formless place. The stellar cloud dispersed to the cosmos. Fielding opened his eyes a fraction wider and tried to focus, but the bank of light before him continued to cast everything in a bright veil. He tried to turn away from the light, but it seemed to be everywhere. The power of its spell over his senses was above him, behind him, in any direction he looked.

Fielding gasped, stretching a foot forward. Then a second step. He lunged, as if the fog of brightness would lift with his movement. But it did not. He stumbled and fell forward, catching himself with his hands, the claws of the bear digging into the loose stone. He was hot and anxious and breathing heavily, and he didn't know which way to turn. If only he could see clearly. But it wouldn't happen that way. Sight came gradually, in increments. Wavy line became hard contour. Suggestion of shape yielded to identifiable form. It would be the small things that would come into focus. And that's all he needed. A toehold on reality. Something, anything, to edge him back to the visible world, to allow him to get his bearings.

He looked toward the ground, toward the base of the column of light, and finally, something began to set itself apart from the perpetual glare. It was a dark shape, rounded to some extent, in the same position as the twin bolts of fire that had blinded him. Fielding recognized the skull in his memory before actual sight confirmed the nature of the object. It was the skull resting on its upper jaw, except that it had changed. Its entire top half was gone, having been reduced to ash. Still resisting the flames was the nasal cavity and the protruding upper jaw, the exposed teeth in a sardonic half grin. It was a display of macabre humor, the laughter of the ancients, taunting him, telling him his ashes would join theirs. There was no escape.

Escape! Fielding turned and, reaching a hand to the side wall, began to lead himself toward the exit. He had managed just a few steps when the fire erupted in another streamer, aimed not at him but the rock wall along his path. It was a concentrated shaft of intense heat, and at the point of impact it flared out in fingers of flame, reaching for the cracks and crevices, boring into the stone, transferring its energy directly into the petrified sediment of forgotten seas. The rock absorbed the heat, and inside it began to change. It began to expand. It cracked first along the edges; then, in an escalation of sound, the rock exploded, splintering into a hundred pieces, sending stone shrapnel in a 180-degree arc away from the wall.

Shards of broken stone peppered Fielding, rocking him backward, knocking him off his feet. Though heavy fur softened the blows, he hurt in a dozen places. But there was no time to recover. He had to keep moving. Toward the far limit of the cavern. Toward the dot of light that faded in and out of his vision like a beacon on a fog-shrouded shore.

He rolled over to his knees, and while he was still on all fours, a second explosion of rock erupted up out of the floor. Fielding grabbed his head, falling to his side. He turned angrily back toward the fire, as if there were something he could do to strike back. He had already done what he could. He had arranged to complete the destruction begun six hundred years earlier. When would it be done? he shouted angrily within the confines of his thoughts. How much fuel was there for the flames to feed upon?

The skull near the base had nearly disintegrated. All Fielding could see was a row of bared teeth, and even these were bathed in the yellow aura. It was happening, he told himself. As Jean had read on the ceiling, the bones were turning to dust, exiling the residue of their power from the world of object and reality. Fielding sensed a flickering upbeat to his heart. He looked at the column of fire rising to the ceiling, billowing outward along its concave surface, and he began to notice the change.

The fire seemed a steadier display. It was losing its random action. Lines of deep shadow began to hold their positions. Upward tongues of flames rounded into recurring shapes, joining with the roiling flow of the entire column, bringing discipline to the bulges and flares, the deep fissures and shifting colors. Like water rushing down a rocky streambed, maintaining the same patterned flow, the rising bursts of primal energy took on a motive constancy. And within this constancy appeared suggestions of structure and form, constituent pieces of emerging shapes.

They were coming, Fielding thought. As had happened last night in the woods, when fire rained down out of the trees on his truck and a hundred souls emerged out of the sheet of light. They were coming back, for one last, desperate foray into the corporeal world of cold as well as heat, into the world of flesh and sacrifice, of visible manifestations and spiritual sustenance. They were coming back for him.

But Fielding did not fear them. He had seen their grotesque visages before, and he had become kin with the Ancient Ones. There was nothing they could do to forestall their destruction. Their was nothing they could do to penetrate the magic.

Fielding slowly pushed himself to his feet. He kept his eyes on the recurring patterns, the individual flares that held their positions, the subtle, changeless gradations of color from filmy white to rich yellow-orange, the outline shadings of shadow or soot that provided definition to the emerging shapes. It was as it had been last night in the truck, except much slower. They were weaker, Fielding thought. They were dying.

He watched and waited, suddenly infused with a desire to see the end, to shout out his defiance, to witness the compelling final chapter to the cremation of a people whose evil had managed to transcend the boundary between a state of mind and a wicked materiality. He focused on the burning images taking substance from the rising wisps of color and heat. He looked for signs that the creatures of the fire were emerging, but though the suggestions of shape grew in distinction, they remained unrecognizable. No more than a collection of bits and pieces of suggested form. Disparate elements of a hidden design. Constituent pieces of a *greater whole*.

Fielding staggered back. As his perception changed, the abstractions suddenly became part of a cohesive pattern. Each individual curve carried on into the next. Linear designs ran together. They were all part of the whole.

Despite the intensity of heat, Fielding felt a deadening chill. All the earlier doubts came rushing back. He was not kin to the masters of the fire. He was an archaeologist, an interloper in this realm of non-science, an unpracticed intruder in things he could not understand. How could he have hoped to overcome a power that had existed through the centuries? How could he lay claim to the mantle of the Ancient Ones when his soul had never been washed with the blood of the first peoples? And his most serious misjudgment of all, how could he have thought he could destroy the evil by bringing it to life?

Cowering below the full manifestation of the emergent form, Fielding struggled to resist the building anguish. He groped for a reply to the questions, and though he had little capacity for reasoned thought, somewhere buried beneath the doubt and the fear was the knowledge that the strategy for the second fire had not been part of his interpretation. It had been the interpretation of Jean Shawshequay. And she had seen. She had remembered. She had been there.

She saw her people dying. She remembered the pain herself. And she was there. She was bound to the pyre at the sacrificial altar; she was amid the flames and fury of the massacre with her wrists tied behind her back, and she was constricted by the stone ceiling across the yoke of her shoulders.

Place as well as time had become a dimensionless plane where substance yielded to the ephemeral nature of fire and fire became substance. It blended with living tissue. It coursed through her veins. It became the transmitter of neural signals. The fire had stolen into her body and she had entered the fire.

Her cousins in the flames were failing, but the power was not. It was growing stronger as it distilled into a single force. *She* was growing stronger as the men that had ignited the pyre gave up their lives. She felt the rock at her back, the energy surging through her limbs, through the tendons in her neck, bursting with incandescent fury in the center of her skull. Raising her face toward the enveloping black, she shouted out her anger, her hatred, her unceasing rage at the continuing sacrilege, at the renewal of the massacre, at the sounds of her people dying. Her head thrashed from side to side, straining at its bonds, bursting forth with a fury directed at the creature of flesh and fur, the cowl-shaped representative of her old foes, the igniter of the second fire.

The fire blasted violently at the ceiling of the cave. Rapid shoots of flame, pointed crests of yellow and red, thrashed back and forth against the carbon-black rock. Witness to this display, Fielding could see the connections between sharp points of light and deep shadows. He could see the shape within the growing violence. He could see the bestial outline of the six-hundred-year-old evil, the source of its intelligence raised wolflike toward the sky. And he could hear its cry of rage, its voice like the roar of the wind cycloning above a forest on fire.

The fire was a single entity, a cohesive force as immense as the cavern itself. Restrained by the arching roof thirty feet above the floor, the fire reached out to either side in glowing plumes of descending flames. Like the body of the fire itself, like the sharp lines and wolflike peaks that thrashed the ceiling at the central height of its form, the side plumes took on their own character, their own substance, their own function. They took on the aspect of free-form limbs.

The thrashing, horned peak of the fire's crest billowed suddenly downward, and in the folds and deep crevices, in the steady darkness of the fire's hidden soul, for a moment Fielding was sure he was fixed by the black gaze that had challenged him last night, except that in scale there was no true comparison, and unlike last night, the curtain of fire did not fade. Instead it grew brighter, angrier, more active, as if its rage had become a fuel itself, adding to its own lethal mix.

It was fire of a rabid nature, and Fielding was touched by the madness. He wanted to run, he wanted to escape, but nothing seemed to connect for him. His mind was a jumble of confusion and fears and misdirected impulses. He had become again a player in another's mythology, with no more control over his own fate than a cluster of stars quitting their constellation.

The fire along the wall peeled free from the crags and splits of stone and reared back. As it did, the heat and light seemed to carry toward its furthest extremity, concentrating at the tip, splaying into a dozen fingers, each one a white-hot dagger of flame. Fielding could only watch as the appendage of pure energy snapped forward, releasing the daggered bits of itself, sending them toward him, seeking to penetrate his puny shield of ancient magic.

Fielding yelled out in shock, falling back. He had been struck. By the flame, by the living manifestation of the evil itself. Near his waist and again at his ankle, Fielding felt the sting of the fire. More than a sting, it was a puncture, a stab wound from a heated blade whose burning threatened to spread wider, deeper. Like the fangs from the dead camp fire, the pain refused to lift.

Fielding emitted an inarticulate syllable that carried the extent of his pain, his surprise, his fear throughout the closed chamber, rising in volume to match the heated rush of the beast's roar. And it was his scream more than anything that helped him resist the tearing feeling from the burning incision that released him from his paralysis.

He looked and saw that the other appendage had coiled, its light concentrating at the tip. Fielding turned as it flung its tipped daggers, and this time he could feel even more impact along his side and at the back of his neck. It was growing stronger. He was growing weaker. He had to get out. Fast.

Fielding was lunging, tripping, scrambling over the rock debris and uneven floor toward the far wall. He was no longer a figure of mythology, no longer a creature of mixed design. He was nothing more than a man desperate for survival, a human being cast into a realm that existed in another place and another time, a world where evil turned incarnate and voices from the grave breathed life into its power. Voices that were carried on the wind, the heated flash that rushed through space with the throaty breath of a carnivore, the hiss of a serpent, the dying gasps of a legion of demons. Fielding could hear the carnivore, the serpent, the legions from Hell. He could hear the wind!

The fire was suddenly all around him. He was enclosed in a pocket of flame. He was cupped within the palms of the beast. He was trapped within the grasp of the creature of fire. And it was contracting around him, closing in, squeezing tighter.

Horizontal bands of red and yellow and orange and white blended together into new variations of color, then separated back into their constituent shades. There was a frantic urgency to the motion, a flickering, flitting action to the flames. It was a display of frenzy, a wild, circling, ravenous band of energy that throbbed with nervous tension, each pulse leaving it a fraction closer, a degree hotter.

Fielding could feel the heat, and he could feel the tension. He was being drawn into the frenzy. The fire was taking command. It's rapid flow urged on the pace of his blood through his veins. The jittering flashes and fades of the light became the action of his nerves. The confusion of colors brought new turmoil to his thoughts.

It was winning. It was killing him. It was stealing his breath. The fire spun closer. He could barely breathe. He could barely move. The only constant remained the action of his legs. He was laboring forward, the lack of oxygen, the weight of the robe, the intensity of the heat, making every move sluggish. He felt so heavy, so very heavy. His thighs burned, not from the fire, but from the exertion. And then the circle of fire began to change. It broke in the center. It pulled back, revealing clawed digits that raked against the rock wall. The wall!

It was a black expanse of ancient soot, and with the glare of the fire it appeared to be a flat field of absolutely no definition. It was total darkness, total contrast, except in one tiny regard. At the center of the field, framed by the hooked scimitars of flame angrily clashing against the stone, was a single point of light. It was the beacon in the fog. It was the flashlight on the edge of the pathway out of the inner chamber.

Fielding reached toward the smooth metal tube, the claws of his own second nature making it hard to grasp. He turned the light around, focusing it into the slit of stone, ready to dive into the narrowing jaws. But Fielding did not move.

The exit was a passage with room for man or beast, but not both. He would have to shed his dual nature. He would have to relinquish his kinship with the spirits of the good people of this land. He would have to confront the evil alone.

Fielding acted fast, trying to outrace the pace of his fear. He swung a leg up to the lip of the aperture, then hefted himself up. He was going to go in feet-first, and he had to turn to face the boiling semicircle of flames. The fire seemed to sense his intentions. It surged forward, coming close to the fur of the bear, probing for weakness, reaching for the soft flesh underneath.

Fielding started to edge backward into the hole, and as he did the fire reacted. It sent feelers of flame along his sides, delving into the depths of the stone. Fielding could feel the pressure, seeking to encircle him, to prevent his escape. Then just as suddenly as it had advanced, the fire retreated, billowing into a roiling turmoil of black smoke and flame the color of fresh blood. The color of old blood. The color of the blood of all of those who had died. It became a new element that pushed at the bounds of the properties of fire. It seemed to take on body and mass, a thing of corporeal substance, and from out of this heaving brew it began to expel flaring bits of itself. Darts of blood from the fire-thing shot forward, penetrating the magic, pricking him with their heat.

Fielding could only duck his head and continue inching back. He could feel both the top and bottom of the rock tunnel with his feet, and as he slipped deeper, he had to begin peeling the cloak from his legs. There was no room to maneuver. He pushed with his hands, edging deeper into the hole by minute fractions. The bear hide slipped higher, to his waist, bending in stiff folds atop the small of his back.

Fielding's progress slowed even more. He felt trapped in the neck of the aperture, as if the rock were conspiring with the fire, the crypt with the killer. The heated tempo of despair pounded at the sides of his head. It flared with new heat throughout the core of his body. Fielding grunted with effort, to push himself backward, to overcome the inner turmoil.

He was more than halfway through the narrow part, and the cloak itself was now working against him, piling up on his back, constricting his passage. Fielding reached for the chest strap of feather and leather and wrenched it from its stitching. He shoved and moved a few inches in one thrust. But that was as far as man and beast could go together. Fielding pulled the clawed forelimb from his left hand, and the fire burst forward into the narrow tube of stone. He pulled his arm back, under his stomach, shielding it from the flames. Then with his other hand, he jammed the claws of the bear against an edge of rock, he bunched his fist, and tore his fingers from the ringlets sewn into the underside of the paw.

The head and upper jaw of the black beast of the forest came loose. Fielding pulled his head free; he grabbed the fur and stuffed it forward in the horizontal chasm of jagged rock. The fire reacted in a frenzy, shooting tendrils of corded flame past the gaps, lashing around Fielding's shoulders, digging with a thousand razored teeth into the flesh of his arms. But still, he moved backward, faster now. The jaws of the stone tunnel were opening. First his feet, then his knees, were into the next chamber, groping at blank space, seeking a hold, wriggling, flailing, anything, to get him out.

As Fielding fell to the ground outside the entrance to the inner chamber, the narrow streaks of flame changed. Rather than looping, grasping cords of fire, they became fluid lances that stabbed and thrust in fury as blind as it was frantic.

He had to close the hole. He had to seal the entrance. Ignoring the flaming assaults, Fielding grabbed the half can of kerosene, and as he had planned, he hoisted it up and into the natural crevice between granite and limestone. He stuffed it deep into the aperture, pushing the two-and-a-half gallons of flammable liquid against the fur of the black bear. Then he turned and began to run. But he was not alone. The fire continued its pursuit.

Tentacles of flame reached into the next chamber, bypassing the robe, engulfing the can of kerosene, flashing against the arched ceiling streaked with ocher and chalk markings. They lashed against the back of the fleeing figure, sending him flying, all the while calling for more energy from the inner chamber, and the light and heat did flow, coming in waves, each spurt lapping at the heated metal of the can, rushing over and around the can, causing the liquid inside to rise in temperature, to expand, to near its point of combustion.

Fielding staggered to his feet. He was burned and hurting and victim to continuing assault, but he kept moving. He passed under the stylistic representation of the early Ojibwa sacrificed in the flames. He could see his own shadow, a tortured silhouette playing off the far wall, the end of the tunnel, the rise to the network of crevices that led to the surface.

He saw all of these things, and then he did not. The eighteen pounds of liquid explosive blasted every sense from his awareness. Everything went white and black, loud and silent, at the same time. He was sailing through the air, he was at rest against the stone. He was awake, he was unconscious. He was in pain, he was at peace. He existed only at the extremes, and in this world of opposites, he had no way of knowing if he was alive or dead.

The explosion blew inward as well, filling the enclosed chamber with rolling waves of pressure that blasted against the black walls, that boiled upward toward the curved ceiling, forcing its energy into the deep crags and narrow cracks of stone, seeking release. And release it found, bursting through the matted floor of the sinkhole, erupting in nearly a dozen different places with balls of fire blackened by the accumulated grit and soil of centuries, opening holes that the slow forces of erosion and forest decay had conspired to fill.

As these new avenues of ventilation belched kerosense fire, the subterranean entrance into the chamber of bones, the narrow natural aperture that had been blocked for so many years by stones stacked by hand, was sealed again. Granite and limestone chunks broken apart by the blast collapsed, blocking the passage, cutting off the light, casting the outer tunnel into utter darkness.

He was alive.

Whatever the confusion in his world of extremes, Fielding was conscious of life. He didn't know how long he had been near the brink, but he was certain he was back now.

The only way he could tell if his eyes were open or closed was by touching them. When the tip of his middle finger brushed against bare eyeball, he winced. He pulled his hand away and felt a slick substance along the fleshy skin below his small finger. He felt it with his other hand, then reached back to his head. The blood was still flowing, and that's what told him he had been out minutes, not hours.

He was stiff, and every part of his body ached. But it wasn't the condition of his muscles and joints that was strangest. It was the sound in his ears, the sound that in keeping with his world of opposites blanked everything out. He wasn't deaf, because he could hear the explosion. It continued to echo in the center of his head, exerting pressure, pushing at the confines of his skull.

Fielding remembered his own tortured silhouette playing off the far wall, and then the force of the blast had shot through the tunnel like the barrel of a gun and he had joined his shadow. He had been thrown up against the wall.

Through this process of deductive reasoning, Fielding realized exactly where he was in the dark. He knew what he would have to do to get out.

He rolled to his knees, able to move only with greater difficulty than when cloaked with the heavy bearskin. It was more than dark inside the cave. The air had a gritty feel to it, and he coughed. The air was choked with rock dust, but there was one saving grace about the total darkness: There was no fire.

Groping, he felt the rock wall, then slowly began to ascend. It was strange, not being able to hear the tinkling of pebbles he dislodged, the clink of his buckle against the rock, the sounds of his own grunts. All the subtle noises were lost to his ears in the continuing turmoil of the explosion.

He pulled himself up to the next level, where he could smell the bats. And as he reached forward, dragging himself fully over the edge, he could feel them. Tiny winged bodies that had lingered too long after dusk littered the floor.

Fielding came to his feet and moved forward on stiff legs, his arms outstretched. When he felt the rock, he sidled into the narrow slit that led into the network of crevices. He paused, trying to review in his mind the path he had followed before, but beyond the second turn, or the third, the continuing force of the explosion in his head made it too painful to think. He could only react. He could only grope blindly ahead, hoping direction would come to him in stages. And so he began to move, feeling the sharp edge of the rock, groping across black cavities, trying to decide if that's where he should turn, or should he cross the gap and continue ahead?

He became aware of the crinkling feel of certain areas of his skin. It was the mark of the fire, but the burning feeling that refused to lift seemed somehow insignificant, compared to the pain in his head. The constant pressure. The continuing concussion of the blast. He could hear it still. He could feel it, the noise that stabbed into his ears, sinking deep into his brain, then exerting new pressure, expanding, seeking to get out, to reignite the force of the explosion itself inside his skull.

Fielding banged flush into the rock. He had been moving too fast. He half turned, then shifted sideways out of the dead end. He groped about, but he had no idea where he was. He had no idea which way to turn. If only he could get back to the central path, back to where he could pick up the familiar passage.

Fielding felt the rock as if searching for clues, as if his tactile sense would somehow translate visual images to his brain. But it was a foolish exercise, not because of any failing with his sense of touch, but because of an inability to think. Because of the pain. Because of the explosion.

Fielding screamed, grabbing the sides of his head. He couldn't hear his own voice, but he could feel it in his throat, a raspy, burning sensation that tore at pink tissue already chafed with the heat of the fire, the grit of the particles in the air. And he could feel the scream in his head. It only increased the pressure. It increased the flow of his blood. Each throb in his temples became a hammer blow, each attempt at reasoned thought yielded panic, and each new bit of panic careened out of control, pounding without mercy at the gray matter inside his skull.

He felt the sting of salt in his eyes. Tears mixed with blood on his cheeks and dripped onto his chest. He was moving before he formed the thought to press on. Reflexes were taking over. There was nothing else he could call upon. He had become a creature of the dark, a species without sentience that existed in a world it could not see or hear. It was alive for only a brief time, its only purpose a mad struggle for survival. It fought against the odds, it thrashed vainly about, seeking that one key to existence that would allow it to live, that would allow it to continue its struggle.

Fielding pressed against the petrified sediment of the prehistoric sea, the rock crypt of countless creatures, the jagged stone wall of the cave. His hands groped at the surface, and as they did, his tactile sense tried to send a message. The muscles in his fingers tensed. The tension was transmitted to his brain. It was a nub of stone, smooth from centuries of people climbing over it, using it as a handhold.

Fielding raised his foot, feeling with his toe for a ledge. He wasn't thinking. He was reacting, carried on instinct, and carried on this lone drive, he rose higher up the face of the rock. He could feel it leveling out above him, he could feel the dirt on the floor, and he could feel the change in atmosphere.

When his head passed through the barrier between the constant subterranean chill and the air from the surface, the pressure inside him began to change. The hammer blows eased, the careening panic slowed, and controlled thought began to return to his mind. He was nearly at the surface. He was almost out. His ordeal was over.

Fielding scrambled into the earthen cove of dangling tendrils, roots and matted cobwebs. He pushed through it all, forcing himself into the crescent-shaped gap, emerging out of the cave between the cleft of boulders.

Stumbling, staggering, groping for stone, for roots, for spiney stems of plants, he pulled himself away from the cave, from the tunnel of ancient paintings, from the chamber of fiery massacre. He collapsed first to his knees, then fell flat on his chest to the ground. He was in all manner of pain, but the only sensation he could feel was that of relief. He had survived. He had escaped the chamber of death. And he could see!

He raised himself on his arms so he could look around. It was night, but the all-pervading darkness had vanished. He could see the outlines of stone chunks in gray relief. He could see the lacy fabric of ferns, the solid essence of tree trunks, and he could see the delicate, fluttering nature of the leaves. The leaves that played on the wind, that flickered like lobes of flame in a camp fire, that caught on their glassy surface the light of the forest, reflecting it in an excited, multihued display.

Fielding could see the green of the canopy, and he could see the reflected light dancing in the motion of the leaves. He could see the yellow and reds and shades of orange in between. He could see the fire! He could see it in the leaves, and rising to his knees, scanning the floor of the sinkhole, he could see it on the ground, erupting from the earth, billowing into the night air.

Coming fully to his feet, Fielding moved farther from the cleft of rock, farther into the leafy realm of this hidden spot of forest. It was a hellish spectacle he witnessed, plumes of fire belching from the earth, stabbing with rapid, pointed spikes of flame at the trees and brush, at the dry vegetation and combustible tinder long devoid of life, reaching toward the sky, tearing asunder the peace of the night, pushing back the dark, returning him to the cave, to the world of fiery horror and visible evil.

Fielding reacted with little renewed sense of dread and danger. He had been drained of those feelings, and instead he could feel only despair. And surrender. It wasn't fair. He had been master of the second fire. He had finished the cremation that had been initiated six hundred years ago. And yet the fire was here. It had escaped the crypt. And it was growing larger.

Fielding continued stepping forward over spongy mats of soil, moving deeper into the center of the pit. He was oblivious to the danger. Indeed, it was as if he welcomed it. As if he would welcome the touch of the fire. He admired its purity, the singleness of its purpose. It was consume and die. There was no pain, no morality, no choices that had to be made.

As he moved onto the field of fire, as he smelled the burning leaves and black soil being turned to ash, he watched the action of the flames. Arching curls of jagged light snapped at the air, rising higher with each upward lunge, reaching toward the trees, toward new tinder, catching on dead branches, racing on tiny legs along the bark, carrying themselves into the crowns of oaks, the pyramidal peaks of pines, turning leaves to a network of veins and needles to slender brown cinders. It was a display of power and primal energy, an inferno building, as fire does, on its own heat and spreading into new sources of fuel. He looked for repeated patterns; he expected them, but Fielding could see no suggestion of hidden form. He could see no beasts of Dantean description seeking to take control of the flares and bulges, the spikes and soaring tongues. He could only see the fire, the flickering, flashing, gyrating madness of the fire, as it should be. As it would be, released to follow its own course. Released from the power of the otherworld. Released from the core of evil that had stained this place for so many years.

It was the sound of the fire that displaced the explosion in his ears. They were so much alike, at first he didn't notice. The roar of the flames supplanted the echo of the blast. The cracks and snaps of disintegrating wood became the sharp reports of the explosion. The waves of radiated heat replaced the pressure in his head.

His hearing returned not with the same distinct clarity as his vision, but in slow increments. He began to distinguish the sound of his own footsteps, the raspy rush of his own breath, the snapping of twigs as he brushed them from his face. And he began to hear other things. He began to sense a variant in the constant turmoil of fire and thrashing leaves.

It carried a jittering, disturbing feel into his chest, and before he could identify the source of the variant of noise, he was falling victim to the fear, to the terror, to the panic that was carried on the rippling swells of sound, that flooded into his ears, that was alive in the tremulous tone of the *screams*.

She was here! My God, she had come to the pit!

Fielding spun in place, his eyes rapidly flashing between the flames, into the dark, looking for her. He began to move, the creaky stiffness of the blast, the burning sensation of the fire, no longer a constraint. He lunged over the soft ground, his feet sinking into the soil. He vaulted over downed trunks; he flailed at dense thickets of brush. All the while coming toward the center of the sinkhole. Toward the sacrificial altar of the early European tribe. And of Johnny Penay.

Fielding broke into the clearing, and as he did, as he looked ahead, he found he could not move. It was as if he had been thrown flush into a wall, as if he had been shot again through the barrel of the subterranean tunnel by the force of the blast and flattened against the rock ascent. He was breathless, he was stunned, he was transported to a land of disbelief.

It was a medieval scene before him, a group of wooden stakes on a bed of wood, and strapped in the center, the figure of a woman writhed in terror. She was screaming, struggling, pulling at the ligatures that secured her to the wood. But she could have no effect on them. She was helpless and vulnerable and easy tinder for the flames. The fire, reverted to its normal properties, had entered the inner circle. It bore into the base of the poles, it followed the surface of the logs higher, lapping at the wood, sending its heat closer to the flesh of her wrists.

She screamed as the upward peak of the fire stabbed at her skin, and Fielding broke toward the pyre. He covered the ten paces in the flash of a heartbeat, but in the realm where a single heartbeat is the difference between life and death, it seemed to take an eternity to near the pyramid of logs, the circle of fire, the tortured, tormented figure of Jean Shawshequay.

Fielding ran toward her as if he didn't see the fire, as if he didn't see the danger. All he could think of was to get to her side, to join her, to tear her free. He didn't see the charred remains near the outer perimeter of the fire. They were black like the soil, like the burnt logs; Fielding's foot caught on the remains, and he sailed forward.

He hit the ground heavily, rolling to his side. His face was directed back at the charred obstruction, and he saw the blackened skull, the empty orbits of eyes, the mouth frozen in eternal horror.

Fielding came to his feet. In his last, desperate act, the man had grabbed a hatchet, digging it into the earth, seeking to halt his backward slide.

Fielding wrenched the hatchet out of the ground, then broke the dead grasp of the thing that used to be a man. The ashy flesh flaked away, the bones cracked, and he had the hatchet for himself.

"Please, help me. The fire!"

He didn't know if it was a plea directed toward him, or a sound as meaningless to her ears as her screams of terror and panic and pain. Her face contorted by her struggle, she already looked beyond the boundary of sanity. And with the fire reflecting off her cheeks and forehead, off the gleaming enamel of her teeth and in the whites of her eyes, for a second it appeared as if she had joined herself to the flames, as if she had already exchanged her substance for the everlasting kinship of the fire.

Fielding broke through the outer circle, coming into the black hole at the center of the pyre. The heat practically stole the air directly from his lungs, and he grabbed out for the log for support. But the log was afire. He recoiled, clenching his hand to his chest, almost falling backward.

Jean was aware of him now. She was screaming with a heightened urgency. Shouting conflicting commands. First to leave her, to save himself. Then for him to hurry. To get them out of there. To cut her bonds.

Fielding dipped under one of her outstretched arms. Reflexes were taking control again. Pushing him forward, directing his actions. The sound of the fire raging all around had entered his head, boiling up against the inner parameters of his skull, returning the pressure of the concussion to what it had been before.

He swung the hatchet, and the rope snapped; one arm flung free.

The flames were inside the triangle formed by the poles. They were greedily sucking in the new tinder, flashing through the dead grasses and twigs, the broken branches and hewn logs.

They were streaking into the black air, cutting the darkness with yellow scythes that slashed and stabbed in a frenzy of expending energy, all the while seeking more fuel, all the while flashing closer to the woman, to the man.

Fielding waved his hand, holding the hatchet in an attempt to clear away the smoke. But that only caused it to swirl more angrily, cupping around his forearm, seeking to wrap him in a hazy brown shroud. He turned toward the other stake and took a step. His foot snagged between the logs, and suddenly he was falling forward, weightless, his arms flailing at nothing but air.

His hands crashed through the tangle of brush and tinder, and he was face-to-face with the fire, the suffocating draw of the turbulent heat, the turgid boils of particulate matter. It was advancing. He was failing. Fielding fought to tear himself free, to bring himself upright, to pull back from the inward bulge of the fire. The dead vegetation scraped at his knuckles, it twined behind his elbows, but Fielding succeeded. He freed himself from its grasp. He pulled back. He was leaning upright, balanced on his knees.

He looked at his right hand, and his bladed tool, the hatchet, the black-handled instrument he had wrested from the dead man's hand, that had failed once to deliver its user from the flames, was gone. He looked frantically into the mesh of grasses and leaves and tangled twigs. Then upward, at the slumping form of the woman who had yielded the last of her conscious energy. At the tight circles of hemp that secured her wrist to the stake. At the flames that rose in sheets of frantic activity all around, that billowed from all sides, carrying their elemental heat along the outer rise of the poles, coming together above their heads in a single peak at the point of the pyramid. Entombed in this failing space, each breath was the breath of fire, bringing not life but diminishing chances for survival. Survival!

Fielding surrendered his instincts to the most primal drive, freeing his mind from the constraints of fear and pain and swelling pressure. He became a creature of the light, a species alive with but a single purpose. And as he continued to move under the veil of fire, as his reflexes commanded the almost involuntary action of his muscles, he sensed that that single purpose had been achieved. He sensed that as a creature of light he had no more need to struggle. It was no longer necessary to endure the hardships.

He was in a dying place, a place where kin of his dual nature of bear and man had given up their lives, beginning their journeys to the village of souls. It was a place of sacrifice, and somehow it seemed fitting that with the single purpose achieved, with the joining of the second fire to the first, there be a final sacrifice. It seemed fitting that he surrender his life to the fire of the ancients. It seemed a fitting sacrifice for the peace of future generations.

In his painless, strangely satisfied foray into the world of light, Fielding sensed it was right that if it was to end for her, it end for him as well. It seemed fitting that if the fire was not to be cheated, it take them together. It seemed fitting that the smoke of their combined existence rise into the night sky as a single plume.

Epilogue

A DEAD FOREST has a smell of its own. The fire lingers in cinders and cellulose skeletons, giving the air that shares the same space a solid feel and a taste that congeals on the back of the tongue. Even after a year, when it rains, the gray odor of wood turned to charcoal, the ash of ancient sacrifice, incinerated bones, and earthy soil pungent with the aroma of rot and decay, emit a new pall of thickness and death.

The sinkhole was a black hole. The fire had destroyed it all. Denuded tree trunks, blackened and deeply scorched, stood like dead sentinels over barren ground reduced to its rocky core, and the rock itself, the reservoir of fossil and sediment, was so thoroughly stained with carbon residue that it appeared to be stone retched upward from the belly of the planet.

From above, the Cave of Bones was a round scar in a sea of green; it was the imprint of a cloven hoof; it was a lasting mark seared into the soul of this place by a force of such consummate evil that it transcended the bounds between state of mind and true corporeal existence. It was a fitting monument to the people who had come here six centuries ago, and to the events that had transpired.

Atop the knoll near the rim of the pit a small fire burned in front of a figure in a deerskin cloak and mask. Behind him was a round-humped sweatlodge resembling the structure that had exploded in flames a year and a day before. The being of dual natures, seated on the dirt, stared into the flames, looking and waiting for the visions he had never had the opportunity to seek when he was younger, that his father had said awaited him.

His visit to this place was the first in a long while. After the fire there had been a flurry of interest by the authorities, but that interest was short-lived. What the sheriff found proved to him that he had been right all along about Penay. The man's final, bizarre ritual of human sacrifice confirmed that he was behind the other killings, and the fact that the last fire had flashed out of control, engulfing him and his cohorts, put an end to the investigation. Though it had all ended as far as the sheriff was concerned, people still tended to stay away from the geological curiosity in the woods. Myths are born out of lesser things than rumors and fears, and once alive in the collective soul of a village, they have a tendency to outweigh any authoritative presentation of the facts.

Archaeological interest in the site died as well. A note at the end of a quarterly journal declared that the proposed excavation at what was thought to be a significant Late Woodland site had been canceled. Closer investigation and more exhaustive sampling had determined that it was not a significant site at all. It turned out to be nothing more than a nineteenth-century fur trappers' camp, the one-paragraph note stated.

Except for the hunched figure that was part man and part fleet animal of the forest, it seemed as though the world had shunted this place aside. But like the smell of the fire that lingered in the ash and the burnt trees, the things that happened here were destined to reverberate through time. They were events too compelling to fade simply into memory. They became part of the place of their occurrence, dwelling in the blank spaces, living on in the subtle noises, resonating forever on the strength of the emotions expended by those who had been victims of the final fire.

The experiences of that night would not die. They were fated to be replayed again and again, each time like the last, a changeless cycle that repeated the tension, the pain. And the terror.

The fire was the sole constant. It surrounded her, she was inside of it, she was the fire. She could feel the flames eating into her flesh, and yet she could feel the power as it stole the flesh of the others. It was a world of paradox, of contrasting images and emotions charged with the passions of revenge and threatened extinction. The emotions built to such an intensity that the world of paradox continued even after the competing visions merged. She remained unaware of the change because of the force of events, because of her panic. And because of the fire.

The fire remained the sole constant. The whispery suggestions that had seized her will were silenced. The vision of black rock and yellow heat beating against stone vanished. And the fused figure of man and bear was no more. Though she had been released from those worlds, the fire did not disappear. She was still inside of it. She was still part of it. And she was still threatened with extinction.

But there were differences, and though sight was proving to be a false ally, somewhere in the back of her mind she perceived the change. She realized that the fire offered not strength, but death. She realized that there was no life in the flames. She realized that the pain she felt was not a six-hundred-year-old memory, but rather a real and current phenomenon.

The fire was moving closer. She tried to turn, but she was immobilized. She looked up, and for a second she thought she was back in the dream. Her wrists were lashed to slanting wooden posts. Her mind was thrown into confusion, but she didn't have time to reason it through. She had no energy to waste on figuring out what had happened. There was only one matter of importance. Getting free. Getting away. Escaping the flames.

She tugged on one arm, then the other, trying to squeeze her hand through the ropes. She strained, pulling harder, the hemp cords digging into her skin, cutting off the flow of blood, the feeling in her fingers.

Her chest sagged as she gulped in air. But the air itself seemed aflame, and it brought little relief. She twisted her neck as far as she could, looking over her shoulder. She was enclosed in a circle of fire, strung from a three-legged frame. The flames rose in rapidly flashing sheets of excited energy, higher than her head near the outer ring. She looked down and gasped. She was standing on a pile of kindling and brush and dried wood that was drawing the ring of flames inward. The fire progressed at a slow creep, and yet sparks jumped ahead, igniting new circles of flame, which began to expand at their own pace.

She tugged again at the ropes, twisting her body, seeking to break the bonds, to pull the posts down, to do anything that would change the situation. But the only changes were within her. Her heart beat at a faster tempo; the blood in her veins rushed through her system; her lungs could not deliver enough oxygen. She felt light-headed, drifting again as if in a dream. But this time there was no relief in secondary worlds or remote eras. She was trapped in the present, at the center of a raging inferno. A billowing, blasting fury of destruction. An advancing wall of color and heat.

This was the final world. The final vision. The last truth. She was going to die. She was going to burn to death.

Madness rushed in on panic's shouted urges. She lost all

method to her struggle, all cohesion to her thoughts. She was reduced to her only means of resistance. It welled up in her chest, surged through muscles straining with effort in her neck, and erupted from her mouth. It was a scream of madness and terror, of pain and panic. It was a declaration of ultimate protest, a cry of frustration and defiance and fear. It was a final thrust back at the flames with the only weapon she possessed.

But the flames heard not her cry or her protest, nor did they react to her defiance. She could see them moving forward at their own pace, lapping up the slanting rise of the posts, taking deeper hold of the thick lengths of wood. She looked past the stakes, beyond the circle of fire, at the open space outside the waving curtain of light. She wanted to ignore what was happening. She wanted to imagine herself free and cool and no longer at danger. She wanted to disregard the pain. She wanted the fire to take her fast.

The light she stared into was a medium of varying intensity. It was a constantly shifting series of advances and retreats, of incendiary bursts and weakening flickers of flame. But despite the changing nature of the fire, despite the varying magnitude, wherever she looked it was bright. The nature of the fire, which could not change, was that it gave off energy. It gave off light.

Except in the very center. There was a shadow, a slender bank of darkness obscured by the flames. It was a bipedal form, a moving creature. A memory from the other world came rushing back. She reacted with renewed fear. The fire was coming alive.

But even as the fear formed in her mind, she realized it was an irrational reaction. The thing of the fire was dead. She had been released. That horror was over.

"Please," she heard herself shouting. "Help me!"

And the shadow—the man—advanced. He came through the wall of flame, entering her diminishing space. At first she didn't recognize him, so altered seemed his appearance. At first she didn't care who he was, so desperate was her position. But when she realized who he was, the frantic workings of her mind changed again. She urged him to get out. To save himself. She didn't want him to die. But he ignored her pleas. And then she saw the glint of metal. A knife, a blade, an ax. "Hurry!" she screamed, giving in to the panic, letting the terror take control once again.

He moved behind her, and she twisted her neck as far as she could. The metal thing in his hand rose and fell, and her hand

dropped free. When her arm fell, she fell with it, her legs offering no support. A blast of hot air rushed into her face as the fire
surged toward her. She was closer to the flames. She could feel
their effect on her skin. And dangling from one arm, she was
losing her grasp on things hard and real. She was slipping away.
The light was fading. Her vision was failing. She was moving
out of the center of the sun, drifting into space, floating into the
blackness of the universe, falling into the depths of starless sky.
She was sinking into oblivion.

That's how it ended for her then. And that's how it ended in her
dreams. It was the same, except that in her dreams there was no
gift of unconsciousness. She remained frozen on the brink, with
no escape from the burning. No escape from the terror, unaware
of the man's continued efforts to free her. It all continued to
build, until she was thrust violently back into the world of
wakeful nightmare.

The light switched on and there was the usual moment of
confusion. She was sweating and breathing heavily, and her
eyes flashed about in panic. But then it quickly settled into a familiar pattern. The walls, the plaster ceiling above her head, the
moist feel of the sheets and her bedclothes. And Fielding was
there too, watching her, waiting for her to come out of it. As she
had after the last dream and the dream before that. He had been
through it with her every time, and he knew the pattern as well
as she.

Gradually her composure returned. The heaves of her chest
eased. And she asked the question she had asked a hundred
times before. "Will it ever go away?"

Fielding didn't answer. He couldn't answer. Instead he told
her what was most important, as he had every time. "They're
gone," he said. "And they're never coming back."

She settled her head back on the pillow, looking at the ceiling, taking hold of his hand. She disagreed with him. Not about
the things of the fire, but about what was most important.

Getting on with her life was most important. Guiding the expansion of the museum she now directed was most important.
Getting continued good reports from Lindsey Verhoven's new
family was most important. And of course, Christopher Fielding was most important.

The dreams? Everybody had bad dreams. She was strong
enough to live with them for as long as necessary. Already, they

came less frequently, and each time he was there for her, as he had been that first night in the circle of flames. As he said he would be every other night into the future.

The ties to her people's past were strong. That kinship could never be replaced. But there was nothing deeper than her ties to this man. He was kin to her now, a kinship stronger than blood or genes or shared history.

They were kin of the fire.